GOD DON'T PLAY

GOD DON'T PLAY

MARY MONROE

KENSINGTON PUBLISHING CORP.
http://www.kensingtonbooks.com

DAFINA BOOKS are published by

Kensington Publishing Corp.
850 Third Avenue
New York, NY 10022

All Kensington titles, imprints and distributed lines are available at special quantity discounts for bulk purchases for sales promotion, premiums, fund-raising, educational or institutional use.

Special book excerpts or customized printings can also be created to fit specific needs. For details, write or phone the office of the Kensington Special Sales Manager: Kensington Publishing Corp., 850 Third Avenue, New York, NY 10022, Attn. Special Sales Department. Phone: 1-800-221-2647.

Dafina Books and the Dafina logo Reg. U.S. Pat. & TM Off.

ISBN-13: 978-0-7582-0347-2
ISBN-10: 0-7582-0347-0

First Hardcover Printing: September 2006
First Trade Paperback Printing: August 2007
10 9 8 7 6 5 4 3 2 1

Printed in the United States of America

ACKNOWLEDGMENTS

Thanks to Karen Thomas for being such a super editor.

Thanks to Andrew Stuart for being the best agent in the world.

Thanks to L. Peggy Hicks, Roxann Taylor, Gerry Martin, and Jennifer Dyer at Tri-Com Publicity and Maureen Cuddy at Kensington Books for arranging my book tours and setting up my radio, magazine, newspaper, and television interviews.

Thanks to everyone at Kensington Books for making me feel so special (especially Jessica McLean!).

Joan Schulhafer, publicity director at Kensington, I can't thank you enough for taking time away from your busy schedule to accompany me for the first two weeks of my 2005 *In Sheep's Clothing* homecoming book tour. Let's do it again!

Please enjoy *God Don't Play*, and visit my Web site at *www.marymonroe.org*

Peace and blessings!

CHAPTER 1

My worst nightmare began with a blacksnake and a cute envelope. I had no way of knowing that my life was about to fall apart on the most beautiful day that we'd had all year.

The bold morning sun was shining down on my freshly painted house like a lighthouse. I had just had some of the best sex that I had had in years, and there had been no one else in the same room with me.

"You give good phone sex. You should call me up more often," I teased my husband, Pee Wee, as I'd struggled to catch my breath before hanging up the telephone on the wall next to the refrigerator in the kitchen. I couldn't remember the last time I'd enjoyed sex standing up, and nibbling on a Pop-Tart at the same time.

"Well, it is the next best thing to me bein' there," Pee Wee told me, whispering so that his cousins in the next room at his cousin's house couldn't hear him. "Did you get naked like I told you?"

"Uh-huh. Naked as a jaybird," I lied, smoothing down the sides of my muumuu. There was no way I was going to shed my clothes in the middle of my kitchen floor. It was hard enough for me to get naked in my own bedroom. But I did remove my shoes.

"Did you stick your fingers where I told you to stick 'em?" Pee Wee asked with a moan.

"Uh-huh," I mumbled, lying again. The only thing that I'd stuck my fingers in was in that Pop-Tarts box. However, I had massaged a few other spots on my body like Pee Wee had instructed, and that had been enough for me.

I had enjoyed my passionate telephone tryst with my husband, but I was glad when it was over. Not only did I feel downright ridiculous doing some of the things to myself that he'd ordered me to do, but I had started getting cramps in my legs. And I wanted to clean myself up and put on some fresh underwear.

With a satisfied smile on my face, I stepped out on my front porch to retrieve the mail. A large butterfly that had wings every color in the rainbow landed on my hand.

The sun felt good on my face as I clutched my mail and shook the butterfly off my hand. I waved to the friendly, good-looking White couple from down the street as they walked by, pushing their homely toddler in a creaky stroller. Everybody on our block, except for the husband, knew that the homely toddler's daddy was the homely insurance man who made house calls.

A large, light-skinned man that I didn't recognize, with his black hair in large pink foam rollers, waved to me from a shiny black Lincoln that was cruising down the street. I yelled at a stray dog who had decided to lift his crooked leg and water the prizewinning rosebush in my front yard.

My biggest concern that day was trying to decide what to do first: get my nails done, go shopping, do the laundry, or treat myself to lunch at one of my favorite restaurants. I was in a frivolous mood so I didn't want to do anything that was too serious, like go pay bills or visit my fussy parents. But the bizarre uproar that I was about to face would cancel everything else that I had planned to do on that beautiful Saturday. From that point on, my life would never be the same again. What happened to me on this day would haunt me for the rest of my life, because it was the beginning of the end for me in some ways. And it all had to do with a blacksnake and a cute envelope.

There was nothing that unusual about the cute envelope that had arrived in the mail that morning in late August. I had almost missed it among the usual stack of bills and other unwanted junk—like the Frederick's of Hollywood catalogue with the picture of a beautiful young blonde woman in a white negligee on the cover.

I laughed when I saw the catalogue, wondering what the world was coming to for *my* name to end up on the Frederick's of Hollywood mailing list. I had to give them credit for advertising muumuus, waist clinchers, capes, bras with cups large enough to hold forty ounces of beer, long flowing nightgowns that looked more like parachutes, and other inducements every now and then to appease us full-figured gals. But almost everything else that the mysterious Mr. Frederick—who probably looked like Buddha or worse himself—sold was for women half my size and even smaller. On the first page inside the catalogue were some "one size fits all" panty hose. Yeah, right. The see-through gowns and low-cut blouses were outrageous enough, and I had absolutely no use for crotchless panties. I'd probably be wearing diapers again before I broke down and put on a pair of crotchless panties.

I was not surprised when I flipped the catalogue over and saw that it was addressed to Jade O'Toole, my best friend's sneaky teenage daughter. Some of the clothes that the girl wore every day showed just as much skin as the frocks she ordered from Frederick's that she hid from her parents, so I didn't know what the big deal was. But I didn't have a teenager yet, so I couldn't really judge the behavior of the "in your face" music-video generation. They had their own culture and Jade kept it in my face. I had allowed her to take too many liberties with me so it was too late for me to revise my position in her life. I was no more of an authority figure to her than a cat was. She had started using my address without my knowledge or permission. I shuddered when I thought about what that girl might do next.

CHAPTER 2

The catalogue that had just come in my mail for Jade was not nearly as shocking as the foot-long vibrator that she had had delivered to my address a few weeks ago. It had also arrived on a Saturday morning but in a plain brown envelope and by registered mail, delivered by one of the nosiest brothers in town. My mailman and I socialized with some of the same people, so he took the liberty of greeting me with a sly grin on his face when I opened my front door.

"Good morning, Moshay," I said, my face burning with shame as I read the return address on the package that he held in front of his wide chest like a bib. One of his sausagelike fingers tapped the return address. There was only one adult toy store in town and most people knew the address by heart. Even me. But only because it was next door to the dry cleaners I used.

"Same to you, Annette. Um . . ." Moshay paused and nodded at the package, the same grin still on his face, which was covered in beads of sweat. Almost everything on his face was too big: his eyes, his nose, his chin. His short, stout body resembled a barrel. But he had a lot of confidence for such an ugly man. He flirted with me every time I saw him. "You lookin' mighty nice today. I ain't seen you in church lately. I guess you been keepin' yourself busy takin' care of that husband of yours, huh?"

"I guess I have, Moshay," I said, reaching for the package. I tapped my bare foot and glanced at my watch so that he would know I was getting impatient.

It didn't take much to encourage Moshay Dixon. He tried to get too friendly with too many females. Back in high school, he used to crawl around on the floor in the lunchroom to peek up under girls' skirts. He had a wife and a mistress now, and all the local hookers loved him to death.

Moshay glanced around and even over my shoulder before he spoke again. "You need to sign for this first," he whispered.

I didn't know why those companies still bothered trying to hide adult products in plain brown wrappers. When it came to sex, there were very few secrets left anymore. But even though I was a married woman, and what my man and I did in our bedroom stayed in our bedroom, I didn't want anybody making assumptions about my private life. Especially my mailman!

I snatched the package out of Moshay's hand and gave him a stern look. It was hard enough to keep secrets in a small town like Richland, Ohio. Before Moshay finished delivering mail for the day, I knew that everybody on the block would probably be wondering what I'd ordered from the sex shop.

Ten minutes after I'd signed for the package, Jade called me up.

"Auntie," she said, panting like she had just finished running a footrace, or, knowing Jade, fucking her young brains out. She let out a deep breath before continuing. "I'm expecting an important package today," she informed me, speaking in a low voice. "From that, uh, specialty shop on Sawburg Avenue," she added, now whispering so low I could barely hear her.

"You mean that dark little place that sells all that *nasty* shit?" I snapped. If I had told Jade once I'd told her a thousand times, I didn't feel comfortable discussing sex with her. But Jade paid me no more mind than she did anybody else.

"They're having a big sale, in case you're interested," Jade told me.

"I'm not!" I yelled, forcing myself to sound disgusted. The truth of the matter was, I wanted to laugh. If nothing else, Jade was very entertaining. There were times when she was the only one who could amuse me. "Your order arrived a little while ago." I glanced at the package on the end of the coffee table in my living room where I'd dropped it. "And what would you be ordering from a store that sells only adult products?" I teased, wrapping the telephone cord around my fingers. I frowned when I realized my nails were screaming for a manicure. I released the telephone cord and balled my hand into a fist so I would not have to look at my tacky nails.

"Huh?"

"Never mind, you nasty little thing, you," I laughed.

"Oh, Auntie, get yourself on the ball. This is the nineties. Kids grow up a lot faster than they did when you were young."

Jade's comments made my thoughts wander but not in a pleasant direction. It seemed like I'd never been "young." I had spent my childhood dealing with things that a lot of adults wouldn't have been able to handle. I pursed my lips and shook my head as Jade continued.

"Sex is not what it used to be, Auntie." She had a way of representing herself that made me feel like I was the child and she was the adult. "You ought to know that by now."

"Sex is no different now than it was a hundred years ago. As far as I know, people are still doing it the same way," I said, swallowing hard. I wondered what Jade would say if I told her I'd had my first sexual encounter at the age of seven. Even though it had been rape, sex was still sex. "There is just a lot more of it going on," I scoffed.

"Well, everybody is doing it," Jade insisted, with a moan that made me blush.

"Not everybody, Jade," I said sadly. "There are people my age who still have a hard time dealing with sex." And I was one of them. I tolerated sex, even when it was good. If I had not married such a patient and passionate man, I'd have kept my legs closed for the rest of my life. "And for the record, a lot of men don't care if we enjoy it or not. As long as they get what they want out of it . . ."

"Boo hoo," Jade sneered. She paused and let out a giggle. "That's why they make vibrators," she practically sang.

I let out a disgusted sigh, making sure it was loud enough for her to hear. "Where are you?" I asked, hoping she could tell how impatient and exasperated I was. I didn't even like to discuss sex with my doctor, my husband, or my adult female friends—let alone a youngster like Jade.

There was a lot of noise in the background on Jade's end. Car horns blasting, people yelling, dogs barking. The train tracks that divided Richland into almost two equal parts were just a mile from my house. I could hear the train whistle blowing from my end and from Jade's. It gave me an eerie feeling because I didn't like trains. Every time I saw or heard one, it reminded me of the segregated train that my mother and I had been forced to ride on when we moved from the South to Ohio. If I couldn't travel by plane when I had to go out of town, I either drove my car or I took the bus.

"I'm at a pay phone right outside the train station. Listen, I'll be there in a few minutes to pick up my package. If my mom happens to drop by, don't let her see it! And please don't open it!"

CHAPTER 3

I was standing in my doorway when Jade stumbled up on my front porch ten minutes later. She paused and roughly wiped the soles of her brown suede boots on my well-worn welcome mat.

"Auntie, what are we going to do about that stray dog who likes to leave his calling cards all over your yard? Eeeow! My boots are practically ruined! And how am I going to get rid of this unholy stench?" she asked, screwing her face up like she was in pain.

Jade gently brushed past me and entered my living room, her huge green eyes darting from side to side. She crept across the floor like a burglar, her long black hair swaying down her back like a horse's tail.

Jade worshipped her body and so did a lot of the horny little boys she ran around with. She liked to show it, and she liked to share it. She had on a snug-fitting, pale pink halter top that didn't even come close to hiding the nipples on her firm, perky breasts. Her jeans were ripped on both knees and on the sides of her crotch. And if the rips were not provocative enough, the jeans were so tight I could see the split in her busy little pussy.

"I'll get some warm water and some rags for your boots before you leave," I offered, following Jade to my sofa, wondering how she could breathe in such tight clothing. I didn't have a problem with females wearing sexy clothes. I wasn't even jealous. But I had a problem with the ones who chose to "advertise" and then complained when men came on to them.

"I would have been here before now, but this dirty old man who was waiting to use the pay phone tried to pick me up," Jade complained. She rolled her eyes, but I rolled mine even more.

"Oh, really? I wonder why," I said with a smirk. I lifted the package addressed to Jade off my coffee table and handed it to her. With wide, anxious eyes, she snatched it out of my hand so hard the wrapping ripped in several places. Just like her jeans.

I don't know why Jade had ordered me to not open her package. She finished opening it right in front of me. I almost fainted when she shook out the long, plastic battery-operated vibrator. It was curved on one end like a sword. And from the size of it, I decided that it probably felt like one, too. I didn't want to think that a petite young female like Jade required such an ominous-looking device.

"Girl, you ought to be ashamed of yourself!" I exclaimed. I looked around my living room to make sure my nine-year-old daughter, Charlotte, had not snuck into the room. She was also a sneaky little devil, a habit she had picked up from Jade. "Do you really need that damn big-ass thing?" I hissed, hands on my hips.

Jade blinked and looked at me like I was speaking Greek.

"It's for a friend, Auntie. I babysit for her. You know that White girl Jimmy Lipton met and married when the navy sent him overseas? The girl with the buck teeth? Poor Jimmy. What a shame! Married to a girl who looks like a talking mule!" Jade paused and shook her head. "I know the boy could have done better. He's no Eddie Murphy, but he didn't have to settle for such a dull frump. Especially with all those pretty girls up for grabs down there in Australia where he's stationed now." Jade paused just long enough to sniff and catch her breath. "I feel so sorry for that poor girl, too. A plain Jane like her never learned how to look out for herself in an emergency. Anyway, me and a couple of my friends put our money together to buy this for her," Jade said, holding the vibrator up in front of my face, shaking it back and forth like a pendulum.

"Did this girl ask you and your friends to buy this thing for her?" I asked. I gave Jade a puzzled look before I frowned.

"No," Jade said with an indifferent shrug.

"Well, don't you think that giving somebody something like this, when they didn't ask for it, might offend them?"

"Why?"

"Maybe she's not into things like this, Jade," I said, nodding toward the vibrator, glaring at it now like it was a bomb. "I would scream if somebody gave me one of these damn things," I added with a shudder.

"You'd scream? That's right." Jade nodded vigorously, clapping her hands like a seal. "That's the right idea, Auntie. That's what it's supposed to make a woman do," Jade said in a voice too serious for a child of her age. I gave her a horrified look and my mouth dropped open, but before I could speak again, Jade continued. "Oh, I don't have to worry about offending Plum. See, she's from France so she's very broad-minded."

Jade unzipped her yellow canvas backpack, designed by a European designer with a name I couldn't pronounce. In addition to a platinum American Express card in her own name, the yellow backpack was one of the things that she never left home without. With a loud sniff, and the tip of her tongue parked in the corner of her mouth, she stuffed the vibrator into the backpack. Her eager eyes shone like diamonds.

"If you want one, let me know. I can get the next one for half price," Jade said with a giggle and a wink. "But a great big woman like you would probably want one of the great big ones, though, huh?" Jade paused again, tilted her head to the side, and gave me a serious look. "But a bigger one will probably cost more. Now what color—"

I cut Jade off. "Girl, I don't need anybody's fake dick!" I hollered, waving my hands, forcing myself not to laugh. Then I slid my knuckles along the side of Jade's head and chased her back out the door.

I returned my thoughts to the present moment, the Frederick's of Hollywood catalogue still in my hand. I laughed out loud before I tossed it aside, so that I could sort through the rest of the mail.

The only thing that made the envelope stand out was the fact that it was pink and small. Like the kind used to send invitations or cards. I guess that's why I'd decided to deal with it first. I was impressed to see that the sender had taken the time to type my name on the envelope, but it seemed odd that the person would not include a return address.

My birthday had just passed a week ago and belated birthday cards were still trickling in. The day before, I had received one from my half sister in Miami. And the day before that, I had received two from Miss Nipp, my first-grade schoolteacher. She was senile and in a nursing home now and I was the only one of her students she still remembered. Miss Nipp couldn't even remember the names of her remaining family members. It gave me a good feeling to know that there were people who still acknowledged me after almost forty years.

I plopped down hard on the new living room sofa that had just been delivered a few days ago. It was the best birthday gift that I had received, and the most practical. It was the kind of gift that only a mother would give. Especially a mother like mine. But at least this was something I could use. The canning jars that she'd given me last year were in my basement, still in the box.

At forty-five, I needed very few things that I didn't already have. My husband made good money as one of the three Black barbers in town and my promotion to supervisor at the Mizelle Collection Agency had moved me up to a tax bracket that was downright scary.

I loved my job as a bill collector, but it had taken me a while to get used to it. Now it was almost as entertaining as Jade. I never thought that I would benefit so much from people not paying their bills. And getting them to pay their bills was another story. The excuses that people gave were outrageous, like they couldn't find their wallets, somebody had stolen the money that they had planned to use to pay their bill, or they didn't have a stamp to mail their payment. I had heard every excuse but one about the family dog eating the money. Some people even swore that they'd paid their bill, but that they'd misplaced the receipt and would fax it to us as soon as they located it. That bought them a brief reprieve, and it also meant job security for people like me. I had to laugh to myself when I thought about all the times my mother had made me lie when I was a child when mean bill collectors called our house asking for her. Now I was one of those bill collectors who often had to get mean with folks, hoping that it would encourage them to pay their delinquent debts. It was an unpleasant but necessary job.

Like I did in every other situation, I made the best of my job. Life was too short. I was grateful and surprised that I'd made it to forty-five with my sanity intact.

Instead of a sentimental birthday card that I had expected to find, with a spidery note or a neatly typed message from Miss Nipp, the pretty pink envelope contained a sheet of perfumed pink stationery. There was a picture of a white dove in the upper right-hand corner. Both the sheet of paper and the envelope were rose-scented. The text had been typed in a crisp, bold font. I fanned my face with the envelope and the roselike fragrance was even more potent. But the pleasantries ended there. I gasped so hard that hot, foul-tasting bile rose in my throat as I read with my eyes stretched open as wide as they could stretch:

Greetings, Miss Piggy:
You are in trouble up to your receding hairline! Who in the hell do you think you are? It's time for somebody to put you in your place. You are nothing but a fat, slimy, middle-aged, stinky, bald-headed, rusty-necked black cow! Don't you know that by now? And you need to start acting like one and stay in your place. If you know what's good for you, with your nasty stinking self, you will crawl back up under that rock where you came from and stay there or else! And guess what? I am going to make sure you do just that! Bitch!
Signed, me: your worst nightmare

"My worst nightmare?" I asked in a loud voice. "What in the world . . . ?" My mouth dropped open and my heart started beating so loud I could hear it. I turned the sheet of paper over, blinking at it so hard my vision got fuzzy and my eyes burned. There was no signature, of course, or anything else that might have identified the sender. I went back out on my front porch, looking in every direction. I even stumbled out to the sidewalk in my bare feet and looked around some more. Puzzled, I returned to my living room.

"What in the world is this?" I managed, talking to a big, empty living room. An empty house, for that matter. Pee Wee and Charlotte were in Erie, Pennsylvania. My father-in-law's grave was located there in a family plot where we would all end up someday. Every year on the anniversary of the fussy old man's death, Pee Wee drove the three hours to Erie from our house in Richland to place fresh flowers on his father's grave.

I looked at the telephone on the end table next to the sofa but I quickly decided not to call my husband. He had lost his mother when he was just a child, so he had been very close to his daddy. Visiting his daddy's grave was enough to put him in a somber mood. And if that wasn't enough in Erie to drag him down, he had some relatives over there that were so obnoxious they could bring down a satellite. The last thing I wanted to do was add to his burdens. Especially with something this off-the-wall.

I read the message again, blinking hard as my eyes continued to burn. Then I laughed. I mean, what else could I do? I read the message a third time, more slowly this time to make sure that it said what I thought it said. Then I blinked some more. My eyes were burning even harder, but I suddenly stopped laughing. If this note was for real, I had an anonymous enemy whose mission was to destroy me—and that was nothing to laugh about.

I folded the sheet of paper and slid it back in the cute little pink envelope. I looked at my hands, turning them over. Three chipped nails and ashy skin made them look like bear claws to me. Had I not received the pink envelope, I would have been on my way to the nail shop by now.

"Who sent me this damn thing?" I asked the empty room, glaring at the envelope. "And why?"

CHAPTER 4

I stumbled to the telephone. I felt like I was already drunk, even though I had not drunk even a beer. But I would—and I wouldn't stop with just one beer! In the meantime, I needed to talk to somebody about the very strange piece of mail that I had just received.

My life story would have made a good made-for-cable television movie. It had all of the necessary sensational elements: rape, murder, prostitution, poverty, betrayal, and even more. I had survived it all. People were always telling me how strong I was. I guess it was hard for anybody to believe that somebody as big as an ox could be weak. My size didn't matter when it came to feeling pain or anything else that I considered negative. Receiving a nasty piece of hate mail was the worst thing that had happened to me in a long time. All I wanted was a normal, peaceful, and happy life, and I thought I had finally achieved that. I resented the fact that somebody else had decided that I didn't deserve what I had.

"Damn, Pee Wee, I wish you were here," I said, talking to the wall. As soon as I got those words out, I was glad that my husband was not with me. He was my best friend, but there were a lot of things that I couldn't share with him. The same was true of my elderly parents. But there was nothing I couldn't share with Rhoda Nelson O'Toole.

She was more than my best female friend. She'd been my life-line for over thirty-two years. She could not have known me better had she been able to read my mind. She was half my size but twice as strong. We shared some secrets that were so complicated you needed a pie chart to explain them. And so serious they could have put us both in prison for a very long time. But I'll get to that later.

Other than the police, the ambulance, and the fire department, Rhoda's number was the only other one I had on speed dial. My mother would have made a huge fuss about that if I'd been stupid enough to tell her. Not that I cared more about Rhoda than I did my own blood, but, well, there was no way I could explain what Rhoda meant to me. Not to my mother, my husband, or anybody I knew. When I thought about how important Rhoda was to me, I re-called some lyrics from an old Curtis Mayfield tune called "Pusher-man": *I'm your mama, I'm your daddy, I'm that nigger in the alley* . . . That old song, which the local R&B radio station still played on their oldies-but-goodies hours, was referring to a drug dealer. Right now Rhoda was the fix that I needed. I pressed the buttons for her number so hard on the telephone in my living room that the ball of my index finger throbbed.

"Woman, please be home," I chanted. "Please be home. I need to talk to you."

I had never meant to hurt anybody before in my life, but appar-ently I had done *something* that had pissed off at least one person. The innocent-looking envelope that had entered my life so calmly had struck me like a torpedo. I whipped my head around and looked toward the front door, wondering where the sender was at the moment, hoping that he or she did not occupy a residence too close to mine.

All of a sudden it occurred to me that the note had to have been sent as a joke. That had to be it! What else could it be? Like the black plastic snake in a gift-wrapped box addressed to me, which somebody had left on my desk at work a few days ago. I had laughed about that, and so had my co-workers. I still didn't know who had sent that to me. Now I had to wonder if the blacksnake and the nasty note were related.

"Hello," Rhoda answered on the third ring.

I was having trouble responding. I opened my mouth and my lips and tongue moved, but nothing came out but a few drops of dribble, sliding down my chin like poison.

"I said, hello!" Rhoda snapped. "Is anybody there?"

"Hi, it's me. Can I come over? I have something to show you," I muttered in a voice that sounded like it belonged to a timid child.

There was a moment of silence before Rhoda replied. "I was on my way out the door," she said softly. "You don't sound too good, girl. Is somethin' wrong?"

"Uh-huh," I replied, still sounding like a timid child. My heart had not thumped half as hard and loud during my phone sex session with Pee Wee as it did now. And there was no telling when I'd make it to the nail shop now. But the claws on my hands were the least of my worries.

"Well, why don't I just come over there instead?" Rhoda asked, her slight southern accent sounding more prominent.

"Okay, but hurry up," I said, breathing hard and loud. I didn't realize I was sweating, too, until a few drops fell off my face onto my ashy hand.

There was a long pause before Rhoda spoke again. "You sound serious. Don't you want to tell me what this is about?"

"Well, it's probably nothing, but I think I've pissed somebody off," I said in a flat voice, making a mental note to put some lotion on my hands.

"Well, you are pissin' me off by bein' so mysterious. Exactly what are we talkin' about here?"

"I just received something in the mail," I stated, sucking in my breath. I had to clear my throat before continuing. "And it's not very nice. As a matter of fact, it's downright mean. Maybe you can convince me that it's nothing to worry about."

CHAPTER 5

"Well, if it's not a dead chicken, I could probably convince you that it's nothin' serious," Rhoda chuckled. "Or one of those fierce-looking dolls with pins sticking out of it. There is a lot of shit bein' sent through the mail these days. I'm glad that a lot of that useless junk doesn't come to my address," Rhoda said, releasing one of those proud snorts that smug people were known for. "I'm so glad that I don't have to worry about openin' my mailbox and findin' none of that shit."

Like your teenage daughter's sex toys, I thought to myself. I wondered what Rhoda would say if I revealed that information to her. I didn't really want to know, so I put that thought out of my mind right away.

Rhoda was, without a doubt, one of the most intelligent people I knew. But there were times when it seemed like she was a little dense, or slow, when it came to recognizing a serious situation. I didn't like her initial response to the peculiar information that I'd just shared with her.

"This is not a joke, Rhoda. Well, it could be a joke, but I don't know who would find something like this funny."

"Annette, what the hell are you talkin' about?"

When Rhoda was impatient, she didn't even try to hide it. I could even hear her drumming her fingers on a hard surface.

"This morning I received one of the meanest notes I ever received in my life. As a matter of fact, it is *the* meanest note I ever received in my life. A few kids used to pass me nasty notes in school but this is not kid stuff."

"What do you mean by 'received'? Who sent it to you?" Rhoda demanded.

"I have no idea who sent it to me. They didn't sign it with a real name. And they didn't include a name or return address on the envelope. It came in the mail this morning in a cute little pink envelope, smelling like a rose." I don't know how or why, but I let out a sharp laugh. "It was typed and it looks so . . . professional. Like somebody really gave this a lot of thought." I bit my bottom lip and looked around my living room, paying close attention to the corners and other hiding places where a bogeyman might lurk.

"Auntie, did you tell Mama about the blacksnake yet?" It was the voice of Jade.

She had the annoying habit of eavesdropping on some of my telephone conversations with Rhoda. I had a problem with that because there were many things I felt that Jade didn't need to know yet. Even though she was a very mature seventeen-year-old. Complaints and even punishment didn't faze Jade. This girl thought that the world revolved around her, and that she could do whatever she wanted to do. It was no surprise that she did do whatever she wanted to do, and with little or no consequences.

"Girl, get your ass off that phone!" Rhoda yelled.

"Yes, ma'am. Anything you say," Jade said with an irritating whine. Then she let out a loud sigh before she slammed the extension down. She had her own telephone in her bedroom with a separate line. But she was such a busy little body that she liked to be all up in her mother's business, too.

"You'd better enjoy Charlotte as much as you can now. Another Jade is what you have to look forward to," Rhoda told me with a heavy sigh. "I swear to God, sometimes that girl makes me itch all over! I just wish that she was more like her big brother," Rhoda added.

I never took Rhoda seriously when she "complained" about

Jade. Because Rhoda bowed down to Jade like she was royalty. She didn't even convince me that she was serious. Rhoda's only other child, a handsome young man named Julian, lived in Mobile, Alabama, where he owned and operated a shoe-repair business. It was no secret that the boy was as gay as an Easter parade. Rhoda was as proud of him as I was. Her only regret was that Jade was her only chance to have grandchildren, and that had a lot to do with the fact that Jade was treated like she was made out of gold.

"She'll be mad at me for a little while, so I'd better take her to the mall with me," Rhoda said, almost choking on her words. "And let her pick out somethin' expensive and pretty. Poor thing. She must be havin' her period." Rhoda sighed so much when it came to Jade, you would have thought she was on a respirator.

"Can you hurry on over before you go to the mall? And, uh, leave Jade in the car when you get here, if you don't mind. I don't want to upset her."

"Girl, you are scarin' me." Rhoda paused and let out a mild belch, then complained vaguely about a chipped nail. "And what's this about a blacksnake?"

"Oh. I didn't think that it was anything to get upset over when I got it, but now I don't know." I tilted my head and sucked in so much air my lungs felt like they were going to explode. My eyes were on the evil note still clutched in my hand. It took me a few seconds to compose myself. Rubbing my chest I said, "They had a little surprise party for me at work last week. I came out of a staff meeting and there was a cake on my desk with one candle on it, and a pile of birthday gifts." My voice trailed off as I recalled how I'd jumped and shrieked when I'd opened the box and saw the fake blacksnake.

"And where did the blacksnake fit in?" Rhoda wanted to know.

I swallowed hard. "Well, after I had cut my cake and given everybody a slice, I started opening my gifts. I'd received more than a dozen, and I think it was like the fourth or fifth one I opened. There was a clock radio for my desk, a Macy's gift certificate for a hundred dollars, and some perfume. I got some other really nice stuff this year, too. Of course, the office troublemakers didn't give me anything, but they were first in line to get a slice of my birthday cake." I paused and sucked in my breath, raking my fingers through my knotty hair. "It was a long, flat box, wrapped in gold paper with a white bow. It couldn't have been cuter. Anyway, I popped open the box, unwrapped the gold tissue paper inside, and there was a fake snake. A two-foot-long, black, plastic, shiny fake snake coiled up like it was ready to strike. It looked so real, I thought it *was* real at first. I even screamed and dropped it. Everybody, except for me, thought it was funny," I said stiffly, recalling how disgusted I'd felt at that moment.

"Who sent it?"

"That's just it," I said, flinching. "I don't know. Nobody would admit it. I don't have any proof but I think it was José, the Puerto Rican maintenance man. He sent one of the file clerks some flowers with painted-on faces for her birthday last month. The faces looked demonic. Everybody laughed about that, too. Even me."

"Well, flowers with ugly faces are one thing. A blacksnake is another thing."

"But it was a *fake* snake," I said, forcing myself to laugh. "If whoever sent it really wanted to be mean, they would have sent me a real one," I insisted.

"Well, did you ask that Puerto Rican José if he sent you a fake blacksnake?"

"Yes, I did. He said he didn't send it," I managed. "You know there were a few folks who didn't like me getting my promotion— Carla Henry, Bev Carson, and a few others. They gave me dirty looks and moved to another table in the cafeteria when I tried to sit with them the other day. And Jade told me that she heard a couple of those wenches talking about me like a dog in the ladies' room just yesterday."

"Oh? Look, I don't want my child to be exposed to that kind of foolishness. People like that could be a bad influence on her. They talk about you in front of Jade?" Rhoda sounded serious and angry.

"Oh, you don't have to worry about anybody being a bad influence on Jade," I said dryly.

"What's that supposed to mean?" Rhoda sounded worried now.

"Nothing," I mumbled. I found it hard to believe that Rhoda thought Jade was so innocent.

"Then why did you say it?"

"Jade's not that weak. But she likes to know what's going on around her. Uh, she likes to hide in one of the ladies' room stalls with her feet in the air so that the office blabbermouths won't know she's present. You know how nosy our girl Jade is," I reminded her.

"Tell me about it. But I was just like her when I was her age," Rhoda confessed.

"I remember," I clucked. I ignored an ominous chill that moved across my face, by just thinking about how much alike mother and daughter were. Not only did they look, act, smell, walk, and sound alike, they also thought alike. It was almost like they were the same person. But as far as I knew, Jade had not killed anybody.

Rhoda had.

CHAPTER 6

While awaiting Rhoda's arrival, I made sure that all of the windows and the back door in my house were locked. I drank three beers in less than ten minutes, draining the last bottle with a mighty burp. I regretted drinking all that beer because it didn't help me one bit. I didn't even get a buzz. All it did was make me run to the bathroom twice within fifteen minutes to empty my bladder.

I didn't hear Rhoda pull up in her silver Volvo SUV—her last year's birthday gift from her parents—when she and Jade arrived about twenty minutes after Rhoda and I finished our telephone conversation. They galloped up onto my front porch, stomping like runaway mules. I flung open my front door and they entered my house, both scowling like prosecutors.

As usual, except for height, Rhoda Nelson O'Toole and Jade looked like supermodels. They had inherited their deep green eyes from Rhoda's father's Caucasian mother. But other than the color of their eyes, there was nothing else in their appearance that identified them as biracial. Rhoda and Jade were both as dark brown as I was.

Their faces were beautifully made up, and their tight jeans and bibbed white T-shirts showed off slim, taut bodies that women with my body type couldn't develop even with black magic. Their skin was so smooth and flawless it looked like it had been sprayed on. You had to look really closely to see the fine lines around Rhoda's eyes and mouth. But even that didn't give away her true age. I knew women in their early twenties who had more lines on their faces than Rhoda had.

Good skin was one of the few things that I had going for me. I had my share of fine lines and wrinkles, but you had to look really hard and closely at me to see them.

My hair was another story. When I didn't hide my brittle ends, kinky knots, and bald spots under a scarf or a wig, I kept my hair neat and dyed jet black to hide the stubborn gray strands that sometimes seemed downright invincible. Rhoda's long hair, cascading down her narrow back like a silk scarf, was just as jet black and lush as Jade's. Maybe even more so, because Rhoda had pampered hers longer than Jade had. It pleased me to know that Rhoda had to dye her hair, too, to hide the gray. That wasn't much of a consolation, but it felt good to know that nature had only laid the groundwork; Rhoda had to work hard to remain beautiful.

Even after all the years that I'd known the beautiful Rhoda, standing next to her I sometimes felt as unattractive as a pile of horse shit. I had been fat and plain for as long as she'd been beautiful. It was the one thing that I knew I would never get over. But Rhoda's opinion of me was decidedly different.

"Annette, you look amazin," she assured me as she air-kissed both sides of my face. "Forty-five years old this month and your skin is still as smooth as a baby's butt."

Her comment made me feel warm all over because I knew that she was sincere. My good skin was due to good genes, Ivory soap, and warm water. Rhoda spent a fortune on wrinkle creams and facials, and had vowed to get a face-lift as soon as she felt she needed one.

I had slipped into a fresh muumuu and a pair of comfortable shoes, but I was still on edge. I didn't know what Rhoda had planned, but I was hoping that it involved something that required me to leave my house. It had begun to feel like a chamber of horrors.

A flimsy, red-checked bandanna covered my head. The line in

the nasty note about me having a receding hairline had sent me running to the bathroom mirror. I didn't know what constituted a receding hairline to most people, but I didn't agree with the person who had sent me the note. However, the remark had made me self-conscious enough to cover my whole head. It didn't bother me that I looked like a straight-up mammy next to Jade and Rhoda. That was nothing new, and I was used to it.

"Hi, Auntie," Jade said, covering my cheek with hungry little kisses.

Her warm, wet lips made my face tingle. It puzzled me when, out of the corner of my eyes, I saw Jade wipe her lips with the back of her hand after kissing me. I smiled because she smiled.

"Uh, you taste kind of salty and sweaty," she explained, realizing I'd seen her wiping her lips. "And, by the way, you could use a serious facial, Auntie."

"I could use a lot of things, baby," I said sadly, drifting back to my sofa where I plopped down so hard my thighs vibrated.

Jade and Rhoda looked at each other and shrugged. Jade swiped her lips again, holding on to her yellow backpack with both hands. She protected it like it held mankind's greatest secrets, hiding it in a spot in her bedroom where even Rhoda couldn't find it. Other than the Frederick's of Hollywood catalogues and the other risqué items that she decided she had to have, I didn't know what else Jade concealed in her backpack. Frankly, I didn't want to know. However, one time when she accidentally dropped it in front of me, the lid flew open and a package of condoms fell to the floor. Before Rhoda could see what had dropped out, I'd kicked the package of condoms up under the bottom of my sofa, nodding as Jade gave me a conspiratorial wink. I knew that I was part of the reason Jade was the way she was. But compared to some kids, Jade was still a good girl. And I was so proud of her.

I grabbed Jade's hand and pulled her onto my lap, the same way I had done since she was a very young child. Rhoda stood over me with her arms folded, with the same scowl still on her face.

"Where's the note?" she asked, looking around my living room.

I nodded to one of the end tables by the sofa.

"Mama said that it's probably from somebody who is jealous of you," Jade announced, patting my shoulder and rocking back and forth on my lap. She felt as light as a feather, but she was as solid as a brick. "I said, 'Horsefeathers!' to Mama," Jade hollered. Even though she sounded and looked profoundly bored, I knew in my heart that Jade was just as concerned about my well-being as Rhoda was.

While Rhoda was looking in another direction, I slid the Frederick's catalogue under the pillow next to me. With a frightened look, Jade took a deep breath, held her finger up to her lips, shook her head, and quickly snatched the catalogue from under the pillow. Within seconds Jade had stuffed it into her backpack.

Clearing her throat, she continued talking. "Yeah, somebody is straight-up jealous of you, Auntie."

Jade spoke with such authority she almost had me believing every word that came out of her mouth. But after I gave her comments some thought, I had a hard time believing that anybody was jealous of *me.* I could feel an incredulous look slide across my face. "Jealous? Jealous of me? What in the world do I have for anybody to be jealous of?" I asked, waving my hand.

I noticed a slight frown on Jade's face when she noticed my nails.

"Uh . . . uh . . . that's the same thing I asked Mama," Jade stammered, nodding so hard her eyes blinked. "I mean, what do you have that would make anybody jealous?" Jade made a sweeping gesture with one hand, holding on for dear life to the strap of her backpack with the other.

I was horrified when I saw the lip of a beer bottle peeking from an unzipped pocket on the side of the backpack. Jade's eyes followed mine. She gave me a contrite look before she slung her backpack around to the side, her back to me and Rhoda as she zipped it up.

"Jade's got a point," I said in an offhanded way, with an acute sadness tugging at my heart. It was a struggle for me to remain composed, but I managed to curl my lips into a weak smile. I wasn't trying to be sarcastic and my feelings didn't feel hurt. Jade was not malicious or insensitive. At least, not on purpose. She was sophisticated and mature when it benefited her, but she was still young enough to use her youth as an excuse when she crossed the wrong line.

Rhoda read the note in silence. There was an amused look on her face when she looked up. "I know you aren't takin' this seriously." She laughed in a way that sounded like it was coming from some place other than my living room. Like a hollow cave or some place equally bleak.

"Why shouldn't I?" I asked, gently pushing Jade slightly to the side.

"Girl, this is about as serious as a chain letter I received last month that said I was goin' to have nine years of bad luck if I broke the chain," Rhoda said, hands on her hips. "I threw it in the trash and that's just where this belongs."

Rhoda lifted an eyebrow and winked at me as she ripped the note and the envelope into tiny pieces. Then she waltzed across the floor to a wastepaper basket next to my entertainment center, and let the pieces fall in with the rest of the trash. Strutting back across the floor rubbing the palms of her hands along the sides of her jeans, she gave me a triumphant look. "Now. That's the end of that," she said, folding her arms. "What did you do with that snake?"

I turned to Jade and dipped my head, as if offering her a cue to speak again. She ran with it.

"Oh, I took care of that myself," Jade told Rhoda, sounding excited. "I put it back in the same box that it came in, and then I had the maintenance man take it to the Dumpster." Jade eased up from my lap. "Auntie, why don't you come to Cleveland with us? After we finish shopping, we can go have a real nice lunch at that deli on Superior that you like so much. You can eat all the fried chicken, liver, greens, ribs, oxtails, corn bread, black-eyed peas, and all the rest of that stuff you like to eat so much—as much as you want. My treat."

Eating was the last thing on my mind. As a matter of fact, just hearing Jade name all the items on that soul food smorgasbord made me nauseated. I had to hold my breath for a moment to keep from throwing up.

"I don't think so," I said firmly, shaking my head and my hand. "I have a lot to do around the house before Pee Wee and Charlotte come home tomorrow," I stated, wobbling up from the sofa.

"Well, can we bring you something back?" Rhoda asked.

"I'm fine now. You all go on," I said, nodding toward the door. "Thanks for coming over here and I am sorry it had to be for something so foolish."

"Are you sure you're all right now? You want to spend the night with us? We should be back home before dinner," Rhoda said, her arm around Jade's shoulder.

"I'm fine. Just call me when you get back home," I said, easing them out the door.

The note had shaken me up, but after a few hours and a long nap I felt fine. Pee Wee and Charlotte weren't due home for another day so I still had plenty of time to do the laundry and clean the house.

Around four that afternoon, the telephone rang. Expecting to hear either Rhoda or Jade on the phone, I answered in a cheerful voice.

"Hello, bitch!" It was a woman's voice.

My heart must have skipped two beats. I got so light-headed, I had to lean against the kitchen wall. The same way I had leaned against it when Pee Wee had talked dirty to me on the telephone a few hours earlier. A low, disguised whisper made it impossible for me to recognize the harsh voice. There was no noise in the background. Just the raspy breathing of a person who obviously needed to get a life, and stay out of mine.

"Who is this?" I asked, my hand trembling. "Are you the same one who sent me that snake, and that nasty note?"

"You're damn right I am the same person who sent you that blacksnake and the note, and you can expect a lot more from me before I get through with your big, sloppy black ass!"

There was so much contempt in the voice on the other end of the line, it made me flinch. Even so, I tried to sound pleasant. I felt that it would be to my advantage to do as little as possible to provoke my tormentor. "What do you want? What did I do to you?"

"You'll find out soon enough!"

Before I could say another word, the line went dead. Tears that I couldn't hold back formed in my eyes, blurring my vision. For a moment the black telephone cord looked like the fake plastic blacksnake that I had received on my birthday. I gasped and threw the telephone to the floor.

I checked all the windows and doors again. I even went down to my basement to make sure all of the windows were closed and locked there, too. I stumbled upstairs to the master bedroom and grabbed the baseball bat that Pee Wee kept on the floor by his side of the bed. My hands were shaking so hard I could barely hold the bat, let alone use it if I had to.

I left all of the lights on in the house, and I rushed out the front door like a bat flying out of hell. The house that I loved so much and had spent so many memorable moments in, not all of them good, was the last place on earth where I wanted to be alone right now.

CHAPTER 7

"Auntie, are you all right?" Jade's voice woke me up. She tapped on the dusty window on the driver's side of my two-year-old Mazda.

After Rhoda had received her nice new SUV, I had dropped hints all over the place, hoping my mother, who now had more money than she could spend, would get me one, too. She ended up getting me the sofa instead and then reminded me about all the times when she and I had walked five miles each way to get to and from the Florida shacks we once occupied, and told me how I should be grateful that at least I had a vehicle, period. I still longed for one, but every time I saw Rhoda's chic SUV I knew that if I really wanted something better I could get it myself. Gifts to myself from myself didn't have the same effect as gifts I received from somebody else, though. It did a lot for me to know that other people cared about my feelings.

That was why it was no big deal for me to sit in my car in front of Rhoda's house all that time waiting for her to come home so that I could talk to her again. Besides, I felt safer in my locked car on the street than I had felt in my locked house. I looked at my watch and trembled when I realized I'd been sitting in front of Rhoda's house for over three hours, asleep for the last two.

"Auntie, what's the matter? You look like you saw a ghost," Jade said, squinting her eyes to see me better.

I rolled down the window and unlocked my door, happy to see Jade and Rhoda, even with the horrified looks on their faces.

"What is goin' on, woman? How long have you been sittin' out here?" Rhoda asked, opening my door.

I had not bothered to ring the bell on Rhoda's front door, even though I knew her husband was in the house. His Thunderbird, along with several other vehicles, occupied the driveway.

Rhoda's handsome Jamaican husband, Otis, was from a well-to-do family. He was my husband's closest friend, and I'd known Otis almost as long as I'd known Rhoda and Pee Wee. But I'd always been careful of what I said to and around him. I had never gotten over the fact that he'd been the first and only male to come between me and Rhoda back when we were in high school, when I first realized how important Rhoda was to me. I used to be very possessive of her time, but over the years I had learned to compromise. I saw Rhoda when it was convenient for her. Even if it meant I had to sit in my car on the street for hours at a time.

"Uh, I just got here," I lied. "I was so tired, but I didn't mean to go to sleep. I just . . . just closed my eyes for a few minutes." I yawned, then forced myself to smile. I had slept with my head against the steering wheel. Now my forehead was so numb it felt like I had lost the top part of my head. "I guess I was more exhausted than I thought."

Rhoda had parked her SUV on the street in front of her house. She and Jade had shopping bags from some of the most expensive stores in Cleveland.

"Why didn't you wait for us inside? Otis is home," Rhoda said, a quick glance over her shoulder toward her house. She waved at her husband, who was now peeping out the living room window with both hands shading his eyes. She set one of her shopping bags on the ground and grabbed me by my wrist, practically pulling me out of my car. My feet felt heavy, like my body didn't want them to move. I felt like I was rooted to the spot I stood in, like an old tree.

"I didn't want to bother Otis and his company. I didn't mind waiting outside," I mumbled, with a wave of my hand. Rhoda and Jade looked at each other, then at me. "I . . . I . . . got a phone . . .

phone call," I stuttered. The voice coming out of my mouth sounded nothing like my own. I was beginning to feel like a visitor in my own body.

I didn't feel like myself because I was still confused, and I was truly frightened now. I was mad, too. Mad as hell. I wasn't the bravest person in the world, and I had only had to defend myself on a few occasions in my lifetime. But I was prepared to do whatever I had to do to protect myself.

I couldn't think straight. There was an eerie sound buzzing in my ears and a storm of a headache pounding at my brain. I thought I was going crazy. I thought, at that time, that Rhoda was my best and only ally. "The same bitch who sent me that blacksnake and the note called me at my house."

"How do you know it was the same person?" Jade asked, her eyes wide with anticipation.

She had two shopping bags in each hand and a shoe box under one arm. Her yellow backpack was dangling off her shoulder like a vine. And she had on a different shade of lipstick from the one she'd had on earlier, which told me that she'd had her makeup done, too. Rhoda had done the same thing. She even had on a pair of long, curly false eyelashes. It was no wonder they had been gone for so long!

As in awe as I was of beautiful women, I was glad that I was so low maintenance. After a five-minute shower, it took me ten minutes to do my makeup and hair, and then wiggle myself into one of my many muumuus. I didn't own a single belt. There was no point, because I had no waistline. And the one pair of jeans that I'd had the nerve to buy ended up as the top part of a backyard tent that Jade and some of her friends made. I had a few suits that I wore to work and a few other fancy outfits that I wore to weddings and funerals, but floor-length dusters and muumuus suited me just fine most of the time. Rhoda and Jade took at least two hours to put themselves together each time before they left their house. Even just to go to the corner store! It frustrated me to no end to have to endure all that pussyfooting around, when I really needed to talk to Rhoda ASAP. But like I said, she was really the only person I could talk to about everything. Therefore, I had no choice but to wait for her to come home. She gave me her undivided attention as I spoke.

"Oh, it was the same person, all right. She told me so," I said, giving the hood of my car a quick slap that was so sharp and hard it made the palm of my hand throb.

"Why, that bold bitch!" Rhoda roared, stomping her foot.

I let out a triumphant sniff, glad to see Rhoda so fired up. I knew that whatever it was I had to deal with, Rhoda would be with me all the way.

"This bitch knows where I live, where I work, and my phone number. I need to stop this and I need to stop it now before . . . before somebody gets hurt, real bad," I whimpered. I didn't have to worry about Pee Wee getting hurt. He had survived Vietnam, so I knew he could take care of himself. My main concern was my daughter. I could get over my tormentor terrorizing me, but there was nothing that I wouldn't do when it came to protecting my child. I had to put a stop to this foolishness, and I had to put a stop to it now.

Or at least before Pee Wee and Charlotte got dragged into it.

CHAPTER 8

Rhoda glanced toward her house again, clearly getting impatient with me. "Do you want to come inside and talk about it?" she wanted to know.

I nodded. "I tried to call Pee Wee but he had already left. I don't know if he's coming straight home and I don't want to be in the house by myself. Not now," I said. "I don't know what this person wants from me. I don't know what this person is capable of doing, and I don't want to find out, until I know what kind of maniac I'm dealing with," I snapped.

"That's it! That's it!" Jade said through clenched teeth. "I'm going to go inside and call the cops! We are not going to let this heifer do this to you, Auntie!" Jade yelled, her bottom lip trembling. "Are we, Mama?" Jade lowered her head and gave Rhoda a tentative look.

Rhoda pressed her lips together so hard that it looked like one had disappeared. There was a faraway look in her eyes before she blinked. Then she and Jade stared into one another's eyes, like each was reading the other's mind. That was one time that I was glad I didn't have that ability myself. I didn't really want to know what was going on in those two heads.

"What?" Rhoda spoke and shook her head like she was just coming out of a trance, and in a way I think she was.

"We're not going to let this sorry skank keep this up. Are we, Mama?" Jade asked, rotating her neck so hard her hair fluttered.

"No, we won't," Rhoda said in a calm, easy manner followed by a quick smile. Rhoda's smile disappeared when she looked at me and saw the exasperated expression on my face. "Don't worry." She tapped my foot with hers and offered another smile. Then her voice got deep, her eyes more intense as she glanced up and down the street.

"If this bitch is crazy enough to step onto my property, I'm crazy enough to straighten out this mess myself." Even though I weighed more than Jade and Rhoda put together, literally, I felt safer with them than I would have with anybody else I knew.

One thing I could say about Rhoda was she would stop at nothing to handle her business. I had learned that early in our relationship. It had a lot to do with how important she was to me. She took no prisoners and didn't have to because she had a shoot-to-kill attitude. I didn't condone that attitude but I did feel that a person had to do what a person had to do, when he or she felt threatened.

When I couldn't face one of my battles on my own, I always knew that Rhoda would face it with me. I was not proud of the fact that I was so dependent on her, but had she not been such a powerful crutch for me to lean on, I wouldn't have made it this far. I didn't know what I expected Rhoda to do about my present situation. But it meant a lot to me just to have her emotional support. And since I didn't even know who or where my tormentor was, confronting her face-to-face was not an option. At least not yet.

I held up my hand, looking away from Rhoda to Jade. There was no smile on Jade's face. She looked as grim as I felt. "I don't think this is a police matter, Jade. I don't have all the evidence anymore and I can't even prove that this person called me up and threatened me," I said, trying to sound strong. The truth of the matter was, I felt as weak as a kitten.

"She threatened you?" Jade and Rhoda yelled at the same time. Rhoda replaced her smile with a look of horror.

I nodded so hard my neck ached.

"Come on. Let's get you inside and have a few stiff drinks," Rhoda said. "I've been waitin' for an excuse to pop open a bottle of the brandy my mother-in-law sent me for my birthday." She picked up her shopping bags and beckoned me to follow her and Jade, but my feet still felt so heavy that I couldn't move right away. Rhoda and Jade started to inch toward their house, the sharp heels of their boots click-clacking on the concrete sidewalk.

"Can I spend the night? Or will one of you come spend the night with me?" I begged, dragging my feet, with my flip-flops sliding every which way, as I moved toward Rhoda and Jade.

"Well," Rhoda began, giving me some of the same looks of pity that I received from my mother. "My husband's friend from London is still here and he's straight-up nosy. If you don't mind him askin' you all of your business, you're welcome." Rhoda leaned toward me and rubbed the side of my arm. "You remember Ian Bullard?"

I nodded. "The one we call Bully," I said, wiggling my nose because the man in question was also Rhoda's former lover and had fathered one of her children. It had been years since Rhoda and I had discussed her indiscretion and I wanted to leave it that way. But this was one time when I didn't care who I had to deal with to get what I needed. And right now, I needed to be with Rhoda. "I just don't want to be alone tonight," I whined, blinking like an owl.

"And you won't have to be alone," Rhoda assured me.

Being that I was such a big ox and Rhoda was so dainty and petite, it seemed like I should have been the motherly one in our relationship. Rhoda couldn't even get her arms all the way around me whenever she wanted to give me a hug. Instead of hugs, she usually just rubbed the side of my arm, like she was doing now. She opened her mouth to speak again but Jade cut her off.

"Spend the night with us, Auntie. Nobody will bother you in our house. Will they, Mama?" Jade asked. "And I can tell Uncle Bully that you have the cramps, or you're going through menopause or some other female thing, so he'll leave you alone."

There was a smug look on Jade's face. One of the few things that I didn't like about this child that I loved so much was the fact that she never let me forget what I was: an obese, middle-aged Black woman who had nothing that anybody would be jealous of. Well, I had something at least one person was jealous of. So much that she took the time to type up a note and send it to me through the mail, call me up and talk crazy, and send me a blacksnake!

"Whoever it is that's giving you a hard time won't bother you while you are in our house. Huh, Mama?" Jade asked, anger flashing in her eyes. She shifted her weight to one slim leg and pressed her lips close together.

I didn't like for Jade to be caught up in this mess that somebody had dragged me into, but she and Rhoda were like a package deal. A lot of the things that I shared with Rhoda, she shared with Jade. I had never had such a close relationship with my mother, which had a lot to do with me getting raped for ten years by one of her best male friends. But I did have a close relationship with my own daughter, even though she was only nine years old. As soon as she had learned how to talk and walk, I'd made it perfectly clear to her that she could come to me with any problem, no matter what or who it was.

"No, they damn sure won't bother you as long as you're in my house," Rhoda sniffed. She lifted her chin and let out a loud breath. Then she spoke so calmly you would have thought she was ordering a pizza. "Jade, sugar, I want you to run into the house and put your bags away. Give yourself that egg facial you wanted to rush home for. Then I want you to go down to the basement and get one of your daddy's guns. Load it up, and bring it to me."

CHAPTER 9

Pee Wee, whose real name was Jerry Davis, Rhoda, and I had been friends since junior high school. We had gone through most of the usual things that kids had to go through during the sixties. But Rhoda and I had experienced some things that set us apart from a lot of the kids we knew when we were growing up.

Rhoda had grown up in a privileged environment, and she had enjoyed being the beautiful and pampered only daughter of a charismatic funeral director. She had lived in the lap of luxury in a big house with an extended family that adored her. If all of that wasn't enough, she was at that time, and to this day, the most beautiful woman in Richland, Ohio.

I had not been as fortunate as Rhoda. I had not even come close.

My father had deserted my mother for another woman when I was three, and had left us in a shack in Florida to fend for ourselves. But being a typical Black woman, my mother did what she had to do so we could survive.

We left Florida and moved to Richland, a small, blue-collar city near Cleveland. My mother did domestic work and that kept us from living on the streets. But when she took in an elderly boarder named Mr. Boatwright, our lives changed for the better, and for the worse. Mr. Boatwright had lost a leg, so he received a nice disability check every month. In addition to paying his rent on time every month, he helped us pay our bills.

And since he didn't have to work a regular job, he was eager to babysit me, keep our house clean, hop around town to shop for groceries, and cook while my mother went to babysit, clean, and cook for lazy, rich White women.

Mr. Boatwright—"Buttwright," as Rhoda called him behind his back—was very prominent in our church so he got a lot of pleasure out of giving me my Bible lessons. He liked to take credit for the times that I stood up to testify in church. And he took a lot of his time teaching me how to be nice and polite to people. But all of that had come at a high price: me. A few months after he'd moved in with us, he started doing whatever he wanted to do to me when I was alone with him.

By that time, he had already broken my spirit by constantly criticizing the way I looked. "Girl, can't nothin' help you! You fat, you Black, you ugly!"

I heard comments like that from Mr. Boatwright so many times that I began to hear them in my sleep.

I had only known Rhoda for a few months when I got up enough nerve to tell her that Mr. Boatwright had been abusing me since I was seven. Rhoda wasn't like any of the other girls I knew at the time, but nothing about her shocked me more than her reaction to my situation. She was horrified and developed a level of contempt for Mr. Boatwright that scared me. She vowed that one day she would make him pay for what he did to me. One thing I could say about Rhoda even back then was, she always did what she said she was going to do. Knowing that made it easier for me to keep my legs open long enough for Mr. Boatwright to have his way with me.

The same week of Martin Luther King Jr.'s assassination, Rhoda put a pillow over Mr. Boatwright's face while he slept. She held it there until he was dead. Rhoda and I were seniors in high school at the time.

I didn't witness, encourage, or participate in Mr. Boatwright's murder, but I felt that I was just as responsible as Rhoda. And to this day, I still consider myself her accomplice.

Everybody thought that Mr. Boatwright had died of natural causes and since Rhoda had made me promise not to tell what really happened, nobody questioned Mr. Boatwright's death.

Rhoda and I finished school and went our separate ways. She married Otis O'Toole and moved to Florida. I drifted around like a rootless gypsy in Erie, Pennsylvania, for a while, before I ended up back in Richland.

People were really not that surprised when my parents got back together after a thirty-year separation. But a lot of people were surprised when Pee Wee and I got married and had a child. My looks had not changed that much over the years. Except the older I got, the plainer and bigger I got. Pee Wee went from being a puny, effeminate busybody to a handsome, strapping man who could have married just about any woman he wanted. And that woman turned out to be me. For years some people walked around scratching their heads over that one. And I was one of those people.

Pee Wee and I had a lovely home and a lot of good friends. We had worked hard for everything we had acquired, including our love for each other. I had a good job that I enjoyed and people who cared about me. As far as life was concerned, I had had a good thing going.

Until now.

CHAPTER 10

As soon as I entered Rhoda's beautifully decorated living room, I felt sick. Or sicker, I should say. My stomach had been in knots and my head pounding like a drum ever since I'd left my house. The way I was feeling, I was in no mood to deal with Rhoda's husband and their houseguest. For all I knew it could have been one of them who had called me up! I once knew a man, when I'd worked for the telephone company, who could disguise his voice to sound like a woman. So that was not so far-fetched. But I was fairly certain that that was not the case.

I couldn't believe how paranoid I had become.

"Uncle Bully's depressed, too. Maybe you and him can cheer each other up, see which one is the most depressed," Jade said with a gleam in her eye. Jade was so young. She had so much to learn about life.

The man that they affectionately called Bully had been Otis's best friend since grade school. It was hard for me to believe that this same man had seduced Rhoda and was now drinking and grinning in her husband's face!

According to Jade and Rhoda, Bully's British wife had run off with *his* best friend. It had upset him so much that he had quit his job as a hotel manager in London and hopped on a plane and come running to Ohio so that Rhoda and Otis could console him.

I had never been one to judge people, but this was one situation that made me uncomfortable. Though I had no proof that Bully and Rhoda were fooling around again, it was enough for me to know that they'd already done it, producing a child.

"I'd rather deal with anybody else today," I told Jade as she escorted me to the kitchen, leading me through a back room so I'd bypass Otis and his company in the living room.

Just like Rhoda and Jade, Rhoda's house was spectacular. Large green plants filled almost every corner in every room. Expensive black-leather furniture and smoked-glass tables dominated the living room. The television in Rhoda's living room took up almost half of one wall by itself. Rhoda had recently replaced the white shag carpets that she'd had on every floor for over ten years. Now, with the carpets being maroon, she didn't insist that her guests remove their shoes at the door. I was so disoriented and I stumbled so much that my flip-flops kept sliding off my feet anyway. I was barefoot by the time I made it to the kitchen.

Rhoda was already in her cute little kitchen, where the walls, and almost everything else, were either yellow or white. She had a large glass of white wine waiting for me when I got there. I gulped it down in one swallow. Not because I was that thirsty, but because I was at a point now where alcohol was the only thing that I could think of that would dull my senses. It would give me the buzz I needed that I hoped would ease my pain. I let out a great belch and handed the glass back to Rhoda.

"I'll fix you a hot toddy after you get settled in the guestroom," Rhoda said, lightly touching the side of my sweaty face. I dabbed at my lips with the tail of my dress.

"I really appreciate you letting me stay here tonight," I sniffed.

Rhoda looked at Jade and they both gave me incredulous looks.

"Annette, you are family. If you can't count on family, who can you count on?" Rhoda asked. "Have I ever let you down?"

I could not remember the last time I'd seen so much compassion on her face. I shook my head and glanced around the kitchen.

"I just wish we knew who that cow was who's messing with you so we could straighten out this mess tonight, huh, Mama?" Jade asked with a furrowed brow. "Do you think she's going to call you up again, Auntie? When you find out who she is, I hope you punch her in the nose and get it over with."

I knew that Jade was way too young to know better, but she was more anxious to confront my adversary than I was! I looked at the freshly waxed kitchen floor and shook my head. "I don't know." I gave Rhoda a pleading look. "I sure hope she does not call me again. I don't need some shit like this in my life. I don't deserve this," I said angrily. "And I won't put up with it. If she calls me again and if I ever find out who she is, she's going to be sorry," I declared, shaking my fist. This was such a bold gesture for me to make, Jade and Rhoda looked like they didn't know whether to laugh or cry.

"That's right, Auntie. And I don't care who she is, or how tough she is, I know a great big woman like you could beat the crap out of her," Jade said, nodding. "Let's hope she's not real big and fat, too," she added with a wide-eyed look.

Like a lot of people I knew, Jade often made being big sound as critical as cancer. But I had to learn to look beyond this type of ignorance. Ignorance was like a cow that a lot of people couldn't stop milking. And some of the smartest people I knew, like Jade, were also some of the most ignorant.

"I didn't say anything about beating anybody up," I clarified, sucking in my stomach, which did me no good. There was nowhere for the thick roll around my middle to go. Jade looked at my stomach and shook her head, her mouth twisted like she was in pain. I refused to think about what she was thinking.

Just then Otis stuck his head in the doorway. He still had a full head of hair, but a lot of it was gray. His strong features had weakened over the years, giving him a jowly, fish-eyed look. I didn't know if they made girdles for men, but he sure could have used one. His unbuttoned shirt revealed a belly that hung over the top of his pants like a bloated apron.

"Annette, Annette, you look . . . You look . . . You don't look your best on this day," Otis yelled, looking at my ashy bare feet. One of my shabby flip-flops was by the stove, the other was on its side on the floor in front of the refrigerator. "To be honest, you look like some kind of hell. Ow! Everything all right for you?" Otis padded across the floor with his long, flat feet covered in a pair of beige socks, and gave me a quick hug anyway, looking me up and down.

"She's fine," Rhoda insisted, pulling me toward the door.

Otis frowned for a brief moment, then gave me such a wide smile, I could see every tooth in his mouth. I could also smell the whiskey on his breath.

"How about something to drink or some food or some conversation? Come! Come and join me and Bully in de living room and see if we can put a smile on that face of yours," Otis invited with a reckless grin and his hand held out in my direction.

"Maybe later. She needs to get some rest now. She's had a rough day," Rhoda said, guiding me out of the room.

Otis shook his head, slid his hands into his pants pockets, and shrugged. He was clearly disappointed and confused.

Before I could get out of the kitchen, Bully darted out of nowhere with a can of beer in each hand. Unlike Otis, he still had a firm, youthful body. Even with his plain blue shirt buttoned up to his neck, I could see a large, well-developed chest. He had rolled up his shirtsleeves, revealing thick arms with blue veins popping out, top and bottom. His smooth skin, rust colored on his body, his face and hands a shade darker, looked just as youthful as the rest of him. The only thing that gave away his age was the fact that he had several patches of gray hair, too. But he was still a very handsome man, and if Rhoda was still fooling around with him, I could see why.

"Ahhhhh, I think I met de lady before," Bully leered, looking at me in a way that made me feel even more uncomfortable.

"You are not a dry, sparse lady and that's a good thing!" Bully hollered. "Lots of you for a man to grab a hold to!" His eyes roamed over me like he was inspecting a side of beef.

Otis was the first person who had told me that large women like me were revered in Jamaica. And he had also told me that his friends and family had made fun of him when he'd chosen to marry a slim woman like Rhoda.

Jade giggled under her breath. Rhoda rolled her eyes and let out an exasperated groan. "Come on, Annette, before you get eaten alive. All the sharks aren't in the ocean."

I stumbled along between Rhoda and Jade, glancing back to see that Otis's frisky friend was still giving me admiring looks. If for no other reason, I was glad for the additional distraction. I had something else to think about other than the nasty note, the black-snake, and the disturbing telephone call.

"Rhoda, I hope this is not an imposition. I feel better now and it might be best if I go on back home. You have enough company in your house," I said. If Rhoda still had feelings for Bully, the last thing I needed was for him to pay too much attention to me.

"Don't even think about it. You are not goin' anywhere tonight. You are stayin' here with us tonight," Rhoda insisted, giving my arm a mild pinch. "Like I said, we are family. I can't speak for that man of mine, but I plan to be right with you throughout this mess. All the way, until it's over."

"And so do I," Jade said through clenched teeth.

CHAPTER 11

I hadn't brought any sleepwear with me to Rhoda's house. Spending the night had not been my original plan. But Rhoda found an old nightshirt that had once belonged to her big, husky son. Even though the boy was gay, he looked like a football player. His huge nightshirt was still tight on me when I put it on. And by the time I slid into bed, bloated from the two beers and the glass of wine that Otis had insisted I drink, the nightshirt felt like a cocoon.

I don't know what time I went to sleep that night in Rhoda's house. But I ended up being sorry that I was able to get to sleep at all. Throughout the night I had so many bad dreams I couldn't tell where one ended and another began. They included everything from me running up and down the streets with blacksnakes hanging off the top of my head like Medusa, to me receiving bombs in the mail hidden inside cute little pink boxes.

I woke up the next day with such a start I almost rolled off the queen-size bed in Rhoda's guestroom. I was stretched out on my back like a seal, with the silky sheets and fluffy white goose-down comforter wrapped around my legs like a single vine. It took me a while to realize where I was and why I was there.

I glanced at a clock on the nightstand and was surprised to see that it was almost noon. I had never slept this late on a Sunday. I went to church only about every two months, dragging Pee Wee with me. But I got Charlotte to go every week with my mother— whom I affectionately referred to as Muh'Dear—and Daddy. Anyway, even on the Sundays that I didn't plan to go to church, I always woke up at the crack of dawn to get Charlotte ready. Even without an alarm clock. This was the first Sunday in years that I had slept so late, and I didn't like it. I hated the fact that my tormentor had disrupted my normal routine. The fact that she hid her identity made her actions seem especially cruel. I felt totally helpless and defenseless. How could I prepare myself for something that I didn't understand and with an enemy that I couldn't see? It was beginning to feel like I was doing battle with a ghost.

I sat bolt upright in bed when I looked to the side of the room toward the door and saw Jade standing there, holding a breakfast tray that contained a plate and a cup of coffee. I will never forget the look on her face, because it was one that I had never seen before. She seemed to be looking at nothing in particular, like a statue. Her eyes reminded me of the eyes I'd seen on a dead woman once; the soul had departed.

"Jade? What?" I tried to untangle the bedding with my legs, but all I managed to do was tangle myself up even more. I rubbed my eyes and cleared my throat because for a moment I thought I was dreaming. The Jade standing across the room did not look or act like the Jade I knew.

She handed me the tray. When she smiled, her face looked like it was going to crack. "You need to eat, Auntie," she told me, rubbing the side of my face. "You had a rough day yesterday."

"Tell me about it," I said, taking a sip of the black coffee. I usually took cream and sugar, but this was one morning that I needed my coffee to be as potent as possible. "Where's your mom?" I asked, sniffing as I snapped off a piece of bacon. I blinked at the steam rising from the plate. There was enough food in front of me for three people. Even a glutton like me couldn't consume eight strips of bacon slathered with redeye gravy, six slices of wheat toast, a dollop of grape jelly as big as my fist, a stack of pancakes, and a mountain of grits with a puddle of butter. As if all of that wasn't enough to kill me, a saucer with about half a dozen thick link sausages that looked like a pile of logs sat on the edge of the tray. With an incredulous look on my face, my mouth hanging open, I looked from the feast in front of me to Jade, then back to the food.

"Is all this for me?" I asked dumbly.

"Uh-huh. I fixed it all myself," Jade said with a nod. "I know how big people like you love to eat."

"Oh. Well, I'm not really that hungry, but I appreciate you doing this for me, baby." I cleared my throat and sat up straighter. "Jade, let me tell you a little something. And I don't want you to take this the wrong way, because it's not really a complaint. Uh, it's more of an observation, but it's something I've been meaning to bring up."

"What?" Jade asked with a worried look.

I could see a pout forming on her face.

"Honey, you are almost grown. Some of the things you say now, you won't be able to say and get away with in a few years."

Jade gave me a surprised look, tilting her head to the side and looking at me out of the corner of her eye. "Huh?"

"It doesn't really bother me what you say to me. But sooner or later, you are going to say the wrong thing to the wrong person, and you will regret it," I said as gently as I could. But an angry look still appeared on Jade's face.

"I don't know what you are talking about, Auntie! I am one of the nicest people I know!" Jade yelled, waving her arms.

Her pouts were a powerful tool that she often used—and it always worked with me. I immediately regretted chastising her.

I nodded. "Yes, you are a nice person. But you say some crazy stuff sometimes." I smiled.

Jade shook her head and waved her arms some more. "Look, Auntie, you need to get some more rest. You are the one talking crazy right now. I gave up a trip to the mall with Debbie Bronson and Kim Jones so I could stay here and be with you. Now you eat! After that, you can use some of my bubble bath. Then, we'll get you back into your muumuu. Which, I washed myself last night after we put you to bed." Jade gave me a wide grin and a quick peck on my cheek.

She wore a tight denim jumpsuit that emphasized her tiny waist, which was smaller than one of my thighs. It was times like these that made me feel like somebody from another planet.

"And another thing, you don't have to worry about . . . you know," Jade assured me. She sat on the side of the bed and touched my arm. I gave her a guarded look. "What I mean is, we are behind you one hundred percent. Me and Mama. The person who sent you that mean note and stuff, she fucks with you, she's fucking with me and Mama."

"Jade, you shouldn't be using words like that," I scolded.

"I know, and I don't use them in front of Mama or Daddy. They know you spoil me and let me get away with all kinds of sh—stuff. If you hadn't talked them into it, they never would have let me intern for you at the collection agency."

"Well, I only agreed to that because it was just for the summer. You'll be leaving for college soon, and I wanted to spend as much time with you as I could." I smiled and raked my hand through Jade's hair. I loved how soft and silky her hair felt. I gave Jade a pensive look and pulled my hand away, rubbing the balls of my fingers together.

"Uh." Jade paused and patted her hair.

"Uh, what?" I asked, giving her a guarded look.

"I've changed my mind." Jade rose and started pacing the floor, munching on a piece of the toast that she'd prepared for me. "Um, I plan to tell Mama and Daddy that you want me to keep interning for you for a few more months. Well, until next year, at least. A lot of kids are going to spend at least a year doing other stuff before they start college. Backpack through Europe, Asia, Africa. My best friend, Cheryl Combs, she's going to hitchhike all over India. Isn't that the coolest thing you ever heard? And you wouldn't believe how many kids from my graduating class decided to do a few years in the military first and then come back to go to college."

"Jade, this is between you and your parents. But if you want to know what I think, I think you should go on off to college now. You've been accepted, and your folks can more than afford to send you; don't pass up this golden opportunity. I wish my mother had been able to send me to Spelman when I got out of school," I said with a sad sigh.

"Well, that's another thing. You and Mama didn't go to college and look how well you two turned out," Jade argued, standing over me like a sentinel.

"Things were different back then, honey. Your mother had it a lot better than me, but she didn't want to go college. She was pregnant with your big brother, and all she wanted to do was get married. Me, I had to get a job and start working to help my mother pay bills. I didn't have the choices you have."

"You mean you won't talk to Mama?" Jade whined.

"I didn't say that. But I don't have a good argument to work with."

"Will you at least give it a try? Oh, Auntie, I don't ask you for much. Please do this one thing for me. If you do, and Mama and Daddy say no anyway, I can live with that. And I promise you I won't ask for anything else for . . . uh . . . for a real long time." Jade gave me one of her puppy-dog looks before she bit her bottom lip. "You can say that it'll be good experience for me to work at your office for a while longer. I will be making my own money, I will be getting some work experience. And it would sweeten the pot if you gave me a nice raise . . ."

"I'll talk to your mother, but you know how stubborn your daddy is." I sighed, rolling my eyes.

"Well, Daddy will go along with whatever Mama says. If you can get to her, Daddy won't have a choice but to go along with my plan."

I let out a deep breath and handed the tray back to Jade with most of the food untouched. "I'll talk to your mother."

A huge smile appeared on Jade's face. "Thank you, Auntie." She turned to leave the room.

"Jade, can you bring me a phone? I'd better call Pee Wee and let him know where I am," I called after her. "I didn't think to leave him a note." I felt my hair. It was so matted and knotty it felt like I had on a spiked helmet.

"He knows you're here. I called him up early this morning myself, and I told him everything," Jade told me, talking over her shoulder.

I gasped and swung my legs to the side of the bed. "Everything?"

Jade stopped and turned to face me again. "Yes, I . . . oh, not that. I didn't tell him about that snake, or that note that somebody sent to you, or that nasty phone call you got. Mama said that you should be the one to do that," Jade said with a distant look on her face.

I let out a sigh of relief.

Jade gave me a pitiful look and returned to the side of the bed. "Auntie, you should tell him as soon as you get home."

I looked past Jade toward the window. August was such a beautiful time of the year in Ohio. A lot of people complained about the heat, but that was one of the things that I enjoyed most about the month. I never waited for Labor Day to arrive; I started having cookouts before the holiday. Like today. A barbecue in my backyard would be a great way to welcome Pee Wee and Charlotte back from Pennsylvania.

Telling them that somebody hated me was one thing that I would put off doing for as long as I could. But I couldn't bring myself to tell Jade that. "Jade, you have to promise me that you won't tell your uncle Pee Wee, Charlotte, your friends, or anybody else about . . . what happened."

Jade tilted her head to the side and made a sweeping gesture with her hand. "I won't. I just told you that Mama said you should be the one to tell Pee Wee," she said with one eyebrow raised. "I don't want to get in your business. You know me better than that, Auntie."

I nodded. "And I will talk to your mother for you as soon as I get her alone. And don't worry, she'll listen to me. She always has."

CHAPTER 12

After Jade left the room, Rhoda wandered in, looking like she had just stepped off the cover of *Essence* magazine. She wore a bright red sleeveless blouse and black jeans, and a pair of shiny, see-through sandals. Her hair and makeup were flawless.

"Are you all right?" she asked, winding her watch, tossing her hair back.

"I'm fine. Uh, let me say this before I lose my nerve," I said, my words almost running together.

Rhoda stopped winding her watch and stood by the side of the bed looking at me with a puzzled expression on her face. "Say it, then." She shrugged.

"Jade doesn't want to go off to college until next year."

"Is that all?" Rhoda said, looking relieved.

"She said that she wants to work for me a little while longer," I said. "But I think the real reason is that she's not ready to leave home yet." I threw that part in on my own because I didn't want Rhoda to think that I was the only reason that her daughter didn't want to leave home.

Rhoda looked even more relieved. "Well, she can stay home with me for the rest of her life if she wants to. If I had my way, both my kids would live with me until I died." Rhoda gave me a wistful look.

"I would give anything in this world for my son to move up here. I tell him all the time that his . . . boyfriend is just as welcome in my home as he is."

"So, will you talk it over with Otis?"

Rhoda waved her hand. "He doesn't want her to go away to school, or any other place, period. It's the grandmothers and the rest of the family, on both sides, that want her to continue her education."

"Well," I chuckled, "this was easier than I thought it would be."

Rhoda decided to treat Jade and me to brunch at the mall, but I promptly declined the invitation. After the pile of food that Jade had placed in front of me, going to brunch was the last thing on my mind.

With Otis and Bully in the house with me, I chose to stay in the guestroom until I felt ready to go home. Two more hours lying in somebody else's bed was about all I could stand. I crawled out of the bed in Rhoda's guestroom, and slid back into my muumuu and my flip-flops.

I joined Otis and Bully in the living room. I forced myself to smile when Bully commented on how melancholy I looked. After a few awkward comments, most of them made by Bully and Otis, I watched a few minutes of the ball game that had them jumping up and down in front of the TV whooping and hollering like hyenas. Sports didn't interest me and being alone with other women's men made me nervous. As soon as a commercial came on I excused myself and eased out the kitchen door.

By the time I made it back to my house, it was so hot and muggy the idea of standing over a barbecue was the last thing in the world that I wanted to do. But it was too late. I had already opened my big mouth and invited Rhoda and her family to the house that evening.

The only good thing about the invitation was the fact that Rhoda's houseguest had declined. "But I will take a rain check!" Bully had yelled before I left Rhoda's house, with a leer on his face that I hadn't seen since Mr. Boatwright. As if I didn't have enough problems already, I didn't want to have to deal with unwanted attention from Rhoda's ex-lover, especially right in front of her face.

Rhoda was very territorial. All I needed was for there to be some friction between her and me over a man! She had told me, with a severe scowl on her face, that Bully's wife had called him up from London earlier that morning. Apparently, the wife had left the man that she had run off with in a flophouse in Paris, and then returned home, eager to resume her relationship with her husband. Rather than go running back to the wife, Bully was going to spend a few more weeks with Rhoda and Otis, after Rhoda had insisted. However, Rhoda had suggested that Bully at least be available to talk to the woman when she called again. Which meant he had to stay at her house to answer the telephone today.

The more personal information that Rhoda kept from me, the more I wondered just what was going on between her and Bully. In the back of my mind, I was thinking that Rhoda was glad to be involved in my latest dilemma so she would have a good reason not to discuss Bully's presence with me. As far as I was concerned, Rhoda could have been fucking the pope for all I cared. I had my own problems to deal with, and I would have done myself more harm than good by pissing her off when I needed her as much as I did now. Until I figured out what was going on and why, I needed to keep Rhoda on my side.

Pee Wee and Charlotte drove up in his Jeep about an hour after I got home. I waited until he did all of his complaining about his relatives in Pennsylvania before I told him about the cookout we were hosting.

"Goddammit, woman. I'm tired and I sure don't feel like entertainin' nobody. You should have checked with me first before you planned this shindig," Pee Wee scolded, standing in our living room doorway with the screen door cracked open, fanning his face with an old issue of *Black Enterprises*. He had on some baggy black shorts and a light blue T-shirt. For a man with such a nice build, he had some of the scrawniest legs I'd ever seen. I enjoyed looking at him when he was naked because there were other things on his body that took my attention away from his knobby legs. I couldn't deal with him in shorts, and I usually told him so. But today I decided to keep my criticisms to myself. Hearing about the cookout had upset him enough.

"It's just going to be us and Rhoda's bunch," I wailed. I was on the sofa. Charlotte sat on the floor in front of me, clamped between my thighs as I braided her long, thick black hair. My daughter was so tender-headed she had to be restrained when it came time to get her hair combed and braided. The more she whimpered and fidgeted around, the tighter I clamped my knees. "Girl, if you'll sit still, I'll be done with you in a few more minutes." I gave her a gentle slap on the side of her head.

"I wanted a ponytail," she pouted. "Jade gave me all those ribbons and things, and I can't wear them with no braids!"

I ignored Charlotte and gave Pee Wee one of my most pleading looks. "They are just going to be here for a couple of hours. And it's too late for me to cancel."

"Shoot! I'll cook up somethin' in the oven, but I ain't standin' out there in all that hot sun no more today," Pee Wee told me. "I did enough of that over in Erie. I want to get some rest now."

I finished Charlotte's last braid and tapped the side of her head, indicating that I was done. She leaped up and like a bullet she shot across the floor toward the kitchen. I waited until I heard the back door slam.

"What happened while I was gone?" Pee Wee asked, joining me on the sofa.

He never stayed mad at me for long, especially when he was feeling frisky. He draped one arm around my shoulder while his hand slid up under my dress. After all these years, his touch still made my flesh tingle and my panties wet. I pushed his hand away. He leaned back and gave me an incredulous look. Pee Wee cupped his mouth with his hand to see if his breath was bad, which it wasn't.

"All right," he said, "tell me what's wrong. You ain't never done that before. As a matter of fact, every time I go off for a few days and come back, you be all over me in no time." He reared back and studied my face. He gave me a quick peck on my neck before he spoke again. "Remember what I told you I wanted to do to you when I called yesterday?" he whispered, nibbling on my ear. I had completely forgotten about the phone sex that we had enjoyed the day before.

I didn't like to brag, but I had a man that I wouldn't trade for the world. Not only was he tall, well built, and fine, he was a great lover, even on the telephone. My only fear was that one day he would take a real good look at me, and see me the way so many other people saw me: fat, Black, and plain. I knew I spent way too much time entertaining negative thoughts about the way I looked, but that was one thing I couldn't control. My confidence level had improved over the years and he had never done anything to arouse my suspicions, but that still didn't stop me from thinking that my life would fall apart sooner or later.

Pee Wee had had a lot of women before he decided he was ready to marry. All of the women before me had been a lot more attractive, so I have always felt that I was on thin ice as far as being able to hold on to my man. Even though he had made it clear that the way I looked didn't bother him, I felt very threatened when I thought about some of his former lovers. One woman in particular stood out in my mind like a knife: Betty Jean Spool. She'd been two years behind us in school, but that had not stopped her from fucking her way through half of the boys in our senior class. She was as fast as she was pretty, and age had not slowed her down or diminished her beauty. She was a cross between a man-eating shark and a snake in the grass. No man was safe around a woman like Betty Jean.

I couldn't count the number of stories that I'd heard about Betty Jean chasing some other woman's man—and catching him. I had some serious concerns now because I'd heard that she'd recently broken up with her husband and was on the prowl again. I couldn't stop myself from wondering just how far she would go to get a man. Especially my man.

With Richland being such a one-horse town, we didn't have that many bars. The Red Rose was the most popular bar and the one closest to my house. It was also the one that catered to a mostly Black crowd.

I spent a few nights a month drinking at the Red Rose with either Rhoda or Pee Wee. I didn't care too much for the place, though, because it brought back some painful memories. Mr. Boatwright used to visit that bar on a regular basis. I couldn't go there without thinking about him sitting at his favorite table, the one closest to the men's room, with his peg leg propped up on a chair. Another major reason why I didn't like the Red Rose that much was because Betty Jean Spool tended bar there three days a week, sometimes working a double shift, prancing around until closing time. When Rhoda wanted to go out for a drink, I always insisted that we go on one of the days or nights that Betty Jean had off. I had a hard time dealing with memories of Mr. Boatwright and her on the same night.

It was a different story with Pee Wee. He usually wanted to go on the nights that Betty Jean worked because that was when most of his buddies went. It surprised me to know that he didn't see how uncomfortable that woman made me. She flirted with him right in front of me! But then again, she flirted with all of the men, so when I complained to Pee Wee, he brought that up.

"That's just the way that woman is. She just do all that sashayin' and grinnin' so she can get bigger tips," Pee Wee insisted.

I didn't make too much of a deal out of it, because I didn't want my husband to know just how insecure I really was.

I was happy that Pee Wee had returned from visiting his daddy's grave in Pennsylvania. I was not happy that he had gone to the Red Rose for a drink right after I'd told him about the cookout I had planned for the evening. I was glad that I had invited company now. I knew that Pee Wee would want to climb on top of me when he returned from the bar, and with company at the house he would have to wait until we were alone.

"Well?"

He had just returned from the Red Rose, grabbing my tittie as soon as he closed the front door.

"Well, what?" I pushed him to the side and turned away from him, dusting off my coffee table with the tail of my muumuu. I had put on a fresh muumuu, but I still had on the same flip-flops that I had worn to Rhoda's house the night before. I had washed my hair as soon as I got home, and pinned it on top of my head. It hid whatever bald spots I had. A wide black headband covered my expanding hairline.

"I asked you what happened while I was in Erie?"

"Nothing happened while you were in Erie," I said quickly. I grabbed his hand and squeezed it, pinching his palm. "Uh, our company is going to be here in a couple of hours. If you're going to fix up some ribs in the oven, you better get started."

Rhoda, Jade, and Otis arrived two hours later. By that time I had showered and slipped into an even fresher muumuu, one with a more festive design, and the suede sandals that Jade had given to me for my birthday.

I was pleased that Pee Wee had fired up the grill in the backyard and cooked a couple of slabs of ribs. Not only that, while I was upstairs worrying myself to death over what had happened to me while he was gone, he had also prepared some baked beans, rolls, and coleslaw.

It felt so good to be among some of the people I loved. I hadn't invited my parents or any of our other friends to join us. There hadn't been enough time, for one thing, and with the way I was feeling, I was not in the mood to entertain too many people.

While Pee Wee and Otis tossed a dusty football back and forth in our spacious backyard, Rhoda, Jade, Charlotte, and I occupied the wooden picnic bench that Otis and Pee Wee had slapped together one afternoon a few years ago. I say "slapped together" because they had been drunk when they made it and it was so wobbly it rocked from side to side every time we sat down or got up from it.

Jade and Charlotte, each dressed in a bright yellow halter top and short shorts, skipped into the house to get more napkins and plates. As soon as the door slammed, Rhoda leaned across the table. "Did you tell Pee Wee about that shit and that telephone call you received?"

I shook my head. "No. Not yet. You know, I've been thinking about that. I really don't know if I will. I'll wait and see if that bitch calls again, or sends me anything else in the mail," I muttered.

"Yeah. Maybe you're right. I guess I wouldn't tell my man either, unless it really got out of hand."

Charlotte bolted from the door and kept running until she reached the barbecue pit. Like me, she loved her some ribs. But it showed on me and since it didn't show on her, I allowed her to eat what she wanted, as long as she didn't overdo it. I did enough of that for my whole family.

"Rhoda, if something happens to me or Pee Wee, will you promise me you'll take care of Charlotte?" I wasn't sure what prompted me to say that.

"Sure. I'd love to raise another child. But what about your mama and your sister in Miami?" Rhoda asked with an anxious look on her face.

"Muh'Dear is too old. So is Daddy. And Lillimae, well, I think she's enjoying her solitude too much to try to raise another child. She kicked her own kids out of the house as soon as they turned eighteen." I paused and let out a quick laugh, but Rhoda remained dead serious.

"What brought that on? You're not sick or anything, are you?"

"Not that I know of. But you know, anything can happen to any one of us."

Rhoda gave me a sad look. "Tell me about it. Every day I wake up, able to move on my own, I wonder how long it'll be before the damage that stroke did to my body gets the best of me." Rhoda smiled. "I'll make a deal with you. If somethin' happens to you, I'll take Charlotte into my home. If somethin' happens to me, you take Jade into your home."

I gasped. "I'd be glad to take Jade into my home," I promised. But something in the back of my mind made me wish I had never started this conversation.

CHAPTER 13

I was feeling real good now. I had almost forgotten about the note and the blacksnake that I had received, and the mean telephone call. No matter how negative all that was, the list of positive things in my life was a lot longer.

I had even gotten over the fact that Pee Wee had gone to the Red Rose before the cookout to have a drink. Even though it was one of the nights that Betty Jean tended the bar.

While Rhoda and I were in the kitchen, gathering napkins and paper plates, Pee Wee staggered in. Dust and dried leaves decorated his face, arms, and hair. He looked like a scarecrow. Between sips from a bottle of beer, Pee Wee told Rhoda that she was glowing like a woman in love.

"Oh, I am. I am a woman in love," she swooned, giving Pee Wee and me a mysterious look. Otis walked into the kitchen just in time to hear Rhoda's response to Pee Wee's comment.

"Of course she loves me. How can she not?" Otis slurred, giving Rhoda a sloppy kiss. They acted lovey-dovey until we left the kitchen and returned to the yard.

Just as I was about to pop open another beer, I heard the telephone ring in the kitchen. Jade was in the kitchen so I didn't make a move to go answer it. She stuck her head out the kitchen window and told me that I had an urgent phone call. There was a frantic look on her face.

Urgent or not urgent, I took my time walking to the kitchen. The last time I had tried to run after drinking a few beers, I ended up flat on my face on the ground with a bloody nose, and scrapes and bruises from my chin to my forehead. As soon as I entered the kitchen, Jade held up her hand, motioning me to stop.

"What did you say? Fuck you, you bitch! That's my auntie you're talking about!" Jade screamed into the telephone receiver. My mouth dropped open and I started moving toward Jade, reaching for the telephone. But before I could reach Jade, she slammed the telephone back into the cradle.

"Who in the hell was that you were cussing at, girl?" I shouted, gripping Jade by her trembling arm.

"Auntie, it was that bitch," Jade sobbed. She rotated her neck and took a deep breath. "Oh, this is real messed up! That . . . That lady was so mean to me and she doesn't even know me! I don't know why she cussed at me. All I did was answer the telephone and I was real nice to her!" Jade fell into my arms, howling like a panda.

"What? Who?" I asked, a hot flash assaulting my face like a flame.

"The bitch who sent you that shit. The same bitch that called you up last night." Jade let out such a strong, deep breath that I felt a breeze on my face. "I told her that if I ever find out who she is, I will beat the shit out of her with my own hands!" Jade flung her arms around me and cried on my shoulder.

I decided I had no choice but to tell Pee Wee what was going on. And Rhoda felt the same way when I summoned her to the kitchen and told her about the disturbing telephone call that Jade had just taken.

"Annette, you *have* to tell Pee Wee. And you have to tell him now. You don't know what kind of person you are dealin' with," Rhoda said, shaking her finger in my face as we stood in the kitchen by the window.

I ignored Rhoda and moved to the sink where Jade stood dabbing her eyes with a wet paper towel. "What else did she say, Jade?"

"She, she called you a black, black cow and a . . . a . . . b . . . b . . . black heifer," Jade stuttered, almost choking on her words.

"Ha! At least we know she's not too bright. Everybody knows that a cow and a heifer are the same thing," Rhoda snarled. "What else, baby?" Rhoda asked, her lips snapping over each word. "Did you hear any background noises? Cars, music, dogs, trains, kids? Anything that might help us figure out at least where this bitch called from?"

"And what good would that do if we don't even know who she is?" I asked.

"Annette, you really need to sit down and think back over the last few days. Or even the last few weeks. Who have you talked with that you might have said something they took the wrong way? At least we know it's a woman, so you can eliminate every man we know."

"I don't know," I mumbled. Shaking my head, I moved to the refrigerator where I snatched out a bottle of beer and removed the cap with my teeth. I slammed the refrigerator shut so hard that a pan on the stove twirled all the way around like a spinning top. "There are a few women at work who are mean enough to do something like this. But not to me. I haven't done anything to anybody at work that would make them want to get back at me," I said thoughtfully. "At least not that I know of."

"Auntie, remember when I told you I heard those cows talking about you when I was in the ladies' room that time?" Jade asked, surprisingly composed now. One thing I could say about Jade was that she was the most resilient human being I knew.

I looked from Jade to Rhoda, shaking my head. "I can think of at least two or three who didn't like me getting the promotion," I said. I suddenly felt even more frightened. It was one thing for me to receive ugly mail and phone calls at home. I felt somewhat protected in my house, as long as Pee Wee was with me. But I was wide open at work. Anybody could walk up to me and start shooting!

"Shit!" Rhoda mouthed, casting me a hard look.

"What if it is one of my co-workers?" I asked in a frightened, hoarse whisper.

"Well, when you find out who the bitch is, you file a complaint,"

Rhoda said. "There are laws against this kind of shit when it happens at work. You used to work for the phone company. So you got some damn leverage. They liked you so much they didn't want you to leave. It ought to be easy enough for you to pull some strings and get them to tap your phone, here and at work. If you find out where the calls are comin' from, you'll find out who is makin' them."

"I've already thought about getting my phone tapped and adding caller ID to my service. But I don't think either one would do any good. I am sure that whoever is doing this to me has already thought about those things too," I said with a heavy sigh.

"Well, I am dyin' to find out who this bitch is," Rhoda hissed.

"I might not live long enough to find out. Especially as crazy as people have gotten in this world. If I'm dealing with a real psycho bitch, filing a complaint wouldn't even cover as much as a Band-Aid." I gasped and leaned against the wall.

For a moment, my mind flashed on every recent work-related act of violence that I knew of.

CHAPTER 14

It was a major struggle for me to get through the rest of the evening. I had lost my appetite, even for alcohol, and it was not easy for me to go on about my business like nothing was wrong. I couldn't say the same for Rhoda and Jade. They were able to put up a good enough front to keep the men from noticing that something was out of order.

It had begun to get dark and the streetlights that lined my street had just come on. After a trip to the bathroom to rid myself of some of the beer that I'd consumed, I went out to my front porch and looked up and down Reed Street, wondering if my new enemy was one of my neighbors.

I lived in a very quiet, respectable, racially diverse neighborhood. Directly across the street from my house was a large beige house with five bedrooms and a garage wide enough to accommodate three vehicles. It was the newest building on the block. It had been built five years ago by the friendly Pakistani man who managed the Second National Bank, where Pee Wee and I maintained our joint checking and savings accounts. Before the Pakistani man and his family moved across the street from me, the spot where he had built his dream home had been vacant for several years. A lot of folks didn't like to talk about the house that had once stood in the same spot. It had been another large house, occupied by a happy family: Rhoda's family. Not her and Otis and Jade, but Rhoda and her parents and other family members. Shortly after they moved out, a wiring situation created a problem that caused a fire, and the house, which had contained the mortuary that Rhoda's daddy had owned, burned to the ground. Whenever Rhoda paid me a visit, she refused to even look at the location where she'd once lived.

For some reason the streetlights that lined Reed Street looked a little brighter than usual and resembled a strange necklace. Every single residence had a large, well-kept front lawn. Other than the Cherry Hill neighborhood across town, this was one of the nicest parts of town to live in. Cherry Hill is where Rhoda, Muh'Dear and Daddy, and Scary Mary—a feisty old madam who was Muh'Dear's best friend—lived. It was clean, almost crime-free, and I felt safe and welcome. Well, I had felt safe and welcome until I received that cute pink envelope with the nasty message inside.

I glanced at my watch, surprised to see that it was almost nine. But it was still warm. As a matter of fact it was warmer than usual, so on my way back in from the front porch I flipped on the air conditioner.

I had turned on the back porch light, but with the light from the bright, silvery moon and the army of fireflies with their yellow tail-lights flashing, we didn't even need the porch light. There were just as many mosquitoes buzzing around as there were fireflies, and the only purpose that those suckers served was to sting us. As much as we all scratched and complained about the mosquitoes, you would have thought that we would have already called it a night. But everybody seemed to be having such a good time. Everybody but me.

I had sat on the hard bench so much, my butt was numb and my muumuu had begun to feel like it was glued to my body. And as annoying as the mosquitoes were, they were a distraction for a while. I was looking for anything and everything that I could focus on, so that I wouldn't have to think about that telephone call that Jade had answered for me. Because when I did think about the call, I thought about the nasty note and the blacksnake.

Fatigue soon got the best of me. I couldn't stop yawning and rubbing my eyes. As much as I enjoyed the company of Rhoda and her family, now I regretted that I had invited them over. I tried not to think about that telephone call, but it stayed in the front of my crowded mind, even more so than the note and the blacksnake.

Had I still been in school, it would have been easier for me to compile a reasonable list of suspects. But things had changed a lot for me over the years. It was hard for me to come up with more than a handful of people, women in particular, who might have a reason to hold a grudge against me.

I recalled a run-in that I'd had with a hostile clerk in a nearby grocery store who had shortchanged me, a hairdresser who had lost her job after I'd complained about a botched perm, and a waitress I'd refused to tip in a restaurant; I could go on and on. I didn't think that I had done anything to anybody that was a good enough reason for them to approach me in such a hostile manner. But apparently they thought I had, and that was what I had to focus on: what I had done, and who I had done it to.

Every time Rhoda glanced at me there was a look of compassion and concern on her face that I hadn't seen since the days of that child-raping Mr. Boatwright. Even though he'd been dead for almost thirty years, that bastard still haunted me.

Rhoda and Jade *seemed* to be enjoying themselves just as much as Pee Wee, Otis, and Charlotte were. They were still running around in our backyard throwing a Frisbee and that damn football from one to the other like it was the Fourth of July. But I knew Rhoda and Jade better than I knew myself. They were just as disturbed as I was about what was happening to me. They were just better at hiding things than I was. Especially Rhoda.

"Auntie, don't you want to have some fun?" Jade yelled as she leaped in the air trying to wrest the Frisbee out of Pee Wee's hand. "It's good exercise." She paused and gave me a curious look as I just sat looking at her like I had suddenly become mute. "Auntie, didn't you hear me? Don't you want to get up off that hard seat and have some fun?" Jade yelled again. "You are already sweating and huffing and puffing like a pig anyway, and you haven't even done anything but sit in the same spot, off and on, ever since we got here."

Jade's long ponytail flopped up and down like the tail on a

Palomino. With all the sweating I'd done, my short, severe hair looked and felt like a thorny skullcap. It seemed like the older I got, the worse my hair got. It was shorter, thinner, and more brittle than ever. Jade had informed me, in no uncertain terms, that if I ever stopped letting my beautician dye my hair and pluck the stubborn hairs from my chin on a regular basis, I would eventually look like one of the Smith Brothers, the bearded men illustrated on the cough drop box. Not only was Jade's comment a little extreme, it was funny and I had laughed about it. If I had let the things that Jade said about my appearance bother me, I would have covered my entire head and face with a ski mask and the rest of my body with a blanket every time I left my house.

After the ugly comment that the note writer had made about my hair, I knew that I couldn't go on without covering what was left of my hair with a wig. I had worn braids for a few years, but I'd removed them after a comment made by a meddlesome Black co-worker.

"Girl, if you want to get anywhere in this company, you better stop comin' up in here lookin' *too* Black. Them braids gots to go if you ever want to get a management position in the corporate world. Remember how many of us moved up the corporate ladder once we got rid of them Afros and Jheri Curl dos?"

I didn't like what my co-worker had said, but I'd taken her advice. Lo and behold, a month after I traded in my braids for a sleek perm, I was promoted. The woman who had thought that she would get the position, even though she'd often come to work with a greasy hairnet hugging her head, stopped speaking to me the same day. My breath caught in my throat just thinking about this particular woman. She had slashed the tires on her ex's car when he left her. If she could do that, she could do anything!

"Auntie, are you listening to me?" Jade yelled, startling me back to the present moment.

"Huh?" I replied, jerking my head around to face her. My face felt like something was crawling all over it. With my hand throbbing like I had arthritis, which I probably did have, I slid it up and down the side of my face. There was warm sweat on my face, not spiders like it felt like.

I sat on top of the wobbly picnic table with a can of beer in my hand with gnats, ants, and flies keeping me company. I offered a weak smile and shook my head at Jade.

"I'd rather just sit here and watch," I told her. My body felt like a huge boulder, rocking this way and that. It was hard for me to shift my body from one position to another and not fall from my seat. Running around like a teenage athlete was out of the question. Especially with what I had on my mind.

CHAPTER 15

That telephone call had really disturbed me. Even more so because poor Jade had experienced my tormentor's wrath. I had ignored the telephone in the kitchen when it rang again about an hour later, glad that the others had ignored it, too. After the ringing had stopped, I shuffled into the kitchen and checked the answering machine. The caller had not left a message. I turned off the ringer and the answering machine before I returned to my spot at the table in my backyard.

"Oh, let old lazybones stay right where she's at," Pee Wee teased. He paused and shook his finger at me. "I'll exercise her sure enough, later on tonight," he threatened, immediately covering his mouth.

"Watch that smutty mouth you got, mon," Otis teased, his Jamaican accent more pronounced than usual. "There is young peoples in de midst."

"Like I don't know what's going on," Jade scoffed, rolling her eyes and slapping Pee Wee's butt with the palm of her hand.

Pee Wee ignored Jade's gesture, not because he knew I was looking, but because he knew that I trusted him. I trusted him with all my heart. I knew that as long as he was married to me he would never do anything inappropriate with Jade or any other female.

Pee Wee was the only man on earth I could say that about. Daddy didn't like me feeling that way, but with his own track record he didn't have a leg to stand on.

"I'm tired!" Charlotte yelled, out of breath. She darted across the yard and fell to the ground, fanning and wiping sweat from her face. "Mama, can I have some beer, too?"

"What's wrong with you, girl?" I asked harshly, giving my daughter one of my meanest looks.

"My throat is dry," Charlotte whined. She screwed up her face, and then coughed and pounded on her chest all at the same time.

"Have you lost your mind? You are a child, and children do not drink beer," I managed, glaring at my daughter like she had asked me for the Hope Diamond.

"Jade drunk some beer!" Charlotte pointed out, stomping her foot.

Charlotte and Jade both had friends their own ages, but they had a special friendship that was slightly disturbing. At least it was to me.

As strict as Rhoda and Otis were with Jade, she still got away with more than a lot of kids her age. I knew that they allowed her to drink a little wine every now and then, falling back on the excuse that some of the most prominent families in town allowed their children to drink wine occasionally.

Rhoda's father had an older half brother, named Johnny, who had returned to his home in Alabama several years ago. This half brother, who happened to be White, was as shady as he could be. Despite his morals, he had been a fun person to be around. And one thing that I could say about Rhoda's uncle Johnny was, even though he was a notorious womanizer, he had never said or done anything inappropriate to me like Mr. Boatwright had done.

Rhoda often visited her uncle down South, usually with Jade in tow. From what I had managed to piece together from stories Jade had shared with me, that same old White man was just as crazy about Jade as he was Rhoda.

All of the kids in our neighborhood had called him Uncle Johnny, even me. This Uncle Johnny had spoiled Rhoda rotten when she was a child. Pee Wee had told me that the same old man had even taught her how to shoot a gun.

In addition to expensive toys and clothes, Uncle Johnny used to give Rhoda big bottles of wine, way before she reached legal age. It had been nonalcoholic wine, but to me, wine was wine.

I felt the same way about beer and as long as I could help it, my daughter was not going to drink beer until she was of legal age. I had enough to deal with. I didn't need to have to deal with a miserable situation like an alcoholic child, too.

"Mama, can I please have a little sip?" Charlotte pleaded.

Out of the corner of my eye I saw Pee Wee about to react. He slapped his hands onto his hips and started moving toward Charlotte with a stern look on his face. But I got to her first.

"Jade's a lot older than you. How many times do I have to remind you of that?" I ignored the sneer that I got from Jade and for once, I was glad she was not my child.

CHAPTER 16

I didn't like breaking up a party, especially one that I had initiated. But I needed some space so I could rearrange my thoughts. And besides, as much as they tried to hide it, Jade and Charlotte had worn themselves out with all that running and jumping around. Pee Wee, Otis, and Rhoda seemed to be dragging, too.

I feigned a headache. In a way, I did have one. My head felt like it was about to explode because it was crowded with so many thoughts. To make it look good, I slapped an ice pack on my forehead and did some serious moaning and groaning. But it wasn't even necessary for me to go to that extreme.

"We should be leavin' anyway," Rhoda told me in a tired voice, walking along with me as I hauled the leftovers to the kitchen. "Bully doesn't like to be alone too much, even in a house as cozy and nicely decorated as mine. Lord knows what that runaway wife of his will say to him. That's when and if she calls my house tonight. You know how tacky British woman can be. They don't understand men like we do, especially if their man is a brother."

I noticed the dreamy-eyed look Rhoda got on her face every time she mentioned Bully. He must possess some very good dick, because for a houseguest he held a very high position on Rhoda's

priority list. She had told me herself that she enjoyed cooking special meals for Bully. Even when she prepared hot dogs or ham-
burgers for dinner, she thawed out a steak for Bully. Jade had
spilled the rest of the beans on him. To me, he sounded like the
houseguest from hell. He left his dirty clothes and toenail clip-
pings all over the house, and he ate and drank like a hog. When it
came to meat, he only ate steak and lamb. And he had to have
bread from a Scandinavian bakery way across town. And as much
as he liked to drink, Budweiser beer and Wild Turkey weren't good
enough for him. He had to have some kind of Guinness brew or
Remy Martin cognac. He was so lazy that when Rhoda wanted to
make up his bed, she had to do it with him in it. That Bully. He
took hour-long baths and chatted for hours at a time on the telephone, racking up hundreds of dollars worth of calls (that Rhoda
and Otis had to pay) to people in Jamaica and London. He even
had the nerve to complain when his meals were late.

"And Lord knows Bully will have made a mess in my kitchen and
I'll be up all night cleanin' it up." It was one of the few times that
I'd seen Rhoda complain with a smile on her face.

"Well, the way my head is throbbing, all I want to do is crawl into
bed," I muttered. "I'll call you from work tomorrow."

After Rhoda and her family had left, knowing I had a headache,
Pee Wee saw that Charlotte got herself ready for bed. And when he
finally came to bed, I pretended to be asleep.

This was one of the few times that I was grateful for middle age.
Especially middle-aged men. In some ways, it had slowed Pee Wee
down more than it had me. With so much beer in his belly and
him being tired from jumping around in our backyard, he was out
like a light in no time, purring like a cat. This was the first time in
years that his snoring didn't bother me. When I finally did get to
sleep, I woke up every half hour or so with thoughts whirling
around in my head like gnats.

I left to go to my job at the Mizelle Collection Agency the next
day an hour ahead of my normal time. That way I didn't have to
see Pee Wee before he left to go to the barbershop that he owned

and managed. He had inherited it from his late father, so it meant a lot to him. He enjoyed his work so much, he often stayed on the premises long after the last customer had come and gone.

We had an agreement that he would get Charlotte up and off to the child-care center that Rhoda operated out of her house during the summer months. I took care of her the rest of the year. I didn't complain about having to get my daughter up and out of the house nine months out of the year when Pee Wee only did it for three months. I looked forward to it. But Pee Wee was such a hands-on kind of daddy that I thought it was good for him to do some of the things that most men left to their women to do.

Other than Mr. Royster, a bowlegged security guard in his late sixties, I was the only one in the office. Over the years it had become my home away from home because it was where I went when I needed some time and space to be alone.

Right after I graduated from high school I had worked briefly as a switchboard operator. Then I moved to Erie for about ten years. But when I returned to Richland, the phone company gave me my old job back. I remained on that switchboard for several more years.

Two years ago I landed a receptionist job at Mizelle's, the biggest collection agency in Richland. Unlike at the phone company, where I'd only been qualified to work as an operator, Mr. Mizelle, the owner, had promoted me to a management position a year ago. They would have given me the moon to stay because I was the third person to fill that position that year. It didn't take me long to figure out why. Even before Shakespeare created Shylock, the ferocious collector in one of his plays, collection agents had been despised. The company often had to bribe and beg employees to stay. Ironically, we shared the first floor of a small office building with the IRS, the only other group I knew of that was even more despised than collection agents. But I felt like some of the other brave people who stayed: it was a job and somebody had to do it.

Some of the same angry people who had to visit the IRS for an audit also visited us on the same day to make arrangements to pay off a bill that they'd ignored until we stepped in. More than a few angry deadbeats had stormed out of the office spewing threats. That's why we had to have a security guard. And an armed one at that.

Mr. Royster's age and the fact that he was so bowlegged fooled a lot of people. But this old brother was sharp and fearless, and he knew how to use that gun hanging off his bony hip. Before he came to work for Mizelle's, he'd worked at one of the downtown banks. One day, a masked man entered that bank, armed with a gun himself. Mr. Royster had saved the day by shooting the would-be robber in both legs, incapacitating him until the police arrived. I felt safe at the office with our bowlegged security guard there to protect me.

My only hope was that he would never have to use that gun on my behalf.

CHAPTER 17

If Mr. Mizelle had not promoted me, I probably would have returned to my old job at the telephone company, or moved on to another place of employment by now. Bill collectors were not very popular in Richland.

Along with the fourteen collectors I supervised, some days I spent half of my time on the telephone. On a regular basis, I heard so many cuss words from the people we had to call that profanity now sounded like a separate language to me. The turnover among the collectors was incredible. By the end of my first month of employment three of the collectors had left that place, running out like somebody was chasing them with a shotgun. And one time a man did show up with a shotgun and threatened one of the collectors.

The verbal abuse that we had to put up with when we called up people was so extreme that I started seeing spots in front of my eyes when I got an angry person on the telephone. And most people did get angry when we called them up and threatened them with legal action for not paying a bill. Muh'Dear used to cuss out bill collectors or avoid them. I'd even done it a few times myself when I was younger and didn't know how to plan and stick to a budget.

After a man I'd called—about his delinquent account with a furniture store—told me to suck his dick and then hung up on me, I started planning my own resignation. That was when I got wooed into staying by Mr. Mizelle himself offering me that promotion.

I was just as surprised as the rest of my co-workers. Especially the ones who had more education than I did and a background more closely related to the business. Gloria Watson, a bitter woman who rarely had anything good to say about anybody else, started rolling her eyes at me the day the announcement was made. Even when I hired one of her nieces as a temporary receptionist, that ungrateful wench continued to hold a grudge against me.

Gloria's behavior did not surprise me. She had a major chip on her shoulder. It got even bigger when the names of several members of her crude, irresponsible family appeared on our list. The old man who had told me to suck his dick was Gloria's older brother, and the father of the niece that I'd just hired.

"As long as Gloria Watson ain't signin' your paycheck, you ain't got nothin' to worry about," Pee Wee had said when I told him.

"I'm not worried about Gloria," I said, forcing myself to laugh. It was easier to laugh about Gloria than to take her too seriously. I came across women like her, some even worse, on a regular basis. My time and energy were too critical for me to waste on their foolishness. But Gloria was in my space so she could not be entirely ignored. "I just don't feel comfortable around her when she treats me that way. If I'd known she was still going to treat me like shit, I wouldn't have hired her niece. I'd have given that temp job to Jade."

Jade had just graduated from Richland High School at the time and was eager to start her first real job. Up until then she'd only earned her spending money babysitting and running errands for me and some of the other neighborhood mothers.

Three weeks after I'd hired Gloria's niece, that lazy devil started showing up two to three hours late—often with alcohol on her breath! Some days she didn't even bother to come in at all. For a while I let all of that slide, but the day I caught her smoking weed in the ladies' room was the last straw.

"You know, they say that your own folks can sometimes be your worst enemy," Gloria said, talking with her back to me in the break room. It had been two weeks since I'd fired her niece, but the tension between us was still like a poisonous gas.

I noticed how Gloria had waited until we were alone. She had become so disgruntled that the only time she spoke to me was when she had to, or when she had something to get off her chest. My firing her niece had upset her more than it upset the niece. As a matter of fact the niece had grinned and sighed with relief. She didn't even seem to mind being escorted out of the building by our bowlegged security guard.

"What's that supposed to mean?" I asked, not even bothering to look up from the box of Kentucky Fried Chicken that I had picked up for lunch.

Gloria was just as big as me. But the way she pranced around the office, wearing outfits I wouldn't wear to a Halloween party, you would have thought that she was as petite as Jade. For the past year she'd been bringing in Weight Watchers' lunches and going to the gym down the street three times a week on her lunch hour. She was firmer now and didn't jiggle as much, but she was still a very large woman and the biggest bitch I knew.

"You know what I mean." She paused and sucked on her teeth until I looked over at her, standing there with one hand on her hip and a scowl on her face. "Black folks oughta be tryin' to help other Black folks get and keep a job."

"If you are talking about your niece, anybody else would have fired the girl a long time ago. I warned her several times about her tardiness and it did no good. What was I supposed to do, let her continue to work here just because she's Black?"

"That ain't what I said. She's got three kids and she needs a job more than you and me do. You didn't have to fire her. Yeah, she was late now and then, but at least she came to work."

I gave Gloria an incredulous look. "Is that how Black folks are supposed to look out for each other? She didn't follow the rules, and I was not supposed to do anything about that? Well," I said, rising, "if you were the boss, you could supervise your way. Until then, let me do my job the way I think it should be done. And, by the way, I'd appreciate it if you didn't spend so much time on personal telephone calls. It sets a bad example."

I didn't wait around to see Gloria's reaction. I waltzed out of the break room and returned to my office and shut the door. I couldn't ignore the increased tension between myself and Gloria.

The note, the blacksnake, and the telephone call probably had come from her! If not her, then *who?*

CHAPTER 18

I felt pretty stupid just sitting in my office alone—so early in the morning that all of the lights on the floor in my area were still off, except the one above my desk. I must have looked pretty stupid, too.

"Mrs. Davis, is everything all right?" Mr. Royster asked for the third time in the last half hour. "Can I get you a cup of coffee or something? I just made a fresh pot."

The security guard had a pained look on his face. I had never seen anybody as bowlegged as him. Not knowing that much about the condition, I wondered if it was painful. From the look on Mr. Royster's face, it looked like it was a strain for him to stand or walk. With his leathery dark skin and bushy mustache, he reminded me of Daddy, even though Daddy was close to eighty now. Daddy often had the same look of pain on his face. In his case I knew that it was because on any given day something on Daddy's body was aching.

I cleared my throat first. "I'm fine. And a cup of black coffee would be nice."

I waited until Mr. Royster disappeared around the corner before I resumed my thoughts about Gloria. She hadn't been the only one who had had issue with me firing her niece. To my surprise, Pee Wee considered it a bad move on my part.

"A triflin' girl like that ain't goin' to be able to get another office job in this town. She'll be pickin' beans for the rest of her life. And don't forget that's what you used to do," Pee Wee reminded me, as he lay on his back in our bed, naked and frisky. His hands couldn't stop moving all over my body—poking, prodding, and squeezing, no matter how many times I pushed him away.

"And I'd still be pickin' beans if I had acted the way Candace Watson acted." As if picking beans had been the worst thing I'd done to get paid. I didn't want to remind my husband about my brief stint as a prostitute shortly after I got out of high school. "You can hire her if you feel that sorry for her. I am sure a successful Black businessman like yourself can put your reputation, business, and sanity on the line just to keep another Black person employed." I didn't like being so sarcastic and it wasn't something I wanted to do. But the sarcastic comment that I had made to Gloria in the break room about her niece had made her even more upset with me, and that was what I'd wanted. It was my way of reminding her that I was still the boss lady. As a supervisor I didn't think I'd be that effective if I let my subordinates walk all over me. But sarcasm from me usually didn't even faze Pee Wee. It usually took something pretty extreme to get a serious reaction out of him.

As soon as we ended our tense discussion about my firing the useless receptionist, things got really physical. It had been a while since Pee Wee had kept me up most of the night. When he finally climbed off of me, with both of his hands still prodding, poking, and squeezing various parts of my body, we both went to sleep smiling.

I considered myself one of the luckiest women in the world. Pee Wee was the kind of man that any woman would have been proud of. Not only was he good looking and great in bed, he was sensitive, generous, hardworking, and smart. His temperament was one of the many things that I loved about him. But there were times when he truly got on my nerves. Like when I told him that I was going to hire Jade to replace the slovenly receptionist I'd just fired. I had already run this by Rhoda and Otis. Jade had just graduated a few days before. She was scheduled to head off to college in September. Now, I had to admit to myself that it had not been my idea to hire Jade. I loved the girl. I loved her as much as I would have had she been my own daughter. But she had her moments and was a real piece of work by anybody's standards. Once she set her sights on something, she didn't stop until she got it. It took her a year of whining, moaning, and begging, but she eventually pestered Rhoda and Otis until they purchased her a car—a year-old Tercel.

And as soon as Jade had found out that I had fired the temp receptionist, she made a beeline to the same temp agency and signed up.

"Auntie, call up the Marchoke temp agency, ask for Pam Jackson, and request me for the receptionist position you currently have open. I am willing to work overtime at a moment's notice, as long as it doesn't interfere with anything else I have planned. I expect to be able to take time off when I need to, like my birthday, or if I need to stay home and help my mom run her child-care business. But that's only if my absence does not cause any hardships . . ." Jade paused, but because I had no comment to make at that moment, she continued. "And, because the temp agencies don't offer holiday pay or sick leave pay, I need a salary that will make up for that," she instructed me over the telephone that same day.

Just like that. Like she had been sitting back waiting for this particular job to become available.

"Let me think about it for a while," I said, so taken aback I wasn't sharp enough to just say no.

"Good. But make it a short while. I would like to start on Monday," Jade chirped. I was impressed with her level of enthusiasm. It had been a long time since I'd come across somebody so eager to work. From the determined tone in her voice, I knew that she wasn't going to let up until she got her way.

I didn't waste any time discussing this with Pee Wee first because I didn't want his input. But I decided to let him think that it had been my idea to hire Jade. "Uh, I told Rhoda and Otis that I'd like to hire Jade to replace that receptionist I had to fire. It's so hard to find good help these days . . ."

"Oh, shit," Pee Wee laughed, giving me an incredulous look from his side of the bed that Sunday night.

I had agreed to let Jade start her new job that Monday morning like she had requested. I had even agreed to all of her other demands, making her promise not to share that information with the other employees that I supervised.

"This will be good for Jade. With my other collectors quitting left and right, we need all the help we can get. And Jade speaks Spanish so she could even help make some of the calls to the Spanish-speaking folks. It's amazing how many of them forget how to speak English when a bill collector calls them." I paused as I groped for more words. "Rosita Menendez is the only other Spanish-speaking collector we have right now and the way she's been complaining, I expect her to run out of that place screaming any day." I was rambling now. "Rhoda taught Jade how to speak Spanish when she was little. And when they lived in Florida, most of Jade's friends were the children of the Cubans and Puerto Ricans who worked in the orange groves that Otis's family owned. She even speaks it without an American accent."

"And how would you know she speaks Spanish without an American accent? Unless there is somethin' you ain't told me, you don't speak nothin' but English yourself."

I rolled my eyes. "I know because the Cuban lady who does our nails said so," I snapped.

"Yeah, but do Jade speak the language good enough to be doin' it on a job?" Pee Wee wanted to know. "With all the slang these kids use today, knowing Jade, she speaks Spanish like them Cholos over on Willow Street."

"Well, the girl won't be dealing with any diplomats from Madrid or Argentina. She'll be dealing with some of those ignorant Puerto Ricans that come up here to work on the farms, and then jump into a cesspool of debt right off the bat. You wouldn't believe how many of them run out and get new cars and charge accounts they can't afford. One man we call on a regular basis lives in his car."

"And how do y'all call him if he's livin' in his car?"

"On his cell phone, of course, which he can't afford either!" I snapped. "I'm going to have Jade start right away."

Jade showed up that following Monday morning, eager to begin her first real job. Not only was she dressed to kill, she had her own expensive-looking black leather briefcase in addition to her beloved yellow backpack.

CHAPTER 19

Even I didn't carry a briefcase to work. The large black shoulder purse that I always carried around was cumbersome enough.

Rhoda thought it was cute that her daughter was so enthusiastic about her first real job. "My baby. My baby girl is growin' up! It seems like it was just yesterday that I was escorting her to kindergarten," Rhoda said, almost sobbing. As soon as I told Jade I would hire her, she and Rhoda stormed the mall and many other expensive stores along the way. "I want my baby to look as good as the rest of those young women office workers."

"It's a small-time collection agency office, not Wall Street. I am the supervisor, and even I don't go to work dressed like my life depended on it," I chided Rhoda.

"I doubt if I could talk Jade into wearing muumuus to work like you do," Rhoda said with a sharp sniff.

"For your information, I do have a few suits and other business attire. But at my work, we encourage people to dress more for comfort as opposed to style and fashion. The owner from the main office even wears jeans and plaid shirts when he comes to visit our branch."

Rhoda gave me a horrified look and shook her head. But even

hearing that didn't stop her from spending thousands of dollars on a new work wardrobe for her baby.

Rhoda was the one who had bought Jade the expensive leather briefcase with her initials on the handle. Jade carried her briefcase like it contained some of the most important documents in the world. A week after she'd started working for me, she confessed that all her briefcase contained was a can of hair spray, a jar of Noxzema, a few issues of *Essence* magazine, and an extra pair of panty hose. It was her yellow backpack that contained her most important props, like her wallet, her diet pills, her makeup, some romance novels, and anything she didn't want her parents to see.

As I sat there thinking about Jade's yellow backpack, I had to wonder if it still contained that Frederick's of Hollywood catalogue that she had stuffed in it on Saturday, the day I'd received that nasty note.

I glanced at my watch and didn't realize that I'd been sitting in my office reminiscing for more than an hour. All of the lights were on now, and I could hear people buzzing in the cubicles outside my office. I had a lot of work to do, so I planned to stay in my office with the door closed for as much of the day as I possibly could.

Our office area was fairly small. Other than my corner office and the ladies' room, there were not many places where I could hide when I needed to be alone. The break room was like Grand Central Station throughout the day. I knew how stressful it was for the folks I had on the phones making the telephone calls. That was why I didn't complain when most of them had to run into the break room for water to either drink or splash on their faces, after being on the telephone with some of our more difficult debtors.

I had thought that it would be easier for me to be at the office instead of in my own home. I changed my mind the minute Gloria Watson rolled into the office, half an hour late, with rollers still in her hair. Even though I had advised her not to come to work looking so slovenly, she still did so. It had been easy to fire her niece. But firing Gloria was a different story. For one thing, she was known for filing frivolous lawsuits. She had gone after the city bus company because she felt that they always arrived in her neighborhood late, if at all, because they didn't like Black folks. With Gloria, when something didn't go her way, she blamed it on racism. She had also filed discrimination claims against an airline, several department stores, and the restaurant where we'd had last year's Christmas party luncheon. Her latest target was Mizelle's. She felt that they routinely tried to collect from more Black and Hispanic folks than they did White folks because they were racist. I didn't even bother to remind her that it wasn't the collection agency who selected the people we went after, but the stores and banks.

Of all of the lawsuits that Gloria had instigated, she had been lucky with only one. And even that one had been settled out of court. It had been more of a nuisance payoff. A fried-chicken place had given her a few thousand dollars to appease her when she complained that they served reheated chicken to minority customers.

Mr. Mizelle was a kindhearted, fair-minded old man with a face like a lobster and thin hair the color of mud. He and his wife had adopted four Black children and one of his own daughters was married to a Puerto Rican. He didn't have a racist bone in his body. Even though he'd hired a lot of minorities, whom nobody other than the farms would hire, Gloria was still a concern of his.

And mine.

I realized just how much a thorn in my side Gloria was when she entered my office that morning without knocking.

"Hey there," she mumbled, with the same tight look on her face that usually indicated severe constipation. It had been a while since she'd greeted me with a simple hello. "Um, I got a doctor's appointment this afternoon. I have to leave right after lunch."

I sniffed and rose from my seat, hoping she couldn't tell how frazzled I was.

"No problem. But since you came in late, again, this morning, you can make up that time, and the time for this afternoon, by working through lunch today. Otherwise, we'll have to dock your pay."

"Can't I come in this weekend to make up the time? You know I can't afford to have y'all messin' with my paycheck." Surprisingly, Gloria spoke in a gentle, low voice. "You bein' a sister, I am sure you can relate to that." Gloria lifted her chin and looked at me with her eyes narrowed into slits. "You know how we got to look out for one another. I don't care how nice these peckerwoods seem around here, they still want to see us down and out." I looked at Gloria, trying to read the mysterious expression on her face.

"I'm sorry you feel that way, Gloria. Except for getting cussed out by some of the people I call, all of my experiences here have been positive," I said firmly.

"Well, don't let that fool you. You and me about the same age. We can't just up and run off and get hired anywhere we want no more. Most people want to hire them cute young girls like Jade. My cousin Florene, she smaller than me, and she can't get a decent job nowhere. Last place she applied at, that trendy clothing store at the mall, they said her size would be a concern. Not only were they concerned about her for safety reasons, they didn't think it would be the right image for the people who come up in there to buy them youthful clothes. A big she-bull like her ought to have known better. I know *you* know what I mean," Gloria concluded with a sneer.

I nodded. "Give me a list of your calls. If you decide to make up the time this weekend, just let me know so I can leave that information with the security guard."

As soon as Gloria left my office, I shut the door and locked it. I called Rhoda.

"I think Gloria is the one," I said.

"The one what?"

"The one who sent me that shit in the mail. The one who called my house yesterday when Jade answered the telephone."

"Well, did you confront her about it?"

"No, not yet. I need more evidence first. If what I think is true, I am firing the bitch. She can sue me to kingdom come. I am not putting up with that kind of shit from her or anybody else."

"I hear you, girl. But I do wish you'd share this with Pee Wee."

"I will," I said weakly, knowing that I would hold off on that for as long as I possibly could.

CHAPTER 20

It felt like I was on needles and pins every day for the next two weeks. One morning I woke up moaning, with my arms covered in scratches. Throughout the night I had dreamt of long, slimy blacksnakes crawling all over me, and then biting me with their fangs and wrapping their coiled bodies around my neck.

Every time the telephone rang, I almost jumped out of my skin. Most of the time I let the answering machine screen my calls and if the caller happened to be somebody I didn't feel like talking to, I let the machine record a message. It disturbed me even more when the machine recorded a few hang-ups. And once I received a two-minute recording of some heavy breathing!

The mailbox on my front porch had become just as much of a nightmare as the telephone. I held my breath each time I went to retrieve the mail. I sweated so much when I chose to answer the telephone or check the mailbox that I had ruined three of my best silk blouses. And because of all the sweat clogging the pores on my head, my hair had taken on a life of its own. It was in a state of shock and it did what it wanted to do, not what I wanted it to do. I could keep my pink sponge rollers in my hair for two days in a row and my hair still wouldn't curl. And unfortunately, I made more trips to the liquor store than I should have. I felt like a stranger in my own body.

I became abrupt with some people, snapping at them for some of the most insignificant reasons. I'd yelled so loud and with so much contempt in my voice at a young teller at my bank for not moving fast enough that their armed security guard had approached *me* with his hand on his weapon. I was coming undone and I didn't know how to stop it.

Things that had always annoyed me seemed to annoy me even more. Like the leaky faucet in my kitchen sink, the stoplight at the corner that seemed to stay red for five minutes, bubble bath that didn't bubble enough, and even something as minor as the squeaky springs on my bed.

"Pee Wee, if you don't fix that sink and get us a new bed, I'll find somebody who will!" I barked at Pee Wee, as I trotted out of the kitchen before he had time to reply. He fixed our leaky sink the very next day, and by the weekend we had a brand new bed.

"Happy?" he asked.

All I could do was nod and look for something else to complain about.

I felt bad about taking out my frustrations on Pee Wee. But apparently my sudden and odd behavior didn't bother him that much, because he didn't comment on it. At least, not at first.

When three weeks had passed without a note or a telephone call from my antagonist, I relaxed. I felt like I had just been released from a dungeon. As far as I was concerned things were back to normal. One thing I was really glad about was the fact that Pee Wee and I were making love again, and I'd been the one to initiate that. During my previous weeks of despair I had wanted to have sex about as much as I wanted to have shingles. Every time Pee Wee had looked at me, my flesh crawled and knots formed in my stomach. It didn't do him a damn bit of good to strut around naked dangling his dick in front of me like it was a carrot, or to play with my titties. I just could not get excited.

As mysterious and complicated as the female body was to most men—not that a man who didn't have a medical background would know the difference anyway—I took advantage of Pee Wee's ignorance, and decided that I would milk that cow until it couldn't be milked any more. I feigned every malady I could come up with. I held Pee Wee off with fake headaches, backaches, stomachaches, constipation, bladder infections, a yeast infection, vaginitis, and toothaches. Some nights I'd claimed two or three of the discomforts on my list at the same time.

When he suggested that my ailments were probably due to the beginning of menopause, I fell back on that excuse, too. I had had a few hot flashes, sprouted a few stray hairs on my chin, and skipped a few periods, so I wasn't that far from the truth. But that fact of life gave me something else to be down in the dumps about: I was getting old.

I was no longer a young woman, anybody could see that. But my memory was still sharp enough for me to remember most of my life, which had started in a small town outside Miami. Daddy had run off with a White woman when I was a toddler. My mother had dragged me from Florida onto a segregated train that carried us to Ohio. For a long time the only person we could count on was Scary Mary. Of course Mr. Boatwright had always come through for us— if you didn't count his nasty ways.

I don't know what I would have done if Rhoda had not helped me abort old Mr. Boatwright's baby when I was sixteen. But the most important question I couldn't answer was what would have eventually become of me if Rhoda had not smothered Mr. Boatwright to death that night so many years ago.

Mr. Boatwright's murder was the most difficult secret that Rhoda had asked me to keep. But he had been only one of her victims! If everything she had told me was true, her list of victims included her troublesome grandmother, an ex-cop who had shot and killed one of her brothers, a pregnant White girl who had threatened her other brother with a rape charge, and a child molester who had raped and killed the young daughter of one of our friends.

I didn't condone murder or violence, but there had been times when I'd been forced to protect myself. I was glad that I had never done anything as extreme as Rhoda had done to the people who'd provoked her.

Besides, I was way too humble to play God.

CHAPTER 21

Time had brought a lot of changes in my life and the people around me. About ten years ago, after a thirty-year separation, my mother had allowed my daddy back into her bed. People new in their lives had a hard time believing that they had ever been separated. They seemed that natural together. And that was exactly how they had been before Daddy had run off.

The White woman that my daddy had left us for eventually deserted him and their three biracial children. After being in an interracial relationship in the South at a time when it was still segregated and sizzling with racial unrest, the White woman had decided that she wanted to enjoy all the advantages of being White after all. She not only turned her back on Daddy, she also turned her back on the three kids that the ill-fated relationship had produced.

"Like I tell you, girl, and everybody else, time and time again, 'God don't like ugly,'" Muh'Dear said with a laugh when she heard the news about the woman leaving Daddy.

And if that sweet revenge was not enough, the White woman's death in an automobile accident years later brought another caustic comment from my mother. "See there? That home-wreckin' hussy had it comin,' and now she won't be bustin' up nobody else's marriage."

I was glad that Muh'Dear's bitterness and anger had not rubbed off on me. I had felt bad for everybody involved, even the White woman who had broken up the happy home I'd once known. But I had not been the only innocent young victim. There were three other young people with the same blood I had, who had to piece their lives back together, too.

Two of my half siblings had careers with the military and lived in Germany. I didn't communicate with them that often, but I spoke to my half sister Lillimae in Florida on a regular basis.

Other than Rhoda, Lillimae was the only other female I felt I could confide in. I had chatted with her several times in the last few weeks. I guess I must not have sounded like my old self to her, because she'd asked me several times if something was wrong.

"Big sister, you don't sound like yourself lately," Lillimae had told me the last time I had called her, a week after I'd received the nasty note in my mailbox. "Whatever it is, you know you can talk to me about it. And if you need to get away from it all, you are always welcome to come down here for a few days."

I couldn't bring myself to tell Lillimae what was on my mind. It was enough to have Rhoda and Jade in on it. I don't know what I would have done had they not been there for me.

Jade liked to bat around town in her cute little Tercel. Two or three times a week she insisted on picking me up in the morning and taking me to the office and back home at the end of the day.

"Auntie, I am glad to see you smiling like your old self again," Jade said to me. She had picked me up for work five minutes earlier that Monday morning in September.

"I just hope I can keep smiling," I said, with a smile that stretched across my face like a river. I let out a loud sigh. Not a sigh of sadness, but one of relief. I couldn't remember the last time I'd felt so frisky. I was even thinking about sneaking away from work later that morning and going to the barbershop to seduce my husband. If he had customers, I'd wait. But then I'd have to call work and make up a good enough lie that it would get me out of work for as long as it took me to take care of my business. I wasn't just smiling now. There was a wicked grin on my face. "I'm just glad that whoever sent me that shit and called my house found something better to do with their time."

Jade had her eyes on the road in front of her, but she still ran a red light. "Maybe they are harassing somebody else now," Jade suggested. There were no other cars in sight so I didn't react to Jade's careless driving.

"I don't give a shit what they are doing or who they are doing it to. That trifling bitch didn't know who she was fucking with when she started that mess with me," I said, my lips snapping so brutally that spit flew out of my mouth. "I wouldn't want people to know I didn't have anything better to do with my time. You have to be pretty sorry and pitiful stoop to that low."

Jade glanced at me as she leaned forward and gripped the steering wheel, driving with so much determination and skill now you would have thought that she was driving an ambulance.

A few moments passed before Jade spoke again. "Did you ever find out who it was?"

I had closed my eyes and leaned my head back. It was just a little past eight in the morning, but the sun had already turned on its autumn heat, which was just as warm as it had been in August. The only difference was it was a lot more muggy. I didn't know why people in our part of the country called this time of year Indian summer, but it sounded exotic. It was a better time to have picnics and cookouts because some of the annoying bugs and grasshoppers had already disappeared to wherever they go to this time of the year.

My mind was a million miles away but I could still hear Jade's voice. It took me a while to respond to her last question.

"No, I don't know who she is and I don't care. A sorry bitch like that doesn't even deserve any more of my time. I just wish she had kept that shit up long enough for me to find out who she was, so I could have straightened her ass out." It was rare for me to display anger, but when I did it scared me. I must have scared Jade, too, because I noticed her bottom lip trembling. "Sugar, don't mind me acting like this. I wish you hadn't got dragged into my mess. I know how much that telephone call upset you that time. You are like a daughter to me, and I wouldn't want to see you upset any more than I would my own daughter."

"Auntie, if that bitch ever starts to fuck with you again, she'll be sorry."

I nodded and smiled some more. "In the meantime, you watch your language, girl." I tapped the side of Jade's head and we both laughed. "And keep your eyes on the road. You almost jumped that curb just now."

Right after I commented on Jade's driving skills, an old memory shot through my mind like a cannonball. Rhoda had been a horrible driver when we were young. Her daddy had bought a used Mustang for her. Before she had learned how to maneuver the vehicle properly, she had knocked over mailboxes and run into more trees with it than anybody I knew. She had used that same car to mow down the ex-cop who had killed her brother. The man's death had been listed as a hit-and-run. Nobody had questioned Rhoda about the severe dent in the front of her car that she'd come home with that same day. But by then, every body shop in town had worked on Rhoda's car.

Once again, she'd gotten away with murder.

CHAPTER 22

Before we were married, I had told Pee Wee about Rhoda's crimes even though I had promised her that I wouldn't. However, some of the secrets I carried around like a sackful of rocks eventually got too heavy for me to handle by myself. I trusted Pee Wee and I knew that my secrets would be his secrets. His response had surprised me. He had been so amused and nonchalant the day I told him, I regretted doing so. I still didn't know if he believed me or not. It was something that we hadn't discussed in years. I wanted to leave it that way.

I knew enough about crime to know that there was no statute of limitations when it came to murder. Even though Pee Wee was no longer the type of person who ran all over town spreading rumors and gossip, I had no way of knowing whether he would leak that information anyway. I knew that there was no guarantee that we would remain together. I had a concern that if he married another woman he might share what I'd told him with her. Only God knew what would happen then. Information like that usually found its way to the authorities. And I had every reason to believe that if Rhoda went down, I'd go down with her. At least for Mr. Boatwright's murder. I gave things a lot of thought now before I shared them with Pee Wee. Like the mess that was going on in my life now.

I had also told Pee Wee about Mr. Boatwright abusing me and the fact that out of desperation I had sold my body to some of Scary Mary's clients so that I could raise money to leave home. I really don't know if he believed any of that, either. It had also been years since we'd discussed that confession. The only other person I had shared this same information with was Lillimae. She had believed every word I told her. I couldn't explain why I had not called her when I got that note in the mail. But even though this was something I didn't want to share with my husband, I knew that sooner or later Lillimae would pry it out of me.

I called Lillimae from my office but got her answering machine.

"Hey, little sister, it's Annette. I need to talk to you. Please call me back as soon as you can. I know you are at work now, but don't call me at home tonight because I can't talk. Tomorrow, when you can take a break, call me at the office." I hung up and let out a loud, deep sigh, feeling better already. As soon as I hung up, someone tapped on my door and opened it before I could respond.

"You want to join me and Mom for lunch?" Jade asked.

"Oh, no, sugar. I'm going to run across the street to McDonald's and grab a salad, I said, sucking in my stomach. Tell your mom I'll see her at the beauty shop this evening, and afterwards we'll go for drinks."

As hard as it was to believe, Rhoda and I got our hair done at the same place. What was even harder to believe was the fact that even though she had four times as much hair as me, they charged me the same amount that they charged her. Rhoda got her hair done once a week. I only had to go every other week. So there was some justice in the world of beauty. My monthly hairdressing bill was half of what she paid. But even on the weeks that I didn't have to visit my beautician, Rhoda and I had a standing date to meet up at the Red Rose for a couple of drinks.

"OK," Jade said, her big green eyes slowly looking over my head. "Auntie, no offense, but don't you think you should consider going back to braids? And the longer and thicker the better. Uh, people are laughing at your bald spots. From the front, your hairline looks like Harry Belafonte's."

"My hairline looks like Harry Belafonte's? What . . . I . . . what bald spots?" I asked with a profound gasp. Both hands flew up to my head, patting and feeling around. I plucked my purse out of my desk drawer and fished out my compact.

Jade shut the door and moved over to my desk. "You can't see them, but other people can," she informed me. "Especially in the back . . . and on the sides."

I gave Jade a thoughtful look before I rolled my eyes upward. "I don't have a receding hairline."

"I didn't say you did." She rushed around my desk and stood behind me, her fingers raking through the top of my hair. My skin tingled as she inspected my scalp with the tips of her fingers. "But, I swear to God, these bald spots need all the attention you can give them," Jade complained. "Just look this mess!" Jade walked back from around the desk, shaking her head.

"Who has been laughing at me?" I asked quietly. "Other than Gloria Watson, I mean." Gloria made fun of a lot of people, so whatever she said about me usually didn't bother me.

Jade shrugged. "Well, her mostly. She cracks jokes when she's got an audience."

"Uh-huh." I shook my head and shifted in my seat. "You go on to lunch. Paula Barton is out again today and she left a long list on her desk. I'm going to have to make some of her calls."

"I can help you make some of the calls when I get back, if you want me to," Jade offered, heading for the door. "Now you just sit there and relax."

I didn't like the fact that Jade, at times, held such a high position of authority in my life. There were occasions when I felt like I was the child and she was the adult.

Muh'Dear and a lot of other adults I knew complained that Jade was too mature for her own good, and that it would eventually cause some problems. Not just for Jade but for other people in her life.

"And don't worry about that bitch," Jade said. "Me and Mama, we got your back." Jade gave me a firm nod before she left my office, gently closing the door behind her.

I was worried about *that bitch*. But I was worried about Jade, too.

CHAPTER 23

W hat Jade had said about people laughing at me didn't really faze me that much. A lot of people had said a lot of stupid shit about me, and to me. Some had even been brazen enough to say it to my face. I had been used to it for a long time. However, mean and nasty comments still hurt, but I got over it all a lot easier and sooner than I had when I was younger.

I had a lot more going for me than some of the people who took it upon themselves to criticize me. My job as a supervisor at a respectable company was one of the many things that I had going for me. Despite the negativity that I had to deal with, I still felt blessed.

There was only one other enclosed office at Mizelle's. Our bookkeeper shared that cramped little fishbowl with a wall of files and Mr. Mizelle, my boss, when he visited. And that wasn't very often. It was a privilege for me to have an office all to myself when the other employees had to work in tacky little back-to-back cubicles. The four cubicles along the wall had windows, and those cubicles were almost as coveted as my office.

My promotion had included a cash bonus of three thousand dollars that I had used to buy myself some new office furniture. The company had a budget that covered furniture, office supplies, and a few other miscellaneous items, but the company didn't want to pay for what I wanted. I got myself a large red oak desk with a matching file cabinet. I even purchased some ethnic artwork for my walls. I loved plants but I didn't have much luck with them. I had to replace the plants in my house on a regular basis because I couldn't keep them healthy and looking good. I did the same thing at the office. A large, framed grinning portrait of me, Pee Wee, and Charlotte was the only photograph that I had on top of my desk, even though we took pictures all the time.

I removed the latest issue of *Ebony* magazine from the top drawer on the side of my desk. After I glanced at the table of contents and didn't see anything I was anxious to read about, I dropped it back in the drawer. As much as I liked to read, women's magazines especially, I hadn't done much reading in the last couple of weeks. It angered me to know that the person who had chosen to harass me had caused me to make so many changes in my routine.

I rolled my chair around just far enough so that I could look out the window behind my desk. There was not much of a view: just the side of another dreary gray building and a few naked trees. Fallen leaves covered the ground like a thin brown blanket with jagged edges. I leaned forward toward the window so I could see the corner of the Chinese restaurant where Jade and I often ate lunch. Despite the fact that there was nothing that interesting to see, I sat and stared out my office window.

I sat there wondering if I would ever find out the identity of the woman who had targeted me. But then I had to ask myself: what good would it do me to find that out? My instincts now told me that it probably wasn't Gloria Watson. She had not done anything out of the ordinary that I was aware of. But I didn't want to rule her out. I let out a sigh that was so strong it fogged up part of the window, forming a large, steamy *O*.

I lost track of the time so I don't know how long I sat in the swivel chair behind my desk, as stiff and mute as a statue. When I finally stood up, my legs almost folded. My head was spinning and I couldn't understand why I was so dizzy. I decided that I was going through some kind of an aftershock and my body and mind had to readjust. That little note, the blacksnake, and the telephone calls had done a lot of damage to me. And I knew that it would all stay on my mind for a long time to come.

Just before noon I decided to leave the building. I walked briskly past the cubicles near my office, flipping a folder in my hand. I looked busy and in a hurry and that's the way I wanted to look. I didn't even want to talk to anybody unless I had to. My workers were pretty independent and reliable. I knew that they did what they had to do without me breathing down their necks.

With my purse swinging off my arm like a pendulum, and my legs aching like I'd been kicked, I trotted the one block down the street from our office to McDonald's. I was so preoccupied, I crossed the busy street without looking both ways for traffic, and an eighteen-wheeler missed mowing me down by just a few inches.

That incident was responsible for my stomach feeling something other than hunger pains. I decided to not pick up the three Big Macs that I had planned to eat for lunch because I had to stand in the order line for so long that by the time I got up to the counter to give my order I had lost my appetite. I was annoyed because I had wasted twenty minutes of my lunch hour.

"I don't want to order anything. I keep forgetting that I'm on a diet," I told the young girl behind the counter with a sheepish grin on my face, my chin tucked in.

"I don't blame you," the girl hollered, with a frown on her face as her heavily made-up eyes roamed all over me as I turned to walk away. Her reaction made me feel twice as big as I really was. I waddled to the restroom, sucking in a stomach that wasn't going anywhere.

Before I left the restroom, I looked at myself in the full-length mirror on the wall, raking my fingers through my hair. I was horrified at what I saw. I had left home without putting on any makeup and my hair looked like I'd been flying. The buttons on my blouse were buttoned wrong. I had on a flowered blouse and a plaid skirt. I looked like a humongous piñata. I wondered why Jade hadn't also commented on my attire. Realizing how tacky I looked, I was afraid to go back out in public. But I did. I couldn't have felt more uncomfortable walking back to work if I'd been naked.

People gave me the usual looks of disgust that they gave other obese people, but my weight was their problem. I had stopped obsessing about it a long time ago. Diets didn't work for me, my doctor said I was in good health for a woman my size and age, and my handsome husband couldn't keep his hands off me. I knew that Jade and Rhoda, both being a size four, thought that being slim was the greatest thing in the world. They suffered a lot to remain thin. Three years ago when Rhoda returned from a cruise eight pounds heavier, she fasted on water and juice until she got back to her normal weight, which took three whole weeks. The fast had almost killed her, but to a person as vain as Rhoda, it must have been worth it.

I didn't envy Jade and Rhoda for their beauty. If anything I felt sorry for them. Especially Rhoda.

In Rhoda's case, nature had given her a lot. But it had taken much more away from her.

CHAPTER 24

I was thankful that nature had not chosen to disrupt my good health, so far. I was obese, there was no doubt about that. But that was an affliction that I could have controlled better, had I tried. When I compared my health to Rhoda's, I decided that I was the lucky one after all.

Unlike Rhoda, I had never really been sick or incapacitated a day of my life. Death had even come knocking on her door; lucky for her she was too sick to open that door and she'd escaped death that time.

Even though she was still an extremely beautiful woman, Rhoda's deterioration had begun right after she had given birth to Jade. Breast cancer had claimed both of her breasts, but she had learned to live with that disfigurement. She wore clothing that hid it so well, even I didn't know until she told me. But that was just the beginning.

About ten years ago she suffered a stroke that had almost killed her. Of all the places on her body to be affected, it had to be her beautiful face. To a vain person like Rhoda, that was as good as a death sentence. For several months one side of her face was so contorted that she'd looked like a leering gargoyle. She also had some paralysis and speech problems. After two intense years of physical therapy, she recovered. At least on the outside. Her face resumed its original appearance, but for several years after, her left eye wouldn't close and tears streamed from it at the most inconvenient times.

"I finally got my husband to fuck me after a two-year dry spell and right in the middle of it, my damn eye up and starts floodin' like Niagara Falls," Rhoda complained. Rhoda's marriage suffered, to say the least. She and Otis would go for weeks at a time not speaking to each other.

But Rhoda's marital problems had started long before her physical problems, so she couldn't get any mileage out of that. Time had not healed the wounds in Rhoda's marriage. In some ways she and Otis lived separate lives. They were more like roommates than husband and wife. It pleased me on the occasions when they showed some affection toward one another, but they were rare.

Before Rhoda's stroke, right after giving birth to her first child, Rhoda gained a lot of weight and had a hard time losing it. Her husband had found her repulsive, and started to ignore her in the bedroom. But some men found Rhoda's weight gain attractive.

The man who had found Rhoda most attractive was her husband's best friend, Bully. For several weeks they had fucked the hell out of each other—once even in the same bed where she slept with Otis. Rhoda had told me all of that out of her own mouth.

After Bully had moved on and married some English woman, Rhoda discovered she was pregnant with his baby. Since Otis had not touched her in months, she knew that if she wanted to save her marriage she had to come up with a plan. She got Otis drunk and dragged him to bed. When he woke up the next morning naked, she was in his arms. Self-inflicted scratches on her thighs had convinced Otis that he had made love to her. She'd even scolded him for being so rough.

A month later when Rhoda told Otis she was pregnant, he was jubilant. By then she had lost most of the weight from the first baby, but he professed that he didn't care how much she gained this time. She gave birth to her second son and regained her original figure in no time, with the help of an aggressive and expensive personal trainer. Her marriage was wonderful again. But Rhoda's bliss was short-lived.

Things fell apart again when the little boy died shortly after his birth. Rhoda was devastated. She then seduced Otis several times a day until she got pregnant with Jade. When the cancer claimed Rhoda's breasts she fell into a bottomless pit of depression. Otis didn't neglect her this time, but she neglected him, and that drove her husband into the arms of another woman.

They had worked through their problems and managed to stay together for the sake of Jade and her older brother, Julian. Jade was almost grown now and Julian was on his own. The marriage that Rhoda and Otis had now was more like a relationship of convenience, a sham and a shame. I didn't know what Otis did on his own, but Rhoda was as busy as a bee.

Even though Rhoda avoided the subject, I had a feeling that she and Bully had resumed their affair, right up under Otis's nose.

Since Bully had come to town, Rhoda paid even more attention to Jade. But something told me that that was just a smoke screen. Even if it was, Jade was still the center of Rhoda's universe. As far as Rhoda was concerned, Jade could do no wrong. But I knew things about Jade that I didn't want to know. Things that I had promised myself I would keep from Rhoda for as long as I could.

Rhoda often bragged about how Jade was going to be a virgin until she got married. Well, unless Jade knew how to perform a miracle, being a virgin on her wedding night would be impossible. I didn't have the heart to tell Rhoda that Jade spent more time on her back than a quadriplegic does. Like so many other young girls hot between their legs, Jade regarded sex as a pastime. Like hanging out at the mall with her friends or getting one of her weekly egg facials.

"Auntie, I love tall boys to death. They make the best lovers," Jade had swooned to me a couple of years ago in my living room during one of her frequent visits.

"Girl, you'd better leave those tall boys alone if that's all they are good for. Sex is at the root of a lot of society's problems. It's even a crime in some situations," I said, recalling the many rapes I had endured at the hands of Mr. Boatwright.

"Oh, not getting sex ought to be a crime," Jade laughed.

I dismissed Jade and her comments, and forgot all about that conversation until I received a frantic call from her, begging me to come give her a ride home from the Rolly Stark clinic where she'd just had an abortion. She was fifteen at the time.

"Auntie, you have to come get me! Paulie got scared and left me here at the clinic by myself!" Jade had sobbed.

"And what did you go to the clinic for?" I asked, glad I was home alone so I wouldn't have to explain anything to Pee Wee about Jade, once I found out what she needed to explain to me.

"Uh . . . I . . . I found out last week that I was a little pregnant. Remember that party you dropped me off at a couple of months ago at Lolly Hawk's house? Well, something happened to me that night, but I didn't expect to get pregnant! Shoot—I just wanted to have some fun! Honest to God. Me and Paulie don't want really want a baby right now," Jade told me. She broke down and cried for two minutes straight before I could speak again.

"Does your mother know about this?" I asked in as calm a voice as I could manage. This was the most stunning piece of information that Jade had ever shared with me. I couldn't believe my ears as she told me the whole story.

The baby's father, a boy who still walked around with a snotty nose and who hung out in the neighborhood on his bike, had become nervous in the waiting room. He had left in such a hurry that he'd left behind one of his shoes. This was a boyfriend that Jade had kept a secret from everybody, including me. The boy didn't even have a driver's license or a car, so he and Jade had planned for him to escort her in a cab to *my house* where she could recooperate from her abortion. This had been planned without my knowledge or consent. Now I was sorry that I had given Jade a key to my house.

The whole situation stressed me out from the beginning to the end. But the thing that seemed to bother Jade the most was the fact that she had been brought to my house in a cab. Like buses, dollar stores, and food stamps, cabs were on a long list of things that Jade didn't tolerate.

With my support, she got through that traumatic experience intact. But as soon as she was up and about, she slid into a series of affairs with several other boys, some in college. That was all done behind her mother's back, but in my face. It made me feel like I was more than just a conspirator. I felt somewhat responsible for what Jade did, because I didn't do much to prevent her from doing it. The few times I did try to interfere, Jade wasted no time reminding me, "You are not my mother! You can't tell me what to do!"

I loved Jade with all my heart, but I was glad she wasn't my daughter. I predicted that one day she would break Rhoda's heart clean in two.

I didn't like Jade dragging me into her sordid lifestyle. One of my fears was that if and when Rhoda found out that I had been cloaking for her daughter, she would read me the riot act. And she had every right to. But since I'd given Jade a job, she had been behaving herself quite well and I was proud of her again.

CHAPTER 25

As I strolled down the aisle that separated the cubicles, I saw Gloria Watson and several others female employees in a huddle in Tami Barber's cubicle. Gloria didn't like Tami, claiming that Tami thought her shit didn't stink because she was a natural blonde. Yet Gloria had dragged her chair into Tami's cubicle, too. The women were poring over some Avon brochures. They didn't notice me as I grabbed a thick red folder off Gloria's desk and returned to my office.

Lately I had gotten in the habit of keeping my office door shut. Not because I thought I was such a big muckety-muck, like Gloria had called me in the ladies' room one day, but because I enjoyed the solitude that, in an office environment, a person could only get behind a closed door.

In the red folder that I'd plucked from Gloria's desk was another red folder, one that she had obviously tried to hide. In it was a three-page list of names and telephone numbers of people who had failed to pay their bills. "Shit," I said with a chuckle, falling down into my chair so hard my tailbone ached. I never knew what to expect from these people who had ended up on our shit list. We encountered all types of personalities.

I straightened up in my seat and cleared my throat, frowning as

I scanned the list of names. I recognized a few names of people I had attended school with, and a woman I used to go to church with. But the name that almost leaped off the page was the name of my gynecologist. I drew a line through his name. I'd let one of the other collectors contact him. Just a month ago I'd read a disturbing article about an evil, vindictive doctor who had injected some of his patients with the AIDS virus, after they had complained about him. My mother had taught me that you didn't piss off the people who held your life in their hands—like doctors, cops, and people who worked in restaurants who prepared your food. I had to cover my mouth to keep from laughing out loud when further down on the list I spotted the name of my hairdresser.

I dialed the number of the first name, took a deep breath, and braced myself.

"Mmmmm, hullo." The voice on the other end of the line was the very pleasant, almost sexy, voice of a man who sounded like he was in his forties or fifties, and a little on the impatient side. "Who this is be callin' here while I'm tryin' to sleep?" He didn't sound too educated, either.

"May I speak to Marvin Dunn, please?"

"This him! If you sellin' septic tanks or some other such mess, I ain't buyin' nothin'," the man barked.

"Uh, yes. Hello, Mr. Dunn. No, I am not selling anything. As a matter of fact, this call is in reference to something you've already purchased. Some stereo equipment from Hardee's Electronics at the Melden Village Mall." It made no difference how polite I was. Some of the people that I called still behaved like raging pit bulls. "How are you doing today, Mr. Dunn?"

"Well, you must have the wrong Marvin Dunn 'cause I ain't bought nothin' in six months! Shoot! I been eatin' peanut butter and jelly all week 'cause I can't even scrape up no money for no meat or nothin'."

"Yes. Well, it's been six months since you made the purchase that I'm calling you about. In fact, you never made the first payment on the account you opened. But the merchant is willing to work out a payment plan."

There was a long pause before Mr. Dunn replied. I could hear people laughing and cussing on the other end of the line as well as

B.B. King singing the blues. Background noises revealed a lot about the people we had to call that they didn't want us to know. It sounded like Mr. Dunn and some of his friends were thoroughly enjoying the stereo equipment that he had purchased and now couldn't, or wouldn't, pay for.

"I axed who this is?" he hollered.

"This is Annette Davis at Mizelle's Collection Agency," I replied in a crisp voice.

There was another pause and B.B. King stopped singing, but the laughing and the cussing continued. Finally, there was a loud grunt before I heard another word.

"Uh-huh. This me."

"Mr. Dunn, I am calling because you are six payments behind on your account with Hardee's Electronics. Your account has been turned over to us for collection. Is this something that we can we discuss right now? Is this a good time for you?"

"Naw, this ain't no good time for me to talk. I got company right now."

"Well, when is a good time for me to call you again?" We had been trained to remain pleasant, no matter how difficult a call was.

"I don't know! What's good for you might not be good for me!"

I rubbed my eyes and sucked in some air. "Sir, we'd like to work out some payment arrangements, and we'd like to do that as soon as possible. Our client has been very lenient with you. Even though you already had bad credit, they opened an account for you in good faith . . ." Taking a debtor on a guilt trip sometimes worked.

"Uh-huh and I sho 'preciate that. I intend to pay 'em," Mr. Dunn said sharply. Gone was the voice that had sounded almost sexy. "But like I said, I got company right now!" he boomed.

"Well, like *I* said, when is a good time for me to call you again?"

"Shit! Ain't no time a good time for you to call me!"

"It'd only take a few minutes for us to make some payment arrangements, and since there is no other good time to call you, I suggest we settle this right now."

"How did you get this telephone number in the first place? I changed my phone number last month."

"We got that information from the two references you listed when you opened the account, sir."

"Well, this is a unlisted phone number!"

"Would you like to discuss some payment arrangements now, sir?"

"Would you like to discuss kissin' my black ass? I ain't got no money! My boy just got out the hospital and them damn mother-fuckers at the insurance company won't pay the whole bill!"

"Sir, you don't need to shout. And I am sorry to hear about your son. But you still have an obligation to settle your debt with Hardee's Electronics."

"And you have a obligation to kiss my black ass!" Mr. Dunn roared before he slammed the telephone down.

I let out my breath and called the next name on the list. "This is Annette Davis. I am with Mizelle's Collection Agency. May I speak to Jerry DeFazio, please?"

"I . . . *He* don't live here no more!"

"Do you have a number where he can be reached?"

"Naw, I ain't got no number where he can be reached!"

"Can you tell me where he works now?"

"Get your ass off this telephone, lady!" This individual hung up on me, too.

I hung up the telephone and stood up and stretched for a few moments, rubbing my ear. The last caller had yelled so loud at me, my ear was still ringing.

I couldn't understand why people got so upset when they had to be called about bills that they knew they still owed. I dragged myself back to my seat and was just about to call up the third person on my list when my telephone rang.

"Annette Davis," I said in my most professional voice.

"Good afternoon, bitch!" the caller whispered. It was a voice that was all too familiar. There were no background noises. If anything, the background was so deadly silent, it reminded me of a tomb.

I sucked in my breath and stood up. "Who is this?" I asked, knowing I didn't want to hear the answer to my question.

"You know who it is, you black-ass bitch!"

The harsh language that I had just listened to from the people I had just called was bad, but I didn't take it personally. What I was hearing now was a direct assault. A huge lump immediately formed in my throat, and it was a few moments before I was able to speak. My voice came out sounding like a croak. "What do you want from me?"

"I want to see you gone, bitch!"

"What the hell do I have to do for you to leave me alone?" I whimpered, balling my trembling hand into a fist.

"I want you to let your man go."

"What did you say?" I gasped, looking at the telephone in my hand with so much contempt you would have thought that *it* was responsible for this vicious call.

"You think you got your man sewed up, well I got news for you. He'll be with me soon. *He loves me!*"

"Fuck you! I don't believe anything you say!" I seethed. "My husband does not cheat on me!"

"Oh, yeah? Well, I'll send you some proof, bitch!"

I gently placed the phone down on my desk and rushed out of my office. If Gloria was the person responsible, and if I ran fast enough, I'd catch her red-handed!

Gloria and Tami Barber were still fawning over the Avon brochures. I ran back into my office and picked up the telephone. She had hung up.

On one hand I was relieved to know that Gloria Watson was not my tormentor. But on the other hand, I was totally alarmed all over again to know that she wasn't. This meant that I still had a serious problem.

I was right back where I started.

CHAPTER 26

Rhoda didn't have to work. Her husband made good money as the lead foreman at Richland Steel. He was heavily insured so that if anything happened to him, Rhoda would be set for life. But Rhoda had more than one egg in her basket.

Her daddy had owned and operated the only Black funeral home in Richland. He had retired several years ago, and he now lived with Rhoda's mother and other relatives in New Orleans. He had made a lot of money over the years burying folks. I recalled the last year that Mr. Nelson operated his funeral service before he retired. People had been dropping like flies. Some days he got in two bodies at the same time. I had a dream one night about dead bodies falling out of the sky and landing on Mr. Nelson's front lawn. I never told anyone about that dream.

Rhoda's older brother, Jock, lived with her parents in New Orleans and had to have twenty-four-hour-a-day care. He had come back from Vietnam so severely shell-shocked, he would never be able to fend for himself again. And since she had no other siblings still alive, Rhoda would inherit the bulk of her father's estate once he and Rhoda's mother passed on. Rhoda would be a very wealthy woman someday, one way or the other.

Rhoda didn't have any money problems now. But she operated

the child-care center out of her home anyway because she loved
kids.

I felt comfortable knowing that my daughter was in Rhoda's
care. Rhoda had a couple of women from the neighborhood helping her with the kids. That way, Rhoda wasn't confined to the house.
She could go out and go shopping or meet me and Jade for lunch.

One thing I could say about that girl was that she was dependable. When she was supposed to be in the office, she was in the office. She was a good receptionist, too. I had already decided that if
she chose to not go on to college the following year, I would love to
keep her on. And I would do whatever I had to do to make her a
permanent employee.

The vicious call had come in at twelve thirty. Jade was due back
from her lunch with Rhoda at one.

I couldn't wait. I ran out to the parking lot and stayed there until
Rhoda returned with Jade. They seemed surprised and alarmed to
see me standing in the parking lot with a wild-eyed look on my
face.

"Auntie, what is it?" Jade said, jumping out from Rhoda's SUV
before it even stopped. I must have looked pretty desperate for
Jade to jump out of a moving vehicle. She ran over to me, on the
tips of her toes like a ballerina, and wrapped her arms as far around
me as she could. "What's the matter, Auntie?"

Rhoda parked and leaped out of her vehicle. Jade was practically holding me up as I leaned against the side of the building,
swaying like one of those naked trees I stared at outside the window of my office. A man in a shabby brown suit left the IRS office
next door looking more distressed than I was. He got into the car
parked next to Rhoda's SUV, slamming his door so hard the window rattled. I waited for him to drive away before I spoke again.

"She called me again," I managed.

"Who?" Jade and Rhoda said at the same time.

"The same woman who sent me that note. The same woman
who called my house that day we had the cookout," I said, shaking.
Rhoda and Jade looked at each other, then back at me.

"She called you at work?" Rhoda asked, her eyes wide and angry.

I nodded. "She knows where I work. That's where she sent me
that blacksnake." I sniffed and looked toward the door. "I thought

. . . I thought it was Gloria." I paused and looked at Jade. "You know how much she hates me."

Jade nodded. "I know she does. You said you *thought* it was her? What do you think now?"

"Well, while that bitch was still on the telephone, I put the telephone down and ran out to Gloria's cubicle. It wasn't her." I swallowed so hard I saw a few spots in front of my eyes. I had to blink hard and then rub my eyes to make them go away. "She and Tami were ordering Avon and eating lunch and probably didn't even know that I was in the office at the time. It wasn't Gloria. It never was her." I was disappointed. Had it been Gloria, I could have laid this puppy to rest now.

"What did the bitch say this time?" Rhoda asked. "Did she give any hints or ideas as to who she is, and why she is doin' this damn shit?"

"No, she didn't. She . . . she disguised her voice like before," I stuttered.

"Are you sure it was her? Maybe it was one of those deadbeats you called," Rhoda said, looking at Jade.

I shook my head hard. "It was the same woman. I recognized her voice. She just said she wanted me gone." I blinked and shook my head again. "Gone where? Why? Who in the world would want me out of the picture, and why? This is some crazy shit!" I couldn't bring myself to tell Rhoda yet that the woman had claimed she was having an affair with my husband and was going to prove it.

"Why don't you take the rest of the day off? Let me take you out for a drink. Then we'll go get our nails done," Rhoda said, gently rubbing the side of my face. "Jade, honey, go get your auntie's purse and let everybody know she's with me."

"Yes, Mama," Jade said, rubbing my back.

Jade gave me a quick peck on the cheek. Then she took off running without another word, clutching her ever-present yellow backpack like it was the Shroud of Turin.

Rhoda folded her arms and stared into my eyes, which by now were itching and burning so bad I was scared to blink. "Annette, if you don't tell your husband about this, I will."

CHAPTER 27

"Well?"

"Well, what?"

"Well, do you want to have a drink or not? You sure look like you could use one," Rhoda said, not trying to hide her impatience.

I had been drinking a lot lately. But I'd been doing it in secret. In my case that was a lot more dangerous. I didn't care if I made a fool of myself when I was alone. However, I wanted to be more in control of my actions when drinking with a partner, which meant I couldn't overdo it.

"I guess I could use a small glass of wine," I told Rhoda. I felt like a crippled woman and I must have looked like one, too. I limped along as Rhoda led me by my arm to her SUV.

The small glass of wine that I had at the Red Rose Bar didn't really help me that much. It made me so paranoid I didn't even want to discuss the situation that had sent me to the bar in the first place. Rhoda slurped up two piña coladas.

"Well, if you don't want to talk about this shit, there's no need for us to stay up in here. One more drink and I'll be blind drunk anyway," Rhoda decided, glancing quickly at her watch. "Come on.

We can do better than this." She dropped a few bills on the table and waved me out the door.

We walked the two blocks from the bar to a nail shop near Miss Rachel's beauty shop and got our nails done. Instead of going home after we left the nail shop, I went with Rhoda to Miss Rachel's for her to get her hair washed and blown dry.

There were only two other beauty shops in town that catered to Black women. For many years Miss Rachel's had been the only one, so it was still the most successful. Most of the clients were the old-school regulars like Rhoda and me. When Miss Rachel died nine years ago, her daughter, Claudette, took over the business. And she depended on some of her mother's most loyal customers to keep her in business. With so many Black woman wanting braids, weaves, or perms, there was a lot of business. But there was a lot of competition, too. The other two beauty shops were located in the Melden Village Mall, located one exit off the freeway from my house. They stayed in business because that's where a lot of the younger women went to get beautiful. But not Jade. Miss Rachel's was the only beauty shop that Jade thought was good enough for her.

I had never been to any other beauty shop myself because I enjoyed visiting Miss Rachel's. Claudette was a charming person, but I couldn't say that for some of her friends. Like Betty Jean Spool, one of the two beauticians who worked for Claudette.

Everybody knew that Betty Jean had dated Pee Wee before he married me. And everybody had expected him to marry her.

Betty Jean and I got along as well as one might expect under the circumstances, but I wasn't stupid enough to let her touch my hair. I wasn't as superstitious as I used to be, but I still had strong ties to the South. That was where I'd heard a lot of stories, while sitting on somebody's front porch, about the things that people could do to harm a person if they got some of their hair.

Voodoo gobbledygook was not as common among the folks in Ohio. But the few spooky stories that I did hear from time to time involved members of Betty Jean's wild clan. She had a one-eyed cousin who'd slowly poisoned her husband to death, and a great-aunt who had tossed a dead chicken through somebody's window.

There were other stories, but I tried not to think about them unless I had to. It seemed like evil took a special interest in me. Before my marriage I'd been through hell on earth. I had been happy and trauma-free now for more than ten years. But I was not going to make it easy for Betty Jean, Gloria, or anybody else who wanted to turn my life upside down.

Whenever I made an appointment to get my hair done at Miss Rachel's, I insisted on having Claudette.

The minute Rhoda and I entered the beauty shop and I looked into Betty Jean's eyes as she stood over an old bat named Mabel Brisbane curling her limp gray hair, I immediately suspected that Betty Jean was the one who was harassing me. The way she looked at me made my flesh crawl. It seemed like she was trying to let me know with just a look that she was the one after me. And it made a whole lot more sense for it to be her than it did for it to be Gloria Watson. Well, at least now I knew for sure that it was not Gloria. I made up my mind within seconds, while Betty Jean was still giving me the evil eye.

Now I needed to find out why. I had a hard time believing that this was all about a man, but it was not that far-fetched. Therefore, I had to keep that in the front of my mind. I knew that Betty Jean was not jealous of my job, like Gloria was. Had my tormentor been Gloria, she would not have gained much by getting rid of me. Even if I dropped dead, Mr. Mizelle wouldn't give my job to an oaf like Gloria. He had even told her as much. Betty Jean wanted something from me that meant a whole lot more to her than a job did. She could get any job she wanted. And any man.

Everybody knew that she still had some feelings for Pee Wee. It hit me like a ton of bricks: she wanted Pee Wee back. This *was* really about a man! My man! And the only way she could get him was to get rid of me.

Unless I was dealing with some sick stranger who had chosen me at random, Betty Jean *had* to be the bitch who was trying to destroy me!

CHAPTER 28

One thing about a small town is that if you know everybody else's business, everybody else knows your business. But only if you put your business out there.

Betty Jean Spool's older brother, Lester, was a violent drug dealer who double-crossed everybody he came in contact with: the people who supplied him with drugs as well as the people who bought drugs from him. Everybody felt that it was just a matter of time before he ended up dead or behind bars. Betty Jean was very close to her brother and was all up in his drug business, helping him spend the money. We all expected her to follow him when he went to jail.

She was the one woman that Pee Wee didn't like to discuss in my presence. He didn't like to admit that he'd been involved with a woman with such a shady background. After she'd broken up with Pee Wee, she married a construction worker from Sandusky. She divorced him within a year and then she married another man five months later.

Betty Jean and I had a harmless, unofficial feud going on, ever since Pee Wee had married me. She used to tease me with playful threats about how she was eventually going to get him back. Betty Jean would always laugh when she said it, and I would laugh right along with her because I never took her seriously. A few times when I got mad at Pee Wee, I'd go into the beauty shop and ask her to come get him. It was all a joke. I knew that I had nothing to worry about as for that woman taking my man. But knowing her history with men, I had always kept one eye on her, and one eye on Pee Wee. I didn't think of it as a joke now.

"Annette, girl, looks like you didn't get here a minute too soon," Betty Jean said with a smirk. She had a soft, high-pitched voice. Back in high school when we had talent shows, she used to do a good impression of Diana Ross. "I could see them naps risin' up on your neck as soon as you stepped in this door."

"She doesn't have an appointment today. She's with me," Rhoda clarified, dropping down onto the first vacant seat she came to. I eased down onto the green vinyl love seat near the door. A lot of women hated Rhoda because of her long, thick black hair and Rhoda loved to flaunt her beautiful hair in front of those women. In addition to Claudette and Betty Jean, there were three other women in the shop. They all seemed to be interested in every move that Rhoda made, giving her that look that jealous women give to beautiful women. To me that look resembled a cross between a smirk and a scowl.

All eyes were on Rhoda as she leaned back and shook her hair, running her fingers through it the way White girls do. "I can't do a thing with all this mess on my head," Rhoda remarked, with a grimace on her face that couldn't fool a fool. "If it wasn't for my man, I'd cut it all off . . ."

"Well, you know we'll hook you up," Claudette said, breaking the tension that had suddenly covered the room like a fog.

Even though Betty Jean was attractive, she needed a lot of props. In school she had padded her bra with socks and told everybody who would listen that she was saving her babysitting money so that someday she could get her breasts enlarged.

When her drug-dealing brother gave her five thousand dollars for a graduation gift she gathered all of the girls in a circle in the girls' locker room and yelled, "Now I can go get me them titties!"

In addition to her surgically enhanced breasts, she wore a natural-looking hair weave. She worked out regularly at a nearby gym so the rest of her body looked nice, too. I couldn't even begin to compete with a woman like Betty Jean.

If she really wanted to repossess Pee Wee, it would have been easier for me to just hand him over to her on a platter. But I loved my husband. I didn't want to turn him over to a woman who would no doubt chew him up and then spit him out as soon as she saw somebody she liked better. She had had her chance with him.

My eyes burned every time I looked across the room at Betty Jean. When I couldn't stand to feel the pain in my eyes any longer, I focused my attention on other things around me. She looked away every time I tried to look in her eyes.

The beauty shop had gotten rather shabby over the years. The floors were gummy, the light from the two gooseneck lamps was dim, music from a tired blues station in Cleveland was the only station the radio could get, the furniture didn't match, and some of the equipment was outdated. But like I said, it had always been the most popular beauty establishment in Richland because Miss Rachel had been a good businesswoman and a down-home girl to the bone. And she had always provided free beverages and snacks, not to mention credit.

Miss Rachel's customers as well as their offspring remained loyal to her memory. Claudette had promised her mother on her deathbed that she would not update the shop as long as she owned it. With the attitude she had, Claudette would never have to worry about her clients deserting her for the newer shops.

"Oh? If you ask me, Annette, it's a damn shame you don't have an appointment today," Betty Jean said with a wink. "I guess Pee Wee ain't as particular as he used to be."

"I would say he's more particular now than he was when you knew him," I said. Betty Jean laughed, I did not. I could see that I was making her nervous, and that gave me a little more gumption. "How have you been?" I asked.

"Fine," Betty Jean said sharply, looking around the room.

"Uh, Annette's not feelin' well," Rhoda explained, nodding in my direction.

"I can see that," Betty Jean sneered, adjusting the lightbulb in one of the lamps.

Even though my eyes still burned when I looked at Betty Jean, I stared at her so long and hard that everybody in the shop noticed it. I could see that I was making her nervous; I was making myself nervous, too. Confrontations did that to me.

"Annette, you actin' mighty strange. Even for you," Betty Jean said. "Now, if you got something to say to me, why don't you just go on and say it? You been looking at me like I got two horns and a tail ever since you walked in that door." Betty Jean had a tuft of Mrs. Brisbane's hair in one hand, her other hand on her hip.

"I don't have anything to say to you," I said, rising. "I don't have anything to say, period." I didn't know what else to do after my outburst but run. Rhoda followed me outside.

Rhoda caught up with me and spun me around by my arm. "Annette, please get a grip on yourself. I know you are upset, but you can't be takin' it out on any of these women. They are all worse off than you."

"That's just it. They want what I have. At least Betty Jean does. You remember how hot and heavy she and Pee Wee were at one time?"

"Of course I remember. It was no secret. But that was a long time ago. He married you. He loves you. And from what I hear, she's with the man she wants to be with." Rhoda rolled her eyes. "He's somebody else's man, but that's beside the point."

"Well, if it's not Betty Jean who is tormenting me, who else could it be?" I asked through clenched teeth.

"I don't know. That's what I am goin' to try and help you find out. You thought it was that Gloria Watson, and then you found out today that it wasn't her."

I looked at the ground as I spoke. As luck would have it, I was standing in some dog shit. I scraped the soles of my shoes across the ground and moved to the side. "The caller said something today that I didn't want to tell you. She wants my husband. That's what she said on the phone today."

"What?"

I nodded and blinked at Rhoda to hold back my tears. I was a strong woman, but I wasn't Superwoman. I had to do whatever I could to hold myself together. I knew that if I broke down I would probably never recover. "That's what this is all about."

"Don't get ahead of yourself. This could still be a prank."

"I want to go home. I know now that I can't keep this from Pee Wee any longer. Not if it involves him. If he's involved with another woman, I am going to make him tell me."

CHAPTER 29

It was a little past eight when Rhoda parked in front of my house after we left the beauty shop. A mild wind was blowing dust and dead leaves all around, but the weather was still nice enough for people to be sitting on their front porches. My street was busy. There were whole families occupying almost every front porch on my block. Little kids of all different colors and sizes, some naked to the world, were running up and down the street screaming and tossing balls. I saw one little boy waving a stick, terrorizing that same stray dog that liked to piss on my rosebush.

The good-looking White couple that lived down the street stopped next to Rhoda's SUV so she could admire that homely baby that they liked to parade around town in his squeaky stroller.

"Oochie coo," Rhoda cooed, tickling the baby's thick neck as the mother held the baby up to the window on Rhoda's side. "What I wouldn't do to have another baby to raise," Rhoda said longingly. She kissed the baby's bloated pink cheek before the couple left. "Well, here we are. I'll call you tomorrow," she said, turning to me. I was still strapped in my seat, staring at the neighbors with envy. They all looked like they didn't have a care in the world.

It didn't dawn on me until then that I had not called Pee Wee to let him know my whereabouts. Even on the days that Rhoda and I typically got together after I got off work for drinks or whatever, I still called him to remind him to pick up Charlotte from school and to take care of dinner. It had been our routine for years.

"Shit, I forgot to call Pee Wee! He's probably wondering where I was all this time," I hollered before I climbed out of Rhoda's SUV.

"I got your back," Rhoda said with a wave of her hand and a look of confidence. "You know how I do things. I called him at his barbershop before I even picked you up from your work. He knows where you were," Rhoda smiled.

See? That's what I meant. Rhoda had me covered.

I breathed a sigh of relief. "Thanks, girl," I said, opening the door on my side. The only thing I didn't like about SUVs was that they were so high off the ground. And as clumsy as I was, I had to move as slow as a snail getting in and getting out. My nails had dried hours ago but I still held my hands up at an angle so I wouldn't scrape off my fresh nail polish. It took me longer than it usually did to unhook the seat belt and slide my legs to the side. "Rhoda, I'm so sorry to be such a deadweight," I huffed.

"Annette, don't look at yourself that way. I don't. You take all the time you need," Rhoda said gently, giving me a playful tap along the side of my head.

I hit the ground with the kind of thud that you might expect a piano to make. Then I rushed across the sidewalk that led to my front yard. I was glad to see that Pee Wee had cut the grass. He had also removed some of Charlotte's old broken toys off of the porch. Rhoda waited until I had made it up to my front door before she blew her horn, waved, and drove off.

I stopped and looked at my mailbox like it was a tumor. Even the good Lord knew that I was afraid to look inside. But it was something that I had to do, whether I wanted to or not. With fear gripping me like a bear trap, I stared at the top of a long brown envelope peeking out over the top of my mailbox. Like most husbands, Pee Wee couldn't be bothered with certain aspects of domesticity. I had to threaten him just to get him to let the water out of the bathtub after his baths. Unless he was expecting a check or a letter from his hometown, he ignored the mailbox. Last year I went to New York for three days with Rhoda and Jade to do our

Christmas shopping. When I returned home our mailbox had three days' worth of mail in it.

I sucked in my breath and plucked out the contents of the mailbox. The dim porch light, provided by a forty-watt lightbulb with a yellow glow, was surrounded by moths and gnats. I flipped through the mail. There was a credit card bill, a flyer asking for a donation from some charity that I had never heard of, another Frederick's of Hollywood catalogue for Jade, a flyer from that adult sex-toy shop on Sawburg advertising a half-off sale, and a coupon for a free massage from a massage parlor in Cleveland. That was addressed to Jade, too. I shook my head, surprised and glad that I was still able to laugh over Jade's antics after the rough day I had had.

I had only been standing in the same spot on my front porch for a few minutes, but in my neighborhood that was a few minutes too long. My neighbors knew me well enough to know that I wasn't the type to stand on my front porch by myself unless I had a damn good reason.

On any given day or night, on both sides of us and across the street, nosy neighbors peeped out of their windows every time they saw or heard somebody coming or going. Like some of them on their front porches were doing right now, all probably wondering why I hadn't gone inside my house yet.

Before I opened my front door, Betty Jean's leering face flashed across my mind. So did the face of Gloria Watson. I looked at the mail in my hand and wondered if I would have to add another name to the list I had already compiled.

Pee Wee had turned on the front porch light and his Jeep was in the driveway, so I knew he was in the house. He had not put on the light in the living room. I flipped the switch as soon as I stepped in the door, expecting to find him slumped in a chair in front of the television with a beer in his hand. The television was on but the living room was empty.

I followed some muffled voices into the kitchen where I found him and Charlotte sitting at the kitchen table. There was a half-finished Snow White puzzle on the table. Pee Wee looked up, his hand full of puzzle pieces. There was a look on his face that I decided was guilt. I held up my hand just as he opened his mouth to speak.

"Charlotte, go to your room," I ordered, my jaw twitching. I slung my purse over my shoulder and dropped the mail onto the kitchen counter.

"Why come?" Charlotte wailed. I was glad to see that she was already in her pajamas.

The kitchen sink was full of dirty dishes. Fast-food containers and empty Pepsi cans littered part of the counter. There was a skillet on top of the stove that contained a flat sheet of corn bread with some lumps on one side. The mess in the kitchen told me a familiar story. Pee Wee had attempted to cook dinner. I could smell the greens he had burned.

"Annette," Pee Wee began, rising, holding up his hand, too.

The more I looked at him, the more he looked like a guilty man. I held up both hands.

"You just hold it right there," I said firmly, my eyes following Charlotte with a stern look until she disappeared from the kitchen. I heard her stomp all the way upstairs to her room.

"Annette, I need to tell you—" Pee Wee started again, plopping back down into his chair so hard it almost rocked to the floor.

"You . . . you no-good . . . punk!" I shrieked, shaking so hard I got dizzy.

"Huh?" Pee Wee gasped.

"Shut up! Just shut up!" I hollered. I shot across the floor in Pee Wee's direction. Without attempting to say another word he covered his face with his hands, but he couldn't conceal his guilt with a hood. "You no-good, two-timing whoremonger!" The brutal words flew out of my mouth like flies. "You think you can make a fool out of me? Well, I got news for your black ass! I am not going to take any shit from you!" I was talking so fast and hard that my teeth accidentally bit into my tongue hard enough to draw blood. I swallowed the salty blood and rotated my tongue a few quick times until I could no longer taste any blood.

Pee Wee gasped and uncovered his face. There was such an incredulous look on his face, it looked like a mask. His eyes were stretched open so wide it looked like they wanted to pop out of his head. His mouth dropped open and he stared at me so hard it felt like a heat wave had entered the room. He shot up out of his chair, kicking it backward. I had known this man most of my life and I could count on one hand the number of times I'd seen him angry.

"What in the hell—"

"Shut up!" I shouted, my hands on my hips.

There had never been any violence in our relationship. As far as I knew, Pee Wee had never hit a woman in his life.

I had only resorted to violence two times in my life: During my senior prom a girl who had bullied me all through school threw some fruit punch on my prom dress. The sucker punch that I surprised her with sent her to kingdom come, scattering a few of her teeth along the way. Several years later, my ex-fiancé, Jerome Cunningham, attacked me when he found out I had turned a few tricks during my teens. I had retaliated by giving him the beating of his life. I was proud of the fact that I had not raised my hand to anyone else since then. But I would if I had to. Even if it was Pee Wee.

"How long did you think it would take before I found out?" I demanded, shaking my fist in his direction.

"Found out what?" Now his hands were on his hips. He still had on the shirt that he had worn to work, but he had on a pair of pajama bottoms and his favorite house shoes.

"About you and your bitch! I know all about it and before I let you make a fool out of me, I will divorce the hell out of you! I will take everything you own but your citizenship! Then I will take Charlotte to Florida and you'll only get to see her when I say so! I don't have to take this shit from you! Just like I got you, I can get me another man. You black-ass nigger!"

For a moment it looked like Pee Wee was going to laugh. He narrowed his eyes and shook his head and the most incredulous look I'd ever seen on his face appeared.

"What in the world . . . Woman, *what in the hell are you talkin' about?*"

CHAPTER 30

"I know you are having an affair!" I lifted my hand to slap Pee Wee, but he grabbed my wrist and held it so hard it felt like I'd been handcuffed.

"I don't know what in the hell you are talkin' about!"

Just then the telephone rang.

"I bet that's your whore calling again!" I snatched my hand from his and ran to the telephone. "HELLO!" I yelled. There was some dead silence at first. Just as I was about to yell again I heard a nervous, low whimper.

"Annette, baby, you need to get over here." It was Muh'Dear. She had never sounded so weak in her life.

"Muh'Dear, what's wrong?"

"Didn't Pee Wee tell you?"

I glanced at Pee Wee. The guilt was gone from his face. I couldn't decide what the look on his face said now.

"Didn't Pee Wee tell me what?" I asked, looking into Pee Wee's eyes. "Muh'Dear, where are you?"

Pee Wee came and stood next to me and took the telephone. "Your daddy had a heart attack. He's at the hospital," Pee Wee said. He rubbed the back of his neck and let out a loud sigh. "The doctor said he might make it through the night, and he might not."

"What did you say?" I didn't even recognize my own voice. I wondered if I was having an out-of-body experience. I shook my head and looked around my cute little kitchen. Pee Wee and Otis had painted the walls a pale yellow, and that looked good with the bright white new stove and refrigerator we had bought a few months ago. There was a large calendar on the wall with a very good likeness of Dr. Martin Luther King Jr. on it. For a second it looked like the picture on the calendar was moving. I prayed silently that I would not lose my mind until I found out what had happened to my daddy, and straightened out the mess between me and the woman who wanted my husband. The insides of my mouth suddenly tasted like metal and my teeth felt like rocks.

"Your daddy had a heart attack while he was sittin' at the table eatin' dinner this evenin'," Muh'Dear was saying. "I know it was them day-old turnip greens what done it. I put too much pork in 'em this time. Girl, I been callin' all over town lookin' for you. Them hens at the beauty shop said you'd just left when I called there. You just now gettin' home?"

"I . . . I went out for a drink with Rhoda after I left the beauty shop," I mumbled. "Is Daddy all right?"

"Girl, did you hear what I just said? The man had him a heart attack! Folks don't have heart attacks when they 'all right' and you should know that by now."

"No," I said, shaking my head. "My daddy is as strong as a bull. He . . . he had a heart attack? Are you sure?" I covered the left side of my chest because a sharp pain had just shot through it. I thought I was having a heart attack, too. I managed to compose myself. "My daddy's in the hospital?" I asked in a hoarse whisper.

"That's what I been tryin' to tell you," Pee Wee said gently. He looked away from me and said something to Muh'Dear, then he hung up the telephone. He pursed his lips and sucked on his teeth, looking at me like he was seeing me for the first time. "Now this other shit you talkin' about, whatever the hell it is, it's goin' to have to wait until later," he declared in a firm voice, moving toward the door.

I nodded. "I . . . I guess it can wait," I stammered.

"Let me get in my clothes so we can get out to that hospital," he told me, glancing at me over his shoulder as he left the kitchen.

Rhoda and Pee Wee accompanied me to the hospital. Jade had given up a date to stay at my house and babysit Charlotte. Otis was one of Daddy's fishing buddies, and he had wanted to come to the hospital with us, but Rhoda had made him stay home to keep their houseguest company. I wondered just how much longer that man would be referred to as a houseguest. Especially since O.J. Simpson's so-called houseguest, Kato Kaelin, had given houseguests such a bad name. These were the thoughts going through my head as we marched through the hospital corridor. I almost mowed down a few people in hospital gowns who already looked like they'd been mowed down enough. I had decided that if I could distract myself enough, I wouldn't spend too much time thinking about my real problems.

"It's about time you got here," Muh'Dear said in a gruff voice as soon as we entered Daddy's room. *It was the same room where my beloved stepfather had died.* As soon as I realized that, I felt like I was going to faint. Somehow I managed to remain reasonably composed.

Muh'Dear sat on the side of the bed that Daddy was propped up in, already looking like he had been embalmed. My heart jumped when I saw him, and then I almost threw up. I had to cover my mouth and my nose for a moment. The smell in the room was overwhelming. It was like a combination of mothballs, urine, and that harsh antiseptic odor that was so common in hospitals.

"And not a minute too soon," said Scary Mary, the most obnoxious senior citizen I knew.

As annoying as Scary Mary was, I loved this woman with all my heart. From the time that I was a toddler, she'd been there when Muh'Dear and I needed her the most. In all the many years that she'd been in our lives, she had never revealed her real name or her age; both varied from one year to the next. She had had several husbands, and there was some question about her legal last name. Some folks said she called herself "Mary X" on paper. She was now somewhere in her eighties, but she was still as spry as a colt. She had always been vague about her background. Other than her middle-aged, severely retarded daughter, Mott, the only "family" that she claimed were Muh'Dear and me, and the five jaded prostitutes who worked for her.

"It took you long enough to get here, girl," Scary Mary huffed. Her narrowed eyes looked more like slits. She cleared her throat and clenched her false teeth, flipping her tongue up and down to make sure they stayed in place. After she adjusted her fluffy red wig, she sniffed and scratched the long scar that she'd sustained in a fight several generations ago on her long, reddish brown face. She occupied a chair facing the bed with her long, flabby legs crossed. I had to wonder what store clerk had been able to talk this old crone into buying the black-leather pants she wore so proudly. "I guess you had better things to do, huh?" Scary Mary pinched some lint off her sweater and flipped it to the floor.

"I just got the message," I wailed, leaning over the bed to feel Daddy's forehead. He felt like a piece of wood. Pee Wee stood at the foot of the bed. Rhoda was right behind me, literally breathing down my neck. "Daddy, are you all right?" I asked. Before he could respond, I turned to Muh'Dear. "What happened? Is he going to be all right?"

"He old, that's what happened," Muh'Dear sighed.

Mixed in with all the other irritating scents in the room was the smell of alcohol. But not the kind you'd expect to find in a hospital. Out of the corner of my eye, I saw Scary Mary whip a brown paper bag from one of the pockets on the plain blue smock that she had on over her pink cashmere sweater. She took a few quick sips from a pint-sized bottle in the bag before she slipped it back in her pocket. I rubbed my nose and pulled the covers up to Daddy's neck.

Daddy was asleep but from the way his face was twisted and the fact that he was breathing so loud, I decided he was in pain. "Daddy, I'm here. Everything is going to be fine," I said weakly, turning back to Muh'Dear.

"It's his heart," Muh'Dear said before I could ask again.

I felt a twinge in my own heart. "Just like my stepdaddy," I muttered, wishing Scary Mary would offer me some of whatever it was she had in the bottle in that brown paper bag.

CHAPTER 31

As much as I hated hospitals I didn't want to go home. One, I didn't want to leave until I was able to speak with Daddy. I had to put all of my concerns aside so that I could focus on him.

But Daddy was under so much sedation it was unlikely that he would wake up before the next morning. Another reason I didn't want to go home was because I didn't want to have to finish the confrontation I'd started with Pee Wee a couple of hours ago. I had no choice but to tell him about what I'd been going through with the woman who was determined to take him from me. No matter what, it had come to that now.

I tried to keep things in perspective. Despite the nasty little situation with my anonymous tormentor and Daddy's medical problems, I still had a wonderful life. I was thankful that I still had my health, a good job, and a beautiful daughter. And I had survived some serious obstacles. Most people would have already checked themselves into the nuthouse if they had been in my shoes.

But the last ten years had been especially enjoyable. I was thankful that nobody could take that away from me. I had worked hard for everything I had: my job, my marriage, and my sanity. I had too much to lose and nothing to gain by letting some ignorant jackass disrupt my life. However, I did know where to draw the line. If I was facing a losing battle anyway, I wanted out of it as soon as possible. One thing I had to say about myself was that I didn't stay anywhere where I wasn't wanted. And that included relationships. If my husband had grown tired of me, I was not going to try to hold on to him. But like I'd felt from the beginning of this mess, I wouldn't make it that easy for him or his whore.

I was glad that Rhoda was in the car with Pee Wee and me. She had folded herself into a corner on the backseat directly behind me on the passenger's side of my car. But the ride home was still difficult. Nobody talked.

When we dropped Rhoda off at her house, she looked at me and winked. "Uh, if you get a chance call me later tonight. I'll be prayin' for your daddy," she said. "'Bye, y'all," she added with a crooked smile. She gave Pee Wee a light pat on his shoulder.

One thing I had to remind myself was the fact that Pee Wee and Rhoda had been best friends before I came along. He had been the one that she had shared all of her secrets with then. They were still close and I didn't know for sure, but I would have bet good money that Rhoda shared things with Pee Wee now that she didn't even share with her husband or me. If I had to give Pee Wee up, it would have a profound impact on my relationship with Rhoda. I couldn't stand to think about that, too.

"I'll call you," was all I said to her.

Pee Wee and I rode in silence for about five minutes. He started tapping the side of the steering wheel with his fingers, another one of the many little things he did that annoyed me, and I had told him about it time after time. He stopped when I shot him a hot look.

"You ready to talk?" he asked, clearing his throat.

"It can wait," I said flatly. "My main concern is my daddy."

"No, it can't wait, goddammit. I'm just as concerned about your daddy as you are. But you came at me with some pretty serious shit before we left the house, and I want to know what that was all about."

"Why don't you tell me?" I barked, glaring at him again.

He glanced at me briefly, but seemed to prefer keeping his eyes on the road. He cleared his throat again and gripped the steering wheel, ignoring the twenty-mile-an-hour speed limit.

"Will you slow down? All we need now is a speeding ticket on top of everything else," I said, glancing at the side mirror.

"And just what is it you want me to tell you?" he asked, slowing the car down to a crawl.

Now I was concerned that we'd get a ticket for driving too slow. But since there were no cars immediately behind us and I didn't see any police cars around, I didn't say anything about that. I had other things on my mind that needed to be said.

"Are you having an affair?" I asked, looking at the side of his head. He gasped and almost ran off the road.

"Woman, who in the hell would I be havin' a goddamn affair with?"

"I have a pretty good idea, but I want to hear it from you!" I yelled, my eyes still on the side of his head. He turned just enough to see me and keep his eyes on the road at the same time. His mouth fell open, he eyes blinked hard and fast. "Whoever the bitch is, she's been sending me all kinds of shit through the mail. She called the house the other day and today she called me at my office."

"And she claims she's havin' an affair with me?" This time Pee Wee glanced at me with an amused look on his face. "I'm flattered as hell. I guess I ain't the gray-haired old fossil I thought I was, after all."

"So is it true?" I mouthed. I wanted to slap the daylights out of him, but that would have been too mild. Then I wanted to stomp him into the ground. I surprised myself at how easy it was for a nonviolent person like me to be having such violent thoughts.

"Hell no, it ain't true!" he bellowed, slapping the dashboard so hard the radio came on. He flipped it back off, mumbling and laughing under his breath.

"You can sit there on your black-and-gray ass and laugh all you want to. But I bet you won't be laughing so much by the time my lawyer gets through socking it to you."

"Is this all because you want a divorce?"

"This is because of you and some woman. And if what she's claiming is true, I am through with you."

"I tell you what, you ask this mystery woman to prove that I'm fuckin' her. Then we'll go from there. Put some proof out there."

The last thing I wanted was to hear from the mystery woman again. Especially if she had proof that she was having an affair with my man.

"If there's proof out there, I will get that proof. Now, I'm through talking about this shit tonight," I insisted. I sniffed and twisted my body in my seat, so that I was pushed against the door on my side. The car was as silent as a tomb the rest of the way home.

I had enough to keep my mind occupied. I tried to pretend that Pee Wee was not in the car with me. I was worried about Daddy, and Muh'Dear too, for that matter. She seemed to be in good health but she didn't look so good anymore. And even though she never talked about it, I knew that the pressures she had endured over the years had finally taken a major toll on her. She had reached her limit. Now that my stalker claimed that she had proof that she was involved with my husband, I had reached my limit, too.

I stole a glance at Pee Wee. He was steering with one hand. I couldn't imagine what was going through his mind. From the look on his face, he was as miserable as I was.

CHAPTER 32

When Pee Wee and I got home from the hospital, he went straight to bed. Jade had put Charlotte to bed. One thing I liked about my daughter, though she was no cherub and needed a good whupping every now and then, was the fact that she was fairly independent. She didn't want to spend all of her time hanging around with me and Pee Wee. She loved school. And the time she spent with Rhoda and Jade was a real treat to her. As a matter of fact, sometimes Charlotte chose to be with Jade over me. That didn't bother me because Jade often chose to be with me over Rhoda. So there was some balance in my confused life. But there was a downside. Jade was spoiled rotten and sneaky and I didn't want Charlotte to pick up too many of her bad habits. That was the only thing that I really had to work hard at to prevent.

"Is your daddy going to be all right?" Jade asked as soon as I sat down next to her on the sofa.

I ignored the XXX-rated movie that she had been watching on the VCR when Pee Wee and I walked in. I was thankful that she had the sound on mute. Pee Wee kept a stash of dirty movies in a box in a corner behind some more boxes in our bedroom closet. It had been years since that box had been opened by him. And I certainly had no reason to open it myself. I hated pornography. But when he was younger and friskier, he liked to get wild and crazy with Otis and some of their other male friends and watch those nasty-ass movies. They would get freaky after a ball game or a fishing trip. Rhoda had assured me that it was no worse than them going to a strip club, and a lot safer. For Jade to have found those movies she had to have done some serious snooping. I didn't have the strength to go into that with her now, though. Not tonight. But I made a mental note to throw out every single pornographic movie in that damn box, first chance I got.

I was surprised and glad when Jade reached for the remote on the coffee table and turned the movie off without me having to tell her to do so.

Jade's yellow backpack was on the floor right next to her feet, bulging with God knows what. There was a can of Slim•Fast on the coffee table right next to an empty beer can. Both cans contained smudges of Jade's plum-colored lipstick. She saw me looking at the beer can. "Uh, I got thirsty and couldn't find any soda," she said, ending her weak defense with a loud hiccup.

"Did you look in the refrigerator? I just put two six-packs of Coke in there yesterday," I said tiredly.

"Hmmm," she replied, a puzzled look on her face. "I didn't even see that!" Jade sat up straighter, sliding her backpack a few inches away with her foot. "Is your daddy going to be all right?" she asked again, with an anxious look on her face.

Like the rest of us, Daddy was guilty of spoiling Jade, too. He was good with cars and electronics, so whenever her car—or the VCR or TV in her room—needed maintenance, she called up Daddy and he went running over to Rhoda's house with his toolbox.

"I sure hope so," I sighed, fanning my face with the *TV Guide.* "I didn't get to keep him long when I was little, and it looks like I might not get to keep him long now," I said, trying not to think about the thirty years that Daddy was missing from my life. "Did Charlotte give you a lot of trouble?" I asked, forcing myself to smile. I had licked off all of my lipstick and licked my lips so much they were now dry and threatening to crack. My trying to smile didn't help. But I managed to keep a weak smile plastered on my face just for Jade's sake. "I'm surprised you were able to get her into bed before I got home," I said, looking at my watch.

"Oh, but she went kicking and screaming. And even then only because I agreed to read to her. I had to promise her two movies at the mall, and a day at the park, too," Jade said, glancing at the floor. "I hope you don't mind if I spend the night," Jade said with a sniff, giving me a long, hard look, as if she was daring me to say no. "I brought my pajammies, and I already called Daddy and told him to tell Mama you wanted me to spend the night." Jade dipped her chin and gave me an anxious look. "Is that all right with you?"

"You know I don't have a problem with you spending the night here as long as it's all right with your mama and daddy. But tomorrow is a workday and don't you have things you need to do to get ready for work tomorrow?" I asked, pushing a strand of Jade's hair off her face.

Jade let out a deep sigh before she let out a sudden sob. "Auntie, I need your help. Uh . . . I got another *little* problem that I need you to help me out of."

"What is it, child?"

"I just found out . . . Um . . . I don't know how it happened!" Jade rose. "I was using the pill and everything!"

"Jade, don't tell me you are pregnant again!" I hissed, glancing toward the stairs to make sure that Pee Wee or Charlotte had not crept back to the living room.

Jade nodded so hard one of her false eyelashes came unglued. "Madeline Green is having a swimming party at the Y next month, and I can't be seen in my bikini with my stomach poking out like a melon. I'm going to make an appointment for . . . um . . . that thing. I'm getting rid of it. I need you to go with me and drive me home. And . . . um . . . to pretend to be my mama." Jade paused and adjusted her eyelash, securing it back in place with her long nails. Blinking both eyes, she continued. "You have to help me, Auntie!"

I threw up my hands and shook my head. "Jade, I have to think about this. I already have a lot of heavy shit on my plate these days. If something happens to you, and I'm involved, your parents would probably run me out of town on a rail! I wish you would stop dragging me into all the messes you seem to get yourself into!" Jade often made me angry, but I rarely showed it. I loved her so much that the last thing I wanted to do was disappoint her.

"But what about that time you got pregnant when you were a young girl! You got rid of yours and you didn't even go to a real doctor like me!"

One thing I regretted was sharing too much of my past with Jade. True, I had experienced an unwanted pregnancy when I was a teenager, and Jade's own mother had tried to help me abort it by forcing a whole bottle of whiskey down my throat while I sat in a bathtub full of hot water. I'd ended up in the hospital anyway and lost my mother's respect. However, Jade's situation and mine were as different as night and day. Sleeping around with whoever she was sleeping with was a long way from what I went through. I had had old Mr. Boatwright, my live-in rapist, to thank for my predicament.

"I don't know what else to do," Jade sobbed, grabbing my hands and placing her head on my bosom. I couldn't stop myself from rubbing her back.

"It'll be all right, honey. If you really need my help, I'll be there for you." I sighed and gently lifted Jade's head and looked in her eyes. "What about the boy?"

"What about him?" Jade asked, with a look of complete indifference on her face now.

"Does he know? Can't he go with you? Does he want you to have this abortion?"

Jade dropped her head. "When I told him, all he did was cuss me out and call me a slutty whore." Jade sucked on her teeth and gave me a serious look. "Just goes to show you can't trust too many people these days. I don't know what this world is coming to."

"I see boys haven't changed much over the years," I said sadly, swallowing a huge lump in my throat. Boys had changed over the years, but they had only gotten worse. Although the same thing could be said about girls.

"Huh? Is that how it was when you told the boy who got you pregnant?"

"Uh . . . yeah. It was something like that." Jade didn't know all the facts about that pregnancy. She didn't need to know that a man old enough to be my grandfather had sexually abused me throughout my childhood, and I would never tell her. I prayed that Rhoda wouldn't either. "Let's get some sleep and we'll talk more about this in the morning," I said, my arm around Jade as I led her to the guestroom upstairs. "And I'm telling you right now, if you get yourself into a mess like this again, I am going to be the one to tell your mama. Do you understand me, girl?"

"Yes, I do, Auntie," Jade said, giving me a peck on the cheek.

It was the same thing she had said, and the same thing that I had said, the last time she got pregnant.

CHAPTER 33

I was convinced that nobody knew Rhoda like I knew Rhoda. She had a very close relationship with various members of her family even though her parents lived in New Orleans, and her favorite aunt, Lola, lived in Alabama. But she was particular about what she shared with them. There was no doubt in my mind that Rhoda's family was totally unaware of the dark side she had that I knew about. There were even times when it seemed like I knew her better than I knew myself. I could predict her actions more often than I could predict my own. My relationship with Rhoda had always been this way. Now I was in a similar situation with Rhoda's daughter.

About ten years ago, I had had no contact with Rhoda for several years. We had reconnected at a funeral and promptly resumed our friendship.

Jade was seven when she entered my life, but there had been two sides to that child even then. She had been just as cute as a button and one of the most likeable children I'd ever met. But she was also self-centered, secretive, and manipulative back then, too.

She had not changed. Well, I guess you could say she *had* changed: she was even more self-centered, secretive, and manipulative now. I pitied the man she married. He was going to have his work cut out for him. But knowing Jade, she'd latch on to some lovesick fool that she'd pussy-whip so fast he wouldn't know what hit him. The bottom line was, history was being repeated. Jade was Rhoda all over again. But I thanked God that it was in a much less sinister way. I was convinced that my influence would help keep Jade from duplicating her mother's homicidal behavior.

Jade was the daughter I dreamed of having, and until I gave birth to Charlotte I treated Jade like a daughter. It was bad enough that Rhoda and Otis had already spoiled the girl rotten, but I had to go and jump into the mix with both feet.

I was the one who Jade had run to when she got her first period at thirteen. "Oh, Auntie, I don't know what I would do without you. I don't like what's happening to my body!" she had wailed that day in the middle of one of my cookouts, angry and embarrassed to discover the bloody stain on her new white shorts. It was doubly bad to her, because Pee Wee was the one who had noticed it first. Right in the middle of a volleyball game. "And to let Pee Wee see me like this!"

"Don't think he hasn't seen this before. You'd be surprised what men, especially men his age, already know about us females," I chuckled. I gave Jade one of my old housecoats, which wrapped around her three times, to put on until I washed and dried her shorts. "Don't you think you should call your mama so she can pick you up?" I asked, gently scrubbing the bloody crotch of Jade's shorts.

"I don't want to go home yet," Jade said with a smirk. "I can't leave until I beat Pee Wee at a few games."

I was glad that Jade got along so well with Pee Wee. She loved babies and being around Charlotte, who was a fussy five-year-old at the time, and it kept Jade out of trouble. Or so I thought.

A month after Jade's first period, she came to me again with another personal crisis. I came home from work and she was sitting on my front porch with her schoolbooks in her lap and a look of terror on her face.

"What's wrong now?" I asked, dragging my feet as I walked toward my front porch. I had a hard time moving when I encountered unpleasant news. From the look on Jade's face, I expected to hear the worst. I covered my heart, which had started racing like mad, with my hand. Then I braced myself.

"Nothing," she said with hesitation, following me inside.

"Then why the long face?" I asked, my arm around her shoulder.

"I bled again," she stammered.

I gasped. "Well, honey, you are going to bleed a lot more in the next thirty or forty years. According to nature, you are a woman now. I know a smart girl like you knows that by now," I chuckled. "They were teaching sex education when I was in school, back in the Stone Age, and I know that these days they are telling you kids a lot more than they were telling us. If you don't talk to your mama, I will. You will need to know how to take care of yourself every month."

"I know everything I need to know. Mama knows I know. She even took me to the drugstore and bought up a bunch of tampons—yuck—and she gave me that 'keep your legs closed' talk. And what she didn't tell me my friends did."

"Then what's your problem? You say you're bleeding again, but didn't you know that was coming?"

"I had my period again last week."

"Oh. Well, if you are bleeding again already, you might need to see a doctor. The first few periods are irregular, but you should still see a doctor just to make sure everything is all right."

"Lo'Reese Freeman said you bleed the first time you have sex."

"You will," I sighed. "And you can expect it to hurt like hell," I said over my shoulder. Jade followed me into my kitchen where I snatched two sodas from the refrigerator, handing one to her.

"I did," she said with a sheepish grin.

"You did what?" I asked, already knowing the answer and not liking it one bit. Jade dropped her head and giggled under her breath. "Jade, you are still a baby! You don't have any business getting that close to any boys right now. You have all the time in the world. Don't grow up too fast, baby."

"But I really like this boy and he likes me. He let me ride on his bike. He gave me a dollar. And he said I was the prettiest Black girl in the world." Jade sniffed and stuck out her chest. "This boy only likes White girls, so getting him wasn't that easy. Especially for a girl as dark as me."

"Jade, boys will tell you anything and everything that they think you want to hear, just so they can fuck the hell out of you. Excuse my language, but that is exactly what it comes down to. Sex is a double-edged sword. It's 'fucking' when it's with the wrong person. It's 'making love' when it's with someone that you care about, and someone who cares about you."

"But guess what? I care about Jeffrey Rollins and he cares about me. Honest to God. I think about him all the time, and he thinks about me. He told me so."

"I am sure he does think about you all the time. All of the other boys would too if you let them get in your pants. Listen, baby, you need to forget about boys right now and concentrate on school and growing up. You have lots of girlfriends and they can offer you a lot more than any boy can right now. The main thing is, you can do whatever you want with your girlfriends and a girl can't get you pregnant."

From that day on, Jade surrounded herself with female friends and I was glad to see that.

I had no idea what *that* was going to lead to.

Unlike Jade, Rhoda had not had many friends when she was a teenager. Had it not been for Pee Wee, Rhoda would have been the loneliest girl in her class until I came along. As a matter of fact, Pee Wee and I were the only friends that Rhoda had until she met Otis and married him as soon as we finished high school.

Our classmates had despised all three of us for different reasons, the same classic and typical reasons that kids had used for centuries: Rhoda was too pretty and her family had too much money, Pee Wee was too sissified and he was friends with a dark horse like Rhoda. Me, I was an even more popular target because I had more of the typical flaws that attracted bullies: I was fat, Black, ugly, shy, and poor.

It was a damn shame that a lot of the girls hated Rhoda back then because of her looks. But Jade was just as beautiful and it didn't seem to bother the other girls. Old Mr. Boatwright had convinced me that the only reason Rhoda had befriended me was because I was no threat to her. "With that bald head and butt-ugly face of yours, ain't no girl got to worry about you givin' them no competition. And if that ain't enough, that big, fat-ass blimp you call a body is."

At the time, I didn't care if what Mr. Boatwright said was true or not. His opinions were so off-the-wall that I could not take him seriously. And it didn't matter what he thought of me anyway, because Rhoda had chosen me, and only me, to be her best girl-friend. And in all the years that I had known Rhoda, she had never made an issue out of the way I looked.

I couldn't say the same for Jade and her prissy little friends. One thing I learned early in my relationship with Jade was that she did not tolerate unattractive people. All of her girlfriends looked like living Barbie Dolls.

Jade had started watching her weight at the tender age of eleven. Two years later she had attempted to wear makeup at thirteen, but Rhoda nipped that in the bud right away. "No makeup and no dating until you are sixteen," Rhoda had declared.

CHAPTER 34

As strict as Rhoda was with Jade, Jade pretty much did and said whatever she wanted anyway behind Rhoda's back. Especially when it came to me.

"Auntie, I love you to death, but I'd rather be dead than be as big as you are." She had just turned sixteen. Jade blinked and shook her head with a look of pity on her face. "Geraldo had a man on his show one day that was so fat, he had to tie a bath rag to a stick to bathe himself. And if that wasn't bad enough, he had to squat over his bathtub when he had to go to pee or . . . whatever."

Jade and I were having lunch at Mickey's Pizza Parlor in the Melden Village Mall. "Now I don't want you to think that I am trying to be funny or anything like that, but I can't tell where your chin ends and where your neck begins," Jade inserted. She was nibbling on a spinach salad, taking small, dainty bites. "I feel so sorry for you, Auntie."

Her bold comments had taken me by surprise, but I refused to let her know that. I responded in a very casual manner. "I am used to being big. I've been this way all my life." I let out a slight yawn before snapping another slice of the small pepperoni pizza in two with one bite.

"But don't it make you mad?" Jade asked with a frown on her face.

I laughed. "It wouldn't do me a bit of good to get mad about being fat. I'd be mad every day for the rest of my life because I know by now that I will be this big, if not bigger, until the day I die." The last thing I wanted at this point in my life was to have somebody else feeling sorry for me. Despite my appearance, I was happy.

I didn't know what all went on in Rhoda's house when I wasn't there. But whatever it was, it was enough for Jade to not want to be present. The reasons she didn't like to be alone in the house with her parents came out a piece at a time, usually during lunch at the mall, like today.

"I like spending time with you, Auntie. Mama and Daddy don't even sleep in the same bed anymore. And when they do talk, it's just to fuss and cuss each other out."

"Uh, that's kind of personal, honey. You shouldn't be exposing your family business like that. Not even to me."

"But you are family to me. And when I am around you and Pee Wee, I don't have to listen to a lot of cussing and fussing. Ever since Mama had that stroke, she's been mad with Daddy. If I didn't know any better, I'd swear she blamed him for it." Jade's eyes rolled slightly to the side, and she stared off into space for a few moments with a distant and sad look on her face. It was obvious that her mind was on something now that was more disturbing to her than my weight.

I cleared my throat to get her attention back. "Jade, there are things going on with your parents that you don't know about. But at your age, you should not try to figure it out. Your parents love you, and part of the reason they stay together is because of you."

Jade returned her attention to me. She gave me a stony look, and then blinked so rapidly that I thought she had something foreign in both eyes. But I realized she was just trying to reorganize her thoughts. She seemed to be having a hard time getting her words out. "Auntie, I think my daddy's fooling around on my mama," she muttered with a hint of anger.

"Well, unless you know that for sure, you shouldn't repeat that to anybody else. I don't even need to hear stuff like that. False accusations can do a lot of harm to innocent people," I said in a stern voice. "What makes you think your daddy is fooling around? Have you been snooping into things that don't concern you again?"

Jade bowed her head and nodded. "Last week I found a telephone number on a napkin from that Red Rose Bar in my daddy's pocket when I was looking for some loose change. I called the number and a lady answered. She had an accent."

I shrugged. "Maybe she's somebody from Jamaica that your daddy knows."

"Uh-uh. I don't think so. I know everybody he knows from Jamaica. The woman sounded kind of . . . uh . . . trashy. And a real snooty bitch, too, I might add."

"That doesn't mean anything. It could have been a friend or a co-worker. You don't know all the facts, so you should not upset your mama with that information."

Jade gave me a guarded look. "Last year when we went to Jamaica to visit Daddy's folks . . . Uh . . . I saw my mama kissing a man on the beach."

I stopped chewing. "So? That doesn't mean anything either. I've kissed men other than my husband and it was all quite innocent."

"Yeah, but you don't look like my mama does in a bathing suit, and this man had been looking her up and down all day. That man . . . Uh, it was my uncle Bully, my daddy's best friend from Jamaica. And when Uncle Bully kissed my mama, his hand was rubbing up and down her butt and squeezing on it, too." Jade paused and a cold, hard look appeared on her face. "I couldn't face my friends if my parents got divorced. That's so . . . so . . . lower class. It's not fair!"

I held up my hand, which was a useless attempt to calm Jade down. Her lips were trembling. Tears began to form in her eyes.

"Jade, life is not fair," I said gently, more disturbed by what she had just said about me not looking like Rhoda in a bathing suit than I was about Rhoda's indiscretion with that rakish Jamaican they called Bully. "Whatever you saw, I am sure it didn't mean much to your mother."

Jade sniffed and dabbed at her eyes and nose with a napkin. "That's not all. I heard some of what they said."

"What did you hear?"

"And let me tell you something else that I found out." Jade paused and glanced around. "That baby that Mama had before I was born that died . . . Uncle Bully was that baby's father."

My face froze. As far as I knew, I was the only person who knew that Rhoda had had an affair with her husband's best friend and had his baby.

"Who told you that?" I asked, with my eyes stretched wide open.

"Nobody told me. That's part of the stuff I overheard Mama and Uncle Bully talking about that night on the beach in Jamaica. And that's how I found out about that ugly woman that my daddy had an affair with before we moved here from Florida."

"Jade, I don't need to know all your family business. I will forget what you just told me, and I would appreciate it if you didn't tell your mama what you just told me. Are you good at keeping secrets?"

Jade nodded but a strange look slid down on her face like a curtain. "Are you?"

"Am I what?" I asked, holding my breath.

"Good at keeping secrets?"

I shrugged. "I guess I am." I added with a chuckle. "Is there something else you want to share with me?"

I had never seen Jade look as radiant as she did at this moment. "Auntie, I'm in love again. I am in love so hard it hurts. And it's for real this time."

I gave Jade a puzzled look as she rose from her seat. I didn't realize she was crying until she wiped her eyes and nose with the tip of a napkin.

"Is it that bad?" I asked, wondering who Jade could be in love with so much that it reduced her to tears.

Jade shook her head. "I'm just so happy I can't stand it. I never knew that true love could be so deep. I'll be right back," she sniffled before she trotted across the floor, leaving me more puzzled and confused than ever.

While Jade was in the ladies' room I moseyed back up to the

counter and ordered myself a medium-sized pepperoni pizza, thinking that I should have ordered a larger one in the first place. The same counter girl who had taken my original order waited on me again, giving me the same look of disdain that I usually received from fast-food counter workers. I expected it from the younger, slimmer ones. But this one was almost as large and old as me. I ignored the way she lifted her thick eyebrows when I ordered a large Diet Coke.

By the time Jade returned to the table, I had finished that pizza, too, and was quietly sipping on what was left of my drink.

"Now, where were we?" Jade asked, sitting down with caution, adjusting her low-cut sweater.

"You were telling me about your newest love," I told her, clearing my throat.

"This is the real thing, Auntie. I really mean it," Jade squealed.

I sniffed, wiped my nose and greasy lips with a napkin, and gave Jade a serious look. I could see that she was prepared to shift into a defensive mode by the way she pressed her lips together and narrowed her eyes. I decided that I would not be too critical on her this time, not that it would have done any good.

"Well, even if you are in love for real this time, you better keep your legs closed. Babies and abortions are no fun. Some women get abortions, then later, when they really want to have children, they can't," I told Jade, speaking in a tone of voice that was both firm and gentle at the same time.

"I won't have to worry about any of that," Jade said with a smug look. One thing I could say about Jade was when she gave me this type of look, she usually had something to tell me that I didn't want to hear.

"Oh? Is this the kind of boy who wants to save himself for his wedding night?"

Jade shifted her eyes. "I'm through with *boys.*"

"Oh? Well, I hope you are not involved with some forty-year-old fool who can't get anybody but a young girl. Men like that usually end up making a fool out of young girls. Those men are not responsible because they never matured themselves in the first place. Your mama and your daddy would have a fit if you get involved with an older man, and I would, too!"

Jade was looking at me with her mouth hanging open and her eyes bugged out. "Auntie, what is the matter with you? Do you think I'm crazy?"

I gave Jade a puzzled look and a shrug.

"Me with an old man in his forties? Chicken skin! Yuck! My flesh crawls just thinking about it!" Jade said, with tears in her eyes.

"What, then?" I asked, getting impatient.

Jade folded her arms and placed them on the table with a dreamy look in her eyes now. For a brief moment she actually looked shy and demure.

"It's not a forty-year-old man, Auntie. Jeez! I don't even like to sit too close to people that *old*. All old things do for me is remind me that we have just so much time to do what we need to do. I don't want to waste my time, ticktock, ticktock, with some dusty, musty, crusty, rusty old fossil. Anyway, they usually have some old, contagious disease or some musty smell." Jade paused long enough to shudder. "I don't even wear old clothes."

"Uh-huh. Well, you might want to move to a table across the room to finish your lunch," I smirked, kicking Jade's foot under the table.

She gave a dismissive wave. "You know when I talk about old people I don't mean you. You are special! Just like my mama and my daddy. And Pee Wee is an OK dude for an old man. You really lucked out when you reeled him in."

"That's good to know. And I'll be sure and let Pee Wee know that, too," I said, unable to hold back a rapid string of mild belches. That got me another look of pity from Jade. "So exactly what is it you are trying to tell me?" I glanced at my watch. As much as I liked spending time with Jade, I had other things that I needed to attend to.

"You got somewhere else to go?" she asked with a pout. "I thought you wanted to spend the day with me, Auntie."

"Jade, I have a family and a big house to take care of. And I do have other places to be and other things to do. Saturday is the only day in the week that I can do all those things. Doing a little window shopping with you and us having lunch is one thing, but I didn't say I'd spend the whole day with you. Now, if there is something you are trying to tell me, you need to tell me now."

"I'm not *trying* to tell you anything. I am telling you, I am through with members of the opposite sex. They are boring and everybody knows how they like to use females. Even you."

I gave Jade an impatient look and shook my head. "Well, believe it or not, I am still confused. If you have something to say, please just come on and say what it is." I slid my tongue across my lips and glanced at my watch again to add some emphasis.

"There is this girl." Jade reared back, scratched her chin, and then winked. She looked around before she continued, leaning forward now and speaking in a very low voice. "I've been looking for somebody like her all my life." There was a faraway look in Jade's eyes and a mysterious smile on her face. She bobbed her head and looked around again, like somebody just waking up from an erotic dream.

My diet drink suddenly tasted like turpentine. I slid the container to the side of the table, then I folded my arms and placed them on the table, like Jade. We were staring at each other, eyeball to eyeball.

"Pardon me?" I asked, refusing to take my eyes off Jade's even though she attempted to look away. I looked at her like I was seeing her for the first time and in a way, I was. "Jade, are you . . ."

"Shh! Don't talk too loud. I just saw Curtis Booker from my school walk by. He is the biggest-mouthed boy in the world." Jade reared back again and sucked in her breath, a sparkle in her eye.

Ever since we sat down at the shiny white metal table near the counter, males of all ages slowed down when they walked by, grinning in our direction, nodding, tipping their hats. I knew that their attention was not aimed at me. I pretended like I didn't see them, but Jade enjoyed being admired. Just like Rhoda. She tilted her head back and shook that pile of black hair on her head until she had all eyes on her, just like Rhoda always does. One unruly lock fell across her face, almost covering her eye. "I swear to God, men are all the same. I wish they would stop being so obvious," Jade sighed, removing the hair off her face and tucking it behind her ear.

"I know what you mean," I said, wiping a wet spot on the table with one of the soiled napkins.

"Anyway, don't tell my mama I told you this," Jade clucked. "She told me how she grew up thinking that Pee Wee was gay until he started fucking up a storm with women, so I know she'd be OK with me being a lesbian. She is real liberal when it comes to certain things, so she feels that gays are just as good as regular people, except for being gay." Jade paused and without the aid of a mirror, she applied a fresh coat of lip gloss, pressing her lips together afterward to even it out. "But Daddy and his family wouldn't be too happy about it. You know how the West Indians are. They are just like the Spanish. Too emotional. They get hysterical over the least little things. The way they carried on when my big brother came out of the closet was a scandal and a shame! You would have thought we were Spanish! I just want to ball up and cry when I think about poor Maria Cortez, this Dominican girl who sits behind me in English class. Her daddy had to go to the hospital when he found out she liked girls."

I looked at Jade in a way that must have made her uncomfortable, and that was not easy to do. She crossed and then uncrossed her legs two times. She blinked hard a few times, and then tucked her bottom lip into her mouth.

"What?" she asked, twisting in her seat. "Why are you looking at me like that?"

"Girl, you are just full of surprises," I said in a tone of voice that was sharper than I wanted it to be. Jade flinched and looked disappointed. I blew out my breath and gave her a concerned look. "Who is this girl you think you are in love with?"

"Auntie, she's so smart and so pretty and so fly. She really is. I mean, she's just like me!"

"So basically, you are telling me that you are in love with yourself?" I was teasing now.

"Something like that," Jade said.

She was serious so I became serious again, too. I cleared my throat before I spoke. "You know, this could be a phase. I never told anybody, but once upon a time, I had a crush on a female. I got over it." I saw no reason to tell Jade that her mother was the female I'd had "unnatural" urges for. "Kids your age are still confused about what they like."

"Please promise me you won't tell my mama? I know she likes gay people, especially since my brother is one and all, but I don't know if I'm ready for her to know about me, too. All she talks about with my grandmothers and other folks is how she can't wait for me to make her a grandmother. Can you imagine that?"

"No, but why are you telling *me* something this, uh, sensitive? I would think you'd want to keep this lesbian thing a secret. Unless you are planning to 'come out,' as they say."

"Because Noelle, that's my lady, and I need a place to meet. I really want to make a good impression on her, see? She's got too many folks in her house and you know how gloomy it is at my house. Besides, Mama is always around."

"My house is not a motel, Jade. I have a husband and a daughter, and I don't want them in the middle of something like this."

Jade shrugged. "Oh well. Then when Noelle and I want to spend some time together, you can rent us a motel room. When we tried to get a room the other day, they asked for ID and a valid credit card. Like, how many sixteen-year-olds walk around with credit cards." Jade gave me a disgusted look. "I swear to God, some adults can be so . . . so . . . dense. Don't these motel people know that if we really want to get a room, we will find a way? They should just give us what we want in the first place. Just like the folks who sell alcohol. They know we are going to get what we want one way or the other! Like they didn't do the same things when they were kids."

I was no longer interested in Jade's company. I had heard more than I wanted to hear about her love life.

"Jade, as an adult, I have to maintain a level of responsibility. A lot of adults feel the way I do. I already do things that I shouldn't do on your behalf. Letting you receive questionable items at my address is one thing, but I am not going to rent motel rooms for you."

"I'll pay you back . . . if I have to," Jade said, a desperate look on her face.

I held up my hand and shook my head. "It's not about the money for a motel room. If you and this girl Noellen, Norelle, Noreen, or whatever her name is, want to be together, you are going to have to figure out how to do so by yourselves. I am not getting involved." I was getting impatient. "Let me get you home right now before you drop another bomb on me."

CHAPTER 35

Jade never mentioned her "alternative lifestyle" to me again. After a few weeks had passed I was convinced that she was over it. I guess that's why I reacted the way I did when I came home one day a month after Jade's true confessions and found her upstairs in my guestroom in the bed. And she was not alone.

As soon as I entered the room, I slammed the door shut. Then I stood there in a state of shock with my back against the door. About five different thoughts jumped to the front of my mind at the same time. The one that concerned me the most was the fact that my young daughter could have entered this unlocked room. Or anybody else. When Muh'Dear, Daddy, and Scary Mary visited my house, they roamed all over the place, being nosy. It would have been right up their alley to peep into my guest bedroom just to see if I was keeping it clean. Another thing I thought about was the fact that I didn't know the girl Jade was with. What if she was some she-thug whose real motive was to come case my place so that she and her friends could come back later and commit a robbery?

I had to rub my eyes to make sure they were not playing tricks on me. I reached behind me and locked the door and then I stood there with my hands on my hips.

Jade was on her back splayed like a frog, naked to the world, with the head of her companion bobbing up and down between her thighs.

"Jade, what in the world are you doing, girl? You get your nasty little self up off my bed!" I shouted. Pee Wee and Charlotte were downstairs in the living room, slumped in front of the TV watching reruns of *The Jeffersons.*

When I had come into the house, Pee Wee had mumbled something about Jade being upstairs. There was nothing unusual about that. The older Jade got, the more time she spent at our house. She even had her own key and as far as she was concerned, she could occupy our guestroom any time she felt like it and that's just what she did. And the reason she came and went as she did was because we'd always let her. Well, that was more my doing than Pee Wee's. He wouldn't even allow his relatives to get that comfortable when they came to visit.

"What are you doing in my house?" I stood by the side of the bed with my arms folded. I was horrified at what I'd walked in on. But I was even more disturbed by the fact that Jade and the girl she was with glanced at me and kept right on doing what they were doing! I snatched an *Essence* magazine off the nightstand and swatted the other girl's naked butt.

"Auntie . . . can't you see I'm busy?" Jade panted, pausing long enough to moan.

The girl was unbelievably bold! I had expected her to jump up, grab her clothes, and run, apologizing profusely to me.

The look of ecstasy on Jade's face frightened and embarrassed me. Nobody had ever seen that look on my face. Not even when I had worked as a prostitute and did everything I could to make my tricks think I was having a good time. I usually made love to my husband in the dark. But even when we did do it where he could see my face, he never saw me make faces like the ones Jade was making now. In addition to being horrified and frightened, I was jealous!

"This is the last straw! I told you my house was not a motel! You can do whatever you want to do with your girlfriends or boyfriends, but not in my house!" I hissed, yelling loud enough to make Jade think I meant business. I leaned over the bed and low-

ered my voice. From what I could tell, these two hussies had no de-
sire to leave that bed until they were good and ready. I swatted the
other girl's butt again. This time harder. When that didn't get a reaction, I grabbed her arm and pulled her around to face me.

"What?" the girl squeaked. The entire bottom of her face was
covered in Jade's joy juice. "Lady, what is your problem?"

I could not believe that a stranger could talk to me like this in
my own house—

"How dare you two nasty little things come into my house and
behave this way?" I snarled.

Jade stopped moaning, squirming, and panting long enough
to speak. "Auntie, what are you doing? I never knew you could be
so . . . so rude! I know you like to get your pussy eaten just as much
as the rest of us," Jade said in a serious tone of voice.

"Look, girl, you, your little friend, and your nasty language need
to get up out of my house. I told you I wasn't going to be a part of
this."

"Auntie, what is your problem? If I didn't know any better, I'd
swear you were not getting enough loving yourself these days. You
need to talk to your man about that." Jade let out a deep sigh and
rubbed her girlfriend's shoulder. "This won't happen again," Jade
said.

"You are damn right it won't," I yelled. "I want both of you to get
up and get your little nasty-ass selves dressed and go home. Lickity
split!" I immediately wished that I had not used that particular
phrase. Jade giggled, her friend gave me a thumbs-up sign.

"Lickity split, lickity split," Jade said in a singsong manner, slowly
sliding her tongue across the top of her bottom lip. The longer
they stayed, the more horrified I became.

"I'm sorry, Auntie," Jade finally said with her head bowed.
Looking up she added, "I really am. Can you leave us alone so we
can get dressed?"

I left the room stomping, but as soon as I reached the landing at
the bottom of the steps, I tried to act as normal as possible. Pee
Wee and Charlotte glanced up from the television as soon as I entered the living room.

"Is Jade all right? She said she had real bad cramps and couldn't find her key to her own house and wasn't nobody there to let her in," Pee Wee said, his back to me now. I was glad he couldn't see the disgusted look on my face.

"Uh, she's fine now. I gave her some Advil," I lied.

"I hope she don't make a mess up there in that room," Pee Wee snapped.

"She won't," I said, plopping down on the sofa next to Charlotte. I immediately started tapping my fingers on the top of the coffee table. When Pee Wee noticed, I stopped and gave him a nervous grin.

Every few minutes I looked toward the stairs, hoping to see Jade and her lover. But when another ten minutes passed and they still had not come downstairs, I went back to the guestroom and flung open the door again.

This time I was even more horrified. Jade and her girlfriend were still naked and still stretched out on the bed. But this time it was Jade's head bobbing up and down between the other girl's thighs.

CHAPTER 36

I stood in the doorway of my guest bedroom for just a few moments, trying to adjust to the spectacle on the bed. Again! I blinked and rubbed my eyes.

But other things were going through my mind at the same time. Things that had been even more painful than what I was looking at now. This room had a history that I had tried to put behind me. It was too disturbing. Mr. Boatwright had slept in this same room and he had raped me more times in it than in any other part of our house.

For several years after his death I had used this room to store some of the items that most people stored in their basement or garage. I kept the door shut at all times and the curtains drawn until the room got so gloomy and musty I didn't want to go into it unless I had to.

But after I had finally told my mother—and everybody else who had worshipped Mr. Boatwright like a saint—what he had done to me, my attitude about the room changed. I refused to let it control me any longer. Hell, the room was part of my own house and I was in control. I had already had the room painted several times, each time hoping to cover another painful memory. With the new queen-size bed and the bright new furniture, which had taken me so much time to choose, it looked like a new place. And it really was. It was the perfect guest bedroom. We allowed everybody who used it to treat it as they would a room in their own home and that's exactly what Jade did whenever she felt like it.

Jade glanced around at me and kept right on doing what she was doing! I stared at her in slack-jawed amazement. I had to rub my eyes because it was hard to believe that I was seeing what I was seeing for the second time. The floor on the side of the bed was littered with cute, pastel-colored bikini panties, padded bras, and a pile of other clothing. Jade's ever-present yellow backpack was on the small blue wing chair facing the bed. The bed was shaking so furiously, both nightstands on either side were rattling. I was not surprised to see two beer bottles rocking back and forth on one of the nightstands, clicking against the side of the little white lamp that I'd purchased just a few weeks ago.

Jade's lover, a honey-colored girl with reddish brown hair, and a small, upturned nose, winked at me as she wrapped her long, slender legs around Jade's shoulders. Instead of wasting any more of my time protesting, I just shook my head and shut the door. Pee Wee and Charlotte were surprised but pleased when I rejoined them in the living room and insisted on taking them out to dinner. I rushed them out the door so fast they had to put their jackets on in the car.

Two hours later when we returned, Jade and her friend were gone. I was still furious. I planned to let Jade know that I didn't appreciate the stunt that she had pulled in my house, with my husband and my young daughter right downstairs! Jade was too self-centered and brazen for her own good, and something told me that it would be her downfall. I just hoped that it didn't involve me.

The bed had been made up and they had had the good sense to spray the room with pine-scented room deodorizer. But even that didn't hide the fact that they had also smoked weed in the room. Well, I wouldn't say anything to Jade about her and her friend smoking marijuana in my house. That little indiscretion was a little too close to home. That was one skeleton in my own closet that I wanted to keep there.

I didn't condone the use of drugs, but when I was young I never turned down a chance to share a joint with Pee Wee, a habit he had picked up in Vietnam. Unfortunately, Jade had walked in on us indulging on more than one occasion. I was proud of the fact that I had not puffed on a joint in over five years. And everybody knew that I had given up that particular habit. I couldn't speak for Pee Wee. I didn't want to think about how many joints he smoked when he hung out with Otis.

According to Rhoda, who despised smoke of any kind, Otis had relatives in Jamaica who lived the Rastafarian lifestyle and they smoked marijuana on a regular basis, from the grandfather on down to the kids still in grammar school. Pee Wee never turned down one of Otis's frequent invitations to accompany him to Jamaica for a few days. And now that I thought about it, Jade always went with them.

I didn't particularly like being a middle-aged woman, even though the people my mother's age still called me "young lady." But I was glad that age had rewarded me with a little more common sense. There were some things that I'd done when I was younger that I would never do again. However, there were things I did now that I wished I could stop. Being such a pushover where Jade was concerned was one of them.

Jade didn't come to my house for two weeks after the incident with her and the girl in my guest bedroom. As a matter of fact, I saw very little of her during those two weeks. I missed her frequent visits, but I wasn't about to do anything to bring her back any time soon. Pee Wee seemed relieved not to have Jade underfoot so much.

"That girl spends too much of her time up under you. She got a home and she need to stay in it more," he insisted.

I could tell that he was trying not to sound too harsh because he knew how much I doted on Jade.

"She's not really happy at home," I defended. "You know how boring Rhoda and Otis are these days. He spends most of his time at his job or propped up in his La-Z-Boy with a beer in his hand. Rhoda spends most of her time at the mall and the beauty parlor. Jade is at that age where she needs more attention. Her grandparents on both sides live too far away, and her brother doesn't want to be bothered with her coming down to Alabama to pester him to death."

"That ain't our problem. It ain't our responsibility to make Jade happy. And if she ain't gettin' enough attention from Rhoda, how come every time I look up, that fast-ass Jade is taggin' along to that mall and that beauty parlor with Rhoda? Maybe the girl's problem is she is gettin' too much attention."

I gave Pee Wee a thoughtful look. "Well, I don't really mind paying 'too much attention' to Jade. She keeps me young," I said with a hesitant smile.

"Well, she don't do nothin' for me but get on my nerves. She is still a child, she ought to stay in a child's place. And to tell you the truth, I don't want her comin' around this house when you ain't here. Especially when I got my cousin Steve and the rest of my boys over here watchin' a game. She can't stay out from underfoot, prancin' around us with them short shorts of hers cuttin' into her behind like a ribbon. It ain't healthy."

"What do you mean by that?"

"Annette, you ain't stupid. You know how men are. A woman throw somethin' at a man long enough, he's goin' to catch it sooner or later . . . You know what I mean."

CHAPTER 37

Pee Wee and I didn't argue often. And when we did, I had to tune up my mouth and organize my thoughts to make sure I didn't say something that I'd regret.

I gave him a guarded look, but I didn't appreciate the hot look that he gave me. Still, I didn't want to say anything that I would regret.

"Pee Wee, if I ever hear about you saying or doing something inappropriate where Jade is concerned, I will never ever forgive you. I will hate you for the rest of my life. Even more than I ever hated that sex-sick puppy, Mr. Boatwright, for taking advantage of me. You—You know better." The words that had just slid out of my mouth felt and tasted as foul as a snake must have tasted and I was immediately sorry.

Pee Wee dropped his head, scratched the side of it, and then quickly looked back up at me with a strange expression on his face. I couldn't tell if he was angry, sad, or just plain disgusted. And he had every right to be all three. Without another word, he left the room with me following so close behind him, I stepped on his heels.

"Woman, what in the world has got into you?" he demanded,

whirling around to face me. His eyes had darkened to match his mood.

"Uh, you know damn well that I didn't mean anything by that," I said with a forced grin, touching his arm.

He wasted no time in removing my hand from his arm. I felt like I had been burned, and I wanted to blow on my hand. But under the circumstances, I didn't want to appear too melodramatic. There was enough going on in the room already and I had started it. Now it was up to me to finish it.

"This ain't nothin' to be laughin' about. I got a young daughter and if any motherfucker touches her before she's of age and without her consent, they will have to tie me up and tie me down, stuff me in a barrel, and then throw me in the ocean. Because if I ever get loose, I will kill that motherfucker. You can count on that. I would expect any other man to do the same thing to my black ass, if I was stupid enough to touch his underage daughter. Otis is my best friend, and you know how far me and Rhoda go back. I wouldn't mess with their baby girl. You of all people know me better than that. At least I thought you did. But I could be wrong." Pee Wee paused and gave me one of the most critical looks anybody had even given to me. It was so disturbing and intense that I had to hold my breath.

"I know you would never in your life touch somebody's child. Especially Jade," I said in a thin voice.

Pee Wee slapped his hands on his hips, more anger flashing in his eyes. "Annette, I don't ask you for much. All I ask is that you be a good wife and a good mother. So far we have been real lucky in our marriage. I want to keep it that way." Pee Wee lifted his hand and shook a finger in my face. "But don't you never say nothin' that stupid to me again as long as you live. You know I would never ever put my hands on my best friend's young daughter. Even if Jade was twenty-five years old, I wouldn't touch her with a yardstick. Skinny women don't appeal to me no how. You know that," Pee Wee said, his eyes giving me a quick look up and down.

Pee Wee started to walk away again but he stopped and gave me another angry look. "And another thing, I hope you didn't forget what I shared with you that night you came out about what old Mr.

Boatwright had done to you all them years. I had my own story. Somebody took advantage of me, too, when I was a child."

I bowed my head submissively and left the room. I wanted to hide my face because it was burning with shame.

As hard as it was to believe, I wanted Jade to start coming back to the house. I missed her and so did Charlotte. Now that I had had time to cool off, I decided that I wouldn't bring up the incident involving Jade and her girlfriend in my guestroom. What good would it do anyway? I asked myself. If nothing else, she was the distraction I felt I needed to keep me from getting bored. Had she been present during my last argument with Pee Wee, I never would have said such a ridiculous thing to the man who had all but saved me from a life of despair.

I continued to visit Rhoda at her house, and we visited the nail shop and the beauty parlor together like we always did. I didn't want anything to seem out of the ordinary to her where Jade and I were concerned. She was Rhoda's most sensitive area. Jade was not just Rhoda's daughter. In some ways it seemed like Jade was Rhoda all over again, so I had to be careful how I dealt with them both. I knew firsthand what Rhoda was capable of doing. And if she didn't stop at murder, there was no telling what to expect from Jade.

"I'm glad Jade has finally started spending more time with kids her own age," Rhoda told me over one of our frequent lunches in the same food court where Jade had revealed her lesbian leanings to me. But instead of pizza, like I had enjoyed on my lunch with Jade, I ordered just a salad, like Rhoda. "I can't believe how mature she's gotten these last couple of months," Rhoda said with a shy smile, nibbling on a small piece of lettuce. "She seems so pleased with herself these days. She cleans up her room and other parts of the house without having to be asked. She even volunteers to run errands. Ha! I remember when I used to ask her to go over to Pee Wee's barbershop and let him trim the ends of her hair, and she'd rather get a whuppin'. Now she rushes over for Pee Wee to trim her hair before she even needs it!" Rhoda smiled so warmly, her eyes watered.

"She is growing up," I offered, snapping a carrot in two with my teeth. I was impatient, but I didn't want Rhoda to know that. I knew that after we parted, I'd have to make a beeline to the Mc-Donald's next door to snatch up a few Big Macs. The only thing that salads did for me was make me mad. But Rhoda had insisted that that was all we should order. She was on a tight schedule. We had ordered something that we could eat fast, so that she could be on time for her appointment at a nearby spa for her weekly massage.

"All I want is for Jade to be happy. She's one of the few things that I have to look forward to anymore." Rhoda gave me a pleading look as if she was trying to read my mind. "I hope you and Pee Wee don't mind havin' her at your house underfoot all the time. She'd rather be there more than she would her own house! And such a lovely home Otis and I have made for her!" Rhoda stopped abruptly and touched my hand. "Not that your house is not just as lovely as mine. It is."

I shrugged. "You know we don't mind Jade coming over to our house so much. Charlotte looks forward to her visits. Not many girls Jade's age would spend so much of their time away from their friends."

Rhoda nodded and gave me a pensive look. "Well, you know how things are between Otis and me. He pretty much goes his way, and I go mine. It's a bitch and sometimes I get depressed. I don't like havin' to hide that from Jade. And she is *so* observant. Just like I was when I was growin' up. When she's in the house, she keeps her nose in everything. Always lurkin' around corners, listenin' to my telephone conversations. Whenever Bully calls, I'm usually the one who takes his calls. Poor Bully. That British bitch—the flat-assed girl from London he was stupid enough to marry—treats him like shit, so he calls a lot. Anyway, I have to chase Jade from the house to keep her from sneakin' a listen on the extension. I don't know what that girl thinks she's goin' to hear. Me, I just give Bully some . . . uh . . . marital advice."

"Uh-huh," I said, rolling my eyes. Rhoda was too wrapped up in her own thoughts to notice my reaction.

I was just burning up with curiosity about Rhoda and the de-pressed and neglected Bully: the Jamaican man that Jade had seen her kissing on a beach in Jamaica. Part of his pain was the fact that his British wife was unable to have children. The only child he had ever fathered was the one with Rhoda. I knew in my heart that because of that, and the mysterious death of that child, Bully and Rhoda would always be connected.

One thing I could say about Rhoda was that if she didn't want me to know something about her, she didn't tell me. And I dared not ask. But under the circumstances that I'd been made aware of, it was not that hard to believe that Rhoda had recently resumed a romantic relationship with the man who had fathered her second child.

Rhoda opened her mouth to speak again, pausing to cough. "I want everything to be special in Jade's life. Especially . . ." Rhoda sucked in her breath and leaned across the table. "Especially her . . . first time."

"First time for what?" I asked, blinking stupidly. Rhoda shot me a sharp look. "Oh. That," I managed. "Well, I'm sure her first time will be special," I said with my fingers crossed. "How do you know she hasn't done it already?" I asked, my mouth still hanging open after I'd finished talking.

"Because I know my child. I've raised her well. Jade knows that she can talk to me about anything and everything. I made her promise that she would tell me when she was ready to start havin' sex. That is, if she can't wait until her weddin' night, like I advised her to."

Rhoda chewed more of her salad, not taking her eyes off mine. I was staring at her in disbelief. I found it hard to believe that a woman as savvy as Rhoda could also be so naive!

"Anyway, if she can't wait, and I would understand if she couldn't, with the way sex is all over our kids these days—the least I could do is get her prepared and organized so she won't have any unexpected little visitors. But I know that if that did happen, she'd be as good a young mother as I was." Rhoda stopped at this point and waved her fork at me. "Girl, if you want some good advice, I suggest you get to work on Charlotte now, before she reaches her teens. Be open with her about sex and love. Make sure you explain the difference between the two to her. Charlotte's lucky to have Jade there for her, willin' to explain the things to her that kids would be too embarrassed to ask their parents about. There is nothin' about sex that Jade doesn't know, and she heard it from *me*! So she's got all the facts, and not some goo-goo version from Hollywood or her friends. My girl is informed!" Rhoda laughed, winked, and leaned forward, speaking in a very low voice. "I'll bet Jade will suck a meaner dick than I can, once she gets started. Whoever she marries will be blessed, thanks to me."

"Did your mother tell you all this stuff when you were Jade's age?" I asked in a stiff voice. The conversation was making me uncomfortable, but I knew that it wouldn't be over until Rhoda was ready for it to be over.

"Of course not! My mom was a very dainty, straitlaced, proper woman."

I looked at Rhoda out of the corner of my eye.

"What I didn't learn from hangin' around Scary Mary's whorehouse, I learned from Aunt Lola. It's a good thing some women choose to be sluts. Lord knows she had enough men in her life to practice on. We women have to share bedroom knowledge so we can all have some fun." Rhoda sat up straighter and sniffed. She seemed to be glowing. "I can't even believe it myself when I recall how I once thought that all I was supposed to do in bed with my man was lie there and holler."

"I'll tell my daughter everything she needs to know when she's ready," I said in a heavy voice. A deep feeling of sadness came over me whenever I thought about Charlotte and sex in the same context. I wanted my child to stay innocent and untouched for as long as possible. In my mind, I believed that it would make up for what had been taken away from me at such a young age. I had had more sex before I'd reached my teens than some women had in their entire lifetime.

Rhoda laid her fork down on her half-empty plate and threw back her head and laughed. "Girl, try to explain and describe an orgasm to your young daughter! By the time I got through tellin' Jade about the stars she'll see and the bells she'll hear, she was ready to run out of the room and jump on the first boy she saw." Rhoda laughed so hard, tears streamed down the sides of her face. "It's a good thing she's got such good self-control, huh?"

I took so long to respond to Rhoda's last comment, she leaned forward and tilted her ear toward me.

"Yeah . . . it is a good thing Jade's got such good control," I mumbled, stuffing my mouth with a huge forkful of my salad so I would not have to speak again right away.

"And she'd be lost without you and Pee Wee there for her to fall back on. Annette, will you always be there for my child? Please promise me you will."

That was a question that Rhoda already knew the answer to, but I answered it anyway. "Of course. Why wouldn't I be?"

I was glad that Rhoda couldn't see the cold, hard lump that suddenly formed in my throat.

CHAPTER 38

Jade leaped back into my life with both feet. She showed up one Saturday morning at my door with a large single white rose wrapped in pink tissue. "Auntie, this is for you. I am so sorry for doing what me and my girlfriend did in your house. It won't happen again. Honest to God," Jade said, crossing her heart with her fingers.

On top of everything else, Jade considered herself a devout Christian. When she remembered, she said grace before each meal. Even if it was just a salad at the food court with her friends. It didn't bother her that some of her friends made fun of her vague relationship with God, but it bothered me when she told me. I knew the difference between right and wrong, and I didn't try to make deals with God when I wanted to do something that I already knew was unacceptable. I was not perfect, not by a long shot. But as hard as it was to do in our current world, I tried to be as good a person as I could be.

Jade had a warped sense of what religion was really about. Just like old Mr. Boatwright. Some Sundays he would rape me just before he left the house to go to church—and with Muh'Dear across the hall in her own room getting ready to go to the same service!

He thought that it was all right to rape me as long as he prayed a little harder and longer when he got to church.

Jade didn't go that often to the Baptist church that we all belonged to, but she read the pocket-sized Bible that I had given to her on her thirteenth birthday, and she knew about as much about scripture as I knew.

"Well," I began in an uncertain voice, "you better not pull another stunt like that one. At least not in my house!" I said sharply.

"I know, Auntie. But guess what? I've already asked God to forgive me, and I know He has! He's never let me down . . ."

"Jade, you know before you did what you did that it was wrong. But you went ahead and did it anyway. Then, you prayed about it. Let me tell you something, honey, God don't play. If you want to play games, you pull out that Monopoly board that I gave you for your birthday two years ago. Don't play games with me, or with God. Now, I usually get over things pretty quickly, but I am a worm compared to God. You have to go to Him with something that's coming from your heart. And you'd be better off if you remembered that."

"I know, I know," Jade sang. "God and His mysterious ways. It's a wonder He hasn't zapped us all back to wherever it is we came from," she scoffed, rolling her eyes. "But I will say my prayers before I go to bed tonight and ask Him *again* to forgive me for what I did in your guest bedroom. She sniffed and clutched her yellow backpack, giving me a curious look as I accepted the rose. "Please forgive me, Auntie. I had to look all over the place to find a white rose. White is the one that stands for peace, isn't it?"

"I don't know. I only buy red roses," I said. A pensive look appeared on Jade's face and she blinked hard. For a minute I thought she was going to cry. "But the white ones are just as nice. Maybe I'll start buying them, too."

Jade's face lit up and she didn't even wait for me to invite her in. She brushed past me and slunk into my living room and plopped down on my sofa the way she always did, hugging her yellow backpack against her chest like it contained diamonds and gold. Like nothing had changed.

I gently closed the door and followed her, taking tentative steps like I was the guest and she was the lady of the house. "From now on, when you are in my house, I expect you to behave yourself, girl," I said, my voice weakening by the second. I was so glad to have Jade back in her old position, I sat down next to her and grabbed her hand. "And, uh, just how is your . . . girlfriend?" I asked, immediately pressing my lips together right after I finished my last sentence.

"Gone. She's back with her boyfriend."

"And what about you?" I asked, looking at Jade out of the corner of my eye.

"Me? Oh, I'm going to take it easy for a while. Love is such hard work. I don't know how you do it." Jade let out a sharp laugh and looked around the room. "By the way, where is that husband of yours?"

"He drove over to Erie to see some of his kinfolks," I said, glad that Pee Wee wouldn't be back for a few days. I needed time to readjust to Jade and I knew he would, too.

He called just before Jade left to go home. As luck would have it, Jade answered the phone, greeting the caller in a singsong manner. "Pee Wee, you are so funny! And you got the funniest laugh."

I couldn't imagine what it was that Pee Wee had said to Jade when Jade answered the telephone. But from her reaction, it was something cute and amusing. At least he was in a good mood, I thought. I loved it when Pee Wee was in a good mood. But something told me that it wouldn't last too long this time.

As soon as I pulled the telephone out of Jade's hand and identified myself, Pee Wee released a loud string of foul words that I had not heard him or anybody else use in years. He was so hot that I could feel the heat on my ear. I was glad when he finally spoke in a normal voice.

"Please don't tell me that that gal is back in my house actin' like she's at home," Pee Wee complained bitterly.

"Uh, it's good to hear from you, baby. Don't let Charlotte eat too much candy," I said evasively, altering my face with a fake smile.

"Please tell me she just dropped by to say hello and don't plan on comin' over again any time soon," he continued in a weary voice.

"Well, I wish I could say that." I gave Jade a fake smile as I patted her shoulder. She stood next to me with her ear cocked as close to the telephone as she could get it. I held the telephone closer to my ear and gently pushed Jade to the side, ignoring the look of contempt she gave me.

"Shit!" Pew Wee exclaimed. "Annette, you listen to me, and you better listen to me good. You are goin' to rue the day that you didn't put your foot down. Somebody needs to sit that girl down and talk some sense back into her head."

I was getting exasperated and I wanted him to know that. "Why don't you do that?" I snapped, my fake smile still plastered on my face.

"Yeah, right! Like Jade would listen to me! You are closer to her than anybody else, other than her mama, and we know she ain't goin' to straighten the girl out. As far as she is concerned, the girl couldn't do no wrong if she tried."

"Uh-huh. That's nice, baby."

"I know she's standin' right up on you, so you can't say what I want you to say. But you know I'm right. We got enough problems without Jade addin' to 'em."

"What do you mean by that? What problems?" I asked with concern, praying that Pee Wee would hang up soon.

"Look, I don't have the time or the patience to go into that right now, but you know what I mean. It ain't easy keepin' a marriage on the right tracks these days with so many outside influences. The way Jade drops in on us with her friends, you would think we were runnin' a youth hostel or a cheap hotel. I didn't like her bringin' that girl to the house that time and then goin' straight upstairs after I told her not to! I know your mama left the house to you, but I am your husband and this house is my home now, too. I should have some say in what happens in it."

I was really getting concerned now. "Maybe you should discuss this a little more with me when you get home, because I don't think we are on the same page." I looked at Jade and blinked.

"I've said all I had to say about this for now. When I do get home, all I want is some peace and quiet. And I hope that's somethin' I'll be able to enjoy with nobody present but you and Charlotte."

"I'll let you go, baby." I hung up before Pee Wee could say another word. "Jade, Pee Wee said to tell you he's glad to know you're keeping me company while he's gone," I lied.

"Auntie, can you help me out again?" Jade asked.

I had to shake my head and return my thoughts to the present. I was glad that for a few minutes I had been able to put Daddy's dilemma out of my mind. Even though I had just replayed some of the most unpleasant incidents and conversations that had occurred over the last two years.

"Yes," I mumbled. "But I don't want anybody to know that I know about this. Rhoda would never forgive me if she knew that I helped you get rid of her grandchildren."

"What my mama don't know won't hurt her."

"Well, Jade, sometimes what we don't know *can* hurt us. Remember when you had those venereal warts and didn't know it? Who knows what damage they might have done to your system if you hadn't found out when you did and got treated?"

As far as I was concerned, getting pregnant was not the worst thing that could happen to Jade. Not that that would have been a walk in the park, either. There were diseases out there that I was hearing about for the first time, and she'd already had one. At the rate she was going, AIDS was just around the corner. I knew that it did me no good to try and talk some sense into Jade's head. She was too far gone for that. But I couldn't go to Rhoda and talk to her about Jade. It was too late for that, too. I knew Rhoda well enough to know that she would be furious if she ever found out how much information about her daughter I kept to myself.

I was thankful that there was a light at the end of a very long and dark tunnel. Jade would be leaving home eventually to continue her education—and in an out-of-state college at that. At the very least, Jade would be removed from my orbit in about a year.

"When do you plan to get this taken care of?" I wanted to know, wishing that I had had enough gumption to flat-out refuse her request.

"Friday. Right after work. We can leave the office together a little early, and get this mess straightened out in time for me to be home to watch the *I Love Lucy* reruns."

"I'll try to be there for you."

"You'll try?" Jade gasped, with terror in her voice. "What do you mean, you'll 'try'? Didn't you just say you would be there with me and make sure I got home all right?" Jade let out a loud disgusted sigh. "Auntie, you know how these abortion people do their thing! They won't let me leave the clinic by myself after it's over."

"Well, can't you take a cab?"

"A *cab*? What do you think I—a cab? Auntie, you know I don't fool around with those dingy, loud, scandalous-looking cabs driven by people who wear diapers on their heads and can't even speak proper English," Jade hissed, glancing around. "That's almost as bad as riding around on a Greyhound bus. I don't want anybody, even people that don't know who I am, to even think that I am broke and trifling enough to be in a cab or on a bus. I would drop dead before I let my friends see me like that." Jade's tongue snapped brutally over each word. For a second, I thought she was having a panic attack. "Anyway, if I do go home in a cab, with my luck Mama and Daddy and Uncle Bully will be peeping out the window and see me. The first thing they will want to know is why I'm coming home in a cab when I left home to go to work in your car with you. By the way, you'll have to pick me up to take me to work that morning, since I won't be able to drive my car afterward."

I rolled my eyes and let out a disgusted sigh of my own. "Jade, my daddy just had a heart attack. I don't know what's going to happen in the next couple of days. As much as I love you and want to help you out, I have to put my daddy first. I hope you understand that."

"I do, I guess," Jade said with a severe pout on her face.

"If you don't mind now, I need to call my sister in Florida and let her know about Daddy. She might want to come up here," I said, lifting the telephone from the end table by my end of the sofa.

"Yes, ma'am. Tell Miss Lillimae I asked about her," Jade said over her shoulder as she headed for the steps to my guest bedroom with that pout still on her face.

But this time, I didn't care about that pout. It had finally lost its potency.

CHAPTER 39

"It's so good to hear your voice again, girl," my half sister said to me when I called her at her home in Miami. "I was thinkin' about callin' to check up on you and Daddy anyway. Y'all both been on my mind a lot lately. I had planned to do so on the weekend when the rates are so much lower."

"Well, Daddy's out of the dark, but I don't know what is going to happen next. He's got a good doctor, and he says that Daddy is still pretty strong for a man of his age."

"Is he in good enough shape to talk if I call him tomorrow mornin'? To tell you the truth, I don't want to see him if I don't have to. I would rather wait to see him when he gets well. After all them years he lived with me, sick almost every other week, I don't think I could stand too much of it right about now. Me, I been wrestling with fibroids and a high blood pressure myself."

"Lillimae, you don't have to explain anything to me. I know you love our daddy just as much as I do. If I wasn't already in Ohio, I wouldn't want to come see him lying in a hospital bed either."

Lillimae took a long time to respond. "But if he gets any worse, I'm comin' up there even if I have to come on a dogsled. No matter what, I would like to see him, and hug him at least one more time before . . . before he leaves us."

"Lillimae, Daddy is not going to die any time soon. I promise you that. I didn't call to worry you. Muh'Dear tried to talk me out of it because she didn't want you to worry yourself."

"No, you did the right thing. I am glad you called me. And I expect to hear from you every day as long as he's sick. Do you hear me? You don't sound too hopeful to me. Now, is there anything else botherin' you?"

"Uh, no. It's getting late so I will let you go. Why don't you call the hospital and talk to Daddy yourself in the morning? In the meantime, I will be praying."

At least one of my prayers got answered. Daddy made a miraculous recovery and according to his doctor, would be almost as good as new. It was a different doctor, but the same thing had been said about Rhoda when she had her stroke ten years ago. She had made a recovery that was so complete, only the people who knew her knew that she had had a stroke.

"See there, I was right. I been tellin' y'all that the more ornery a person is, the longer he, or she, lives," Scary Mary observed with a chilly grin. "Look at me. Look at Rhoda. God couldn't strike her down with a stroke!"

If what the old madam said was true, my days were numbered. At no time in my life could I have ever been described as ornery. I was too passive for my own good and I had suffered because of it. But I could not change who I was, and I didn't really want to change this late in the game. I didn't know what I was going to do about other personal issues, but right now, my biggest issue was my daddy.

I went to visit Daddy at home the day after he got discharged. It pleased me to see that he was looking and feeling much better, although he looked even older than his seventy-nine years. He had lost his handsome looks a long time ago. Like so many other Black men, he had really let himself go. But for a man who had just had a heart attack, he looked as well as could be expected.

"I don't care how good you feel, you are not drinking any beer or anything else with alcohol in it," I scolded, ignoring the petulant look on my daddy's sweaty face.

"You a little too late for that, girl," Muh'Dear informed me. He snuck and drunk up three beers last night before I could even get his dingy black ass in the bed. As soon as I turned my back on him he was drinkin' like a carp! It was a damn shame, and I told him so to his face."

I shot my mother a hot look, then an even hotter one in Daddy's direction. There was now a blank expression on his face, like he had just woken up from a long sleep.

"How did that happen?" I yelled, punching Daddy's pillows and roughly pushing his knotty head back on the bed. He blinked and then lowered his eyes like a naughty child. He scratched the side of his head, then patted his brittle white hair back in place.

"Scary Mary slid through here and hooked him up while I was lookin' the other way. She done had two heart attacks herself, and she is still tickin' better than Big Ben, so I guess beer can't be that bad on no heart patient after all," Muh'Dear croaked.

"Well, if I see any beer in your hand I'm calling Dr. Peterson," I threatened. "I got enough to worry about."

The telephone rang and Muh'Dear stumbled out to answer the extension in the hallway outside of Daddy's room. Just as I was about to open my mouth to continue scolding Daddy, I heard Muh'Dear speaking in a loud and angry voice.

"Who the hell is this? Don't you be usin' that kind of nasty language with me, you trollop! That's my daughter you talkin' about!" Muh'Dear shouted.

Daddy gave me a puzzled look. His sorry eyes looked like they had been pushed halfway back in his head. I gasped and stumbled out to the hallway and snatched the telephone out of Muh'Dear's hand. As soon the caller realized I had come on the line he, or she, slammed the telephone down. I stood there listening to the dial tone, and blinking at the phone in my hands.

"Muh'Dear, who was that? What did they . . . say?" I asked, as if I didn't know already.

There was a stunned, wild-eyed look on my mother's face. Like she had just witnessed a crime, and in a way, she had.

With a click of her teeth she told me, "I don't know who in the world that rude and crude devil was. Some wench with a mouth as nasty as a outhouse! I ain't heard such mean-mouthin' since I quit cleanin' and cookin' for some of them mean old White heifers in

Florida! This hussy that just called here, she said you and me both was nothin' but cheesy-ass whores, and she was gwine to teach you a lesson you ain't never gwine to forget." Muh'Dear's mouth was hanging open. "What did you do to make some woman that dog-gone mad?"

The incredulous look on my mother's face was so extreme, it disturbed me almost as much as the telephone call. I wrung my hands and gave my mother a pleading look. I was taking too long to respond.

"Talk to me, girl! I already got one half-dead body on my hands. Don't you ball up and fall out on me, too," Muh'Dear hollered, looking toward the room where Daddy was mumbling under his breath.

I leaned to the side and peeped around the corner of the door and saw Daddy sitting up in the bed looking at me. It was obvious that the telephone call had attracted his attention. He looked more alert than he had in months.

"I didn't want you to find out about this. At least, not this way," I told my mother, beckoning her from the hallway into her dimly lit living room.

Muh'Dear and Daddy spent most of their time at home in the kitchen watching a small color television on the counter next to the microwave oven. They rarely watched the big screen television that Pee Wee and I had given to them three years ago for Christmas. It occupied a corner in the living room, standing as silent and dark as a big oak tree. Like a lot of older folks with nice things, they wanted everything to stay nice. And they thought that they could keep it that way by not using it. There was an expensive floor lamp in a corner facing the big screen television that had only been turned on once because Muh'Dear didn't want the bulb to burn out.

I pulled Muh'Dear down on her living room sofa, which was covered in plastic, next to me with my arm around her shoulder. I wanted to be out of Daddy's hearing range. This was something I didn't want him to find out about either. I told my mother about the blacksnake, the note, and the other telephone calls.

"You didn't want me to find out?" Muh'Dear hissed, looking toward the door. "Gal, what in the world you done got yourself mixed up in? I never heard such cussin' and name callin' as I just heard on my own telephone." Muh'Dear paused and brushed some lint off the plastic-covered arm of her nice beige sofa.

I shrugged. "Some woman has decided to give me a hard time," I said, shrugging again. "I can handle it, though. I don't think it's anything serious enough for me to worry about. She wants to get my goat." I sounded so uncertain that even I didn't believe my own words. And from the look on my mother's face, she didn't either.

There was a frown on Muh'Dear's face. The long, deep lines that had destroyed her beauty years ago suddenly seemed twice as deep and twice as long. In just a few seconds her face looked like it had slid from its original place. "Well, if she callin' *my* house, it don't sound like you handlin' it too good. Who in the world would do something like that to a nice young woman like you?" Muh'Dear stuck the tip of her finger in her mouth to wet it. Then she used it to dab at my cheek. "You ain't never hurt nobody before in your life. Whoever the hell that slut is, she better hope I don't find her out. I ain't so old I wouldn't beat her brains out."

Muh'Dear's face looked like it was dropping lower with each second that passed. She sucked on her teeth and upgraded her frown to a scowl so severe that I removed my arm from around her shoulder and slid a few inches away from her. Unlike me, my mother had always been a feisty woman.

"I have no idea who this woman is," I mumbled, feeling so helpless.

Muh'Dear looked like she was tuning up her brain, trying hard to come up with something that might help me resolve this knotty problem. I now believed it was a lot more serious than I'd originally thought. But I didn't want her to know that. It was enough that I had burdened Rhoda and Jade with my mess.

"Now, baby, you need to think real hard. Somewhere along the way, you done pissed off some woman. Real bad! And the sooner you find out who she is, and what you done to her, the sooner we can whup her ass."

"Muh'Dear, the last thing I plan to do is whup some woman's ass. I'm too old for that."

"Well, I ain't too old! I ain't never gwine to get so old that I can't take care of my business. When I do, you might as well drop me in the ground, and pray that my soul get to heaven in one piece. But I ain't dead yet, and I ain't gwine to set around and do nothin'. Like I said, the sooner we find out who she is, the sooner we, or at least I, can whup her damn ass. I never heard such foul language before in my life. And certainly not about my own child. I won't stand for it!" My mother had to stop talking and catch her breath.

"Muh'Dear, uh, I am sure it's nothing but a prank," I said with a nervous chuckle. "Whoever it is, she will get tired sooner or later, and move on to something else to amuse herself with. In a way I feel sorry for her. She must have a truly miserable life."

"No, she ain't miserable yet. Just let her wait till I get my hands on her!"

"Muh'Dear, this is my business. I wish you would let me take care of it my way."

"What Pee Wee got to say about this mess?"

"Um . . . we haven't really talked about it much yet. I tried to talk to him about it the day Daddy got sick."

The truth of the matter was, the subject had not come up since the night Pee Wee and I had the heated discussion in my car on the way home from the hospital, the night of Daddy's heart attack. Since then, we had been almost like strangers. We only spoke to each other when we had to, and that was one of the most awkward things in the world to do. A few times we had even communicated by writing notes to each other.

"What you waitin' on? Your daddy is gwine to be fine."

"I'll talk to Pee Wee when I get home tonight."

As soon as I walked out of Muh'Dear's house and got in my car, I fished around in my purse until I found a notepad and a pen. Gripping the pen in my hand like a weapon, I immediately wrote: *Dear Devil.*

Before I could figure out what else to say in the note that I had planned to wave in Pee Wee's face as soon as I got home, I realized how ridiculous our little feud had become. I ripped the piece of paper to shreds and tossed the pieces and the pen back in my purse. It dawned on me that a note was the worst way in the world for me to say what I had to say.

Especially since it was also one of the ways that an evil and mysterious individual had decided to communicate with me.

CHAPTER 40

The weather was still warm during the day, but with fall approaching, it got cold enough some nights for us to turn on the heat in my house.

But even with the heat on, it had been really cold in my house since the night I had attempted to talk to Pee Wee about the phone calls. As hard as I tried to ignore the mess I had on my hands, I knew that it would have to be addressed again sooner or later. Pee Wee had made several attempts to deal with it, verbally and with notes, but each time I had brushed him off.

"I am not in the mood to talk about this right now," I had said the last time, dismissing Pee Wee with an angry wave of my hand, while I was still holding a hot frying pan.

"Well, you better hurry and get in the mood, because I ain't goin' to stop until I get this whole story out of you," Pee Wee told me, his eyes on the hot frying pan.

One thing I could say about Black men was that some of them had eventually learned that the kitchen was the last place in the house to provoke a Black woman. There were too many "weapons" within an angry woman's reach in the kitchen. I had just heard a gruesome story about a sister who had flung a pan of hot grease at her husband, then batted his burning head with a rolling pin. My own daddy still had a scar on his neck where Muh'Dear had poked him with a fork when he'd accused her of having an affair with the preacher who was coming to help us eat the dinner that she had just prepared. I was only three when I witnessed that, but there were things in my life that I never forgot.

Like how angry and disgusted I was when I realized I had an enemy.

My perpetrator had taken her assault to another level by calling my mother's house. And as far as I was concerned, she had crossed the wrong line. I had to take some action. But what? And against who?

Either Pee Wee had read my mind or Muh'Dear called him up before I got home from her house. As soon as I entered our living room, he led me to the sofa and pushed me down. I still had my coat on.

"We need to talk about this mess you brought up the other night," he began. He hadn't shaved in days. The stubble on his chin and the sides of his face made him look like a man I didn't recognize. I found myself wondering just how well I did know this man I'd been with so many years.

"Did you get a telephone call tonight?" I blurted, unbuttoning the thin blue denim jacket I had on.

"From who?"

"Muh'Dear!" I boomed. "Did my mother call you tonight and tell you that some woman's been sending me crazy stuff in the mail and she's been calling me up saying all kinds of crazy shit?"

"I don't know nothin' about all that. But I wouldn't worry about it. It's probably some lonely, broken-down woman on the block that ain't got nothin' better to do with her time. Now she sees you over here in this big fine house, driving a nice car, and she wonders how come she ain't that lucky. Folks don't like it when people around them start lookin' like they doin' too good. Especially *us*. Crabs in a barrel don't want none of them other crabs to get out that barrel, and they'll do everything they can to make sure they don't."

Pee Wee didn't seem that concerned about what I had just told him, and that didn't help his case.

"I . . . We've been doing well for years, Pee Wee. Why would somebody decide to start up some shit like this now?" I took off my jacket and draped it across my arm, trying to act as normal as I possibly could. But it took all of my strength for me to keep from losing my temper again.

"You tell me," Pee Wee said with an amused look on his face and a casual shrug. That made his case even weaker, and it was already so thin that I could see through it with my eyes closed.

"No, you tell me, motherfucker!" I snarled, stabbing his chest with my finger.

"Tell you *what*, woman? And I would appreciate you not usin' that foul-ass language in front of me. You know how I feel about women cussin'," he replied, pushing my finger in another direction.

"Yes, I know how *you* feel about women . . ." I sneered. My jacket fell to the floor when I angrily placed my hands on my hips.

"What the hell are you talkin' about, Annette? So far you ain't said nothin' that made no sense."

"Did somebody call this house tonight?"

"Like who? People call this house all the time, woman!" Pee Wee yelled. I could see that he was getting angry. But he was nowhere near as angry and disgusted as I was.

"That bitch who called me and sent me that shit in the mail. She called Muh'Dear's house tonight talking all kinds of trash to my mother. How did she know I was there and not here? I sure didn't tell her where I was going to be tonight and I doubt if she's psychic." I let out a loud, angry breath and glanced around the room to keep from looking at Pee Wee's face. "I don't remember the last time I saw my mother so upset," I told him, looking at him now. There was a look on his face I didn't like. He looked like he wanted to cry.

"And you think I know something about this shit?" he asked in a low, shaky voice.

"I don't know what you know. All I do know is, if you are involved with another woman, you better get out of my life now while you are still able. I refuse to be made a fool of at my age."

"Annette, I don't know who this woman is that keeps callin' you and sendin' you shit in the mail. I ain't perfect, but one thing I don't do is fuck around on you. When I married you, it was because I was through with all the rest of them women I knew. You was the only woman I wanted to spend the rest of my life with. Don't you know that by now?"

"I wish I could believe you."

Pee Wee looked shocked and disappointed. "Why can't you believe me?"

"Because you are a man. You told me yourself, that 'men will be men' that time you were fussing around here about Jade coming to the house too much in her tight shorts. As far back as I can remember, every last man I ever knew thought with his dick! And that's still true today."

CHAPTER 41

Pee Wee started walking, circling me like a predator. "Oh, that's real brilliant," he snapped, blocking my path. "Just because I'm a man, you believe I can't keep my hands off other women."

I tried to walk around him, but he moved every time I moved. He was determined to keep me in place.

"I didn't say other 'women,'" I snarled. "It's just this one in particular . . . as far as I know."

He shrugged. "Well, do you want to tell me who this woman is, or do I have to take a wild guess?"

"Betty Jean Spool never got over you . . ."

"Betty Jean?" He threw back his head and let out a raw laugh that almost brought down the house.

That bothered me. As far as I was concerned, this was not a laughing matter.

"Laugh all you want. She's still got a thing for you!" I announced.

"That's her problem. I got over her a long time ago. Shit, I wouldn't fuck *that* woman again with a staff."

I stared long and hard at Pee Wee, hoping he would break down and confess his affair. But he didn't. He gave me a look of pity and concern. I leaned away when he attempted to kiss me, not because his breath was foul, which it was, but because I didn't want him to touch me again until everything was out in the open. And even then if it was something I couldn't deal with, he would have a long way to go before he could kiss me again.

"Annette, I go to work and back. That's where I am most of the time, when I am not in the house with you and our child. I go to the Red Rose for a drink with my boys now and then. I go fishin' with Otis, and I even spend time with your mama and your daddy, whether you are with me or not. Them things take up all of my time, and then some. When would I have time to be with another woman?" he asked through clenched teeth, pronouncing each word like he was reading from a speech that he had prepared ahead of time.

"I know how men do their thing. If they want to fool around with another woman, they will find the time. Even the president. Remember all that stuff Kennedy did? Before he died, he had women coming in and out of the White House, left and right. He had a beautiful wife, kids, and a whole country to run. He still found time to do the wild thing! Don't you stand there and tell me you can't have an affair, because you don't have the *time*. That's bullshit, and you know it!"

"Oh, shit. Now you are really talkin' crazy. How did we get from talkin' about me to what John Kennedy done? This is about me and you. And I am tellin' you, I don't have no time in my schedule to spend time with another woman."

"My daddy worked from sun up to sun down, but he still found time to be with another woman."

"So that's what this is all about? Your old man ran around on your mama, so you think all men do it."

"*All* of the men in my life. Look at old Mr. Boatwright and how deceitful he was. There he was fucking the living hell out of me and he always had him a few lady friends. Come to find out, my own mama was one of them! If men will stoop low enough to fuck a woman and her daughter at the same time, what will you bastards *not* do? Nothing is off limits! Mr. Boatwright taught me that much."

The look on Pee Wee's face told me that I had gone too far. One of the few things that we rarely discussed was the abuse I had suffered at the hands of the late Mr. Boatwright. This was the second time I'd mentioned it in the same conversation. Though I had finally told Muh'Dear and a few other people about the abuse a few years ago, Pee Wee and Lillimae were the only two people I'd ever told about Rhoda's role in Mr. Boatwright's death. It was such a grim subject that Pee Wee and I rarely discussed that one either.

"Look, woman. I'm tired. And I can see we ain't gettin' nowhere with this conversation. You can believe what you want to believe. If you want to leave me, I ain't goin' to try and stop you."

"I don't want to leave you!" I wailed, moving toward him. My foot got tangled up in my jacket on the floor. I had to lift my foot and shake the jacket off, almost falling on my face. "I don't want to leave you. Not yet! Not until I know all the facts."

"When you find out all the facts, will you let me know 'em, too? Because I don't know shit, and I ain't havin' no affair. So don't you bother me with this shit no more!"

"Don't you care about what I'm going through? I can't sleep. I'm afraid to open the mailbox or answer the telephone. She's even called me at work."

"I don't know what else to say, Annette. I done told you the truth and you can believe whatever you want." Pee Wee got up and headed toward the door, stomping so hard across the floor every lamp in the room rattled.

I didn't hear him come to bed. I managed to fall asleep somehow about an hour later, making sure I stayed on the edge of the bed so we wouldn't touch.

When I woke up the next morning he was gone. I was glad that it was Saturday. I didn't have to go to work, and I didn't have to get Charlotte ready for school. Rhoda called just as I was about to have my second cup of coffee.

"Can your daddy have company? I'd like to drop by and visit him for a little while this morning before I go to get my nails done," Rhoda said, sounding cheerful but tired.

Whenever I detected fatigue in her voice or demeanor I felt sorry for her. Even though she was still somewhat spry and energetic, the stroke had robbed her of the amazing resilience she'd once possessed. I didn't like it when I burdened Rhoda with my problems, and I only continued to do so because I knew that she really wanted to know when something was bothering me.

"He'll be glad to see you. Just don't stay too long," I told her. "Uh, before Muh'Dear tells you, I'd better tell you."

"Tell me what?"

"Yesterday when I was at Muh'Dear's house, that woman called me."

"What woman?" Rhoda asked dumbly.

"Well, it wasn't the Avon Lady," I snapped. "Who do you think I'm talking about?"

"Shit. That . . . that bitch!" Rhoda said under her breath. "She called your mama's house?"

"Uh-huh."

"What did she say?"

"She hung up before I got to the telephone. Muh'Dear answered and got her ears full. Rhoda, I tried to talk to Pee Wee about this last night. I had tried to talk to him when I got home that night from the beauty shop, but we had to rush to the hospital to see Daddy. I have been putting off confronting him ever since."

"What did Pee Wee say last night?"

"He claims he's not involved with this psycho woman and has no idea who she is."

"Shit. Well, somebody knows somethin' about this mess. Look, let's get together so we can talk face-to-face. Are we still on for Miss Rachel's this evenin'? My hair feels like barbed wire."

"If Betty Jean's the one doing this shit, I don't want to see her again until we get straightened out," I said in a tired voice.

"Betty Jean won't be workin' at Miss Rachel's today. She's tendin' bar at the Red Rose all day today and most of tonight," Rhoda informed me. "But you know how Claudette and everybody else at that beauty shop is: they know just about everything about everybody. Maybe Betty Jean has let something slip out of her mouth in front of them since we were last over there. The women at the beauty shop do suspect that Betty Jean is involved with Pee Wee again."

But so far, Claudette and the other women at Miss Rachel's had not been able to provide any hard evidence that would prove that

Pee Wee and Betty Jean were involved. As a matter of fact, so far they had only *suggested* that something was going on, but they only thought that after I had suggested it. However, the things that Betty Jean had said to me at Miss Rachel's the night that Daddy had his heart attack had been enough to send me home in a rage to confront Pee Wee. I was glad that I had not told Claudette and the other women about the notes and telephone calls. In case one of *them* was the culprit.

It didn't take me long to make up my mind. "I'll pick you up right after I drop Charlotte off at my mother's house," I said, trying to hide the excitement in my voice.

CHAPTER 42

Ihad been looking forward to spending the day with Rhoda. I was hoping that after we left the beauty shop, we'd go have a few drinks. As long as it was in any bar except for the Red Rose, so I wouldn't have to face Betty Jean.

Since Jade had decided to tag along, going to a bar was out of the question. However, there was enough room for a compromise. We could do lunch at a restaurant near the beauty shop where they served wine, at least. But I had to wait and see how I'd be feeling after our visit to the beauty shop.

I didn't know what I expected to hear from the blabbermouths at Miss Rachel's. All I could hope for was that on my next visit, they would be able to tell me something that I didn't already know.

I had gotten used to tagging along with Rhoda and Jade to Miss Rachel's, even though I didn't look or feel any different after one of my visits. But that didn't stop me from going.

Next to the numerous Black churches in town, the beauty shop was the best place to meet up with the local gossips to hear who was doing what. You could walk by the place and hear the women inside chitchatting like magpies, even with the door closed. As soon as Rhoda, Jade, and I entered, every person in Miss Rachel's temporarily turned mute.

"Y'all early this evenin'," Claudette said. The nervous look on her face made me suspect that before we had entered the establishment she and her associates had been discussing either my business, or Rhoda's, or both.

"And that means we'll be leavin' early, so you can start back to yip-yappin' about us," Rhoda teased, swatting Claudette with her red silk scarf.

"Girl, you know I ain't never said nothin' about you or Annette that wasn't true," Claudette said with a severely embarrassed look on her face.

"Y'all got any *good* chat to share with me and the sisters this evening?"

There was a fine line between good gossip and bad gossip. At Miss Rachel's you couldn't tell one from the other.

"There's nothin' goin' on in my life worth sharin'," Rhoda said with a shrug. "Listen, I want you to leave the conditioner on my hair at least ten minutes longer this time. I swear to God, I must be premenopausal or something with all these split ends I have to deal with these days."

Claudette ignored Rhoda and turned to me. "Annette, you look like somebody done stole your pocketbook. I ain't never seen you with such a puppy-dog face. I bet your man worryin' you left and right, ain't he?" Claudette paused and looked at every other face in the room before she returned her attention to me. "But that's the price you have to pay for havin' such a hunky man in your bed. I bet you don't need no blankets or no other covers to warm him up. Did you know that Betty Jean had his name tattooed on her butt? Girl, I feel so sorry for you. Ain't havin' a man hard work?"

The other beauty operator—a long-faced woman named Hazel something who claimed that she was still a virgin at twenty-six—along with two customers snickered and stared at me with bated breath. I purposely disappointed them by not bothering to respond to Claudette's last comment.

"I wish I could say all I had worrying me left and right was my husband," I said, plopping down in the nearest chair. Every other chair in the shop was occupied. A sad blues song was playing again on that boxy radio that Claudette couldn't seem to part with. There was a large silver tray with some cheese and crackers on it on the counter next to the cash register. I snatched a can of Diet Pepsi out of a large Styrofoam container on the floor in front by the door.

"Do tell? We like family around here. If you can't cry on our shoulders, you can't cry on nobody's," said a woman I recognized from church. Her entire head was covered in a pink concoction as Hazel furiously massaged her scalp.

"Some woman's been stalking Annette!" Jade blurted. She left her spot by the door and pranced over to the tray, plucking a wedge of cheese and one cracker, holding on to her backpack like she was afraid that somebody was going to snatch it and run.

"Jade!" Rhoda and I said at the same time.

"It's true. Some crazy woman's been calling my auntie saying all kinds of nasty sh—stuff!" Jade blurted. She gave me a sharp, sorrowful, apologetic glance, but she still continued. "This crazy woman even sent some real nasty notes in the mail!" It was obvious to me that Jade was glad to have some attention focused on her now. "My auntie is on the verge of a nervous breakdown."

I was horrified and embarrassed. If I had been half as ghetto as some of the women looking at me right now, I would have jumped up and slapped Jade in the mouth. But I would never do that, and Jade knew I wouldn't.

"What in the world is this child talkin' about?" Claudette asked, with a hungry look in her eyes.

"Anouk, you come from Haiti. You people are into all kinds of crazy stuff. Like snakes and stuff," Jade said in an even more excited voice.

She was addressing a stout, light-skinned woman in her forties with long brown hair on a head shaped like an eggplant. I knew it would have done me no good to try to silence Jade. She was on a roll, and her audience was too riled up for me to interfere, even though I was the subject.

"What you goin' on about, m'dear?" Anouk asked, leaning sideways in the chair she occupied next to the container with the sodas.

Three empty Diet Pepsi cans lay at her feet. Other than the fact that she was Haitian and had left the island after she'd poisoned her husband, I didn't know much about this woman. For all I knew, *she* could have been the one harassing me! I dismissed that thought right away. Because now I was pretty convinced that Betty Jean was the culprit.

"What does it mean when somebody sends you a blacksnake in the mail?" Jade asked.

"Aiyeeee!" Anouk shrieked. "It can mean many things, none of them too good. Tell us who had such a misfortune to receive such a thing so we can pray for her. Tell us now," the Haitian woman said, popping open another can of Diet Pepsi.

Jade looked at me and nodded.

"Sakes alive, woman! I'm scared of you!" Anouk said to me, making a cross with her thick, ashy fingers. She took a long drink, wiped her mouth with the back of her hand, and looked at me long and hard. "Annette, I suggest—no, I insist—that you find out this woman, go to her, and do what you have to do to get her out of your life as soon as you can, or you will truly regret it." Anouk paused and shook her head and her finger at me. "Beat some senses into her. We would all do the same thing if we was wearing your shoes."

Claudette, along with Hazel—the other beauty operator—and every other customer on the premises, then agreed with the Haitian woman.

"I know I would," Jade said with a vigorous nod as she stood in front of me munching on her crackers and cheese.

CHAPTER 43

My husband had changed so much over the years that a lot of people who had known him as a teenager would not have recognized him as a man of forty-five. He was no longer the thin, effeminate teenage gossipmonger who everybody had thought was gay. Even Rhoda and I. We used to sit around making jokes about Pee Wee. It was hard to believe that we had once referred to this hunk as "Miss Pee Wee."

Then, to everybody's surprise, that same sissified frog-prince went to Vietnam right after we all graduated from Richland High. I didn't recognize Pee Wee when I saw him again five years later, when he came to visit me during the years that I lived in Erie. His looks were not the only thing that had changed about him. He didn't run from house to house delivering and sopping up gossip anymore. As a matter of fact, nowadays Pee Wee would leave the room if I even acted like I wanted to gossip. Especially if the gossip involved him.

When I got home from the beauty shop, I lit into him like a wild woman. "I heard something about you this evening. And I don't like it one bit," I said, hands on my hips. I stood in the kitchen doorway, so hot I felt like I was on fire. I jerked my jacket off and sailed it across the room like a Frisbee, where it landed on the back of a chair at the kitchen table where Pee Wee sat in a chair facing the door. Charlotte was in the chair facing him.

Charlotte let out a yelp and rose with a confused look on her face. "Mama, what's the matter?" she yelled, attempting to move in my direction.

Pee Wee looked from me to Charlotte, grabbing her arm. "Char, go upstairs to your room and stay there until I tell you to come back down," he said, kissing her on the cheek.

"Why come?" she hollered, kicking the table leg so hard the table trembled.

"Girl, I advise you to leave the premises right now," I said, shaking an angry finger at Charlotte.

"Dang! How come I gotta go to my room so much these days?" Charlotte complained. "I don't get to do nothin' no more!" she sobbed.

I was sorry that my only child was caught in the middle of my nightmare. But if nothing else, I could keep her from knowing all the details. She would have to face her own obstacles soon enough. Unlike Jade, Charlotte was not mature enough to handle what was happening to me.

"Get to your room and stay there until I tell you to come out," I ordered, clapping my hands so hard my palms stung.

"But I wanna watch TV now," Charlotte whined, shaking her head so hard her long braids flapped.

"Watch it in your room and finish up your homework so you can be prepared when you go back to school Monday mornin'," Pee Wee said gently, scratching the side of his neck.

From the look on his face I could tell that he was not looking forward to another confrontation with me. And I was sorry that it had come to this. But I knew of no other way to sop up this mess that had seeped into my life like a cancer.

"But that TV don't have cable and it ain't in color," Charlotte sniffed, moving slowly toward the stairs. She stomped her feet and mumbled under her breath until she was out of earshot.

Pee Wee let out a sigh that was so strong he almost lost his breath.

"You still on that same trip?" he asked me, rolling his eyes as he gasped for air.

There was a weary look about him. His eyes looked tired, his shoulders drooped. He looked pretty bad but I didn't want to waste any of my pity on him. I wanted to use it all up on myself. I felt that I was the victim in this sorry drama. And if he was as guilty as I thought he was, he didn't deserve any pity from me or anybody else.

"Everybody in the beauty shop was talking about you," I stated, moving closer to him. "You and that Betty Jean Spool."

"What about me and Betty Jean?" he asked, sounding profoundly annoyed just hearing her name. "Is she still one of the biggest whores in town?"

I had learned enough about men over the years to know that this reaction was typical for a guilty man. He seemed a little too calm, which was a classic giveaway. He couldn't even look in my eyes.

"You fucking her, or what?"

"Shit!" Pee Wee sprang from his seat like a frog, walking toward me with a horrified look on his face, his eyes flashing as he looked in mine. The sudden change in his attitude came as such a surprise, I had to move back a step. I had not expected him to shift gears so fast. "Woman, don't you come up in this house gettin' in my face with none of that beauty-parlor gossip! I done told you a thousand times I don't want you bringin' none of that shit up in this house! Don't them damn women at that beauty shop have nothin' better to do with their time? And why *me* of all people? Was it because you went up in there and stirred up a bunch of shit about them damn phone calls you been gettin'?"

"That's just it," I replied, my head bobbing like a chicken. "I know who the bitch is who's been calling me now! And I know why she's calling me!"

"Oh? And would you mind telling me who the bitch is and why she is callin' you?"

"You know who it is, goddammit! You never stopped fucking Betty Jean!" I wagged my finger so hard in his face, my finger got numb.

"What? I'm going back out to the Red Rose and get drunk," Pee Wee shouted, throwing up his hands. "I am not goin' to sit here and listen to this shit. And let me tell you one thing right now!

This is the last time I want you gettin' in my face with this shit! I swear to God, a Black man can't win for losin'!" Pee Wee dismissed me with a wave of his hand and then he slapped the side of his head.

I faced him now with my hands on my hips. "Uh-huh, that's right. You can't wait to get over to the Red Rose where that bitch is tending bar today. I guess that's the best way you can warn her that I know everything now, huh?"

"Where are my car keys?" Pee Wee said to himself, ignoring me.

I followed him into the living room where he searched around for his keys. He found them right where they were supposed to be, on one of the end tables by the sofa. I ran up to him and snatched the keys out of his hand.

"Don't you leave this house until we settle this shit!" I ordered, shaking the keys in Pee Wee's angry face. I got so close to him that the tip of my nose touched his.

"What did them bitches say about me in that beauty shop?" He snatched his padded jacket off the arm of the sofa and struggled to get it on.

"You never stopped seeing Betty Jean!" I threw his keys at him, hitting him in the face.

He rubbed the spot where the keys had hit him, then he picked them up off the floor and kept talking. "See her? Yeah, I see Betty Jean all the time. She gets her hair cut in my shop. I run into her at the mall from time to time. The last time you dragged me to church, I seen her there. Yeah, I do still see Betty Jean. She happens to tend the bar at the only waterin' hole I go to when I want a few drinks. But that's all I do when I'm up in there. Drink!"

"The hell you do. She wants me out of the picture so she can move in with you. But I tell you one damn thing, that low-down wench will burn in hell before I let her take everything I've worked for."

"Who told you this shit? Which one of them bitches! If my daddy hadn't raised me right, I would go over to that beauty parlor and tell every last one of them heifers what I think about 'em. I am surprised that somebody them bitches done trashed ain't burned that bitch-ass beauty shop down to the ground! If I thought I could get away with it, I'd do it! Beauty parlors and Black women is a bad combination! It ain't nothin' but a recipe for disaster. Well, to hell with them heifers. What the hell do they know?"

Pee Wee stopped ranting and raving, but his mouth was still open and his jaw was twitching, like somebody having a mild seizure. I don't remember ever seeing him this pissed off, but he had cooked his own goose as far as I was concerned.

"Every woman at the shop was talking about how Betty Jean's been running all over town talking about how 'fine' you are and how good you fucked her, with her nasty self," I whimpered.

"So?" Pee Wee rolled his eyes. "That was in the past."

"Three different women told me tonight how Betty Jean said she's going to end up owning half of your barbershop. And, listen to this part, she wants to have one more baby before it's too late—by you. If that isn't proof I don't know what is."

"Proof of what? The only thing all that boopity-boop talk proves is that Betty Jean, them bitches at that beauty shop, and you are all crazy as hell!"

With that, Pee Wee pushed me aside. He ran out of the house like he was on fire.

CHAPTER 44

Istood on my front porch until Pee Wee started up his Jeep and roared off down the street, almost hitting a cat that was strolling across the street like it didn't have a care in the world. I waited until Pee Wee was out of my sight before I returned to my living room and called up Rhoda.

"He denied it," I said tiredly, rubbing my forehead as I dropped down on my sofa. It felt like somebody was beating on some drums inside my head. Sweat had covered my face like a wet veil. I had soaked up three paper towels in less than a minute.

"Of course he did. What did you expect him to do?" Rhoda asked. "Hold on, Annette," Rhoda said. I heard some shuffling-around noise in the background on her end. "Jade, go peep in your daddy's room and make sure he's not eavesdropping at the door." Another moment passed before Rhoda returned. "These men." Rhoda sucked in her breath. "For a dollar and a dime I'd leave this baboon I'm stuck with, and go find me some real romance."

"Now don't you start talking about having an affair, too," I said. I wanted to ask Rhoda if she was already having another affair with Bully. But I knew better. If I ever found out what that was all about, Rhoda would tell me when she was good and ready.

"How did Pee Wee react when you told him what you'd heard?"

"Like I said, he denied it. And to be honest with you, he sounded pretty convincing," I said thoughtfully, running my fingers through my hair. I was glad Rhoda couldn't see the uncertainty on my face. "Pee Wee usually doesn't lie . . . unless he has to," I admitted.

"That's just it. He lied because he *had* to. Shit. I know how men's minds work. They don't have *two* heads for nothin'. And it's that one between their legs that controls them most of the time."

"Do you really think that he lied to me about Betty Jean?" I whimpered, silently praying that Rhoda would say something that would give me some hope. The last thing I wanted to do was end my marriage.

"Of course he lied! Did you honestly expect that man to stand there and admit that he's fuckin' his used-to-be whore again? When I found out about Otis and his whore, do you think he admitted he was fuckin' her? Hell, no! I had to snoop around long enough and catch his black ass in the act. Sneakin' out of that wench's apartment when he was supposed to be at work, buyin' groceries for that butt-breathed heifer, and if all that wasn't enough, that black-ass nigger I married helped her pay her bills! That was the straw that broke the camel's back!"

"But what about that thing you did?"

Rhoda hesitated for a moment. "That was different. I needed to get laid."

"I don't like where this conversation is going," I admitted.

"And I don't either," Rhoda said with a burp. "We need to stay focused. What I did is in the past and I've moved on. And, for the record, my man pushed me into havin' that affair with Bully. He should not have ignored me all those weeks just because I'd temporarily lost my shape. But we are talkin' about Pee Wee and his nasty self now."

"I . . . I don't know what to do now," I stuttered.

"You need to pay that whore a visit! That's what you need to do now!" Rhoda yelled. "Like I did that horse-faced heifer who fucked my man." It amazed me how easily Rhoda could condemn men for their alleged actions, then in the next breath make excuses for her own extramarital affair. I had to wonder if the whole world was going crazy.

"I am not going to fight over a man. All I will do is let him, and her, know what I think of them. If my man wants to be with Betty Jean, the queen of England, or any other woman, he can go," I said tiredly. "All I can say for the woman is, she's getting nothing but a man who cheats on his woman. And my leftovers."

"Girl, what's wrong with you? Did you turn in your Black woman's membership card? You givin' us sisters a bad name. We don't give up our men without a fight! I never told you, but my own daddy had him a lady friend on the side a few years ago."

"Your daddy, the undertaker, had an affair?"

"Girl, please. My daddy was the best-lookin' man his age this town had ever seen," Rhoda said emphatically. "The only women who didn't come on to my daddy were the dead ones he dressed for burial. But most of them did before they ended up on that slab in my daddy's mortuary. My mama, sick as she always was, she nipped that shit in the bud as soon as she found out about it. My aunt Lola told me all about how she and Mama went to pay Daddy's slut a visit."

"Rhoda, my daddy had an affair and he even left us for the other woman, but my mama didn't go confront the woman. The women in my family haven't ever done that kind of shit. When my half sister's husband started running around, she packed up his clothes and took them to the other woman's house and dropped off everything on her front porch."

"Well, is that what you plan to do? If you need a ride let me know," Rhoda said, the sarcasm in her voice so thick you could have stirred it with a spoon.

I gave her words some thought. "I am not going to let Betty Jean or any other woman ruin the life I've worked so hard for." A sad smile crossed my face as I tilted my head. "I can still be happy," I said in a weak voice. "I can be happy without a man in my life." I paused and thought about what I was saying. "I got along without Pee Wee before I married him, I could get along without him now. If that other woman wants him and he wants her, they can have each other. But I won't fight her over him." I didn't feel like smiling now. "What I don't appreciate is her sending me that shit in the mail and calling me on the telephone! If I pay her a visit, it'll be to straighten her out about that shit, not taking my man. But I don't want to talk to her about this in the beauty shop."

"Her husband threw her out on her ear, and I know where she just moved to," Rhoda said in a voice so cold it made me shiver.

"We'll go in your SUV Monday after I get off work. I am sure that Betty Jean knows my car, and I don't want her to see me coming," I said, trying to hide how tired I was of this whole mess. At this point, all I wanted now was my peace of mind.

CHAPTER 45

I could not believe how fast my life had begun to unravel. And all in just a matter of weeks!

I took a long, hot bath right after I got off the telephone with Rhoda. Surprisingly, as much as I loved food, I couldn't eat any dinner. As a matter of fact I had not eaten much in the last few days and my clothes felt looser. I knew I had lost a little weight. I didn't know how much and I didn't want to know. I had stopped hopping onto a scale years ago after my weight had rolled up to two hundred and eighty-five pounds.

I wallowed in the bathtub for at least an hour with hot water and bubbles up to my neck. Pee Wee had not come home by the time I went to bed and I was asleep when he did come home. Actually, I wasn't even sure that he did, because I didn't see him when I woke up the next morning and his side of the bed didn't look like he'd been there. One minute I convinced myself that he had slept on the couch or in the guestroom that Jade seemed so fond of. The next minute I decided he had spent the night with Betty Jean Spool, fucking her brains out.

Charlotte was already up by the time I made it downstairs to the kitchen.

"Mama, I already ate some Froot Loops," my daughter told me, as she hovered over the kitchen table making a mess with a coloring book.

"That doesn't look like homework to me," I said weakly, grabbing a jar of instant coffee from the cabinet over the counter.

"Oh," Charlotte mumbled, snapping the coloring book shut.

Her crayons rolled to the floor. I was glad to see that she was dressed and ready to go to school. She looked like a little doll in her bright red jumpsuit, with her long hair in a ponytail that she had fixed herself.

"Mama, where's Daddy?" she asked, looking around the kitchen. She tossed her head so that her hair swung, one of the many habits that she had picked up from Jade.

"Huh? Oh . . . um . . . He had to go open up his barbershop early this morning," I said.

"Why come? He never done that before."

"Some man he knows has to leave to go out of town early this morning, and this was the only time that the man could come get his hair cut."

I didn't like lying to my child, but I didn't know what else to tell her. Just as I looked at my watch the telephone rang. Other than Muh'Dear and Daddy, or some of Pee Wee's folks in Pennsylvania, nobody else called my house so early in the morning. My face froze as soon as I heard the familiar voice.

"Good morning, bitch." It was the voice of doom: the same raspy whisper as before that had come to interrupt my peaceful life again.

I turned so that Charlotte couldn't see the horrified expression on my face.

"Is that Daddy?" Charlotte asked with an excited voice, making a move toward me.

"No, sugar," I replied, covering the telephone mouthpiece with my hand. "You go play with your coloring book," I said, waving my hand toward the table.

Charlotte ignored me and rushed over to stand next to me. My legs felt as heavy as logs as I leaned against my refrigerator. The heat that my refrigerator was generating gave me a rush, but it was the telephone in my hand that had my jaw twitching.

"Is that Grandma, or Grandpa, or Uncle Fred in Pennsylvania?" Charlotte continued, her voice more excited than ever.

I gently thumped the side of her head and she ran from the kitchen howling like a hyena.

"Did you send me that blacksnake, too?" I asked calmly, shifting the telephone to my other ear.

"You asked me that already and I told you I did! I sent a black-snake to a blacksnake. As soon as I find a place that sells big black baboons, I'll send you one of those, too. But knowing you, you might try to fuck it." The voice laughed.

As hard as I tried to place the voice, I had no luck. I prayed that my tormentor would get careless and speak in her regular voice.

"I feel sorry for you," I said, still speaking calmly. I couldn't believe how polite I was. The truth of the matter was, I wanted to coldcock the bitch on the other end of the line. The strange thing about what I'd just said was, I truly did feel sorry for this sick person. But I still wanted to coldcock her.

"*You* feel sorry for *me*? Now that's the craziest thing I've ever heard in my life!"

"Well, you got some serious problems, honey. You are not well and you need to get some help," I said firmly. "I just hope you don't have any children that might suffer because of you . . ."

"Don't you worry about me, you black-ass bitch. You worry about yourself and that little creature of yours that you squirted out of your nasty-ass cunt. That little brat sounds like she's as hard-headed as you are," the caller said with a chuckle.

That did it! I couldn't believe my ears. I could no longer be polite and feel sorry for this warped individual. "Listen, you crazy-ass slut! Don't you drag my child into this fucked-up game of yours!" I hissed.

I glanced out the window over my kitchen sink, admiring the beautiful day outside. It was almost as beautiful as the day that this mess had started.

"Fuck you!"

"I know who you are," I said, my voice shaking. "If I were you, I would stop this shit right here and now. If you do call me again, or send me anything else in the mail, I will go to the police. Do you understand me?" I was about to speak again, but I didn't know what else to say. It didn't matter because the caller had hung up.

I was so stunned I sat staring off into space for half an hour. As soon as I came out of my trance, I called Rhoda's house.

"Hi, Auntie," Jade said, answering in her cheerful voice. "You coming to work today?"

"Yes, baby. Uh, can your mama come to the telephone?"

"She just walked in the room. Hold on a minute. Lunch is my treat today," Jade added. "Here's Mom."

"This is Rhoda."

"That wench just called me again."

"Betty Jean?"

"I think so. She was whispering, but it could have been her," I said with extreme uncertainty. The only reason I had some doubts was the fact that I knew Betty Jean was not the type to play games. If she wanted something, she didn't care who knew about it. But then I had to admit that most people changed their MOs as they got older. One minute I truly believed it was her, the next minute I didn't know what to believe!

"What did she say?"

"The same old nasty shit as before. Listen, I told her I knew who she was."

"Well, did she deny it?" Rhoda wanted to know.

"She hung up right after I told her that."

"Annette, you really need to talk to the phone company. There must be somethin' they can do to help catch this bitch. They have all kinds of ways of tracin' phone calls now."

"Rhoda, I told you already that I've thought about that. And I also told you that a telephone tap and caller ID would be a waste of my time. I don't even think that adding *69 to my service would do any good. This woman is not stupid enough to call me from a number that can be traced or called back if I hit *69. A fool would know that she's calling me from pay phones."

"I guess you're right."

"And if it is Betty Jean, I know she would have thought about something like that already. I just know it's her. It's got to be her, Rhoda."

"You still want to pay her a visit this evening? I got a large can of mace you can use."

"Rhoda, I don't plan to do anything violent. I just want to talk to her. I just want her to stop calling me and sending me shit. That's all I want."

"What about Pee Wee?"

"What about him?"

"If he's the reason she's doing this shit, you need to talk to him, too."

"I tried to talk to him about her last night and he ran. He didn't come home and I don't even know where he is." I paused and glanced toward the door. The last thing I wanted now was for Charlotte to know that I didn't even know where her daddy was.

"He could be with that cow right now as we speak, for all we know," Rhoda suggested.

Her words made me seethe. "If he's still with her when we get over there this evening, that's exactly where I plan to leave his black ass," I said, the words oozing out of my mouth like bad breath.

CHAPTER 46

I tried to keep my mind off of my problems during my drive to work shortly after I got off the telephone with Rhoda. I tried to concentrate on the things that were still pleasant in my life. It was a nice, warm day and there were a lot of things outside of my car that made me feel good. Like all the cute little kids running to get to school on time, the traffic lights that only stayed red for a few seconds, and birds chirping out a concerto. Even the trees, which showed patches of yellow and brown streaked with green, made a positive difference in my mood.

By the time I got to work, I felt more relaxed. It was a bonus to see that Jade had already arrived at the office. She looked so sophisticated and focused, sitting at her neatly arranged desk. I couldn't figure out how she found the time to go out and buy fresh flowers for her desk every workday. With all of her youthful faults, I was still proud of her.

"There's a fresh pot of strong coffee in the break room. I made it myself," Jade said, greeting me at the door. "I am sure you could use it."

"That and something even stronger," I managed, stumbling to my office. I had to pass Gloria's cubicle and for once it didn't bother me to see her annoying scowl. "Good morning, Gloria," I greeted.

She gave me a surprised look. As a matter of fact, she looked downright startled. She was the only person in the office that I didn't speak to unless she spoke first. The chip on her shoulder was so huge, even a simple greeting could set her off. She hesitated before she returned my greeting.

"Uh . . . Good mornin', Annette. That's a nice muumuu you got on today."

"It has been for years," I sighed. I went to my office and shut the door so fast and hard that I had to hop forward to keep from catching the tail of my dress in it. Jade appeared in my office less than two minutes later with a large mug of coffee.

"I am going with you and Mama this evening," Jade announced, looming over my desk like a warden.

My lip brushed the lip of my coffee mug, but I pulled it away without drinking. "Jade, I don't think that's such a good idea. I don't want you to get involved in this mess any more than you already are. I don't know what to expect." I sucked in my breath and took a long swallow of my black coffee. "You know how rough some of those Spool family members are. Things could get ugly."

I didn't have to remind Jade about all the violence that some of Betty Jean's relatives had been involved in. Not only was her oldest brother, Lester, a drug dealer, she had other family members who had been involved in just about every other criminal activity you could think of. Her alcoholic daddy had run off twenty years ago with his male lover. Her youngest brother was in prison for killing his girlfriend. Everybody in Richland was familiar with the bad side of the Spool family. But the Spools were one of the oddest set of people I had ever met. Half of them were thugs, the other half were pleasant, law-abiding citizens that I was proud to know. One of Betty Jean's brothers was a Boy Scout leader and another one was a teacher who worked with kids who had learning disabilities. Both of her younger sisters were nice, quiet women leading respectable lives. One was a nurse, the other one owned and operated a pet shop. The matriarch of the clan, Betty Jean's mother, was a tiny, soft-spoken woman who went to church every Sunday and spent her spare time doing volunteer work at the homeless shelter right along with my mother and Scary Mary. But Betty Jean's maternal grandmother was a sour-faced old crone who carried a gun, and was currently in jail for shooting at her landlord when he'd attempted to collect three months' back rent.

I wondered how things would have worked out if it had been one of Betty Jean's dignified sisters who had been involved with Pee Wee. It was a thought that had crossed my mind more than once. And it was a much easier thought to deal with than what I had to deal with now.

"I went to school with one of those she-devil Spool cousins," Jade said in a gruff voice, interrupting my thoughts. "The bad Spools didn't scare me then, they don't scare me now," Jade said in a slow, controlled voice.

She sucked in her breath and stuck her chest out, a menacing look took over her face. Jade was so much like Rhoda. It was hard to believe that petite women like them were so fearless. But I had figured out that when you snuck up on your enemies the way Rhoda did, size didn't matter. I knew that old Mr. Boatwright would have put up one hell of a fight, had he been awake when Rhoda entered his bedroom to smother him with that pillow, that night so long ago.

"Mama said I can go, so I'm going." Jade stomped her foot, then turned around and sailed out of my office, switching her shapely butt like she had a stick up her crack.

I made sure my office door was locked before I called my house, expecting Pee Wee to answer the telephone. He didn't, so I called his barbershop and he answered on the first ring.

"It's me," I said stiffly.

"I figured that," he grunted.

"I'm at work. You need to pick Charlotte up from school and keep her with you until I get home this evening."

"And why is that?"

"Because I said so."

"No problem."

Every other married couple I knew had their share of arguments and a few had some knock-down, drag-out fights. My own father and mother still did—and they were both approaching eighty! But it took a lot to get a rise out of Pee Wee. And Lord knows I had been pushing him to the edge a lot lately. That man had more self-control than a monk.

A long moment passed before either of us spoke again.

"You still there?" I asked.

"I'm here. Is that all you wanted?"

"Where did you sleep last night?" I asked. "And don't bother lying to me, because I will know. And that will only make things worse," I warned.

Pee Wee kept a radio, a CD player, and a portable television set in his barbershop. I could hear voices and soft jazz playing in the background. I didn't visit the barbershop that often, but next to our house it was one of the coziest places we had access to. There was a daybed with a goose-down comforter on it in the small back room that Pee Wee also used as an office and a retreat for Charlotte. Facing the daybed was another small television set, and a small refrigerator that was always stocked with snacks and beverages.

"I slept at the shop. Why?"

"I wanted to know."

"And I slept alone, in case you want to know that, too."

"You do whatever you want to do."

Pee Wee let out an exasperated groan. He was still pissed off and I was glad. If I had to be miserable, I wanted him to be miserable, too. Had it not been for him I wouldn't be dealing with the mess I was dealing with in the first place! I never thought I'd see the day when I'd be this upset with the only man I had ever really loved.

"What time will you be home?" His voice sounded hoarse and uncertain.

"I don't know. I'll get there when I get there!" I snapped.

"Then I will see you when I see you."

It bothered me that he didn't try to find out why I wasn't coming straight home. Especially after the things I had said to him the night before. As far as I was concerned, if he was innocent, he should have stayed home and defended himself. At least, that's the way I thought he should have behaved. If he was guilty, he still should have stayed and defended himself. Even if he had to do it with more lies. What confused me was the fact that he was not acting like an innocent man or a guilty man. I didn't know what to believe anymore.

CHAPTER 47

Based on the evidence I had, even though beauty shop gossip is about as reliable as the mess you read in the tabloids, I was half-convinced that that Spool woman was the one tormenting me and trying to take my husband. However, in the back of my mind I wasn't so sure. I had known Betty Jean most of my life. She was a man-eating, hard-drinking, hell-raising floozy, true enough, but sending neatly typed notes and making strange calls didn't seem to fit her personality.

She told me once, "I'm from Texas and down there, when somebody fucks with us, we hang 'em high." Betty Jean's threatening comment, though it had not been directed at me at the time, still rang in my ears.

Pee Wee cleared his throat. "You still on the phone?" he asked.

"Uh, let me call you back. I might be home at my usual time after all. I have to go. I just remembered something," I told Pee Wee.

I hung up before he could respond. What I had just remembered was that a woman like Betty Jean Spool might end up beating me within an inch of my life. Especially if I approached her in a way that she considered hostile.

Even though I outweighed Betty Jean by at least a hundred

pounds, the last thing I wanted to do was get into a physical confrontation with a woman like her. It would be just like her to have a switchblade in her bra or some kind of gun in her purse. Going to another woman's home to get in her face, whether she was normal or a pit bull like Betty Jean, was a bold move. And even though I didn't want to fight Betty Jean, just my showing up at her place might be reason enough for her to attack me.

As much as I loved my husband, and as much as I wanted to stop this woman from harassing me, I had to slow down and give this situation a little more thought. I called Rhoda up.

"Rhoda, I don't know about going to Betty Jean's house this evening. I've been giving this a lot of thought," I said as soon as Rhoda answered.

"Hold on," Rhoda said. A few seconds later she was back. "Sorry. I had to grab my tea from the counter." She paused again and slurped on her tea. "Are you tellin' me that you are goin' to let this woman continue doin' what she's been doin' do you?"

"She can do whatever she wants to do. If she wants to send me shit in the mail or call me up, I can't stop her. When I get home this evening, I will have a long talk with Pee Wee. He will have to decide what he wants to do."

"Are you telling me you are not going to fight for your marriage? I can't believe that you are goin' to let this bitch ruin your life. Like I told you, you need to do the same thing that I did to that cow who messed with my man."

"I am not you, Rhoda," I said flatly. The story that Rhoda had shared with me about how she'd paid her husband's mistress an unexpected visit with a stick in her hand still amused and disturbed me.

"I won't argue with that. But I thought you'd learned a few things from me after all these years."

"I have to hang up and get some work done before I lose my job, too. I just wanted to let you know that you don't have to meet me after work," I said, blowing out a breath so hard the papers on my desk fluttered and slid to the edge. It was then that I noticed the small box on the edge of my desk next to my in-box. "I'll call you later," I said, reaching for the box. I glanced at my name that had been neatly typed on a white address label and stuck to the center of the box. I didn't recognize the return name or address.

I ripped open the box and almost fell out of my seat. Inside of the box was a pair of men's boxer shorts. They had been neatly folded. At first glance, I thought they were new. I removed them with the tip of a letter opener and held them up in the air. Not only were they used, the musky smell and a small tear in the crotch told me that. But I had seen them before. On my husband! I flung the shorts back into the box and dialed Rhoda's number again.

"That bitch! That BITCH!" I roared with so much vigor I almost choked on some air that went down the wrong windpipe. But as soon as I was able to speak again, I let out an outburst that rocked my brain. "That no good, man-eating bitch!"

"What is it?" Rhoda hollered so loud it sounded like she was coming through the telephone. "Girl, what is the matter? Did that motherfuckin' bitch call you again?" she huffed.

"She sent me a pair of his funky-ass shorts! How in the hell did she get his shorts?"

"Hold on now! Whose shorts? What are you talkin' about?"

"I just opened a package that somebody had set on my desk. It's got a postmark on it so it had to be mailed here. Our mail guy left it on my desk, I guess. She said she had something to prove she's been with Pee Wee and she did. She sent me a pair of his shorts!"

"Shit! I will pick you up right after you get off work."

"You do that," I said. "And don't be late."

I lifted the shorts with my letter opener again and I dropped them into the wastepaper basket under my desk. You would have thought that I was disposing of a scorpion instead of a pair of my husband's underwear.

"That low-down, no-good wench," I said in a low voice, trying to control my anger. But I was past being just angry. Jade was right: I was on the verge of a complete nervous breakdown. "That cow!" I screamed, slamming my fist down on the top of my desk.

My coffee cup fell over and spilled coffee on some correspondence that I had been neglecting for the past few days. That increased my anger. I wasn't going to let one more day go by without taking a stand. I was going to have a showdown with Betty Jean and I didn't care what the consequences were.

I was being forced to take some serious action. I realized that that might mean I'd have to do or say things that I ordinarily wouldn't.

But as long as I restored my peace of mind, I didn't care anymore.

CHAPTER 48

Being an office supervisor had its advantages. I worked when I felt like it. When I didn't feel like doing any work, I delegated some of it. I could pretty much come and go as I pleased, within reason. I knew how far to push the envelope. The supervisor that I had replaced had been fired for taking too much advantage of the company. Being AWOL on a regular basis was one. That woman used to disappear without notice for days at a time. But the worst thing she'd done, that we knew about, was to have frequent trysts with her lover on her desk in the same office I now occupied.

I liked to seclude myself in my office with the door shut. It was usually because I needed a little time to perform some duties that required my undivided attention. But every now and then I just needed a quiet break. Like today. I buzzed Jade first before I put myself in a do-not-disturb mode.

"Are you all right?" Jade asked, standing in the doorway. "You want some more coffee?"

She looked like a living doll standing there in her baby-blue pantsuit, with matching earrings and headband. I just sat there staring at Jade like I had suddenly become mute.

"Auntie, talk to me."

"I'm fine," I croaked. "And no, everything is not all right." I stared past Jade at the wall, speaking in a low, nervous voice. "Everything is all . . . all wrong," I stammered.

"Is there anything I can do? I can't stand to see you like this."

I offered a reluctant nod. "Hold all of my calls and don't let any-body into my office until I tell you to," I said with my eyes burning. I waved Jade out of my office. Then I immediately placed my head on the top of my desk.

I didn't pay any attention to the time, but I must have stayed that way for at least an hour. All kinds of things were dancing around in my head. One minute I wanted to confront Betty Jean. The next minute I wanted to divorce my husband. I even had a wild notion to pack my bags and run off somewhere. I was in a fever of anticipation. I don't know how I was able to doze off with all the things I had on my mind.

A loud knock on my door woke me up. I wobbled up from my seat, wiping drool from the side of my chin. I took a quick glance in the mirror on the wall next to my door. It was only then that I re-alized I had left home without putting on my makeup. The dark cir-cles around my eyes were so profound I looked like a panda. I was surprised that Jade had not commented on my wretched appear-ance. She usually did.

"The guy from FedEx just delivered a box for you," Jade told me, leaning her head into my office.

I snapped my head around so fast my neck made a cracking noise.

"Did you open it?" I asked, glancing at the trash can. One of the legs of the shorts was dangling over the top of the trash can.

"No, I sure didn't. You want me to?"

"Bring it here. Bring it here right now."

Jade returned in less than a minute, shaking a box that was big enough to hold a basketball.

"Shut the door," I ordered, motioning for her to set the box on the top of my desk.

"It's heavy," she said, kicking the door shut with her foot. She was still shaking the box. It made a thud when she dropped it on my desk. "And whatever is in it . . . uh . . . stinks."

I looked at Jade, then at the box. We received packages every day, usually boxes that contained office supplies. But they were rarely addressed to me like this one was. The return address and name didn't look familiar.

"Aren't you going to open it?" Jade asked with an anxious look on her face.

I sighed first. Then I took my time opening the box with my fingers, cracking two nails.

I flipped open the lid. Inside was a smaller box. Taped on its top was a small piece of white paper with the words typed in small but bold letters: **Have a nice day, bitch**! I snapped the box shut just as fast as I had opened it. "Jade, you can leave now," I said in a low voice. Now this was a situation that was so over-the-top I didn't know whether to cry or laugh. I didn't even realize I was smiling until Jade made a comment.

"What's so funny? What's in the box, Auntie?"

"Just go. This is nothing but some more bullshit and you don't need to see it!"

Jade ignored me and snatched the box out of my hands. She flipped open the lid and gasped before she stumbled forward and fell against the front of my desk. There was such a look of horror on that child's face that I thought she was going to faint.

"Omigod, Auntie! That's . . . That looks like . . . *horse shit*!" Jade cried, pointing at the box.

That's exactly what it was: big, disgusting, dried clumps of horse shit!

Jade insisted on hauling the vile box to one of the Dumpsters in the alley behind our building. When she returned a few minutes later, she closed my office door and locked it.

"This has gone too far," Jade said, breathing so hard she was wheezing.

She paused just long enough to take a deep breath, rubbing her chest as if that would help her regulate her breathing. She seemed to be just as upset as I was, and I didn't like that one bit. I had to do something and I had to do it soon. This nightmare had done enough damage.

"If that shit didn't smell so bad," she declared, "I'd hold on to it and drop it at Betty Jean's front door when we go over there this evening. And if you don't beat the shit out of that bitch, I will."

"What . . . what are you talking about?" I stammered. I had to blink hard a few times to see clearly again. I had temporarily forgotten about my plan to visit Betty Jean's apartment to confront her. My head was pounding so hard my eyes not only ached, but my vision was foggy. I had to blink hard and shake my head to focus. Jade wiped her hands on a wad of paper towels and propped herself up on the edge of my desk, crossing her arms.

"That's about as nasty as you can get, huh?" I managed with a chuckle, my hands clasped across the middle of my protruding belly.

"Auntie, I don't know how you can sit here and laugh about receiving a box of shit. God knows what that bitch plans to send next, with her nasty self."

I leaned under my desk and removed the shorts from my trash can with the tip of a pen and held them up for Jade to see.

"What in the world is that?" she wanted to know, making a face and rubbing her nose. "Looks like somebody's funky drawers."

"That's exactly what this is. I'd know these damn things anywhere. I have been after Pee Wee to get rid of these raggedy-ass things for months."

"What? How? What are they doing in your trash can?"

"This is what was in the package I received this morning."

"What? When?"

"I don't know when it came in, but the box was sitting on my desk this morning when I got in."

"Auntie, why don't you go home? You are making me scared for you. You look like you are about to have some kind of fit or something."

"I don't want to go back home until I talk to Betty Jean. I can't get anything out of Pee Wee, so it looks like the only way I am going to get to the bottom of this mess is by having a showdown with her."

"What if you don't get anything out of her either? What will you say to Pee Wee then? Will you leave him?"

"I don't know what I'm going to do, Jade. What I do know is, this mess is going to end one way or the other. Even if it means I do have to . . . to leave Pee Wee. I can't take too much more of this. I am about to lose my mind."

Jade strolled around to the side of my desk and gave me a hug.

"Don't forget about that other thing we have to deal with, too," she said in a low voice.

"What other thing?"

"I need you to go with me to the clinic to take care of that little problem I told you about. You know." Jade paused and patted her stomach.

I didn't like the fact that Jade was pregnant, but her dilemma did provide me some much-needed distraction. "Go ahead and make an appointment," I said.

CHAPTER 49

I had a hard time getting through the rest of the day. I avoided my co-workers as much as I could. Whenever I had to go to the bathroom, I walked all the way down to McDonald's to use theirs. All because I didn't want to deal with anybody else in the office except for Jade. I noticed the odd looks I got each time I left my office, and each time I came back. But as long as I kept a scowl on my face, the people who worked for me kept a safe distance.

With the exception of Gloria Watson, I had a great rapport with the people in the office. I didn't like behaving the way that I was behaving in front of them. That's why it was so important for me to resolve the situation that had caused such a disruption in my life.

When Jade and I left the office that evening a few minutes before five, Rhoda was already in the parking lot in her SUV with the motor running. I had been too upset to read the daily newspaper that day. That was something I had not missed doing in over ten years. I had rolled my newspaper up like a baseball bat and dumped it and some files I had been too upset to look at into the trunk of my car, which was parked right next to Rhoda's SUV.

By the time I made it to Rhoda's vehicle, Jade had already

folded herself into the front seat. As usual, I "took a backseat" to Rhoda and Jade. Even though it was my pity party.

"I drove by Betty Jean's place on the way over here," Rhoda announced, a stick of celery dangling from the corner of her mouth. There was a Baggie on the dashboard stuffed with more celery and some carrot sticks. Jade snatched a carrot stick out and started chomping. I declined when she offered me some of the raw veggies. The inside of my mouth was so dry, I couldn't have eaten anything if it had been shoved down my throat.

"Her car was in the driveway so I guess she's home," Rhoda reported, munching like a rabbit. She glanced at me over her shoulder.

I didn't like the look on Rhoda's face or her tone of voice. In my opinion, she seemed too excited, and much too eager for us to get to Betty Jean's apartment. The last thing I wanted was for there to be a bloodbath. I was glad that I was in control of the situation, at least I thought I was.

"If she's not home, we'll wait," Jade added, glancing around at me.

"I want to talk to her by myself," I said, holding up my hand. "After all, this is my problem. All I want to do is talk to this woman. I don't want to fight her and I will do everything I can to avoid things getting violent."

Rhoda and Jade gasped at the same time. Rhoda looked at me through her rearview mirror. This time, Jade turned all the way around to face me.

"What if she's got some of her crazy family members in there with her? Do you think those thugs are going to just sit there and do nothing?" Jade asked. "You know about this woman and the crazy side of her family as well as everybody does in this town. They don't believe in talking to resolve their disputes. I was in Kroger's grocery store that time that a clerk accused the Spool grandmother of shoplifting. That old woman pulled out a knife that was as long as my leg. And do you think if any of Betty Jean's family is up in there with her, they won't be ready to take care of business when you knock on that door?" Jade turned back around and reached for more veggies on the dashboard.

"This is between me and Betty Jean, not me and her family. What else could they do but sit there and do nothing? I am just going to talk to her," I insisted again. "I won't give them, or her, any reason to get ugly."

"But, Auntie, what if she does more than talk?" Jade asked, chewing and talking at the same time. She rose up on the seat and faced me again, her elbows on the back of the headrest.

Rhoda made such a sudden stop at a red light Jade almost came over the seat into my lap.

"We are not dealing with a normal person here," Rhoda said, grabbing Jade's arm, and helping her to return to her seat. Those words sounded odd coming from Rhoda. "Remember that time a few years ago when Betty Jean went after one of her own cousins with a box cutter? If she would do something that extreme to a relative, just think what she would do to you. I mean . . ." Rhoda paused and gave me a pitiful look. "She hates you."

"The notes and other stuff she's sent tell you that. But what she sent today leaves no stone unturned," Jade reminded us, directing her attention at Rhoda. "Mama, Auntie received a box of horse shit today."

"What? A box full of horse shit?" Rhoda roared, slapping her steering wheel with her hand. "Oh, this has gone too damn far! That's goin' way overboard! I'd beat the shit out of that bitch just for doin' that!" Rhoda yelled. "Does that sound like a woman that you can straighten out just by talkin' to her?"

"She sent a pair of Pee Wee's shorts to me, too," I revealed, with a hint of relief in my voice. It felt good to get that disgusting piece of news out in the open. "I don't care what Betty Jean says, or does, when I get to her. I can't go on like this. She's not the only one I have to deal with today. Pee Wee will have to come clean, too. If he is fucking that woman, then he won't be fucking me anymore."

Rhoda let out a loud sigh and shook her head. She turned the corner on two wheels as we pulled up in front of the tall brick building in the quiet residential area where Betty Jean lived.

Jade turned around to face me again, one more time. "Pee Wee sure is causing you a lot of grief. Are you going to leave him? I would if I were you, Auntie. You could probably still get another husband, if you really tried. But you have to hurry up."

I didn't answer Jade's question. I couldn't. I just dropped my head. I kept my eyes on the floor until we came to a complete stop. As soon as I looked up toward Betty Jean's second-floor apartment, I saw the curtains in the front window move.

Jade and Rhoda climbed out and stood in front of the SUV, looking like warriors about to do battle—their arms folded and hot, angry looks on their faces.

I walked up the steps to Betty Jean's apartment huffing and puffing, like I was walking up the side of a mountain. By the time I made it to the landing, I was so out of breath that you could have knocked me over with a feather. While I stood there, leaning against the wall next to the door, Betty Jean cracked open the door, smoothing down the front of her tight white blouse. Ever since she bought herself some titties, she couldn't stop drawing attention to her chest.

"You want something?" she asked.

"I need to talk to you," I told her, in a firm but civil voice. "Is now a good time?" I asked politely. And as painful as it was, I smiled.

She shrugged. "What do you need to talk to me about? A hair appointment, I hope."

I shook my head. "No, it's a little more personal than that. I could feel the heat rising from the soles of my feet on up to my face. "There is something I need to say to you."

"Honey, you ain't got nothin' to say that I want to hear. Now, if you don't mind, I got things to do." Betty Jean attempted to close her door, but I stopped her by sticking my foot in the doorjamb. She didn't like that one bit. She already had a frown on her face, but she managed to look even more annoyed and ferocious. She glanced at my foot, then back at my face. "What the hell do you want to talk to me about, bitch?" she demanded, shaking a finger in my face.

I flinched, but I refused to let her know that she was getting to me. "I want to talk to you about my husband."

She blinked and shook her head. "Who?"

"My husband, Pee Wee."

Betty Jean let out a disgusted sigh and cocked her head to the side. It was a weak attempt to taunt me, but she did. "So what do you need to talk to me about your husband for? That man don't do no socializin' with me no more. Not unless you want to count him stoppin' in the Red Rose for a drink every now and then."

Somebody dropped a pan on the floor in a room behind her, so she glanced over her shoulder. I could smell the pork chops and turnip greens that she was cooking.

"Do you mind if I come in?" I asked. "I can see that you are cooking dinner so I won't stay but a minute."

"Yeah, I do mind if you come in. I got company right now!" she snapped.

"Well, let me say what I got to say and I will leave."

Just then, I glanced over Betty Jean's shoulder into the scowling face of Lester, coming into the room wiping his mouth with a dishrag. He had a bandage on his cheek and his right arm in a cast. There were other scratches and bruises on his face. It looked like he had been mauled by a wild animal and I had a feeling that I wasn't too far from the truth.

"That ain't a bad idea. I feel the same way. Shit," Betty Jean barked. I didn't like the direction that her tone of voice was going in.

"Look, Betty Jean, if you and Pee Wee want to be together, I won't stand in the way."

Betty Jean gave me a stunned look. Then her lips curled up at the ends into a cruel smile. She looked me up and down with disgust and then wiped her mouth with the back of her hand, literally wiping the smile off of her face. "Can you believe this fat-ass bitch?" Betty Jean yelled to her brother. "Woman, what the hell you talkin' about?" Betty Jean swung the door open and placed one hand on her hip, the hand she'd used to shake a finger in my face. "I got a man!" she yelled.

Lester was still standing a few feet behind his sister. "What the fuck is goin' on here?" he asked. "Annette, you done lost your mind, or what? You ain't got no business comin' over here, unless you need a few rocks or something else to get you high."

Another man came out of nowhere and stood next to Lester. "Jo Jo," Betty Jean said, "you hearin' this shit, too? This bitch thinks I want her man. Tell her that me and you fin to move to Cleveland and open a coffee shop."

The other man, wearing soiled bib overalls, strode across the floor. He had a few battle scars, too. He glared at me with large, bloodshot eyes.

"What the hell goin' on out here? Who the hell is you?" he asked, revealing two rows of jagged yellow teeth.

I looked around, glad now that Rhoda and Jade had come with me. It looked like I might need them after all.

"Your woman has been fooling around with my husband," I blurted. "Everybody knows about it. She's been sending me all kinds of shit through the mail. A fake blacksnake, some nasty notes. And today I got a box in the mail full of dried horse shit!" I had to stop to catch my breath again. "And a box with a pair of my husband's shorts in it was sent to my office. I didn't come here to fight. All I want is for her to stop harassing me."

Betty Jean guffawed so hard she almost lost her breath. "You let me tell you one thing right here and now, you big black bitch! I don't want your man! I wouldn't waste up a good stamp to send you nothin' in the mail! And how in the world would I get a hold of your man's drawers?" Betty Jean wrapped her arm around her boyfriend's shoulder.

"Let me straighten out this mess," Lester said, gently pushing Betty Jean and the boyfriend to the side. "Look here, you bald-headed, motherfuckin', dyke-lookin' black heifer," he continued, shaking the arm with the cast at me. "I suggest you get your fat black ass away from here while you still able. You don't be comin' around talkin' that crazy shit. I always knew you was one crazy bitch. And bein' married to that punk-ass Pee Wee Davis proves it! If you ever lose a couple of hundred pounds and want you some real dick, you let me know." Lester moved closer to me, yellow spittle flying out of his mouth into my face as he continued his siege. "Now, we expectin' some trouble over here in a little while and unless you want to get caught up in it, you better get your black ass outta here right now!"

"And you better not bring your big black ass over here no more, messin' with my woman," the boyfriend advised.

I glanced around again. Rhoda and Jade were marching up the steps. I was more confused than ever now. Betty Jean looked even more confused. As a matter of fact, she looked downright frightened. And I could understand why. She had another man waiting in the wings and didn't want him to know what she had been up to.

"Annette, is everything OK?" Rhoda yelled, taking the steps two at a time now.

I started to back away. "Everything is fine, Rhoda," I said, my eyes still on Betty Jean's stunned face.

Without saying another word, Betty Jean slammed the door in my face. But even with the door closed I could hear Betty Jean, her brother, and her lover still calling me every vile name in the book.

"What did she say?" Jade asked, squinting her eyes to look at the door.

"She denied everything," I said, my eyes on the ground. "Her brother and her man were standing there so I didn't expect her to do anything other than that."

"She works the night shift at the Red Rose tonight. We can catch her when her brother and her man are not with her," Rhoda said, leading the way back to her SUV.

"Rhoda, I'm through with this mess. I'm going to talk to Pee Wee and then I'm through with him, too. That's all I can do. That's all I want to do now. I am . . . tired. I want some peace back in my life. Whoever Pee Wee's whore is, she's won."

"So you're saying that you don't believe it's Betty Jean now? You don't think she is the one sending you that stuff and fooling around with Pee Wee?" Jade hollered, almost sounding disappointed. "You know it's her, and I know it's her. Even if her brother and her man hadn't been standing there with her, she would have denied it."

"I don't know what to believe, Jade. I just know I can't put up with this shit any longer." I glanced around the neighborhood. "And I won't," I vowed. "Not for Pee Wee or any other man." There was a hot, sour taste in my mouth and my stomach was churning. For a moment it seemed like the ground was moving. "I just want to go home now," I said. "I am so through with this," I said, looking from Rhoda to Jade. "If you don't mind, I don't even want to talk about it anymore. At least, right now. Please take me home."

CHAPTER 50

The ride back to my office, where I had left my car, was silent all the way. But I could tell that Jade and Rhoda were itching to resume the conversation about my situation and Betty Jean's involvement. I was in the backseat again and every time I looked up at the rearview mirror Rhoda was looking at me. Jade turned around to gaze at me so many times it looked like she had her head on backward.

"Don't you want to talk about it?" Rhoda asked, walking me to my car. "I can go home with you. You might need me to be there in case Pee Wee tries somethin' crazy."

"I can handle Pee Wee," I assured her, holding up my hand in her face.

She seemed surprised and disappointed. Rhoda was still standing in the middle of the parking lot as I drove off, still looking surprised and disappointed.

Pee Wee was not home when I got there, and it was just as well. He was the last man in the world I wanted to see. There was a note from him on the microwave oven that said he had taken Charlotte to my mother's house. I called Muh'Dear immediately.

"Muh'Dear, don't ask me any questions. Just say yes or no," I said as soon as my mother answered the telephone. The television was on, but I could still hear Daddy grumbling in the background, as well as Pee Wee and Charlotte chattering like magpies.

"Where you at, gal?" Muh'Dear asked, sounding just as grumpy as Daddy.

"Can you keep Charlotte over there for the night? I'll come by early in the morning to bring her some clean clothes to wear to school. Just say yes or no."

"Yeah," Muh'Dear said with hesitation.

I knew that it took a lot of effort for her not to badger me. "I will call you later and I will tell you everything when I feel like talking about it. I have to go right now because I have something real important I need to do."

"What in the world is goin' on with y'all?" Muh'Dear whispered. "You done lost your mind?"

"I said, I can't talk about it right now, Muh'Dear. I will call you later tonight. You could send my husband home, though." I hung up before my mother could say another word.

It took me just twenty minutes to pack two suitcases. About five minutes later Pee Wee stumbled in the door, looking confused and weary. I was glad to see that he was alone. I was standing in the middle of the living room floor when he walked in the front door. Right next to me on the floor were the two suitcases I had packed.

With his face hanging like a rope, Pee Wee stopped in his tracks. The dark circles around his eyes were so profound it looked like they had been tattooed to his face. He blinked, looking from my face to the suitcases.

"Annette, before you start up again, let me say what I have to say," Pee Wee informed me, a hand in the air. "I done had enough of this shit," he said, moving toward me with his hand still raised. "Runnin' away ain't goin' to do you no good!" he yelled, motioning toward the luggage at my feet.

"I know that," I said coldly. "And I am not going anywhere. At least not yet."

"It don't look that way to me."

"This is *your* shit I packed up, motherfucker. I want you out of my house and I want you out of here now."

Pee Wee stopped and stumbled back a few steps.

"Annette, this is my home, just as much as it is yours, and I ain't goin' no place. I am your husband."

"Correction: this is *my* house. My mama left this house to me. And unless you want to be carried out of here on a stretcher, you best get to stepping right now. Take these bags and go wherever the hell you want to go." I calmly walked to the door and snatched it open. "Out," I said, dismissing him with a wave of my hand. "Before I throw you out!"

With a slack-jawed expression on his face, he picked up the luggage and started to move toward the door, lifting his feet like they weighed a ton each. "I done had just about enough of this shit. I will give you some time to come to your senses. But I tell you—"

Pee Wee didn't get a chance to finish his sentence. I slammed the door in his face while he was still talking.

It turned out to be one of the longest nights of my life. I was glad that I had left Charlotte with Muh'Dear and Daddy for the night. Daddy was doing so much better and he and his granddaughter were best friends. He was the only other person who fawned over Charlotte more than Jade.

For the next few hours I wandered from room to room. I cleaned things that didn't need to be cleaned, I rearranged the furniture in the living room, and I ironed two baskets of clothes. When I couldn't find anything else to do to keep myself busy, I took a long, hot bath. By midnight I was still wide awake.

I finally stretched out on the living room sofa with a blanket. I couldn't sleep and there was nothing on television that I wanted to see, so I turned on the radio next to the sofa. I dozed off and on for about an hour, listening to my favorite local jazz station. The next thing I heard was Anita Baker's melodic voice waking me up. A few minutes later the telephone rang. As I wobbled into the kitchen to answer it, I glanced at the large round clock on the wall facing me. I wondered who could be calling my house at six in the morning, but no matter who it was, it had to be somebody I didn't want to talk to. Like Pee Wee or that bitch who'd been calling me up. I didn't expect it to be Rhoda, but it was.

"Did you hear the news?" she asked in such a high-pitched yell I almost didn't recognize her voice.

"What news?" I asked, yawning. I had already decided to call in sick and to keep Charlotte home from school. I didn't know what I was going to do next, but whatever it was, I needed to be alone so that I could come up with a plan.

"There was a big mess at Lester Spool's place last night."

"So? What do I care? Especially after the way him and his sister talked to me yesterday," I said, sounding as harsh as I could at the moment. "There is always a big mess happening at Lester's house."

"Somebody drove by and shot up the place."

"That's not the first time that's happened. Lester has a lot of enemies. He has double-crossed so many people, it's just a matter of time before he double-crosses the wrong person. Sooner or later. After all, he is a drug dealer," I reminded Rhoda with a bored sigh.

"He *was* a drug dealer," Rhoda said, her voice cracking.

CHAPTER 51

Hearing that Lester Spool had been killed affected me in a way I didn't understand. All of a sudden I felt unbearably sad.

"Oh. Well, I guess it happened sooner than later," I said, surprised that I felt some sympathy for a man who had caused pain to so many people. He was still somebody's child and that was the first thing that came to my mind. Neither of us spoke for a moment. "Do they know who did it?"

"Annette, there is more to this story. Betty Jean was at his house when the shootin' started."

"What? Did she . . ."

"Yes! She and Lester and one of his flunkies. They all got hit! Whoever it was meant business. Lester's house looks like Swiss cheese. It's all over the news. Scary Mary made it her business to drive over to the crime scene. She said that not only did they shoot up the house, Lester's car looks like a sieve. The windows are all shot to pieces. The tires. Everything. Girl, they even shot out the streetlights in front of Lester's house. And poor old Mr. Middleton in that green house next door, a few bullets even ripped into the front of his house. It's a damn good thing that that old man was visiting his grandchildren in Akron."

"I . . . I don't know what to say." I couldn't believe my ears. It sounded too convenient to be true! Even Shakespeare couldn't get away with such a plot! As much as I resented Betty Jean, I didn't want the woman dead! She was somebody's child, too. I just wanted her out of my life. "Rhoda, we just saw her. Are you sure she was involved?"

"Annette, I know what I am talkin' about. I saw the news, but I got a full report from Scary Mary. She's more reliable than the news any day."

"Betty Jean is dead?"

"No, she's not dead, but she might as well be. Lester is, but according to the news report, Betty Jean is in critical condition at the city hospital. Scary Mary just left here and you know she knows everybody and everything that goes on in this town. One of her contacts at the hospital called her up and told her that Betty Jean's just lyin' there with a bullet in her head. They had to put her on life support! You couldn't have done a better job of gettin' her out of your life."

"I didn't have anything to do with this!" I shouted.

"Girl, I know that. I am just sayin', this couldn't have worked out better in your favor. I mean, after what she did to you and hangin' out with her drug-dealin' brother and his thug friends, what did she expect? What goes around, comes around. God don't play."

Of all the people in the world, Rhoda was the last one I expected to make such philosophical comments. We rarely talked about the heinous crimes that she had committed. But for the last five years, on the anniversary of each of the five murders Rhoda claimed to have committed, she would slip into a deep depression and stay that way for days. I avoided her during those times. The anniversary of her stroke was the only other time that I went out of my way to avoid her. Each year, on that anniversary, she slipped into a crippling depression that no one could bring her out of.

"You reap what you sow," I stated flatly. I figured that if Rhoda could get philosophical, so could I.

"So what are you goin' to do now? Are you goin' to try and work things out with Pee Wee now that Betty Jean's out of the picture?"

"I don't think it'll be that easy. Pee Wee's out of the picture, too."

* * *

After hearing the news about Betty Jean I changed my mind about staying home from work. I didn't go back to sleep after I got off the telephone with Rhoda. And since I couldn't find any more chores to do around the house, I called the barbershop. I didn't know what I wanted to say to Pee Wee.

"I guess you heard the news about Betty Jean," I said when he answered.

"I heard," he told me in a low, detached voice.

"I went to see her yesterday," I said with caution. "I know it was a stupid thing to do. She and brother were expecting some trouble and advised me to leave. If I had gone over there later, the people who followed them to Lester's house might have . . ." I paused. "I don't want to think about it. I'm just glad I got away from them before the trouble started. Going to Betty Jean's place was really a stupid thing for me to do," I admitted.

"I am surprised to hear you say that. You been doin' a lot of stupid shit lately."

"I just tried to talk to her. That's all. I didn't have anything to do with what happened to her last night. I just wanted you to know that."

"Well, I didn't think you did. Listen, I want to come to the house and get some more of my shit."

"Oh?" My breath got trapped in my throat and I couldn't speak for a few moments. "Uh, what do you plan on doing now?"

"I don't know, Annette. I'm goin' to spend some time at my cousin Steve's pad. I don't know what I am goin' to do after that."

"I just want to know one thing." I paused and braced myself. "How did Betty Jean get a pair of your shorts, Pee Wee?"

"Didn't you ask her that when you went to see her?"

"She didn't give me a chance!"

"Well, I can't answer that either. Listen, I've been doin' a lot of thinkin' lately. I don't know what else to do about what you been goin' through. I ain't havin' no affair with Betty Jean or no other woman, but you can believe what you want to believe. What I do know is, I am tired of this shit. Right about now, I think I need some space just as much as you do."

"You want a divorce?"

"I don't know what I want. Let's cool off and talk later." Pee Wee hung up.

Jade was already at the office when I arrived, and I was glad to see her. "What time is your appointment on Friday for that . . . uh . . . situation you need to take care of?" I asked her.

"It's at nine. They like to do it first thing in the morning. You can drop me off and pick me up a few hours later."

"I thought you wanted to do it in the afternoon, so we could get off work early and then go straight home afterward."

Jade shook her head. "I changed my mind. I'd rather do it in the morning, then have you drop me off at a motel so I can rest up. You can go back to work and when you get off, you can pick me up and take me home. See, it dawned on me that if I got it done too late in the day, I might still be feeling weird by the time you took me home. You know how nosy Mama is."

"OK." I noted the date and time on my desk calendar, along with a cryptic message so that nobody but me would know.

"I will be so glad when this is over with! I can barely zip up my jeans," Jade complained, waving her arms. I gave her a weak smile and an even weaker nod. "Uh, you want to talk about what happened to Betty Jean, Auntie?"

"Not really. I am sorry about what happened to her," I told Jade. She looked like she wasn't convinced that I really was sorry, but I was.

"You know something, Auntie, sometimes you seem too good to be true. Like those martyrs I learned about in school."

"I'm a long way from martyrdom," I laughed. "I might be a little gullible and too easygoing, though. I just don't like confrontations and a lot of confusion in my life. I will go out of my way to avoid it."

"Whatever. Well, at least Betty Jean won't be bothering you anymore. Mama told me that you and Pee Wee are probably going to get a divorce."

"I don't know what we are goin' to do yet, baby."

"Are you going to stay with him after what he did? What if he does it again?"

"I don't know exactly what he did, Jade. For all I know, the man could be telling the truth about not having an affair with Betty Jean." I took a sip of my coffee.

"Maybe it wasn't her after all," Jade suggested, with a weak shrug. "But I still think you should have beaten her butt. I would have. Just for the way she talked to you."

"I don't want to fight any woman over a man, Jade."

As it turned out, I didn't have to. Betty Jean died from her injuries that Friday, around the same time that I picked Jade up from the abortion clinic.

CHAPTER 52

There were some Black folks in Richland who went to almost all of the funerals for other Black folks, whether they knew the deceased or not. As sad and bizarre as it was, funerals had become a social event in our culture. The last one that I attended was more like a New Year's Eve party, with people dressed in designer knockoffs, grinning and hugging everybody all over the place. The only thing they didn't do was dance.

Daddy was feeling much better now, but the doctor had warned him to limit his activities. However, even if he had been on life support, he would not have missed Betty Jean's funeral for the world.

"That sister made a mean margarita and I'm sho'nuff gwine to miss her when I go back to the Red Rose Bar," he lamented.

He got to the church even before Betty Jean's own family, which included the wild side and the good side. Funerals were family reunions when it involved the Spool family. It was the only occasion when both sides of this odd family got together at the same time.

Muh'Dear didn't go to Betty Jean's funeral. "I done been to three funerals already this month. I'm sick of lookin' at dead folks," she declared. But she did send one of the most elaborate floral arrangements I'd ever seen.

Scary Mary spent more time around deceased people than did

all the funeral directors in town put together. She went to every-body's funeral. She made it her business to pay me a visit a few hours after the service for Betty Jean that Saturday afternoon around four.

"Can you believe that a lot of folks was surprised to see *me* at that church? They thought I was already dead myself," she complained with a bitter laugh, pushing her way into my house before I could even open my front door all the way. "You'd think that by now these folks around here would know that I ain't leavin' this life until I'm good and ready. Some of them same folks that seen me at funerals last year and was surprised to see I was still alive then— they dead! And I went to every last one of their funerals." Scary Mary paused and sucked her teeth. "I sure could use me somethin' strong to drink. And I don't mean no coffee."

"You want a beer?" I asked.

"I said somethin' strong. I know you got some vodka. With all the money you make, you better have some," she insisted, posing with her head cocked and a hand on her hip. She twirled around and loudly cleared her throat, determined to make sure I noticed her new outfit. This was usually how she fished for compliments.

"You look mighty spiffy in that navy blue dress and matching hat," I commented.

"What about my shoes?" Scary Mary asked, holding up one wide, flat foot.

"Those navy blue pumps sure do look good on your feet," I told her.

"They cost me enough," she said, brushing off the tail of her dress. There was a pleased look on her face now.

"I have some rum and Coke. Will that do?"

"I guess that'll do," Scary Mary said sharply, clearly disap-pointed. "But make it nice and strong," she ordered, sliding a gnarled finger across my coffee table checking for dust.

She followed me into the kitchen where I mixed her a large glass of rum and Coke. "Uh, how was the funeral?" I wanted to know.

Scary Mary took a long drink first. Then she let out a loud belch and grabbed a wet dishrag off of my sink and wiped her lips. "Girl, you didn't miss nothin'," she said, tossing the dishrag back into the sink. "Betty Jean looked just as ornery in death as she did in life. She had a scowl on her face like a hit man. Her poor, long-sufferin' mama just cried and cried and cried. She carried on worse for Betty Jean than she did the other day at her drug-dealin' son, Lester's, funeral. Losin' two young'ns so close together is some-thin' no mother should have to go through. Even though them two was two of the biggest devils in town. My poor daughter, Mott, I'm glad she too retarded to break my heart. Praise the Lord. Long as Mott in that home I signed her into, I ain't got to worry about her."

Scary Mary sucked on her teeth and a weary look crossed her heavily lined face. It amazed me that a woman her age still applied so many layers of makeup. In one spot a clump of nut-brown pow-der was almost an inch thick. Rouge applied in large red circles on her long cheeks gave her a clownish look.

"I sure miss the handsome way that Rhoda's daddy used to make up the dead," she went on. "It's a damn shame he already retired and moved away before he got a chance to bury me. Me, vain as I done got to be in my old age, I put it in my will for the undertaker to have 'em make up my face so it'll look as good in death as it do in life."

"Was there a good turnout?" I asked. We returned to the living room, where Scary Mary flopped down on my sofa next to me, kicking off her blue shoes.

"Brother Hampton's funeral was better last week. He had twice as many mourners and Reverend Carter let me sing two solos. I was surprised not to see Pee Wee at the service today. Him and Betty Jean used to be real close," Scary Mary said, looking around. "By the way, where he at? I been hearin' things about y'all. Imagine his strumpet bein' so mean she stole a pair of his drawers and sent 'em to you! But that pile of shit you got sent to you at work took the cake! I hope you don't let Pee Wee get away with that shit. If I was in your shoes, I'd bounce a brick off his head so fast his brains would catch afire. Shit!"

"We're separated," I said tiredly, wishing I had also fixed myself a strong drink. "We need to work out a few things. That's all."

Scary Mary gave me a dry look, like she was disappointed that I didn't reveal more details. "Well, I wouldn't let him stay out there too long if I was you. There must be a heap of women out there just waitin' to snatch him up. You don't need to make it easy for none of 'em. And Lord knows, you need to hold on to that man while you can." She patted my hand and gave me a look of pity. "Once a woman gets past a certain age, she don't appeal to nobody but a undertaker. I'm glad I had my share of attention while I was still young. But in the long run, not a one of my eight husbands was worth my time. I would have been better off sharin' my affections with a cute cat or a parakeet. Besides, I like bein' single."

It seemed strange to be hearing this kind of talk from a woman Scary Mary's age. But she was the only woman in her eighties that I knew of who led such an active life. She even belonged to a gym!

"Well?" Scary Mary dipped her head, crossed her legs, and wiggled her foot at me.

"Well, what?" I shrugged.

"I guess you don't want to tell me the whole story about you and Pee Wee breakin' up, huh?"

I shook my head. "There's nothing else to tell right now. We are separated."

"Temporarily, I hope."

"I hope so, too," I said, forcing a smile.

"Well, after you fix me another drink, I'll skedaddle on home and get me some rest. I ain't no young woman no more," Scary Mary said, a tinge of sadness in her voice. She groaned and rubbed her neck.

Scary Mary stayed another hour and sucked up three more drinks.

CHAPTER 53

There was a loud knock on my front door just as she stood up to leave. I did not recognize the handsome young Black man standing on my front porch, dressed in black leather from head to toe. He looked like one of those exotic Chippendale male strippers.

"Can I help you?" I asked, looking the stranger up and down, frightened and excited at the same time. His pants were so tight, it looked like they had been painted on. I wondered if the healthy bulge in his crotch area was real.

"I'm here to see Annette," he informed me in a deep, sexy voice, hands on his hips. The buttons at the top of his shirt were undone, revealing a ripped chest. He had smooth, light brown skin and close-cropped, jet-black hair. If I didn't know that Will Smith was in Hollywood, I would have sworn that it was him standing in front of me.

"Um . . . I'm Annette. Do I know you?" My eyes twitched, my stomach fluttered.

"Uh," the stranger looked over my shoulder and lowered his voice, "the agency sent me."

I turned around and looked at Scary Mary. She had moved close enough behind me to hear everything. She looked at me with a raised eyebrow and shrugged.

"Ebony Dates," the man said, his voice just above a whisper. But Scary Mary heard him anyway.

"Shit goddamn! You work for Thelma Paxton? What in the world—who in the world had Thelma send you over here?" Scary Mary demanded, standing so close behind me I could feel her hot, foul breath on the back of my neck.

"Somebody better tell me what the hell is going on and you better tell me fast," I said, looking from the stranger to Scary Mary.

"Thelma runs that pooh-butt escort service." Scary Mary pushed me aside and faced the man, with a look of contempt on her face. "What's your name, boy?"

"I'm . . . Long John," the man said, leering at me. "I'm . . . scheduled to spend two hours with Annette today."

"Well, I hate to disappoint you, Mr. Long John. But you won't be spending two hours with me today or any other day," I said firmly, wiping sweat off my forehead.

"Now you look here, Long. You go tell your boss I don't appreciate her tryin' to do business in this part of town!" Scary Mary yelled. "You tell her I been in this business longer than she been alive and I ain't fin to quit no time soon."

"Who sent you to see me?" I asked, unable to take my eyes off the man's handsome face.

He shrugged and scratched his cheek. "I can't reveal that. I just go where they tell me to go."

"Well, I didn't call for any male escort, so you can go back and tell whoever sent you what I said." I gently closed and locked my front door, and peeped out the window until I saw him get in a dark blue Chevy and drive away.

I turned to Scary Mary with a puzzled, amused look on my face. "I bet Jade or Rhoda sent me a male hooker. Jade even suggested I go out and meet somebody to take my mind off Pee Wee." I shook my head. "But this . . . this is extreme even for Jade or Rhoda."

"Well, who else would have sent somebody over here to give you some nookie?" Scary Mary asked.

"Maybe he had the wrong address," I suggested.

Scary Mary shook her head so hard that the wig on her head shifted. It was already on sideways. "He asked for you by name. If Rhoda or Jade didn't try to hook you up, I say somebody else is tryin' to be funny. You got any more spirits?"

"Yeah, but who?" I moved slowly toward the portable bar across the room. The notes and the other crap I had received in the mail were one thing. That was downright vicious and as far as I was concerned, Betty Jean had been behind all that. But she was dead. "Betty Jean couldn't have done it. Not now."

Scary Mary snatched the large bottle of rum out of my hand and poured herself a generous drink. "Sure she could," Scary Mary insisted, taking her time to continue. She let out a deep, wheezy sigh and moved to the sofa where she plopped down with a loud groan.

I felt uncomfortable in my own house. I stood there staring at Scary Mary. The sleeves on my blouse were too long. With the cuffs almost covering my hands, the blouse felt like a straitjacket when I folded my arms. "When you set up a date through a agency, you can set it up weeks in advance. I even got tricks calling me setting up dates for themselves and their friends months in advance. Judge Bernstein set hisself a date up for this Christmas and it's still more than two months away!" she told me.

"I see." I let out a sigh of relief and joined Scary Mary on the sofa. "So Betty Jean could have called up that agency and arranged this way before she died."

"Yep!"

Scary Mary's explanation made a lot of sense, so I put the whole incident out of my mind. My only hope was that that was the only delayed situation that Betty Jean had arranged.

CHAPTER 54

As obnoxious as Scary Mary was, I was glad she had come by. I don't know how I would have reacted to the male hooker at my door had she not been present. She passed the mailman on my porch on her way out and intercepted him. He handed her the stack of mail, so she returned to my door to hand it to me.

Right on top of the stack was the same type of envelope that I had received the first note in. A small, pink invitation-sized envelope addressed to me. There was no return name or address.

"Don't go yet," I begged Scary Mary.

"What?" Scary Mary asked, her eyes on the envelope.

"Wait just a minute," I said, ripping the envelope open as Scary Mary stared at me with her mouth hanging open. It was a small message but it carried a lot of weight:

Bitch,
I am still here. This town is not big enough for the two of us. LEAVE here or else . . .

The postmark was from the day before. Betty Jean had been dead for three days! "It wasn't Betty Jean harassing me," I whispered. "But . . . But maybe she had somebody working with her. One of her crazy relatives. Maybe she sealed this up before she died and left it lying around and one of them saw it and mailed it," I babbled.

"Maybe she did and maybe she didn't," Scary Mary said firmly. "The question now is, if Betty Jean wasn't the one fuckin' with you and fuckin' your man, who is it?"

"I don't know. Can you give me a ride over to Steve Hardy's house? That's where Pee Wee is staying."

I grabbed my purse and a sweater off the back of the wing chair next to my sofa. I put my sweater on so fast I had it on upside down. I adjusted it in Scary Mary's van. She was the only person I knew who drove better when she was drunk than she did when she was sober.

It took us ten minutes to get to Pee Wee's cousin's house where he'd been staying since our last spat.

Scary Mary parked at a crooked angle in front of the large brown house on a tree-lined street. There was a large weeping willow tree in the front yard on one side of the curved walkway. A birdbath was on the other side.

Nobody answered when I rang the doorbell. The front door was wide open, and the screen door was unlocked. Nobody answered even when I pushed open the screen door and called out Steve's name and the names of his wife and kids.

"Get out the way," Scary Mary ordered, pushing her way in, bold as a thief. I followed behind her.

I had been to Steve's house several times over the years, so I knew my way around. I jumped ahead of Scary Mary and had her follow me. We marched through the living room into one of the two downstairs bedrooms. It was empty, but I found Pee Wee in the second bedroom. I didn't know if he was playing possum or if he really was asleep. I ran up to the bed and started beating him about the face and head with my fists. He woke up immediately.

"What the hell—" He leaped up from the bed, grabbing my wrists and holding on to me so tight I couldn't move anything below my neck. "What in the world is goin' on now, woman? What the hell you doin' comin' up in here with this shit!" Pee Wee glanced over my shoulder at Scary Mary. "What's goin' on here?" he asked her. "Y'all drunk or crazy or what?"

"I ain't drunk," Scary Mary said quickly. "And if anybody in this room is crazy, it ain't me," she added, fanning her face with a handkerchief that she had removed from her bosom.

"Whoever the hell she is, she can have your black ass," I yelled. "I am through with you. You got one day to get the rest of your shit out of my house, or I will give it to the junk man!"

"That's fine with me. You are beyond talkin' to and I ain't even goin' to try and do that with you no more. If you ever come to your senses, you come to me. I'm through. You call up the lawyer and we will work out everything. I don't care what you do, as long as I can see my child when I want to. Now you get the hell out of this house!"

In all the years that I'd known and loved Pee Wee, he had never talked to me in such a harsh manner. This was like the final nail in the coffin.

In just a few days I had become a person that even I didn't like. I was so disgusted with myself that I could barely stand to look at my own face in the mirror. No wonder Pee Wee had lost interest in me.

Even after old Mr. Boatwright had raped me for so many years, I had never challenged him physically. But I had hit Pee Wee so hard with my fists that they were now aching and throbbing like I had pummeled a rock.

As far as I was concerned, my marriage was over. I was completely crushed. Even though I had not attended anybody's funeral today, it felt like I had.

CHAPTER 55

After I assaulted Pee Wee in his cousin's house, I instructed Scary Mary to drop me off at Rhoda's house. She stayed just long enough with me to help me tell Rhoda and Jade about the male prostitute who had been sent to my house, which, as it turned out, neither one of them knew anything about.

"It had to be that bitch," I said. "Lord knows what she's going to do next," I said, as Rhoda poured some Epsom salt into a large bowl with warm water for me to soak my throbbing hands. I had told Rhoda and Jade about how I had attacked Pee Wee. That had horrified them as much as the news about the male prostitute.

I was glad that Scary Mary had decided not to stay with me at Rhoda's house. I didn't feel comfortable discussing my business too freely in front of her. She already knew more about my situation than I wanted her to know.

"Pee Wee didn't fight you back when you hit him?" Jade asked me, stirring the warm water with a long spoon, forcing my hands in deeper. "Are you going to leave him now?" We were in Rhoda's dining room, with the door closed so Otis and Bully couldn't hear our conversation. "If I was you, I would. He's got you acting like a fool."

"I don't know, Jade," I said in a weak voice. My hands looked like they belonged on a lobster. Jade handed me a towel. I hated to lift my hands out of the bowl and dry them, but the throbbing had stopped.

"How much more are you going to put up with from Pee Wee, Auntie?" Jade asked, handing me a much-needed glass of white wine.

"He's no prince or no Greek god or nothing. You deserve better. With all the money you make and all the nice things you have, you could probably get you a real cute, real young man," Jade insisted.

Rhoda and I looked from Jade to each other and shook our heads.

Rhoda dropped to the floor and started giving me a foot massage. "Pee Wee is still Annette's husband, baby," Rhoda said to Jade, speaking in an unusually gentle tone. "I've been giving this a lot of thought." Rhoda sniffed and turned to me. "Pee Wee and I have been friends since we were eight, and I love him like a brother. I'd hate to see y'all break up," Rhoda said to me. "But you have to do what you think is right for you. If I were you, Annette, I would try to work this out. If Pee Wee can stop doin' whatever it is that he's doin' with this bitch, he might be worth holdin' on to. Look at me. I could have dumped Otis when I found out about him and his whore. But what good would that have done me? Him and his bitch would have lived happily ever after. Me, I'd have ended up alone . . ." Rhoda paused and wrapped a warm towel around my feet.

"Auntie, I keep telling you, you can get yourself another husband! It makes me so sad to see you going through all this crazy stuff!" Jade hollered. With a frantic, wide-eyed look on her face, she turned from me to Rhoda. "A lot of men like women who look like Auntie!" Jade said to Rhoda.

I didn't even want to know what Jade meant by her comment about women like me.

Jade turned back to me. "What if he gives you a disease, or gets somebody pregnant? Would you stay with him then?"

"I doubt that very seriously," I said. "I would have to draw the line somewhere. But he is still better than some of the other men out there. And I am way too tired to get back in the dating scene."

"Now that you know Betty Jean *wasn't* the one harassing you, what do you plan to do?" Rhoda asked.

I looked from her to Jade, sucking in my stomach. "Whoever this bitch is, she will have to do more than send me nasty notes to make me leave town," I vowed, shaking my fist.

I enjoyed a very pleasant evening with Jade and Rhoda. And it was a good thing I did, because after that night it would be a while before I enjoyed another pleasant evening with them or anybody else.

The very next day, while I was at a nail shop at the Melden Village Mall getting my nails done, somebody slashed all four of the tires on my car in broad daylight in the mall parking lot.

CHAPTER 56

I had to keep in mind that my actions and behavior affected other people in my life. Even if they didn't know the reason I was acting so out of character.

I could avoid Muh'Dear and Daddy, therefore avoid their nosy questions. As much as I wanted to see Daddy and make sure he was following his doctor's orders, it was better for me to call him. That way I could control the situation. The last thing I wanted to do was to break down in front of him and Muh'Dear. But it was getting harder and harder to maintain a level of sanity so that I could take care of my daughter and do my job.

"When is my daddy coming home?" Charlotte demanded when I picked her up from school in a rental car that following Monday evening. I had decided to take off a few days from work. "Did you get a new car, Mama? How come you look so mad?"

"Just get in the car and hush up," I ordered.

I dropped Charlotte off at Rhoda's house for Jade to keep an eye on her because I had to visit my insurance agent.

Once I got Charlotte situated in the house, Jade walked me back to my car, her arm around my shoulder. "Another package addressed to you arrived at the office today. It looks very suspicious," Jade told me with a weary look on her face.

I could see that this mess was beginning to take a heavy toll on this poor child, too. "Did you open it?" I asked with indifference. Nothing my tormentor did surprised me anymore.

Jade shook her head. "There is just no telling what's in it. Do you want me to bring it by your house tomorrow on my lunch hour?"

I shook my head. "That's all right, baby. Whatever it is, it can wait until I return to work."

"Unless it's a time bomb," Jade said with a chuckle.

I shook my head again and laughed, too. My mind flashed on the way Pee Wee's face looked during my surprise attack while he slept at his cousin's house the other day, and that made me laugh as well. I was glad to see that there was some humor in the situation.

"Jade, I know you'd rather be out with your friends instead of keeping me company. I appreciate all you do for me. Thank you so much for being here for me," I said, my voice dropping to a whisper. "I don't know what I'd do if I didn't have you and your mama behind me."

Jade gave me such a strong bear hug, I almost lost my breath.

"Auntie, I love you and I'll be glad when this is all over," Jade assured me with a sob in her voice. "I can't go on watching you fall apart! It's wrong and I wish to God that I could find out who the bitch is who is doing this. I would take care of her myself!"

"Jade, don't upset yourself. It's not healthy. This whole thing will be over soon. I promise you," I said, rubbing her back.

"Oh? Did you find out something else?"

"No, not yet. But I will."

"Oh. Well, if you don't, are you going to get a divorce, or what?"

I hunched my shoulders. "I haven't decided what I'm going to do. Even if I don't file for a divorce, Pee Wee might. I am not going to try to hang on to a man who doesn't want to be with me. If he doesn't want to stay with me, I can't make him."

"I'm glad to hear that. You don't need to settle for that kind of marriage. But Auntie, this happens all the time. It's a biological thing with most men. When they get a certain age, they have to get a younger woman. Everybody knows that. Donald Trump proved it—twice! Pee Wee is at that age when he wants a younger woman.

Men get that itch any time after their thirties. You do know that, don't you?"

I couldn't bring myself to look in Jade's face. I didn't want her to see the pain in my eyes.

"Pee Wee doesn't like younger women," I said. "He told me that himself," I said in an uncertain voice that cracked before I could finish my sentence.

"Of course he'd tell you something like that! I overheard Mama and Aunt Lola talking about that affair that Daddy had that time. Aunt Lola told Mama that one time Daddy told her that he didn't like plain women. Well, that cow he fooled around with looked like Isaac Hayes!"

"James Brown," I corrected.

"Huh?"

"The woman your daddy cheated with looked like James Brown. That's what your mama told me. They even called the woman J.B." I was surprised that I was able to laugh. Jade didn't laugh, though.

"Whatever." Jade sighed and gave me another bear hug. "I just want you to be happy, Auntie."

I didn't go straight home. I did something that I had not done in years. I went to a bar alone. Not a bar where I might run into somebody I didn't want to see, but a dim, dark, country-western type of place on the side of the freeway, near a trailer park. In the bar's parking lot tipsy hillbillies with crooked, chewing-tobacco-stained teeth leered at me as I approached the bar entrance. As soon as I made it through the door and plopped down on a stool at the bar, a potbellied redneck in jeans and a plaid shirt appeared out of nowhere. He sat so close to me our elbows touched.

"'Scuse me, ma'am," he said, tipping a faded beige cowboy hat. His breath had an unholy stench. His dusty clothes smelled like metal. "Have I seen you somewhere before?" He bobbed his head to a Willie Nelson song playing on the jukebox in a corner near the bar.

I ordered a bottle of beer from an exasperated-looking bartender before I answered. "It's possible. I've been somewhere before," I smirked.

"And you're cute, too. Plump as a pheasant. You lookin' for

somethin' in particular?" he crooned, his eyes roaming all over my body.

"I was in the neighborhood and I just came in for a drink." It took me a few moments to realize I was being picked up. "I am meeting my husband in a little while down the street," I said, looking at my watch.

"We don't see gals like you in here too often. You a . . . uh . . . *workin'* gal?"

Thirty years ago I would have been flattered to be asked that question.

"I have a husband and a daughter," I snapped, rising to leave. I took just one sip from the bottle of beer that the bartender had set on the counter in front of me. Then I dropped a few bills on the counter and rose to leave.

I was so disoriented that I got lost trying to get back on the freeway. I turned on the radio to listen to the news, something I had not done in days. I was surprised to hear that O.J. Simpson had been found not guilty almost a week ago of murdering his estranged wife and her friend! That's how out of touch I had been. If Rhoda, Jade, or anybody else had mentioned that story to me, I had completely forgotten it.

Maybe I really had suffered a nervous breakdown! I was certainly not myself, especially today. I couldn't figure out how I ended up on a narrow dirt road. Especially when I could actually see the freeway from where I was. I had not consumed enough alcohol to be drunk, but I lost control of the rental car anyway. I didn't even see that stray horse when it galloped out of a field and onto the road, right in front of me.

There was a tremendous crash and then it got so dark, it seemed like somebody had put me in a room and turned off all the lights.

CHAPTER 57

At least I wasn't dead, or even hurt. If anything, the accident that had just happened had sharpened my mind and made me more aware of what was going around me.

I didn't like having to deal with the police twice within a twenty-four-hour period. It had been enough of an ordeal for me to make out the police report when I discovered that somebody had slashed the tires on my car.

The rental car had not been too badly damaged, but the horse that I'd hit was dead. Rhoda eventually came to pick me up from a nearby fruit stand where I had called her from. A tow truck had immediately come to haul the damaged car away. I was glad the police didn't keep me on the scene too long. I couldn't stand to look at the broken carcass of the horse I'd hit.

"Jade told me you hit a Porsche. Are you all right?" she asked, helping me to her SUV.

She gasped when I started laughing. "I must have sounded pretty wild to Jade. It was a *horse* I hit, not a Porsche." I yawned, even though I was far from sleepy. "Rhoda, I . . . am falling apart," I stammered.

Rhoda stared at me for a few moments and then she laughed.

"Well, thank God you are all right and insured. This could have happened to anybody, you know."

Rhoda took me to her house to pick up Charlotte before she drove me home. I grabbed the mail out of the mailbox on my way in and tossed the stack of envelopes and magazines onto the coffee table.

It was hours later, after I'd fed Charlotte and chased her off to bed, before I went through the mail. There was no return address on the last envelope, but I knew who it had come from. The note read:

Bitch, you are running out of time!

Attached to the note with a paper clip was an old picture of me standing in front of my house next to Charlotte. Rhoda and Jade had posed with us for that same picture, but all traces of them were missing, except for part of Jade's hand, which was on my shoulder. The photograph had been trimmed on all four sides. Pee Wee had taken the picture on Charlotte's first day of kindergarten. I had not seen this particular photograph in years. I could barely remember posing for it, let alone where I had left it. We had several photo albums in the house, not to mention family pictures on the walls and tables. This picture could have been anywhere and anybody could have taken it.

The picture, with me smiling like I'd just won the lottery, had been neatly cut into the shape of a coffin. My face, and Charlotte's, had been crossed out with a huge black *X*. I could still smell the ink from the Magic Marker that the sender had used.

I was glad that Charlotte was not around to see me hyperventilate. It took several minutes for me to compose myself. I was standing in front of the kitchen sink drinking my second glass of water when the telephone rang.

"I want to speak to Annette." I did not recognize the woman's loud, angry voice, but at least it was not the raspy whisper that I had become far too familiar with.

"This . . . this is she," I mumbled.

"This is Daisy Hawthorne. I am only goin' to tell you one time: stay away from my husband!"

My mind went blank for a few seconds. "What? I don't even know you or your husband."

"You are a goddamn liar. We went to school with your fat black ass, and you done called my house buggin' us about a goddamn jewelry store bill. You damn well do know me and my husband, Brady Hawthorne, you whorin' ass bitch! You can play dumb if you want to, but I will—"

I slammed the telephone down and started to walk away. I stopped when I noticed that the indicator on my answering machine was flashing the number of messages I had received. I had *never* received twelve messages in one day. The first two were from Muh'Dear, the next one was from Pee Wee. The next six were from women I did not know. Each one accused me of sleeping with her husband!

I erased all of the rest of the messages without listening to them. The feeling that came over me was one of the worst feelings I had ever experienced in my life. I felt like I was alone in the world. Other than Rhoda and Jade, there was nobody I could talk to about what was happening in my life.

"Thank God you are still up," I said to Jade as soon as she answered the telephone.

"Well, yeah. I left you two messages. I wanted to see how you were doing. You have been through so much lately, and I am so worried about you, Auntie."

"Oh, shit! I erased your messages. I will explain later." I rubbed my chest and my eyes. I could barely feel my legs and when I tried to shift my position, I almost fell to the floor. "I know you have to go to work tomorrow. But as your supervisor, I give you my permission to take tomorrow off with pay."

"Cool! But why would I do that?" Jade asked in an excited voice.

"I was feeling kind of lonely and wanted to know if you'd come keep me company for the night. If you want to go to work in the morning, that's fine. If you don't, that's fine, too. Like I said, you can take tomorrow off with pay if you want to."

"Did something else happen?"

"I got another note in the mail. This one really upset me a little more than the others. And a bunch of women left messages on my answering machine accusing me of sleeping with their husbands. I guess I've reached my breaking point," I said plaintively. "Is Rhoda still up?"

"Yeah, but she's not here. She went for a drink at the Red Rose with some lady from her exercise class."

"Well, can you come over right away?"

"I'm on my way," Jade squealed.

CHAPTER 58

I didn't realize it was raining outside until Jade walked in my front door with a see-through raincoat on over her silk pajamas. In addition to her overnight case, she had her ever-present yellow backpack slung over her shoulder.

"I just put on some tea," I told her, hanging her raincoat on a hook near the door.

"Well, since I don't have to work tomorrow, and since Mama's not here to mess with me, I'd rather have a beer," Jade said, with a cheeky grin.

"Jade, you know I don't like you drinking over here," I scolded, knowing it was useless. "Your mother wouldn't like it either. I am responsible for you when you are with me." I dipped my head and gave Jade a critical look.

Jade blinked her big green eyes, dropped her backpack onto the sofa, and headed for the kitchen with that silly grin still on her face.

Several minutes passed and Jade hadn't come out. She was probably drinking a beer anyway. I was too tired to fuss with her. I picked up the stack of mail, with the nasty note still on top of the pile. I set it aside so I could show Jade when she returned to the living room.

With a groan I flipped through the rest of the stack, praying that I would not see anything else that I didn't want to see. I did. Between my light bill and a car ad was another Frederick's of Hollywood catalogue addressed to Jade.

I picked up her backpack to put the catalogue in it, surprised that such a dainty-looking thing was so heavy. As soon as I opened the backpack out fell a can of hair spray and a paperback romance novel with a longhaired man on top of a half-naked woman on the cover. Because Jade was so neat, I was surprised to see something stuck between the pages of the book, separate from a plastic bookmark toward the end. I flipped the pages, chuckling. I was not surprised, but I was disappointed to see that Jade was reading such trash. On almost every page I looked at, the characters were having sex. That was disturbing enough. However, what I removed from between two pages, where the author had described an orgy in great detail, could just have well been a deadly blacksnake—a real one this time.

My eyes burned as I stared at what I held in my trembling hand: neatly cut parts of the picture that had been clipped from the disturbing picture that I had received in the mail!

I shook my head, then I shook the book. Nothing else fell out. I dropped it onto the sofa and poured out all of the contents in the backpack. A pair of scissors and a packet of small pink envelopes with matching paper, complete with a white dove in the upper right-hand corner, like the sheets I'd received, were the last things to land on my sofa.

From a distance, I could hear somebody crying. I didn't realize it was me until Jade strolled back into the living room with a loud burp. She stopped in her tracks when she realized what I had stumbled onto.

"Omigod! Omigod! Oh, no! Auntie, please!" she yelled, dropping her cup of tea to the floor. "Oh, shit."

I nodded. "Oh shit is right," I said, rising from the sofa with the pieces of the picture in one hand and the pink envelopes and matching paper in the other.

I could not have been more stunned, horrified, hurt, and confused if the Devil himself had walked into my living room.

But a devil *had* just walked into my living room.

CHAPTER 59

"Jade . . . Oh, Jade, baby . . . It was you. It was you all this time. *It was you?*" The words left a bitter taste in my mouth.

With the same soulless look in her eyes that I'd seen when I'd spent the night at Rhoda's house, Jade just stood there glaring at me. And then she nodded.

I swallowed hard and blinked even harder. "Jade, are you sleeping with my husband?" I asked, bile rising in my throat. My voice was so hoarse I could barely recognize it. I couldn't move from my spot. "Jade, talk to me!" I shrieked. I don't know where I got the strength that kept me from falling flat on my face or snapping completely.

"You were never supposed to find out."

Jade's voice was a low whimper at first and there was a frightened look on her face. But that look didn't stay there long. Within seconds her face turned hard and threatening. Her eyes became slits, her lips thin, dark lines that trembled with every blink of her eyes. Her voice changed just as suddenly and sharply as her face.

She hissed, "Why didn't you just pack up your shit and move to China or somewhere before it came to this?" Jade clenched her teeth and chanted, "Why, why, why? Why don't you go somewhere and disappear?" she asked, stomping her foot so hard the remote fell off the coffee table and onto the floor.

I was so profoundly stunned, I could barely talk anymore. In the back of my mind I wanted to scream and fly into a rage like a betrayed woman was supposed to do. But I couldn't. At least not yet. This young woman, this *child*, meant too much to me. And because of who her mother was, this was one situation that had to be handled with extreme caution.

"Jade, are you sleeping with my husband?" I asked again.

In all the years that I'd known Jade, I had never seen such an extreme look of contempt on her face like I did now. The girl I was facing was not the busybody, feisty, but lovable, young woman whom I had loved like a daughter. This beautiful young woman, my best friend's daughter, was now my worst nightmare. Just like she had told me in the first note.

I had pretty much gotten over what Mr. Boatwright had put me through. But not even the rapes and mental abuse that I had endured had prepared me for this level of pain. I don't remember who said it, but I had heard someone say that "your best friend can also be your worst enemy." That's just about how I felt at this moment. I knew that whatever involved Jade directly involved Rhoda. But this, this was something I did not know how I was going to deal with.

"Are you going to answer my question?" I asked.

"Pee Wee needs a woman like me," Jade said, lifting her nose in the air. "He deserves so much more than what you have to offer!"

"Is that a yes or a no?" I asked calmly. "Are you sleeping with my husband, girl?"

Instead of confirming or denying my charge, Jade just glared at me.

"You were not supposed to find out," she whimpered, stomping her foot again.

"What about?" I had to pause and cough to clear my throat. It felt like a huge ball of fire had risen up from my stomach and was trying to get out through my mouth. My tongue felt like it was on fire. "What about that time you answered my phone and . . . it was that . . . person? Who was that?"

Jade gave me an exasperated look. "It was some telemarketer."

"But you . . . It was you who made all the other calls? You sent that male prostitute to my house? You called up all those other women and told them I was sleeping with their husbands? You, you, you?"

Again, Jade gave me an exasperated look. She nodded. "I guess I must have disguised my voice pretty well, huh?"

"You disguised a lot of things, Jade!" I snapped. "And you honestly thought you'd run me out of town and you'd move in with Pee Wee, right? Did you think that it would be easy, girl?"

Jade replaced her exasperated look with one of extreme contempt and impatience. "Something like that! I thought if I got rid of you, eventually I could come out in the open with Pee Wee. I was hoping you'd go away and marry somebody else and wouldn't care. I . . . I know people who end up marrying people their relatives and friends dumped. It didn't bother them!"

"You are a child, Jade," I wailed, refusing to let her see the tears I was struggling to hold back.

"Pee Wee doesn't think so!"

"So, you are sleeping with my husband?" I asked, lifting my chin and sticking my chest out defiantly.

"I gotta get out of here!" Jade shot across the floor and stuffed her belongings back into her backpack. Then, grabbing her raincoat, she ran—so fast that she fell trying to get out my front door.

I ran behind her, tears pouring from my eyes. "I can't deal with this, Jade! I could have dealt with it being anybody but you," I sobbed, wiping my eyes and nose with the back of my hand. "Do you know what this means? Your mother and I have been best friends for so many years, but now—"

"Look, I am sorry you had to find out this way. I am sorry you had to find out, period. But you are just as much to blame for this as I am."

"What the hell is that supposed to mean?" I asked, grabbing her arm.

"Let me go!" She pried my grip away and moved back a few steps until she was out the door on my front porch, with me following. "You didn't know how to treat a man like Pee Wee. You, with your fancy job and your running around with my mom trying to make yourself look important! You are nothing but a big, chunkifiedbutt wannabe! And you don't even know how to dress! Just . . . just look at you! A big fat *rag doll* is what you are and all you will ever be. You and your . . . your tacky muumuus! You don't deserve a man like Pee Wee!"

"Jade, what are you saying to me?" I yelled. By now we were both on the porch steps. "I loved you like a daughter. I love your mom as much as I love my own flesh and blood. I . . . I . . ." I had to stop talking and sit down on my porch steps. I held my breath and swallowed hard to keep from throwing up the sour liquid that had filled my mouth. My chest felt like it was going to explode and for a moment I thought I was having a heart attack. I gasped until I caught my breath.

Jade disappeared into the night like a thief.

It was dark and even though it had stopped raining, it was too cool and windy for me to be sitting on my porch steps for very long. I was shivering as I wobbled up and went back inside.

There was only one thing left for me to do. I packed my other two suitcases. This time with some of my clothes and some of my daughter's. Charlotte was half-asleep as I dressed her but she was wide awake by the time we climbed into a cab.

"Where are we going, Mama?" she asked, looking out the back window of the cab as we drove off.

"We're going to pay your aunt Lillimae a surprise visit in Miami," I said with a cough.

"Oh. When are we coming back home? Jade said she'd take me to the park next Sunday."

"I don't know, child," I admitted.

I didn't know what my future held now. The one thing I did know was that as far as Jade was concerned, things would never be the same again.

I thought that at that point the unraveling of my life was now complete.

But the worst was yet to come.

CHAPTER 60

Muh'Dear once said that if she didn't make it to heaven when she died, she'd settle for the Bahamas. She had visited her favorite place on earth on a regular basis for years. One year she invited me, Pee Wee, Charlotte, and Rhoda and her family to accompany her and Daddy to the Bahamas to spend Christmas with her and Daddy and some of the many Bahamian friends that she had made over the years. We were all going to be traveling first class, at Muh'Dear's expense.

My late stepfather, Albert King, had owned the Buttercup, the most popular soul food restaurant in town. When he died, Muh'Dear inherited the restaurant. She sold it five years ago, after making more money than she could ever spend in her lifetime. After all of the poverty that she and I had survived in Florida after Daddy's desertion, Muh'Dear was determined to live like a queen for the rest of her days. She shopped at the finest stores in town, lived in and owned several houses, including the one I occupied, and she traveled to the Bahamas at least once a year. She was excited about us all joining her on her latest jaunt to the Bahamas that particular year.

A few days before our departure, I came down with the flu and had to cancel my participation. Pee Wee wanted to stay home with me, but I made him go. It had been a rough week at work, and even though I appreciated Muh'Dear's generous invitation, I didn't really want to go out of town for Christmas. I had already seen all I wanted to see in the Bahamas and this year, I just wanted to stay home and relax.

Well, Jade decided she didn't want to go either if I wasn't going. There was no arguing with her. She was only ten at the time, but already used to getting her way.

Rhoda had left a closetful of new toys for Jade that I was to place under my Christmas tree. Just before midnight that Christmas Eve, after I had put Jade to bed, I played Santa Claus. Just as I was placing the last of four new dolls for Jade under the tree, Jade padded down the steps and into the living room, wide awake.

"Auntie!" she yelled, running across the floor waving her arms, almost tripping on the tail of her floor-length Cookie Monster nightgown. "Auntie, are you really the Santa Claus?" she asked. She was so excited, she jumped up and down, clapping her hands like a toddler.

"Well, yes, I guess," I confessed. "I am Santa Claus. But this is something you weren't supposed to find out until you got a little older, young lady," I said, shaking a finger in Jade's face.

Jade lunged for the biggest of the dolls, a beautiful black doll in African attire. Caressing the doll, Jade turned to me with a puzzled look on her face. "Auntie, how do you get into other kids' houses?"

"Huh?"

"How do you get into the other kids' houses to leave their Christmas presents?"

It was my turn to look puzzled. "What do you mean, baby?"

"You just said you were really Santa Claus. I know you are because I caught you putting my toys under the tree! You live here in this house, but how do you get into the other kids' houses?"

"Uh, when I put on my red suit, it gives me magic powers," I said.

"Is it the magic red suit that makes you look like a white man with a long white beard, too?"

"Uh-huh."

"Auntie, I promise I won't tell anybody else who you really are. I love you and one day I'm going to be just like you," Jade said.

* * *

"Mama, why are you crying?" Charlotte asked, her voice bringing me back to the present moment.

"Oh, I got something in my eyes," I sniffed, rubbing my eye. I looked around and blinked. I had almost forgotten that we were sitting in the Akron-Canton Airport along with dozens of other weary travelers, waiting to get on a plane that would take us to Miami. It was the only place that I could run to. I didn't know anybody else in any other state well enough to drop in on them unannounced. But it would have been nice if I'd known somebody in Alaska, because I wanted to get as far away as possible from Richland, Ohio.

"How much longer do we have to wait to get to Miami, Mama?"

I looked at my watch. I had been so preoccupied that I had lost track of the time. It had been more than four hours since Jade had destroyed my world.

"Not too much longer," I replied, with a detached voice.

"I called Jade to tell her where we were going," Charlotte said proudly.

My head felt like somebody had dropped a cement block on top of it.

"*You what?* When did you call that, girl?" My face got hot, and I had a hard time breathing.

A look of surprise swept across Charlotte's face. "When you went to sleep a little while ago. I took some money from your pocketbook and I went to that pay phone over there," Charlotte said, pointing to a bank of phones facing us.

"Why did you call Jade?" I managed. "Why?" I hollered, fanning my face with both hands.

"Because I didn't know the number to call Daddy." Charlotte rubbed her nose and shrugged.

"But why did you call *Jade?* I didn't tell you to call anybody."

"You didn't tell me not to," Charlotte pouted. "Jade always told me that whenever I felt scared I could always call her. And she said if anybody messes with me she would beat 'em up."

"Oh, shit!" I let out an exasperated sigh and glared at my daughter.

"I want to go home! I want to see my daddy!" Charlotte yelled, swinging her feet back and forth in her seat, drawing unwanted attention. I gave a toothy smile to the strangers looking in our direction.

"Listen, baby. Uh, I have a little problem right now, and I really need to get away for a while. We'll go back home when I work out my little problem."

"What problem?" Charlotte wanted to know. She leaped off of her seat and stood in front of me, holding one of my hands in hers.

"I really don't want to talk about it right now. You wouldn't understand it anyway. Now you just be good and no matter what you do, don't you ever call Rhoda's house again without me knowing it. I . . . I don't ever want you to talk to Jade." I almost choked on the words. I had to suck in a deep breath and rub my chest. My heart felt like it was about to pop out of my chest.

Charlotte's mouth dropped open, her eyes bugged out. What I had just said must have been the most shocking thing she had ever heard come out of my mouth. It was.

"Why?" Charlotte wailed, her eyes still bugged out. "Jade is . . . Uh . . . Jade is . . . *Jade*. Why can't I talk to her no more?"

It took me a few moments to come up with a response. "Because I said so." I couldn't think of anything better to say at the time.

I couldn't imagine what Jade had told Rhoda about our showdown. I wanted to put off knowing for as long as I possibly could. What I had found out about Jade tonight was so overwhelming it hadn't really sunk in all the way, yet.

I didn't know how I was going to react when it did.

CHAPTER 61

We had to wait one more hour for the next flight to Miami. By the time we got on the plane and crawled into our seats, I was so disoriented and upset I couldn't even sleep. I was glad that Charlotte was able to doze off right away, though. She slept all the way while I sweated and cried. I looked so distraught when we landed that a flight attendant offered to get me a wheelchair.

I stumbled through the airport like a zombie. I don't even remember getting in the cab that took us to Lillimae's house in Miami's predominantly Black Liberty City.

With Charlotte stepping on my heels, I stumbled up on Lillimae's porch that afternoon. I started pounding on her front door so hard that a woman in the house next door ran out on her front porch waving a whisk broom at me like a sword.

"Lillimae ain't home!" The scowling woman shouted.

Lillimae had told me more than once that I was welcome to visit her anytime I felt like it. She was one of the few people I believed who said that and really meant it. However, dropping in on anybody unannounced was never a wise thing to do. I could have called her before I left my house, or from either one of the airports. But I didn't think do to so. I had so much on my mind that I didn't know if I was coming or going.

"I'm her sister," I said meekly, bowing my head. "Do you know where she is and when she'll be back?"

The woman moved closer to the edge of her porch, grabbed her glasses, which were hanging from a chain around her neck, and held them up to her face, which made her look like a pie with a nose. Shading her eyes with one hand, she looked me up and down before responding. "You and Lillimae is *sisters?*"

"Uh-huh. It surprises a lot of people, until I tell them we are half sisters," I explained.

Even though Lillimae and I looked a lot alike, I was Black. Technically, she was too, but she could pass for White. I had visited Lillimae several times over the years. We had just met ten years ago after Daddy had pestered me until I visited him in Florida.

"She at work at the post office. She usually get home around six," the woman said, her voice much softer now. The scowl was gone from her face, but her face still looked like a pie. "She usually goes for happy hour with some of the post office folks after work, though. Almost every day. I guess workin' at the post office'll make you want to drink."

"Oh." I looked around. The cab was too far away for me to summon him back. "Well," I said, looking at my watch, "I'll just wait for her."

The woman shook her head and went back into her house.

"What do we do now?" Charlotte asked.

"Sit down," I sighed, waving her to the glider on one side of the porch.

"For what?"

"We'll wait here for your auntie," I said, my voice cracking.

And that's just what we did. For three hours we sat on that porch awaiting my sister's return. I felt that I had no other place to go.

Charlotte got fidgety and angry real quick, and I could understand her feeling that way. I encouraged her to go play in Lillimae's front yard. She found a piece of chalk on the ground and had been playing hopscotch for about ten minutes when Lillimae's noisy old Ford crawled down the street. It was just beginning to get dark. I was disappointed to see that Lillimae's battered old car still had only one headlight. With all the noise her old car made and the one headlight, anybody else would have thought that she was riding up on a motorcycle.

"Annette, what in the world is goin' on?" Lillimae yelled as soon as she parked in her driveway. She slid out of her car like a seal, with her muumuu flapping around her body like a parachute. She had told me once that she always changed out of her postal worker uniform before she came home, choosing to get back in a comfortable muumuu as soon as she could each workday. I was glad that I didn't have to wear uniforms to work. I had more muumuus in my wardrobe than anything else.

I was disappointed to see that Lillimae had gained a few more pounds since the last time I'd seen her. She was now dangerously larger than I was.

Lillimae waddled up the walk and stumbled up the steps. I was so tired and weak, I couldn't move from my seat on the glider. I just sat there blinking. Charlotte ran back up on the porch and hugged Lillimae.

"We ran away from home!" Charlotte hollered eagerly.

"So I heard," Lillimae said, looking at me. "I called my answering machine from the Black Oak Saloon to find out that I had nine messages. Your husband called a few times, your mama, and your girl Rhoda. What in the world is goin' on, Annette? Are you in some kind of trouble?"

I rose. "They all called?"

"Yes, they all called, and you better get on that telephone and call every one of them back. What in the world has happened?" Lillimae fumbled in her large denim purse for her keys. We followed her into her neat little living room. "Your husband thinks you might be havin' a nervous breakdown. And Rhoda was beside herself with worry."

"Did Rhoda say anything else?"

"Like what? She wanted to know if you was here. She said her daughter told her Charlotte called her from a pay phone and told her y'all was on the way to visit with me."

"Is that all she said?"

Lillimae shrugged and eased down on her sofa, pulling Charlotte down next to her. Our luggage sat on the floor in front of Lillimae's feet.

"She's worried half to death! I wouldn't be surprised if she came down here with your husband," Lillimae exclaimed, fanning her face with her hand.

Charlotte looked tired and I knew she was. She had slept on the plane, but that had been hours ago. And neither one of us had eaten or drunk anything since we'd left the Miami Airport. Lillimae must have been reading my mind. She gave Charlotte a mild hug before she wobbled up from the sofa and took Charlotte into the kitchen.

"He's coming down here?" I asked Lillimae as soon as she returned to the living room.

"That's what he implied," Lillimae replied, fanning her face some more. "He thinks that if you are losin' your mind, you ain't got no business draggin' this child with you. He told me to call him when and if I seen you. Now if you don't get on that phone and call him up, I will."

"I don't want him to come down here!" I yelled, almost choking on my own tongue.

Just then Lillimae's living room telephone rang. She grabbed it on the first ring.

"It's Rhoda. She wants to speak to you," Lillimae told me.

CHAPTER 62

"Annette, what the hell is goin' on? What happened? Why didn't you call me? How could you just up and leave without sayin' anything to anybody?" Rhoda demanded.

I didn't know which one of her questions to answer first. I didn't know what to say to her. I stood in the middle of Lillimae's living room floor. My hands were so sweaty, I had to use both of them to hold the telephone and keep it from slipping to the floor. Lillimae stood close to me, her ear tilted toward the telephone receiver. I was glad that her arm was around my shoulder. Had it not been, I probably would have slumped to the floor.

"Annette, talk to me!" Rhoda yelled. I could usually hear a hum of activity on her end when we talked on the telephone. Other than her heavy breathing, there was nothing else but an ominous silence.

"I had to get away," I mumbled.

"Apparently! What did that fuckin' bitch say to you?"

"Huh? Who?"

"The bitch that's been terrorizin' you! Isn't that what this is all about?" Rhoda demanded.

"What did Jade tell you?"

"This is not about Jade! This is about you! Somethin' really fucked up had to happen for you to just up and run off the way you did. Pee Wee is on a rampage. He's talkin' about havin' you committed! And to be honest with you, I am with him all the way. You are not well! You need some professional help. But don't you worry, you are not in this alone! Somebody has to do somethin' before you hurt yourself or walk out in front of a bus or somethin'."

"I'm not crazy," I mumbled with uncertainty. I might not have been crazy according to the medical definition, but my mind was not on the right track. And it hadn't been since this mess started with that blacksnake! "Rhoda, what did Jade tell you?" I asked again, the back of my head feeling like it wanted to drop off.

"About what? You didn't tell her why you took off the way you did. She's just as stunned by all this shit as I am. I can't imagine what this stunt is doin' to poor Charlotte. And your poor mama and daddy are beside themselves. I am surprised that your daddy has not had another heart attack!"

"Rhoda, I need to know exactly what Jade told you."

Rhoda let out a loud, angry sigh. "Look, like I said, this is about you, not Jade. I want you, not Jade, to tell me what the hell happened. Now I really regret lettin' my daughter in on this whole mess."

"I can't talk about that right now. Not until you talk to your daughter. I want you to hear it from her."

"Hear *what* from her? What I want to hear needs to come from you! I want to hear an explanation from you!" Rhoda yelled so loud I had to hold the telephone away from my ear. "I can't believe you shared this with Jade and not me. I thought I knew you better than that."

I excused myself and went into Lillimae's kitchen for a glass of water. It took a lot of effort for me to return to the telephone. By that time Rhoda was snorting like a bull.

"Look, Pee Wee is packin' up to come down there to get you to bring your ass back here, so we can get you some help. Whatever you want to talk about, if you do, you can do it then. I'm sorry about yellin' at you, but this is too much. I love you to death and I am not goin' to stand by and let you go to pieces, not if there's anything I can do about it." Rhoda gasped, as if she'd suddenly had a revelation. "Wait a minute! Does this have anything to do with your work? Did Jade do somethin' stupid at the office? She's been actin' mighty peculiar since you disappeared."

"No. This has nothing to do with the office," I mouthed, biting my bottom lip so hard I trembled.

"So then this is about those telephone calls and notes and the rest of that shit from whoever that bitch is, right?"

"Uh . . . Right."

"I figured that. But I can't imagine anything she could have said or done to you, or sent to you, that was so bad you couldn't call me. Haven't I been there from the beginnin' of this shit? Me and Jade!" Rhoda didn't wait for me to respond. "I want to settle this shit just as bad as you do. As far as I am concerned, we are still in this together."

"Where is Jade now, Rhoda?"

"The poor little thing is in her room bawlin' like a panda. You know how crazy she is about you!"

"I'll be home as soon as I can get another flight back," I said calmly and meekly. "The sooner we get to the bottom of this shit, the better. I'm . . . I'm tired," I muttered.

"Don't you leave Lillimae's house. I don't think it's a good idea for you to be roamin' around by yourself. Pee Wee is comin' down there to get you and I just might come with him myself." Rhoda paused. "This has gone on long enough! Do you want me to come with Pee Wee to get you? I am truly afraid that you might flip out even more, and wander off and hurt yourself."

"No, you don't have to come down here. I am fine. Believe me, I am capable of bringing myself back home. Call Pee Wee and tell him not to come down here," I insisted.

"No, you call him. He's your husband. I mean, despite all this shit that's been goin' on, because of him, he is still your husband and this is somethin' you really need to work through with him. I mean, I don't blame you if you decide to divorce him after all is said and done. But the least you can do is get to the bottom of this mess. Believe me, you'll be glad you did."

"Rhoda, I need to get off the telephone now. I really need to get some rest."

"Annette, if you are not back here by tomorrow, I'm comin' down there myself, whether Pee Wee comes or not. Do you understand me?"

"Rhoda, I appreciate all you do for me. I appreciate you wanting to see me through this mess. But . . . it won't be that easy for us to work through this time." An eerie silence followed.

"What's that supposed to mean? I know I don't need to remind you, but we've worked through some pretty serious shit before."

"I know we have. But this time it won't be that easy." I don't know why I was surprised that Jade had not told her mother about our confrontation. "I will call you when I get home so you can come to my house. We can talk then."

"All right."

"And, Rhoda, come alone."

"Oh, you know I wouldn't drag Otis along with me for something like this."

"I know you wouldn't, but I didn't mean him," I choked.

"Are you tellin' me you don't want me to bring Jade with me?"

"Don't bring Jade with you," I said firmly. Every time I thought about what Jade had put me through, my blood boiled. I didn't know what kind of future I would have with Jade or Rhoda after my meeting with Rhoda.

CHAPTER 63

"Lillimae, thanks for letting me use your telephone. I will leave some money with you to cover these long distance calls I need to make," I said after I'd ended my conversation with Rhoda. I was just about to dial when Charlotte ran into the room, nibbling on an apple and holding a large glass of milk.

"Can I go back outside?" Charlotte wanted to know, looking from me to her confused aunt.

"Don't leave the front yard," I told Charlotte, glad she would not be in the room when I talked to her daddy.

I could feel Lillimae's eyes on my back as I turned back to the telephone. I didn't dial until I heard the door slam. Pee Wee didn't answer the telephone at our house, or at his barbershop. I was in no shape to talk to Muh'Dear or Daddy, so I didn't try to reach him there.

"What are you goin' to do now?" Lillimae asked as I slowly returned the telephone to its cradle.

"I'm going to be on the next plane back home," I said, so tired I could barely stand anymore. My legs felt like jelly as I struggled to make it to the sofa in the middle of Lillimae's living room floor.

"What did Rhoda say? And do you think you can tell me what this is all about?" Lillimae asked with her arms folded. She stood over me as I stretched out on my back on her sofa. I was the one fanning now.

"Lillimae, I don't want to put you in the middle of this mess, but I need to talk to somebody."

"I'm listenin'." Lillimae sat down on the arm of her sofa.

"A few weeks ago, somebody started sending me some nasty notes and other nasty shit through the mail." I stopped and rose up high enough to look out the window. I had to make sure Charlotte couldn't hear what I was saying.

Lillimae shrugged and gave me a puzzled look. "Go on."

"The notes were bad. I was threatened and called some ugly names." I paused and shook my head with my eyes closed. I didn't like the look that was on Lillimae's face when I opened my eyes. She was clearly losing patience, and she was one of the most patient and understanding people I knew. "It was a female. She called me up, too. At home and at work."

"And what was the reason? Who was this person?"

"She didn't say it right away. She took her time telling me why she was doing what she was doing to me. Finally, she told me that she was going to take my husband from me."

"Is that all? Girl, do you know how many times my husband's whores called me up and told me they were goin' to take my man and beat my ass if I stood in the way? That's just the way these ignorant hussies behave. They are too stupid to get a man the normal way."

"This was different. This person sent me a pair of Pee Wee's shorts. A used, dirty pair that I had seen him wear a few dozen times. She even called up some other married women and told them that I was fooling around with their husbands. Then they started to harass and threaten me, too!" I was waving my arms and didn't even know it until Lillimae grabbed my arms and held them down. But I kept talking. "She even sent a male prostitute to my house. I don't even remember all the shit she did. I even received a box full of horse shit in the mail from her!"

"She sent you some shit through the mail?" Lillimae screamed.

"Yes!" I exclaimed, blinking to keep from crying. I didn't really need to do that, because I was too angry to shed any more tears for a while.

Lillimae gave me a serious look as she bit her bottom lip. "Damn. Well, it sounds like you had a real cuckoo on your tail. Sounds like it's worse than I thought."

"It gets worse." I coughed to clear my throat, giving Lillimae a look so hard she flinched. "You remember Rhoda's daughter, Jade?"

Lillimae nodded. "She's not an easy person to forget. She's just a younger version of Rhoda. A little too mature for my taste. I never said anything when I was up in Ohio, but I thought that the girl spent too much of her time around grown folks. But she's still a child and it's a good thing she didn't stumble into this mess. If this is as serious as it sounds and she finds out about it, it could have a bad effect on her." Lillimae let out a loud breath and blinked. "If she doesn't already know about this, I don't think you should tell her."

"Jade knows all about this," I said hoarsely, staring off into space. I didn't need to tell Lillimae any more than that. One look from her told me that she knew it all.

"My God, my God. Maybe you better stay down here with me after all. You can't go back there yet, and face Rhoda with this mess!" Lillimae frantically wrung her hands as she spoke. This was the first time I had ever seen fear on Lillimae's face. "Does Pee Wee know it was Jade?"

I shook my head. "You're the only other person who knows. I just found out yesterday and I am still trying to deal with it. Now can you understand why I ran away the way I did?"

Lillimae nodded. "Girl, if I was you, I'd keep on runnin,'" Lillimae said.

CHAPTER 64

The next plane out of Miami that would help us get back to Ohio was scheduled to leave in six hours. I wanted to be on it. I didn't make it, though. Lillimae had insisted that Charlotte and I eat something, and get some rest. Since there was another plane leaving three hours later, I agreed.

And I changed my mind about calling my mother's house trying to locate Pee Wee. I desperately needed to talk to him now. But as soon as Daddy answered, fussing and cussing, I handed the phone to Lillimae.

For five minutes all she said was, "Yes, Daddy" and "I know, Daddy" before she said, "Please put Pee Wee on the telephone." I could tell from the sudden change on Lillimae's face that Pee Wee had come to the telephone.

She told my husband that Charlotte and I were all right. Without any prompting from me, she lied and told him that Charlotte and I had already left to return to Ohio. I was glad that she also told Pee Wee that she didn't know what time our plane was due to arrive.

Pee Wee was doing most of the talking, because suddenly all Lillimae started to say was "Yes, Pee Wee" and "I know, Pee Wee." I motioned for her to conclude the call and she seemed relieved again. Then she hung up and gave me a weary look.

"Girl, your husband thinks you have had, or are havin', a nervous breakdown."

"Maybe I did," I said stiffly. "I don't feel like myself. I feel so strange and light-headed."

"I guess you do, and you should. You must be pissed off as hell with that Jade." Lillimae clucked and shook her head, clearly disgusted. "And as good as you were to that child."

"Lillimae, why didn't I see this coming? The signs were all there. I could have nipped this in the bud a long time ago. It didn't have to come to this," I said.

"You didn't see it comin' because you didn't want to see it comin', girl. You are a good person and somethin' in you wouldn't let you think anything bad about somebody you loved."

"So it wasn't my fault?"

"This was Jade's fault. She's a child, but she's still old enough to know what she was doin'. Don't you dare blame yourself for this." Lillimae gave me a brief hug.

"I don't know how I'm going to deal with Pee Wee now," I mumbled.

"Pee Wee wasn't too happy to hear that I'd let you leave here without . . . a . . . an escort. Somebody to supervise you . . ." Lillimae screwed up her face and let out a short chuckle. "He's concerned that in your state of mind, you might wind up in Arizona or some other place, naked and babbling."

"Believe it or not, I am not crazy. At least I don't think I am. But I've changed my mind about flying back home. I really need some time to think, so I'm taking the train or the bus."

"Now I can't let you do that. You really need to get back home as fast as you can so you can face your husband . . . and Rhoda. You need to get this over with as soon as possible. What if Jade does or says somethin' against you before you can get home to defend yourself? I am sure that that girl is cookin' up more mess that'll make her come out smellin' like a rose."

I gave Lillimae a thoughtful look. "Speaking of roses, she used rose-scented paper when she sent me those notes," I said, blinking to hold back my tears. "Lillimae, how can I ever forgive Jade for doing this to me? I would have laid down my life for that girl."

"I can't answer that one. Like I said, she is still a child, so she can always fall back on that. Kids can't be held too accountable. I bet a dollar and a donut she is sorry as hell about all this now. I would even be willing to bet that this was all a game to her. She might have had a crush on your husband, but I don't think she really meant none of that mean stuff she said in them notes."

"But what about all that other stuff? It took a lot for her to go out to a pasture and gather up some horse shit, then box it up to send to me. That girl is so squeamish and prissy. For her to stoop that low, she had to mean business."

Lillimae nodded. "It don't matter. Don't deal with Jade like you would a grown woman, because it wouldn't be fair to her. Treat her like the child she really is."

"I hope you're right, Lillimae. I hope you're right." It didn't take much for Lillimae to get me to agree to fly back home. She was right. I needed to deal with Rhoda and Jade as soon as possible.

But first, I had to talk to Pee Wee about Jade. I needed to know if he had been with her. It would make all the difference in the world.

CHAPTER 65

I thought that Rhoda was the last person I wanted to face. But I realized I was wrong when the cab that Charlotte and I had taken from the airport to get to home stopped in front of my house. Muh'Dear was peeping out of one of my front windows, Daddy was peeping out the other.

Before I could even get out of the cab, both my parents had stumbled out to my front porch. Daddy was in a housecoat and his feet were bare. Muh'Dear had on a green, shapeless dress with an apron wrapped around her waist.

"Girl, have you lost my mind?" Daddy hollered.

I could tell that he was still weak from his heart attack. He had to rub his chest and cough right after he closed his mouth. Muh'Dear slapped him on his back a few times, not taking her eyes off me.

"I don't have anything to say until I talk to my husband," I declared, leading Charlotte into the house. My mind was more off than I thought. It was only then that I realized I had left my luggage at the airport.

"What? What do you mean, you ain't got nothin' to say?" Muh'Dear screamed, following me into my living room with Daddy close behind her. "You better have somethin' to say after puttin' us through this mess."

"We didn't know what had happened to you," Daddy wheezed, falling onto the sofa next to Pee Wee.

Pee Wee looked ten years older than he'd looked the last time I saw him. Which was the day I pummeled him with my fists at his cousin's house.

"You all right?" Pee Wee asked, rising.

Charlotte wasted no time leaping into his arms. "Daddy, we rode on some airplanes!" she yelled, like we had just returned from the adventure of a lifetime.

"Charlotte, go to your room," I said gently, easing down on the other end of the sofa.

Pee Wee seemed so submissive it scared me. All I could think about was him and Jade being together. The thought was so painful, I almost passed out just looking at him and picturing him on top of her, making passionate love to her perfect little body.

"Again? How come I all the time have to go to my room when I didn't do nothing bad?" Charlotte complained, stomping across the floor.

"You need to get some rest," I said, even more gently. "You've had a very long day."

"Nuh-uh! I don't need no rest!"

"Girl, get up them steps to your room before I get a switch," Daddy said, sounding so weak and hoarse he could barely be heard.

Charlotte shot up the stairs, stomping all the way to her room. Daddy didn't need to take a switch to her, but the way she was howling you would have thought that he had. As soon as I heard her slam the door to her room, I looked from Pee Wee to Muh'Dear to Daddy. All eyes were on me.

"Muh'Dear, Daddy, if you two don't mind, I need to talk to my husband."

Muh'Dear and Daddy frowned and looked at each other and then back to me.

"We ain't gwine no place until you tell us what's wrong with you. I don't care how grown you get, you still a child to me," Daddy said gruffly, sounding much stronger now.

"And another thing, Pee Wee is your husband true enough, but we done had you a lot longer than he has." Muh'Dear paused and gave Pee Wee a smug look.

He didn't even react. All he did was stare along the side of the wall. As a matter of fact, he didn't seem to be reacting much at all since I'd walked in the door.

Before anybody could say another word, somebody started pounding on my front door like they were trying to break the door down. Muh'Dear went to answer it. My first thought was that it was Rhoda. The knocking was so hard and insistent, my mind told me that if it was Rhoda, she was knocking that way because she was just that mad. But I didn't even want to think about what it was that had made her so mad: me running away or something Jade had told her.

For the first time in years, I was glad to see Scary Mary at my door. She was trying to get in the house so fast that she almost knocked Muh'Dear down.

"Annette, girl, folks runnin' around here sayin' you done left Pee Wee for another man," Scary Mary said, almost choking. I didn't know if she was choking on her own breath or if her false teeth had slipped loose like they often did when she got excited.

"I declare!" Muh'Dear exclaimed with a stunned look on her face.

"What happened? That man didn't want you after all?" Scary Mary scoffed, placing her hands on her lumpy hips. "You ought to know by now that Pee Wee is the best you'll ever do."

"I did not run off with another man," I said. "Now can I be alone with my husband?" I asked calmly, looking at nobody in particular. I didn't have to look around to see what I already knew. I could feel all the anger around me.

"We ain't gwine no place!" Muh'Dear roared. Daddy and Scary Mary nodded.

"Not until we find out what's done got into you," Scary Mary added.

She was just as annoying as my parents were. However, her intrusion gave me the courage I needed to stand my ground. "Fine. Stay here," I said, turning to Pee Wee. "Can I see you in the kitchen for a few minutes?"

He let out a deep sigh and nodded.

I shot a warning glance at everybody else. "Y'all can stay here as long as you want to. But I am not saying anything until I talk to my husband *alone*," I said, firmly. "Then I'll tell y'all everything you want to know."

"Is you fin to divorce Pee Wee?" Scary Mary yelled, taking a few steps in my direction. She seemed to be enjoying this drama. Her lips were trembling, her eyes were wide, and a smile was threatening to take over her face.

Pee Wee struggled up off the sofa and followed me into the kitchen with his head bowed.

"Should I have a drink first?" he asked, a stony look on his face. "I know before all this is over with, I am goin' to need a few."

"I am sure you do need a few drinks. I know I do. But I want us both to be sober until after we talk."

"So. You want to start from the beginning and tell me everything that's been goin' on? What made you run off, Annette? Is there another man?"

I gave Pee Wee a guarded look and shook my head. The truth was, I didn't know where to start. For one thing, I was glad to find out the identity of my tormentor. But knowing *who* it was was one thing, knowing it was someone so close to me was almost as unbearable as the abusive telephone calls and nasty notes. I was really beginning to wonder if I was crazy.

One minute I was glad that I had found out what I now knew. The next minute, I wished that she had remained anonymous. I couldn't decide if I was better off knowing, or not knowing.

CHAPTER 66

"I just want to know one thing. Did you fuck Jade?" I blurted out, watching Pee Wee's eyes. He was not a good liar. His eyes usually gave him away. His eyes blinked a lot and shifted from side to side when he was lying. I couldn't remember the last time I'd caught him in a lie. "And don't bother lying to me. She told me everything . . ."

Pee Wee's face froze. His skin was as dark as mine. I don't know if I imagined it or not, but for about five seconds, he was as white as a sheet. When he regained his normal color, he scratched the side of his head and looked at me through narrowed eyes. I was confused because he didn't blink but his eyes did dart from side to side. "Woman, are you standin' here askin' me if I touched my best friend's teenage daughter?"

"That's right. Did you?"

"If I didn't know no better, I would swear that *I* was losin' my mind. I can't believe my ears!" Pee Wee moved toward me, I moved back until I bumped into the refrigerator. "First you accused me of Betty Jean and that was bad enough. But Jade? What in the hell makes you think I touched that *child*?"

"She was the one who was sending me those notes and all the

rest of that shit. She was the one who was calling me up. She was . . . she was the woman who wanted to take you away from me."

Pee Wee's mouth dropped open and he stumbled a few more steps forward in my direction. For a moment I thought he was going to fall flat on his face.

"Jade?" He said her name, frowning like it was an obscenity. "Jade was the one stirrin' up all that shit with them notes and packages and phone calls?" Pee Wee paused and gave me the most incredulous look he'd ever given to me. "When—how could Jade do somethin' like that to you—and to me?" He stopped and rubbed his head, then his stomach. "This is enough to make me sick!" he yelled, stumbling backward this time. "What in the world was she thinkin'?"

"That's what I'd like to know. I treated her like my own child," I sniffed. I didn't even know what I was saying anymore. "I guess her relationship with you meant more to her than her relationship with me."

"What? Well, I didn't put her up to it!"

"Maybe you didn't, but that doesn't mean you didn't fuck her."

"Woman, if you don't get some professional help, I am goin' to have you committed! This done gone on long enough, and I ain't havin' no more of this crazy-ass shit!" Pee Wee was waving his arms like a windmill.

"What's goin' on in that kitchen?" Daddy yelled from the living room. "What's all that racket in there?"

"It's all right, Daddy," I yelled back. I continued speaking in a much lower voice. Even though it was Pee Wee who was the one talking loud enough to be heard outside of the kitchen. "She sent me a pair of your shorts," I said to Pee Wee, almost in a whisper. "Your funky, raggedy-ass drawers!"

"Well, the girl did always make herself at home here—and you encouraged her to do it! She slept and ate here two, three times a week. And I know you think I don't know about it, but I seen more than one piece of shit mailed to this address with her name on it. Just last week that nosy-ass mailman, Moshay, had me sign for a package from that porno shop on Sawburg that was addressed to Jade. I know I shouldn't have done it, but I opened that package! Shit, this is my address and she had no right to be havin' her shit sent here. You know what it was? Some fruit-flavored condoms! I threw that shit in the trash where it belonged!" Pee Wee stopped long enough to catch his breath. It was cool in our kitchen, but beads of sweat had formed all over his face. "She could have walked up in here any time she wanted to and took whatever she wanted—and that's just what she did. If I was stupid enough to be fuckin' around, do you think I'd be stupid enough to leave a pair of my funky drawers lyin' around so somebody could get a hold of 'em? Don't you know me well enough by now to know I ain't that stupid?"

"I figured she was lying," I said in a weak voice with my head bowed. "I just had to hear it from you."

"If you figured she was lyin', why did you come at me the way you did? Let's get one thing straight right now. I love you and I love my daughter. I done lost my mama and my daddy, so you and Charlotte the most important people in my life. I work my fingers to the bone tryin' to take care of you and her. Do you think I would risk losin' all that for Jade, or any other woman, for that matter?"

"What about Rhoda?" I barely managed. I couldn't imagine how Rhoda was going to react when she heard what Jade had done.

"What about Rhoda?"

"I will have to tell her something. She and Otis will need to know all of this."

"Jade is their problem. Let them deal with her the best way they can. I am through with this mess." Pee Wee snapped his fingers, like he was dismissing the whole ugly conversation. He was, because he started walking toward the door.

"Wait!" I yelled. He stopped and glared at me. "Did you bring your things home?"

"I did. But I can pack 'em up and get up out of here again. And let me tell you right here and now, if I do leave again I ain't comin' back. I can take only so much of this foolishness."

"I want you to stay home because that's where you belong."

Pee Wee started walking toward the door again but he stopped to answer the telephone. A deep frown appeared on his face right away. He handed me the telephone and left.

It was Rhoda.

CHAPTER 67

"Annette, I'm on my way over there," Rhoda said in a distant voice.

I could still hear the telephone ringing in my ears. I didn't know if I was experiencing some kind of delayed reaction or what. But hearing Rhoda's voice had an affect on me: I felt somewhat relieved. At least she wanted to hear what I had to say.

"I don't know if now is a good time, Rhoda. I got a crowd here, and it won't be easy to speak in private," I told her.

"So? I don't have anything to say that your company can't hear," Rhoda said evenly.

"But I do," I let her know. "I have a lot of stuff to say that . . . even you might not want to hear."

I didn't wait for Rhoda to reply. I just hung up the telephone and slumped down into a chair at my kitchen table. I didn't know what Pee Wee had said to Muh'Dear, Daddy, and Scary Mary to keep them out of the kitchen. But I was glad that they were still in place when Rhoda arrived ten minutes later.

"Annette, what the hell did you do to my baby girl?" Rhoda hissed as soon as she roared into my kitchen with a jacket on over her white terry-cloth bathrobe.

She had left her house in such a hurry, she had on two different shoes.

"Before I say anything, you need to tell me what Jade told you," I said, rising.

"I got the whole story from her when I told her I was on my way to see you."

"You got *her* story. I can't imagine what her story was," I smirked.

"Look, I know you are havin' some emotional problems, and that is as good an excuse as any. You are not responsible for your actions and I can understand why. But I will be damned if I stand by and let this madness you've been goin' through be blamed on my child!"

"Hold on," I said, holding up my hand. "What was it that I was supposed to have blamed on Jade?" I left my hand up in the air right in Rhoda's face.

"You accused her of sendin' you those notes! You accused her of makin' those telephone calls!" Rhoda let out a maniacal laugh. "And in the state you are in, I am surprised you didn't accuse me!"

"Jade denies doing that shit?"

"Of course she denies it!" Rhoda said through clenched teeth. "Why wouldn't she? She didn't do any of that shit, and I know she didn't!"

"And you believed her before even hearing from me?"

"Look, I *know* my child. I *know* she would never pull some shit like that."

I gave Rhoda a look that made her face drop. "Rhoda, you don't know Jade like I do."

Rhoda was already angry and she looked it. But now she looked puzzled, too. "What are you tryin' to say?"

"I know your daughter better than you do, and what I know is not nice. That's why I didn't want to face you."

"No, you didn't want the truth. That's what you didn't want to face! And the truth is, you need professional help. But rather than admit that you've lost your mind, you think you can use my baby as a scapegoat! I won't stand for it!"

"Listen to me, Rhoda." I had to breathe through my mouth to keep from having a panic attack, but it felt like I was having one anyway. I was surprised that I was still able to talk. "Rhoda, you don't know your own daughter half as well as you think you do. As savvy as you are, and have always been, you have the nerve to walk around thinking Jade is still a virgin! How naive can you get?"

Rhoda gasped so hard she almost lost her breath. "How would you know . . ."

"Because I was with her for the *two* abortions she had!"

Rhoda gasped again, and this time she almost collapsed. With her hands shaking, she pulled out a chair and sat down. "I'll bet it was that Hawkins boy who took advantage of Jade . . . or that Ralston boy."

"Rhoda, listen to me. Jade got around like a record. Just about anybody could have made her pregnant." It hurt me to say those words, so I knew that it had to be extremely painful for Rhoda to hear them.

"Jade would never go that far on her own. It had to be . . . They had to get her drunk or rape her or somethin'!"

"Rhoda, I wasn't there when it happened, so I don't know. But I can tell you one thing, your daughter is not that innocent."

"She made a couple of mistakes. I will talk to her and get the truth. Then I will talk to those boys' families. Both of them are over twenty-one, so I intend to prosecute them!"

"Rhoda, your innocent daughter licked another girl's pussy right in my house in my guest bedroom. I saw her with my own eyes, and it didn't look like she was being taken advantage of."

Rhoda made a noise that sounded like the cries of a wounded animal. Before I knew what was happening, she leaped up from her chair, and was all over me, beating me with both hands at the same time.

CHAPTER 68

Rhoda pummeled me for a few seconds with her fists. Then she started bombarding me with items she snatched off the counter next to my refrigerator. An empty plate cracked in two as it slammed against the side of my head. A pan whizzed past my head, missing me only because I ducked. I was on the floor, lying on my side like a seal, twisting and turning, trying to get up and away.

"How dare you! You lyin' bitch!" Rhoda screamed.

Even though I was being beaten to a bloody pulp, I was still concerned about other people more than I was myself. I didn't yell or cry out for help because I didn't want to disturb Muh'Dear or any of the rest of the folks in my living room. The more Rhoda beat me, the more I pressed my lips together so that I could keep my cries down to a low, kittenlike whimper.

"Don't you know who you are fuckin' with?" She snatched a wet dishrag off the side of the sink and started swinging that at me, too. It cracked against the sides of my face like a whip.

I was the kind of person who would run away from a fight. Everybody who knew me knew that. I had defended myself only those two times along the way, and I had been totally justified. I loved Rhoda. She had been my best friend for many, many years. She had killed for me. But I had to draw the line somewhere.

Just as she was about to come at me, wielding a long-handled fork, I managed to wobble up from the floor, holding the tail of my muumuu, which was smeared with blood from my busted lip and scratches on my face. When I grabbed Rhoda by her wrists and shook the fork to the floor, she gasped and looked totally surprised. There was at least one advantage to being a big woman: I was as strong as a mule.

As hard as she struggled, Rhoda could not get loose from my grip. I shook her for a few moments. She felt and looked like a rag doll in my massive hands. There was a look on her face that I will remember until the day I die. She looked surprised, frightened, and sad all at the same time. When I got tired of shaking her, I pinned both of her arms behind her back and held her there, looking her straight in the eyes. I held on to her wrists the same way that Pee Wee had held on to mine when I'd attacked him in his cousin's house.

In all of the years that I had known Rhoda, I had never seen her show fear. Until now.

"You're hurtin' me," she whimpered with a look on her face that resembled a deer caught in somebody's headlights.

I nodded. "I want you to leave my house," I said, surprised that I sounded so calm.

Before either of us could speak again Pee Wee, Daddy, Muh'Dear, and Scary Mary burst into the kitchen, all looking like wild people.

"What in the world is goin' on in here?" Muh'Dear wanted to know. She looked from Rhoda to me, her mouth hanging open like a dipper.

"Sounded like y'all was tearin' down the house," Scary Mary said, fanning her face with her hand. She almost looked amused as she padded across the floor and stood next to me.

I still had Rhoda in a death grip, my hands around her wrists like handcuffs. She was still struggling to get free.

"Annette, you turn Rhoda loose!" Pee Wee ordered, holding up his hand as he moved toward me. "Y'all done both lost your minds!"

"What she do to you?" Daddy asked me, leaning against the stove, rubbing his chest with his crooked, arthritic hand.

"It's all right," I said, realizing how stupid that sounded even before I got it out of my mouth. It was not all right. I never thought I'd see the day that Rhoda would raise her hand to me. And I never thought I'd see the day that I would do what I had done to her.

Pee Wee pried my hands from around Rhoda's wrists. I think I'd surprised Rhoda more than I'd surprised myself. She had the most incredulous look on her face as she rubbed her wrists and backed toward the kitchen door.

"Will somebody tell me what in the world is happenin' in here?" Muh'Dear insisted.

She dabbed at my lips with a wet paper towel. I was surprised to see the blood on it.

"Y'all in here actin' like savages!"

"I want you out of my house," I said, pointing to Rhoda. The look she gave me was downright frightening. Her eyes didn't blink, nothing on her face moved. "I said I want you out of my house, Rhoda," I repeated, moving toward her.

If anybody had told me that I was the only thing that could frighten Rhoda, I would have laughed. After I'd finished laughing, I would have told them that they were crazy. This was the same woman who had killed and gotten away with it so that she could kill and kill again.

Rhoda left my house through the kitchen door, dragging her tiny feet like they weighed a ton.

I looked from Pee Wee to the rest of the people in the room. "I don't want to talk about this. Not tonight, not ever," I said, moving toward the door.

"Girl, I know you don't think we ain't gwine to get to the bottom of this mess," Scary Mary said, following me from the kitchen back to my living room. Everybody else filed behind her, looking like black sheep.

"Rhoda's daughter was the one sendin' them notes and makin' them phone calls to Annette," Pee Wee said.

There were enough gasps in the room to put out a burning bush.

"Why?" Muh'Dear shouted, a wild-eyed look on her face.

Pee Wee shrugged. "Jade got a notion in her that me and her was goin' to be together if she chased Annette out of town," he explained, looking embarrassed.

There were more gasps.

"What? Why—*you*? What in the world would a pretty young girl like Jade want with a dried-up old fossil like you?" Scary Mary roared. "*I* wouldn't even want you!"

Pee Wee looked at me and snickered. I knew he couldn't help himself.

I let out a painful sigh and then I went upstairs to my bedroom. I crawled into my bed, clothes and all.

CHAPTER 69

I had been in bed for about an hour when Pee Wee finally entered our bedroom.

"Baby," he said, patting the side of my hip. I had my back to him.

"I don't want to talk about what happened between me and Rhoda," I muttered, hoping he couldn't tell from my voice that I had been crying. I had cried so that my eyes became so swollen I couldn't even close them. I was sorry that I couldn't because it hurt to see all the blood smeared on my pillow.

"That's fine with me. I just want to make sure you are all right. You've been through a lot lately."

"I'm fine," I said. I didn't turn over, but I did reach up and squeeze Pee Wee's hand. He squeezed back.

I slept like a baby that night. When I woke up, Pee Wee was sitting on my side of the bed, just staring at me. He smiled.

"I think I need to take you on a vacation," he said. "You need somethin' to fix up your mess of a life."

"In that case, you'd better take me on a vacation to see the Wizard of Oz," I told him, struggling to sit up. "You didn't fuck Betty Jean. And you certainly didn't fuck Jade," I stated. "Just tell me . . . Tell me you didn't," I said with a pleading look.

Pee Wee let out a deep breath, shook his head, and clasped his hands.

"I didn't. Why should I, when I got me a queen like you?" he asked, giving me a look that almost reduced me to tears, again.

"Well, I don't feel like anybody's queen today," I admitted as I rubbed the side of my face, and the top and sides of my head, all of the places where Rhoda had struck me. "Do I have black eyes?"

Pee Wee shook his head. "No, but them scratches don't do much for you. They look like spiderwebs."

I gave him a pensive look. "I can't believe Rhoda jumped on me," I swooned, rubbing the side of my face.

Pee Wee gave me a serious look before he replied, "I can."

"I am going to miss her," I whispered. "We'll never get past this."

Pee Wee stared at me with a half smile on his face. Then he broke into a broad grin, licking his lips with his tongue before he told me, "Yes, you will."

I shook my head and gave him a thoughtful look. "I hope you can forget all this. I mean, all that shit I said about you and Betty Jean, and you and Jade."

"Oh, I ain't worried about none of that," he said, making a dismissive gesture with his hand. "But I tell you one thing, I hope you don't never hit me again. I had knots on my face and head for days."

He laughed. I laughed, even though I was falling apart inside.

"When do you plan on goin' back to work?" Pee Wee asked, gently touching my hand.

"Soon. That's if I still have a job."

"I don't think you have to worry about that. Old man Mizelle called the other night to see how you were doin'. He advised me to keep you off work for at least another two weeks."

"Oh." I stared at a crack on the wall. "What did you say about a vacation?"

"You want to go over to Erie for a few days?"

I grinned and shook my head. "Pennsylvania?" I gasped. "I thought you meant a *vacation* vacation. Like a few days at a bed-and-breakfast in Connecticut or a weekend in Atlantic City." I chuckled, even though it hurt. "I'd rather go back to work."

"Whatever you say, baby. But if you change your mind, all you have to do is let me know."

I didn't sleep at all that night. We made love so many times, I lost count.

CHAPTER 70

When the telephone on the nightstand rang the next morning and woke me up, I assumed it was Muh'Dear or even worse, Scary Mary. Even though I had told them that I didn't want to talk about what happened in my kitchen between Rhoda and me, I knew that they would both badger me until I did.

"Yes," I mumbled. Pee Wee's side of the bed was empty. While I was clutching the telephone in one hand, my other hand grabbed a note he'd left on the nightstand: "Gone to work. Love you," it said. There was a p.s. that said, "I took Charlotte to school. Please get some rest and be ready for me when I get home . . ." I smiled.

"Hello," I said, sitting up.

There was nothing but silence and then a low whimper. "Annette."

It was Rhoda!

"What the hell—" It seemed like every emotion known to man consumed me, all at the same time. I wanted to cry, scream, throw something at the wall. I wanted to run outside and jump up and down. I wanted peace.

"Annette, please don't hang up. I beg of you." Rhoda had never begged me for anything in her entire life. "*I need you!* I have somethin' to say to you."

"You don't have anything to say to me that I'd want to hear, Rhoda!"

"Listen to me! Jade told me the truth last night." Rhoda blurted the words out so loud and fast, it took me a moment to comprehend what she was saying. "She told me the truth about everything. I . . . I'm so sorry."

"You should be," I said gruffly. "You know me well enough to know I wouldn't make all that shit up."

"You're right. And, like I said, I am so sorry." Rhoda choked back a sob.

There was more silence. Finally, I spoke. "So where do we go from here?"

"You've always been there for me. When my . . . When my son died, you dropped everything and you came runnin' right away, all the way from Pennsylvania."

"And I'd do it again, Rhoda." I couldn't describe how I was feeling now.

"I need you to do it again . . ."

"What? What are you saying? You didn't do anything stupid, did you?"

"Other than what I did in your house last night, no. It's my daughter . . . my baby, Jade . . ." Rhoda stopped. She was crying so hard she was choking.

"Rhoda, calm down. Where are you?"

It took her a few moments to compose herself. "I'm at the Richland City Hospital," she said stiffly.

"Omigod! Rhoda, what's happened? Did you have another stroke? Why are you at the hospital?"

It was only a few seconds but it seemed like an eternity before Rhoda spoke again. "My daughter is dyin'. After I confronted her, she ran off and locked herself in her room. Then she . . . She swallowed . . . She swallowed some pills." Rhoda paused. "I'm about to lose her, too. *She wants to die!*"

CHAPTER 71

Rhoda and I were occupying a white plastic table in the hospital cafeteria, trying to eat some hard scones and drink some muddy coffee. After just a few minutes, we gave up. And it was just as well, because a thin film of some slimy shit settled on top of the coffee.

"Jade knows about me and Bully," Rhoda told me in a weak, dry voice.

"Jade knows a lot of things, Rhoda. Too much. She knows too much for her own good," I told her.

"Well, I've already packed Bully's things and I will escort him to the airport myself tomorrow evenin'. He won't be comin' back to my house. He won't be fuckin' me anymore. I shouldn't have let him . . . again. But . . . I just . . . I just wanted to be *loved* by a man, just one more time."

"You are loved, woman."

Rhoda shook her head. "Not the way I need to be."

I didn't remember much about my fight with Rhoda. I remembered grabbing her by her wrists. But she had some scratches on her face, too. And her lip was busted. I felt kind of strange looking at her. Here was a woman not even half my size. She had survived a stroke and lost both breasts. It seemed like she was slowly fading away. And that made me feel so sorry for her. I didn't even think about the fact that she had attacked me in my own house. I didn't know if I could ever get over that. But that was the least of my worries. Getting over Rhoda's attack was one thing. My main concern was getting over what Jade had done.

Interns, doctors, and nurses scurried about, the tails of their white jackets flapping like wings. The friends and relatives of other patients wandered in and out of the cafeteria with that lost look, a kind of desperation, on their faces that I was all too familiar with.

Rhoda and I had left Jade's room on the third floor only after Dr. Beatty, a sad-faced, elderly man who looked like he should have been in a hospital bed himself, assured us that she was going to be all right. She had swallowed a whole bottle of sleeping pills, but her stomach had been pumped. Otis and Bully were still in Jade's room, chanting some Jamaican prayers. Quite a few of Rhoda's relatives were on their way to Ohio: Her parents were coming in from New Orleans, and her son and some others from Alabama.

"What do you mean by that?" I asked, lifting my coffee cup, frowning at the slime. I set the cup back down, my eyes on Rhoda's face. Which, I was happy to see, had more scratches and knots than I'd originally noticed. And since I didn't remember doing anything but holding her by her wrists, I had to wonder what Jade had done to her when she confronted her. That girl!

Rhoda sniffed and lifted her chin. Her eyes were bloodred. "When was the last time your man made love to you?"

I shifted in my seat and looked around. "That's kind of personal. But if you must know, it was last night. It had been such a long time, I felt almost like a virgin again."

Rhoda gave me a pensive look. Then a look that was unbearably sad crossed her face. For the first time, she looked her age. "My husband hasn't made love to me in eight years," she said in a flat voice.

"Oh." I didn't know what else to say. "Uh . . . that's cold."

"Bully . . ." Rhoda dropped her head but she kept talking. "He couldn't keep his hands off me." Rhoda rolled her eyes up toward the ceiling, then at me. "The breast cancer, the stroke . . . Otis couldn't deal with it after all."

"But you stayed with him," I reminded her.

Rhoda shook her head. "He stayed with me. I wasn't goin' any place. Where would I go? What man in his right mind would want me? Just Bully. And to be honest with you, he'd stick his dick in a hog. He is the only man who has called me beautiful since I lost . . . since my cancer. And that stroke! You remember how long I had to walk around with my face hangin' like a basset hound! Bully . . . he called me. He called me all the way from London at a time when I really needed to be . . . needed. When that bitch he married took off, I insisted he come stay with us."

"What about Otis?"

"What about him?"

"You are still with him. How much does he know about you and Bully?"

Rhoda waved her hand and tilted her head. "He doesn't want a divorce. I tried to go that route, but he wants to remain a family."

"But does he know about you and Bully?"

Rhoda shrugged. "Like I said, I'm takin' Bully to the airport my-self tomorrow evenin'. He's goin' back to London to reconcile with his estranged wife. So, I am back where I started. Annette, I have to save what's left of my family."

"Jade's goin' to be fine, Rhoda," I said, squeezing her hand.

Rhoda wiped her eyes and nose with a napkin, then she took a sip of the grim coffee. "What she did to you was wrong. I know it. She knows it. She admitted to me that she was jealous of you and Pee Wee. Y'all had it all. Me and Otis, we have nothin' anymore."

I shook my head. "You still have your daughter, Rhoda. You still have Otis. You have your mama and your daddy and you still have your son. And . . . You still have me."

I went around to Rhoda's side of the wobbly table and gave her the hug she needed. I held her in my arms for five minutes as she cried on my shoulder.

"Do you want to see her?" she asked, gently pushing me away.

"Maybe it would be better if I waited . . ." I began.

"She's still unconscious. She won't even know you're in the room."

I followed Rhoda to Jade's room where Otis was on one side of her bed, mumbling some gibberish. Bully stood with his back to us, looking out the window. There was nothing to see out that window except the other side of the hospital. Nothing but orange bricks. Bully turned as soon as he heard us enter the room, and gave us a blank stare.

Jade was on her back, mumbling some gibberish, too.

"She's delirious," Otis said in an extremely tired and worried voice as he rubbed Jade's forehead. "De doctor man say she will be fine, praises to Jah."

"I'll pray for her," I said. As soon as I said that Jade opened her eyes.

Large tears slid down her cheeks to her lips. She sniffed and licked her lips dry, rubbing her eyes. She gave me a hard, cold look before she shifted her eyes and looked around the room. She let out a feeble moan and then she focused her attention on me again.

"Where am I? Who are you people?" she whimpered through trembling lips. "Am I dead?"

As upset as I had been with Jade, my heart just about broke in two.

Rhoda staggered before she fell into her husband's arms. Bully moaned and placed his head on my shoulder. I stood there, rubbing Bully's back and staring at Jade.

"She's got *amnesia*!" Rhoda sobbed. "My poor little baby doesn't even know me!"

CHAPTER 72

I could not believe how frail and frightened Jade looked. The beautiful head of hair that she was so proud of looked like a thick, tangled spiderweb. Dried snot hung from the bottom of her nose, on both sides. Her dried lips were cracked and bruised, like she had been biting herself.

She looked at me like she didn't know who I was, and for that I was grateful. I didn't know much about amnesia, but I did know that people could recover from it and regain all of their memory. However, I had heard of people who regained only part of their memory, permanently blocking out the things that were too painful. I didn't want Jade to get off that easily. I wanted her to eventually remember every single thing that she had done to hurt me. And I wanted her to remember it for the rest of her life, because I would.

There was a lot of work that had to be done. I knew that I had to face my nosy parents and that busybody Scary Mary, sooner or later. They were relentless. They wouldn't stop until they knew everything about what Jade had done to me.

Then I had to deal with Jade when the time was right, if she regained her memory. Our relationship would never be the same. I seriously doubted that I could continue to work with her at the same place of employment. As a matter of fact, if she did return to work, I planned to fire her immediately. But that wouldn't be the end of it. Jade had been such a huge part of my life that losing her would be like losing an arm or a leg.

Otis and Bully left the room to go to the cafeteria for coffee. A few minutes later a stout, grumpy nurse entered Jade's room with a cup containing some pills, a thermometer, and a chart. She chased us out so Rhoda and I left to return to the cafeteria.

"I don't know what I'll do if I lose her," Rhoda sniffed in the elevator, her head on my shoulder. "She's all I got. She's my only chance to be a grandmother."

"You won't lose her," I said sadly, knowing that I had lost Jade. "You can get past this." I gave Rhoda a firm hug before we left the elevator.

"And what about you?" she asked, squeezing my hand.

I bowed my head. "I've survived worse," I said evenly. "But then you already know that," I said, blinking at Rhoda. Somehow I managed a smile.

"I want you to know . . . I want you to know that what Jade did to you, it won't ever happen again. I promise. But she is still a child, my child, and I can't get past that."

"I know you can't get past that, Rhoda, and I don't expect you to choose me over your child. But don't forget, I love Jade, too. Despite all this, it's not the end of the world. We'll work through it."

"I can't tell you how sorry I am for what I did to you in your kitchen. I just snapped," Rhoda sobbed. She produced a handkerchief from her purse and blotted her eyes and nose.

"I just snapped, too," I said, biting my lip.

Rhoda and I joined Otis and Bully in the cafeteria. I wasn't surprised to see them drinking sodas while two cups of cold coffee sat off to the side on the table.

There was not much to talk about. I certainly had very little to talk about. I excused myself to go call Pee Wee to let him know what had happened.

The one telephone that I was able to locate on the same floor as the cafeteria was occupied. It was near a waiting room so I waited around for about ten minutes, listening to a redneck with a pony-tail yelling into the telephone about an Indian doctor who'd just performed an emergency C-section on his wife.

I don't know what made me do what I did next. But before I could stop myself, I was back in the elevator. I got off on the third floor, and with my head bowed, I padded past the nurse's station back to Jade's room. Despite what she had done to me, she was still that same little girl who had accused me of being Santa Claus.

The door to her room was ajar. I moved as quietly and quickly as I could. I stopped before I got all the way in the room. Jade was not in her bed, but I could hear her. I moved a little closer. She was in the bathroom, singing "I'm Every Woman," and dancing a jig like one of the *Soul Train* dancers! I leaned forward a little more. She was looking in the mirror, mugging like she was in Hollywood, pos-ing for her close-up.

With a heart that felt as heavy as a large rock, I backed out of the room and waited a few moments before I coughed loud enough to get her attention. While I was peeping around the door, Jade shot out of the bathroom like a cannonball and leaped back into the bed and pulled the covers up to her neck.

She immediately closed her eyes and started moaning, "Mmmm-mm . . . Where . . . am I . . . Where am I? Aarrggggh."

I couldn't resist what I did next. I moved over to the bed and stood over Jade with my arms folded. I didn't say a word, but there was a stern look on my face that I wanted her to see. She cracked open her eyes just enough to see me. And as soon as she did, she started babbling some more gibberish. She was still doing that when I left the room.

I went back to the cafeteria and hugged everybody good night. Even Bully. And then I left. I couldn't wait to get back to my house where I belonged.

CHAPTER 73

Charlotte cried when I told her that Jade was going to live with her grandparents in New Orleans for a while.

"But she didn't even come say good-bye," Charlotte sobbed. "Why is she leaving?"

"Well, she's going to go to college down there next year, and she wanted to get used to living there first," I explained.

"Oh," Charlotte said, drying her eyes. "I hope she brings me a present when she comes back."

That was it. Charlotte ran off to be with one of her friends who lived in the neighborhood, and she forgot all about Jade. Well, she didn't really forget about Jade, but she accepted the fact that Jade was not going to be around for a while.

Muh'Dear, Scary Mary, and Daddy had stopped badgering me. But only because I had told them the whole story. I knew that they wouldn't until I did. So I did.

I didn't tell Rhoda or Otis, or anybody else, what I'd seen when I'd peeped in Jade's hospital room that night. I didn't see any point.

It was Sunday, a few days after my visit to Jade at the hospital. Around six o'clock that evening, my telephone rang. I was in the kitchen alone. Charlotte was at the movies with Muh'Dear and Daddy. Pee Wee was in the living room slumped in front of the television with a can of beer and a plate of snacks.

"Auntie?" It was Jade.

"Jade."

"Auntie, please don't hang up. They are about to take me to the airport to go to New Orleans, and I wanted to say good-bye. And I just want to let you know how sorry I am about what happened. I didn't mean to hurt you."

"You did a pretty good job anyway."

"Auntie, please try to understand me. I thought Pee Wee wanted to be with me. I thought that if you were out of the way, me and him could be together. Honest to God, I did!"

"Well, you thought wrong, Jade. Pee Wee is a forty-five-year-old man. A successful man with everything in the world going for him. What did you think *you* had to offer him?"

"Just myself, Auntie. I'm pretty . . . I'm young. I thought he'd be glad to have me. He was like . . . He is like . . . so cute and funny and nice and everything. He looks at you like you are somethin' good to eat. I wanted me a man like that."

"First of all, he looks at *me* like I'm something good to eat. You just said so yourself. That doesn't mean he would have looked at you like that. What you need to do is find you somebody who will look at you the way my husband looks at me."

"I tried to kiss him one time and he cussed at me," Jade sobbed. "That was last year."

"You should have stopped there, Jade. Just because you throw yourself at a man doesn't mean he's going to catch you."

"But he looked at me all the time. Especially when I wore my white shorts," Jade said, defiant to the bitter end.

"Jade, I looked at you when you wore those white shorts. Everybody looked at you when you wore those white shorts. That means nothing. But just because people, men especially, look at you, that doesn't mean they want you. All you are doing when you walk around half-naked is attracting attention. But it's *negative* attention, baby. And believe me, that kind of attention won't get you anything but a baby you don't need, or a disease that might put you in the grave. Life is one game where people don't play fair."

"You mean people like me? Mama sat me down and talked to me for hours that night I . . . that night I . . . tried to kill myself. My daddy jumped in the mix. And even Uncle Bully tried to talk to me and here he is doing the wild thing with my mama!"

"That's your mama's business, Jade. What you don't seem to realize is, you are still a child." There was an uncomfortable pause. All I could hear was Jade breathing through her mouth. "By the way, I'm glad to see that you've recovered from your amnesia," I said.

"Huh? Oh, that? Yeah, I recovered from that! I feel fine!" Jade said, talking so fast she almost lost her breath. Then there was more silence. "Do you hate me, Auntie?"

"No, I don't hate you, Jade. I hate what you did to me."

"I didn't mean any of that mean stuff I said to you that night you found out."

"I know you didn't, Jade."

I wondered if I was just incredibly stupid and gullible, or if I was crazy after all. I had asked myself a thousand times how I could have let something like this happen.

Scary Mary had told me to my face, "Girl, you don't never give no woman, ugly or pretty, young or old, a position of power in your life, your house."

I had given Jade so much power in my life and in my home that it had overwhelmed her. And I had trusted her when I knew in my heart that I shouldn't have. No, I couldn't hate Jade for what had happened, no more than I could hate myself, because I was in it, too.

"Auntie, are you still there?" Jade asked, her voice just above a whimper.

"I'm still here. I was . . . just thinking about something else, that's all."

"I have to go now. Maybe one day, we can forget about this and you'll love me again."

"I still love you, Jade. Nothing can change that."

"Then maybe one day, you'll be my favorite auntie again?"

"Maybe I will."

"'Bye . . . Auntie."

"'Bye, Jade. Have a safe trip."

I hung up the telephone and wiped a tear from my eye. Pee Wee entered the kitchen, chewing and balancing an empty plate.

"I heard the telephone ring. Who was it?" he asked, heading to the refrigerator.

"Huh? Oh. Just some telemarketer," I said, turning my head so he wouldn't see my tears.

"Tryin' to sell you some shit you don't need?"

I was glad that he had his back to me, as he leaned his head inside the refrigerator. I wiped my eyes and nose on the tail of my muumuu. "Uh-huh," I mumbled. "Just another telemarketer, trying to sell me some shit I don't need."

Pee Wee removed two beers. I was glad he handed one to me.

GOD DON'T PLAY

Mary Monroe

ABOUT THIS GUIDE

The suggested questions are intended to
enhance your group's reading of
GOD DON'T PLAY
by Mary Monroe.

DISCUSSION QUESTIONS

1. Annette had a lot of things that other women wanted. She never thought that someone would want to destroy her to get what she had. Do you think that jealousy is one of the worst of the seven deadly sins?

2. Do you think that Annette should have told her husband about the first poison pen letter the same day she received it?

3. Knowing that Rhoda had committed murder more than once, do you think that Annette was asking for more trouble by asking Rhoda to help her identify and confront her stalker?

4. The average woman knows that it is not wise to give an attractive young woman too much power in her house. Do you think that Annette was just as much to blame as Jade for Jade falling in love with her husband?

5. Do you think that if Annette had been more assertive with Jade, she would not have taken advantage of Annette the way she did?

6. For a woman as streetwise as Rhoda, it was very unrealistic of her to believe that her daughter was so innocent. Do you think that Rhoda was in denial or just plain stupid when it came to her daughter?

7. Betty Jean seemed like the most likely one to be Annette's stalker. Did you think that she was the one, or did you guess the identity of the real stalker before Annette found out?

8. Pee Wee had no idea that another woman was in love with him and was trying to destroy his wife. But he had tried to warn Annette that her relationship with Jade was going to lead to trouble. Did you feel the same way?

9. When Annette found out who was stalking her, she went to pieces. Knowing how dangerous Rhoda was, she thought that it was better to run away. How would you have reacted in a similar situation?

10. When Rhoda attacked Annette in her kitchen, did Annette's reaction surprise you?

11. Afer Jade's attempted suicide, she pretended to have amnesia. When Annette walked into Jade's hospital room to comfort her, she saw Jade in the bathroom singing and dancing a jig. That's when she realized that Jade was still putting on an act. Do you think that Annette should have shared this information with Rhoda?

12. Annette was able to forgive Jade for all the pain she'd put her through. Would you be able to do that?

13. If someone you loved betrayed you the way Jade did Annette, would you ever trust another female friend again?

14. With Jade out of the picture, Annette and Rhoda resumed their relationship. But Annette knew that Jade would return some day. Do you think that Annette should have severed her relationship with Rhoda once and for all?

The following is a preview of
Mary Monroe's exciting new novel

DELIVER ME FROM EVIL

Available in stores September 2007

CHAPTER 1

A crude tattoo on his right bicep told the world that his name was
Wade. I recognized prison artwork when I saw it, but he didn't
look like a thug. At least not like any of the ones I knew. There were
no grills of tacky-looking gold teeth decorating his mouth like stale
corn. There was no thick gold chain wrapped around his neck like a
noose. With his neatly trimmed jet-black hair; smoky gray eyes; sharp,
handsome features; and a thin T-shirt and tight jeans hugging his
well-developed body, he looked like a low-income Lenny Kravitz.

Between sips from a can of Coors Light, he puffed on a thick blunt.
A strong haze swirled around his head like a halo. It was some pretty
good shit, too. I welcomed the immediate buzz I got from inhaling
the secondhand smoke. I hadn't smelled weed this strong and sweet
since I was a teenager, more than ten years ago. But within seconds
that halo around his head turned into a dark cloud and was moving
in my direction.

I swallowed a huge lump that was threatening to block my throat.
Then I held my breath as he dialed the number to the video store that
my husband owned and managed.

"Hello . . . Yes!" Wade said in a loud and gruff voice as soon as he
got a response on the other end. It sounded like he had a huge lump
in his throat, too. He coughed and cleared his throat, altering his
voice this time. "I need to speak to Jesse Ray Thurman." He talked

with the blunt dangling from the corner of his lips. "Put him on the phone. Put him on the phone right now," he ordered, a grimace on his face. "Dude, I ain't playing!" He even sounded like Lenny Kravitz.

The telephone, sitting in the lap of a wobbly bamboo chair, was so cheap looking, it resembled a child's toy. The Wal-Mart bag that he had removed it from lay on the floor, with the sales receipt peeking out like a white tongue. But the cheap telephone had a speaker feature, so I could hear my husband's response on the other end of the line from where I stood, a few feet away from Wade.

"You've reached Video-Drama located on Alcatraz near downtown Berkeley," my husband answered, sounding as cheerful and phony as a used-car salesman. "Please hold."

Wade's mouth dropped open so wide, the blunt fell to the floor, scorching the faded carpet. He immediately ground it out by stomping on it with the heels of his run-over, well-worn shoes, which he had probably picked up from Payless or Goodwill. It must have been hell for such a handsome man to be so broke in this day and age. I wondered where he'd gotten the money to buy the weed.

"This motherfucker put me on hold!" he hollered, looking at me with an incredulous look on his face. "What kind of dumb-ass motherfucker are you married to?" he yelled, shaking the beer can at me like it was a weapon.

"He doesn't know I've been kidnapped," I whimpered. My eyes were itching, and the insides of my nostrils felt like they were on fire. I held my breath again. I could barely feel my lips when I spoke. "Give him time . . . He'll be with you in a minute. Please give him time."

"Fuck this shit! You better be right! I ain't got all day! They got another line I can call at that damn place?"

"They . . . they have two lines, but . . . but if you call the other one, you'll just get put on hold again," I managed, my words rolling out of my mouth like rocks. "Please give him time," I begged. The inside of my mouth was so dry, it felt like my tongue had stuck to the roof.

I closed my eyes and prayed that the man who was about to demand a half-million-dollar ransom for my release was not going to run out of patience. I knew from experience that a caller to my husband's business could be put on hold for one minute or much longer and left listening to an instrumental version of "Strangers in the

Night." That was why when I needed to call him up at work, I usually called him on his cellular phone.

"This is Video-Drama," my husband said after what seemed like an eternity. "We are located—"

"Shut the fuck up!" Wade roared, cutting my husband off in mid-sentence.

"Excuse me?" Jesse Ray said, still sounding cheerful and phony.

"I need to speak to Jesse Ray Thurman. Right now!" Wade glared at me with such an extreme sneer, it looked like his face had been turned inside out. He looked raw and more menacing than ever. Now he did look like some of the thugs I knew.

There was a pause before Jesse Ray responded. A pause that was long enough to make my blood pressure feel like it was about to go through the roof.

"Speaking. How can I help you today?" Jesse Ray continued, almost singing his words. "We are here to fill all of your video needs. We've got everything from the earliest to the latest Hollywood hits to—"

"I said shut the fuck up! I got a gun, and I know how to use it!"

My husband let out a gasp that was so loud, it made me jump. "What did you say?"

"You long-eared motherfucker, I know you ain't deaf. I know damn well you heard what I just said. But in case you didn't, I will say it again. I got a gun, and I know how to use it!" I hadn't seen a gun yet, and I hoped I wouldn't.

The hollow silence that followed for a few moments was almost unbearable. It seemed like every sound in the world had come to an end. My body had begun to let me down. It felt like spiders were crawling over every inch of my flesh.

Then there was a muffled hiss. Jesse Ray cleared his throat before he responded. "Who in the world is this?" His voice was almost as hollow as the silence I'd just endured.

Wade leaned his head to the side and sucked in a deep, loud breath. Then he spoke like he was reading a script. "Listen and listen good, motherfucker. Don't you say another goddamn word until I finish. Now, this is the score. *We got your wife!*" He paused, winked at me, and then lowered his voice. "I just wish she wasn't so damn pretty. It's hard to keep my eyes off a woman with such a nice, juicy petite body, such big brown eyes, cinnamon brown skin, and a head full of thick black hair falling across her shoulders. She looks like a film star." He sighed and moaned, sounding like the same obscene caller who had called me up one night a few years ago.

I didn't think that I was "so damn pretty," but I was attractive. The rest of his description was quite accurate. This situation was more about my husband's money than my looks, but it didn't matter. I was still nervous and frightened about how it was going to turn out.

Wade increased the volume on the speaker. Now I could even hear Jesse Ray breathing on the other end of the line. My husband was a healthy man, but by the way he was wheezing, coughing, and clearing his throat now, you would have thought that he was struggling to stay alive. And I guess in a way that was probably true. He worshipped the ground I walked on and had once told me that if I died before him, he didn't know how he'd be able to go on living.

There was another pause before Jesse Ray responded again. "You need to tell me who this is, and you need to tell me now," he said in an impatient and amused tone of voice.

"You'll find out soon enough. Like I just said, we got your wife. And what a fine piece of tail she is! If you want her back with her pussy in one piece, you'll do everything I tell you to do. Now, first thing is, you don't call no cops, and you don't tell nobody else about this. If you do, I'll know about it, and you can forget about ever seeing this sweet little woman of yours again. Any questions?"

Jesse Ray let out an impatient sigh. Then he laughed. *He laughed.* He cackled long and loud, like a hyena. My mouth dropped open, and I stared at the telephone. My life was at stake, and my husband was laughing!

"Man, what the fuck is wrong with you? Didn't you hear what I just said?"

"I heard you," Jesse Ray said, still laughing.

"You think I'm playing? You think this is funny?"

"Hell, yeah, this is funny," Jesse Ray said, mumbling profanities under his breath. "But I got work to do, so you have to call me back at a better time."

I sat there in slack-jawed amazement. I could not believe what I had just heard.

"Harvey, I know this is you. I've heard you use that same voice when you do your lame-ass impressions. I must say, you are beginning to sound more and more like the Godfather, so keep practicing," my husband said in a stern voice. "But don't practice on me. I'm a busy man."

"Shit! Look, I am not playing with you! Damn you to hell!"

The room got so quiet, I could hear the water dripping in the sink in the bathroom across the hall.

"Are you still there, motherfucker?" Wade shouted, kicking over a chair.

"Yes, I'm still here."

"I told you, I wasn't playing with you! Do you understand what I'm saying?"

"And I am not playing with you, either, Harvey. You are my only brother and I love you, but you are one sick-ass puppy, and you need some serious help! I begged you for years to get some therapy, and you didn't. Now look at what you are up to. Now let me get off this phone so I can get back to work."

Wade and I looked at each other at the same time. My mouth was hanging open wider than his. My husband had just hung up.

CHAPTER 2

Wade redialed the number to the video store, one of three that my husband owned and managed. Jesse Ray had worked hard to build his small empire, and he had taken me along for the ride. Not as an equal partner, but more like a paid companion. He never let me forget that it was *his* business, period.

"Woman, you are a lot more trouble than you are worth," Wade shouted at me, giving me a cold look. "You better pray that your old man comes through with that half a million bucks. All this drama I'm going through, I better get paid! What the hell kind of fool did you marry? What kind of man puts his wife's kidnapper on hold?"

"I told you, my husband doesn't know I've been kidnapped," I reminded.

"This is some . . . Hello? Yes, I need to speak to Jesse Ray Thurman," Wade yelled, tapping the top of the telephone with his finger.

"Herro. This is Vlideo dwama." The cute but heavily accented voice that answered this time belonged to Kim Loo, the twenty-two-year-old Korean woman who worked for my husband. Of all the people who worked for my husband, Kim was the most valuable. As his assistant manager in the main store, she was dependable, punctual, trustworthy, and smart. She even took care of all the accounting. Even though Kim was young and had some mysterious affiliations with the local Asian massage parlors, I didn't worry about her working alone with my husband. She looked like a sumo wrestler and had the face of a mule.

"I don't believe this," Wade hissed. He glared at the telephone like it was a pile of shit. He glanced at his watch as I sat there, with my heart beating about a mile a minute. "I said, put Mr. Thurman back on the telephone."

"Misser Turman busy," Kim Loo said. "I happy to assist you. We are located at—"

"Listen, bitch, I need to speak to your boss!"

"Misser Thurman very busy," Kim Loo answered in a shaky voice. In addition to the massage parlors, Kim had also run with one of the toughest Asian street gangs in the Bay Area. She was not a timid girl, but she sounded frightened now.

"Busy my ass. Look, china doll, you put that black-ass nigger back on this telephone right now, or I'm going to come over there and teach him, and you, a lesson you won't never forget!" Wade warned, still looking at the telephone with disgust.

"Misser Thurman reely busy talking to his brother on other telephone," Kim Loo explained. I was glad to hear that she no longer sounded frightened, but she did sound impatient. And under the circumstances, I didn't know which was worse.

My biggest fear was that she would put Wade on hold for ten minutes or hang up on him altogether. Like Jesse Ray, she was probably thinking that this call was a prank or some disgruntled customer. But if Jesse Ray was on the other line, talking to his brother, Harvey, he knew now that the caller he'd just hung up on was not his brother. That gave me some hope. I was almost as anxious to get this "incident" underway as Wade was.

"Shit! I'm going to stay on this phone. You let your boss know that!"

"Who I say is calling?"

"Just tell him this concerns his wife and her whereabouts and her safety," Wade answered with a smug look on his face. "You tell him that I'd like to make him an offer he can't refuse. For the right price, he can have his wife back."

There was some mumbling on my husband's end and, suddenly, a sharp, shrill yell. I couldn't tell if it was coming from Kim Loo or Jesse Ray. But the next voice I heard belonged to my husband. "This is Jesse Ray Thurman," my husband said, sounding more serious now. "Who are you, and what is this all about?"

"You alone? And you better tell me the truth, motherfucker, because I ain't playing," Wade said in a firm and threatening manner. He no longer bothered to disguise his voice.

"Uh, something like that," Jesse Ray replied.

"What the fuck does that mean? Are you alone or not?"

"Uh, my assistant manager is here . . . and a few customers," Jesse Ray muttered.

"Get rid of them motherfuckers. Every last one of them! That chink heifer assistant manager, too!" Wade demanded.

"Please hold on—"

"Hell, no! Hold my ass! This shit has gone on long enough! You put me on hold again, and you won't never see your wife again. It's time to get down to business! Do you understand me, asshole?"

"Yes, I . . . I do understand," Jesse Ray said in a hollow voice. He paused, and I heard Kim Loo mumbling in the background as Jesse Ray dismissed her.

"You get rid of your brother on that other line, too?"

"Yes, I did," Jesse Ray said, then sighed.

"What about them few customers?"

"My assistant is taking care of them," Jesse Ray said sharply, sucking in his breath. "Now who is this, and what is this all about?"

"This is about you getting your wife back and me getting paid."

"Listen, whoever the hell you are. I don't know what kind of scam you are trying to pull, but it won't work on me. Now, whoever the hell this is, if you call here again, I'm going to call the police. I don't have time to play games. Is that clear?"

"Motherfucker! You stop talking crazy! This is for real! We got your wife, and if you want her back, you'll do what I say!"

Jesse Ray let out an exasperated sigh. "My wife is at the beauty parlor. I dropped her off there myself a couple of hours ago."

I sat as still and stiff as a statue, looking from the telephone to Wade. At this point, Wade looked at me and pointed at me, then at the telephone.

"You know what to say," he whispered, shaking a fist and giving me a threatening look.

I cleared my throat and closed my eyes as I spoke. "J.R . . . honey, it's me," I whimpered. "I've been kidnapped, baby, and I'm . . . I'm so scared."

CHAPTER 3

"**W**hat the hell? Christine? Baby, what is this?" my husband asked in a low, steely voice. "Honey, where are you?" Jesse Ray was yelling now, and he sounded terrified. "Are you all right? Have you been harmed?" His voice was trembling so hard, I could almost feel it vibrating through the telephone.

"I'm fine . . . for now. Please do what they tell you to do," I pleaded, with a sob. "If you don't . . . they . . . they are going to kill me."

"*Shit!*" Jesse Ray roared.

"Baby, go into your office so you can have some privacy. I don't want Kim Loo to know what's going on." I didn't plan on it, but I let out a sharp sob and a loud sniff. My tongue felt like it had doubled in size, and it was flopping up and down in my mouth so hard, I could barely talk. "Baby, I'm so scared," I managed.

A few excruciating moments of silence passed, and I kept my eyes closed until I heard my husband's voice again.

"I'm in my office now," Jesse Ray said, breathing hard. He yelled for Kim Loo to hang up the other phone. Then I heard a door slam and a glass crash to the floor. "Baby, talk to me," he bleated.

"J.R., don't let anybody hear anything you say," I warned, scraping my tongue with my teeth.

"They won't. I'm alone in my office, with the door closed," Jesse Ray said in a guarded tone of voice. "Don't you worry about a thing,

Mary Monroe

honey," he told me, his voice sounding tired and raspy now. I could imagine how hard he was sweating. Jesse Ray was the kind of man who got nervous real quick.

"J.R., don't call the cops. Don't tell anybody about this," I said, sounding as hysterical as one might expect a kidnapped woman to sound. "Please get me out of this mess. I . . . I want to come home—" Wade pushed me roughly to the side as he leaned toward the telephone.

"Satisfied? You believe me now? This sound like a game to you now?" Wade asked, screaming toward the phone so hard, spit flew out of both sides of his mouth.

"Yes, I . . . I believe you," Jesse Ray stuttered.

"And by the way, this juicy butt, big-legged woman of yours looks mighty delicious to me . . . yum-yum. If there's a bitch better than this one sitting in front of me now, God kept her for himself. I will do my best and try to be a good boy. Uh, I'll try to keep my hands to myself, but *I am a man.*"

"*Shit!* Don't you touch my wife!" Jesse Ray shouted.

"Then you better get me my money on time before I lose control. And I know, you know what I mean."

"Don't hurt my wife . . . Please don't hurt my wife," Jesse Ray said, this time in a weak, pleading voice.

"That's up to you. You do what I tell you to do, and everything will be all right."

"What do you want?" Jesse Ray asked, his voice trembling. "I'm not a rich man. . . . "

"Bullshit! And Santa Claus ain't got nothing to do with Christmas," Wade said, then laughed. "Brother, you rich enough for me! I got friends in all the right places, so I know just as much about your business as you do. I know what your black ass is worth!"

"How . . . much do you want?" my husband asked again.

"Do you love your wife, my man?"

Jesse Ray hesitated before he answered. And that gave me something else to worry about. "Yes. I love my wife very much," he said finally. "I have always loved my wife, and I always will. She means the world to me." I breathed a sigh of relief.

"Then you'd be willing to pay to get her back." I couldn't tell if the sentence was a statement or a question, because Wade winked at me when he said it.

"I just told you, I am not a rich man. I don't care what you heard about me. I'm a working man," Jesse Ray said, raising his voice again. "I don't know why you decided to grab *my* wife of all people. Especially since the Bay Area is full of men with a lot more money than I'll ever have—and the women they love. Sean Penn's wife, Mick Jagger's daughter. Why my woman?"

"Well, I know about all them rich folks, but I ain't that greedy," Wade said, with a sinister chuckle. "And I don't want to put myself in no position that might attract a lot of attention. I ain't fool enough to snatch no famous person's woman."

"But you are fool enough to snatch mine?"

"Don't you get cute with me, motherfucker! I'm the one in charge here! And I just told you, I know what you worth. I done my homework. You want your wife back. I want my money. It's as simple as that. Do you understand me, motherfucker?"

"I understand," Jesse Ray mumbled.

"Good! Now just to show you that I ain't one of them greedy bastards you read about in the newspaper, all I want is half a million dollars." Wade was as cool as a block of ice. He could not have sounded more casual if he'd been ordering a glass of wine.

Jesse Ray gasped and started coughing. It took him almost a minute to compose himself. "*A half a million dollars?* Mister, you must be out of your goddamn mind! Who the hell do you think you are?"

"I'm the man with the gun and your wife. You'll get me my money, or you won't never see your wife alive again."

"I don't know who the fuck this is, but whoever you are, you are talking like you're crazy as hell!"

"No, brother. You are the one talking crazy."

"Look, be reasonable. This is not P. Diddy or Donald Trump or Bill Gates you're talking to!" Jesse Ray shouted. "I told you, I am just a working man. I live from payday to payday. I buy my suits from Penney's. I buy just about everything else from Wal-Mart. I don't have the kind of money you're talking about!"

I gasped myself because I knew Jesse Ray was lying! We had over two million dollars in the bank. Or I should say, Jesse Ray had over two million dollars in the bank. And that was just the money that I knew about. For a man who worshipped money the way he did, there was no doubt in my mind that he had another fortune stashed away somewhere. For one thing, he had made more than one mysterious trip to the Cayman Islands in the last couple of years. I knew that a lot of Americans hid money from Uncle Sam in island banks.

But I honestly didn't know what my husband was worth. In addition to the money that the video stores brought in, he had invested wisely over the years. He owned an apartment building in San Francisco, and he had made a lot of wise investments in the stock market over the years. These were just the things that I knew about. I was surprised and hurt that Jesse Ray would deny his wealth, knowing now that I was in such an ominous position.

"Well, if you ain't got it, you better get it. If you want to see your wife again. And just to show you I ain't all bad, I will give you till Friday to get me my money. Today is Monday, so you got enough time to do your thing. I will check in with you on . . . say, tomorrow morning, this same time, this same number. Don't you do nothing stupid, like call the cops. Or tell that big-mouthed sister of yours. What's her name? Yeah, Adele. She got a couple of cute kids, so we just might snatch one of them next if we have to."

"Don't you go near my family!" Jesse Ray shouted.

"Then you better do what I say," Wade warned, snorting like a bull. "Don't get your phone tapped, and don't have nobody up in that damn shop with you when I call you tomorrow. You can afford to close up shop for an hour or two. You understand me, motherfucker?"

The silence on Jesse Ray's end was disturbing. It was so complete, it seemed like he had left the telephone. I held my breath until he responded, which was a few more seconds later.

"I . . . I understand," Jesse Ray stammered.

"Like I said, if you call the cops, your bitch is dead. And . . . so is *your mama*. Bye." Wade unplugged the telephone and looked at his watch. "I can't believe it took all this time to get that stingy motherfucker you married to take me serious. I don't know what this world is coming to!" Wade said, with an incredulous look on his face. "You sure know how to pick 'em!"

"You didn't have to say that about his mama," I said, folding my arms. "Miss Rosetta is the sweetest woman I know. You didn't even have to drag her into this mess. You got me, and that ought to be enough," I insisted.

"Baby, I want this thing to work, don't you? If we want to make sure it works, we got to use every trick in the book."

"I hope it does work," I admitted. I moved the telephone from the wobbly chair, and then I flopped down into it. "I don't know what else to do."

"Look, there ain't nothing else for us to do! If he don't pay, you can't go back to him and pick up where you left off. You'd be a fool to go back to that stingy punk. Bottom line is, he'd better come through. You and me both are fucked in the asshole if he don't."

"But what if he doesn't?" I asked, wringing my hands, rotating my wedding ring.

"Then we go to Plan B," Wade said, with a heavy sigh. "I go on back to L.A., and you go with me, if you want to. Somehow we'll make it," he said, with a shrug and a tired look. "Being broke ain't the worst thing in the world."

"Oh," I muttered, looking around the cluttered room. "Wade, do you really love me? Do you love me enough to take me back to L.A. with you and take care of me?"

The tired look immediately disappeared from his face, and he replaced it with a smile, his tongue licking his lips. It was hard to believe that he was the same man who had looked and sounded so mean and angry a few moments ago. "Why don't we trot back upstairs to my bedroom and let me show you."